A BALANCE OF EVIL

A BALANCE OF EVIL

DOUGLAS RENWICK

PROLOGUE

1979

She has no eyes. Her left knee is wounded, but it doesn't matter. A girl of sixteen, pretty, slim, a nice personality, everything going for her. Except she is dead.

It was the dog that did it. It discovered them, lying in wait in their ambush positions. It didn't see them; it sniffed them out. Otherwise, they would never have been rumbled. They were virtually invisible, as you would expect from a team of professionals, specially selected and highly trained in black operations. Behind enemy lines? Hardly. More like bandit country.

They had been there for three days and two nights, having spent the first night of the operation making their way carefully across the border and into their positions. Just eight miles from the drop-off, but it had been slow going, following stream beds and hedgerows, waiting and listening, avoiding any signs of life, hoping the cloud cover would hold.

Their loads were heavy: water, rations, radios, batteries, binos, maps, compasses, spare socks and crap sacks. Flares, first-aid kits, smoke grenades, fragmentation grenades, side-arms and automatic rifles with night-sights, and an assortment of special goodies shared between the team. And ammunition. Non-standard stuff, stable in flight but tumbled in flesh, assuring a one-shot incapacitation.

Their mission? To kill the enemy before the bastards had a chance to collect the Semtex and deliver it to the bomb-maker in Belfast. The team were to destroy what remained at the RV, a derelict farmhouse 250 metres away, including the people.

It was Tim Turnbull's first operational assignment as the boss, the leader, the decision-maker. He said what goes. And when the dog discovered them, he was the one who decided they would remain in their position and carry on with the mission, and achieve it, rather than abort and attempt a highly dangerous daylight extraction. Yes boss, but the girl?

She guessed Seamus had picked up a rabbit's scent, and she came to look, to make sure it wasn't a poisoned fox. She only saw one member of the six-man detachment, heavily camouflaged lying in the shadow of a hedgerow. And she only saw him because he stroked the dog. It was the movement of his hand, hardly ten feet away. Then she saw the gun, pointing at her. He indicated to her to get down, to lie prone on the ground, face down.

A low whistle brought Tim crawling along the ditch behind the hedgerow. He signalled to the operative to do it, just do it. It had all been covered in their briefing: if you have to, do it silently, with the ratchet-wire around the neck. One sharp yank, job done. The man refused. He had a six-year-old daughter.

It was Tim's first kill. His second was the dog. He dragged them both back to the ditch. After the statutory five minutes, he released the ratchet. That's when her eyes opened. Whenever he looked at her, it seemed that she was looking at him and smiling – or was it a silent scream. He tried to close her eyelids – like they do in films – but they would very slowly open again, and she would be looking at him, with that smile forever frozen. Then he had a thought. She's dead. She won't need them.

Afterwards, he felt better. Without those big green eyes, she was no longer pretty, no longer a person. Just a lump of meat.

That night the team sent eight members of the Provisional IRA to a happier hunting ground. After the firefight, Tim made his way back to the ditch, collected the lump of meat and dumped it in an outhouse. He fired one shot from his pistol into its head and one into the back of its left knee. Then they set the detonators and incendiaries and torched the farmhouse.

The mission was heralded as a great success. Eight enemy combatants killed, no casualties sustained. One informant found dead. Two tons of Semtex destroyed along with dozens of small arms and ammunition. God knows how many shoppers on a Saturday afternoon had been saved from a violent, random death.

Much was made of the cowardly and brutal way PIRA dealt with those who betray them. In the Loyalist bars north of the border they praised the skill and daring of the brave boys of the UVF, the Ulster Volunteer Force, whose members were eager to accept the accolades for an action in which they played no part at all.

Tim Turnbull was not pleased. The girl. Remember the balance, he was told by his boss. One innocent life lost, many innocent lives saved. Yes, I can hack this, Tim thought. I can do the business. But he never forgot those eyes.

PART 1

The Story

1

Dan's phone pinged. It was an email.

"Darling, it's from Frances. To us both. . .about Gerald. . . He's died." Dan swallowed. "In his sleep. . . Such a nice guy – and not all that old. Sad, to think we only knew him for a few years. You'd better read it." He passed his phone over to Helen.

From: Frances and Bob
To: Dan Braithwaite
Subject: Gerald Rayner
Date: 28th January 2017

Dear Dan and Helen,

I'm afraid I've some sad news. During last night Gerald our step-father died peacefully in his sleep. As you can imagine, it's been a shock to us all, although to be honest we were expecting it. We just weren't ready for it yet, particularly as he'd been in fine form over the last week working on his "mission possible" as he called it. When Mum said goodnight to him, his last words were "it's going to be a sunny day tomorrow!" Actually, it's rather cloudy here. Hope it's better over there.

I know you will both share our grief, and that you, Dan, were particularly close to him. He's actually left you a package, which I guess is a book he'd like you to read. It's sealed up and addressed to you in Geneva, so I'll pop it in the post tomorrow and you should get it in a couple of days.

Love to you all,

Frances and Bob
xxxx

"What a shame." Helen frowned and closed her eyes for a moment. "He was a lovely man. We'll all miss him. Poor Julie. Widowed for the second time. Do you think she'll come out to the chalet in April? With her daughters and their families? Like last year?"

"I hope so," said Dan. "At least they won't have Gerald to worry about. Sorry, but you know what I mean. Julie didn't want to leave him on his own, but he insisted they all went and did some skiing for him."

"Do you think the accident had anything to do with his. . . Did it shorten his life?"

"Who knows? I doubt it, but we must make sure the kids don't think it was anything to do with them. It wasn't, but they were very fond of him. Especially Lucy. You know what it's like if something dreadful happens to someone you're close to. You wish you'd done something differently. I'm just so sorry we didn't go to see him at the hospital before they went back to the UK."

"I wouldn't beat yourself up about that," said Helen. "He and Julie left so suddenly. None of us had the chance to say goodbye."

Two days later the Jiffy bag arrived. Dan took it into the study and opened it. On top of a thick pile of A4 sheets held together with two rubber bands was a letter to him from Gerald. He noted the date and realised it was three months after the accident.

18th July, 2015

My dear Dan,

It's a bright and sunny day here, and I'm doing well for someone of my age. However, when you read this I'll have 'crossed the bar'. Like

Tennyson, I hope for an easy passage, but also for 'no sadness of farewell' amongst my loved ones of whom you must rank as one of the most cherished, despite the cruel brevity of our relationship.

It must seem odd to receive a letter – and the story that goes with it – on real paper. But I don't trust the internet and email, the cloud and that sort of thing. What I have to say, or rather write, is for you alone. Certainly, I wouldn't want Julie to be burdened in her widowed dotage with hidden facets of my life which I hadn't been able to share with her.

I remember when we first met you. Julie and I were sitting on the terrace of our ski chalet, a glass of red wine in our hands, and you'd just moved in next door. You waved and we waved back, and when we discovered you were English we invited you to join us.

I wouldn't say it was 'love at first sight', but I was instantly taken by the confident way you handled the situation, the strong handshake, the eye contact and relaxed smile, all of which I wasn't very good at when I was a young man. And I suppose I admired the physical youth and vigour which in me was fast fading. Also I felt we were drawn together by the fact we were both cursed with the red hair gene, and possibly shared the teasing and name-calling which we ginger-nuts inevitably suffered in our school-days.

You bounded back to your chalet and soon re-appeared with your wife, explaining you'd left the little ones with your in-laws. I felt a pang of inadequacy; pro-creation was something I hadn't managed despite fifteen years of trying during my first marriage.

We discussed politics and you got me going on my rather naïve views which I normally have difficulty explaining to others, but you seemed to grasp them immediately. You politely asked me about myself and I said I'd retired, having been an engineer in the British army.

Then Helen announced, "Come on, Danny boy, we better get back." Some things in life give me a weird feeling. That was one of them. I can't remember what happened next. By the time we met again I was over it, and I was relieved that my 'weirdness' on that occasion didn't prevent our special relationship from developing over the next two precious years.

Nevertheless, I think I owe you an explanation for my behaviour on that first day; and for me it's important I give you one. You see, it's part of a long story, one which hasn't yet reached its final chapter. I don't mean it hasn't been written; I mean it hasn't yet happened. Should I wait for the hoped-for happy ending? At my age, waiting can be a risky business.

Lots of love, my special one, to you and to those you love.

Gerald x'

Dan took it through to Helen in the kitchen. "Darling? What do you make of this?"

She sat down and read it. She noted the kiss at the end. "Hmm. It's a bit gushing, isn't it? You don't think he had a. . .umm. . .sort of thing about you, do you? And those references to burdens and secrets. A bit odd, if you ask me."

Dan wasn't sure, but said he never got the impression Gerald was gay. It was probably because Gerald realised he wouldn't see them again and was a bit emotional. And old people can get delusional about things, and think things are secret when everyone knows about them.

Helen replied, "Well I hope the story's interesting. I'll leave that one to you."

It took Dan over three hours to read it. Helen had gone to bed. Just as well, he thought, as he didn't want her to see him getting emotional about it when his eyes fuzzed up and he had to pause for a bit. As Gerald had said in his letter, it contained a lot of secrets, ones which he wanted Dan to be party to, to understand.

2

I think I ought to warn you, Dan. This isn't a tale of derring-do, adventure in far-flung lands, narrow escapes and heroic achievements. In fact, by some standards, my army career was rather dull. Which in some ways suited me as I'm a rather unremarkable person.

But a remarkable thing happened to me shortly after I retired. It was in July 1986. I was 43.

Thing! What a simple word to describe what caused my tectonic plates to shift so suddenly and change my life forever. It was four things, and they occurred over four consecutive days. Here they are, in reverse order of magnitude on the Rayner-Richter scale.

I earned – perfectly legally – more money in those four days than I did in the rest of that year.

My wife left me for another man.

I became unwittingly and uncomfortably embroiled in what became a pivotal event in the history of the World.

I met Mrs Grey.

I'll tell you how it started. A friend of mine phoned me one Sunday and asked me to have lunch with him in London the following day. Great, I said, as it was always nice to catch up with Mike and hear his news.

He too had been in the Army, in the SAS, and was at that time working for some security outfit. He was much tougher than I was, a good rugby player and cross-country runner. I'd kept pretty fit, but not super-fit like him. He left the Army about a year before I had, and was nicely settled in as a civilian, albeit in a job with a military flavour to it.

As agreed, I met him at a small Lebanese restaurant just around the corner from his office in Kensington. We had a good chat over lunch about old times and people we both knew. Then he asked me how my newly formed property restoration company was getting on.

"Well. . . " I replied.

"Well, meaning it's going well?"

"Er, no. To be honest, I'm struggling. There's a bit of a lull at the moment. And getting bank finance is a pain."

"I'm sorry to hear that. Look, don't take this the wrong way, Gerry, but would you be interested in earning some dosh on the side?"

"What? Doing what you do? No thanks, mate!" I liked to think I'd grown out of all that sort of thing, but to be honest, it scared me.

"No, Gerry. Nothing like that. It's an engineering consultancy job. Just up your street, actually. Four days. Good pay."

"Tell me more!" I had a small army pension, but I reckoned some ready cash would be useful.

"Nothing more to tell, I'm afraid, but if you want it, you need to report this afternoon to a chappy at the Old War Office Building. I've forgotten his name, but it's Room 109. That's all I know about it."

We talked some more over coffee, sharing news and views, and about when we served together in the same unit. He was the one who christened me Gelignite Gerry, as I'd carried out a big demolition job when we were young officers. To me, it wasn't a great achievement as my preference had always been for making things rather than blowing them up.

We parted company at about two, and I decided to walk to

Whitehall, about half an hour away. When I reached the Old War Office, I told the dear lady at the reception desk the purpose of my visit. After issuing me with a visitor's pass, she took me to Room 109 to meet a retread – a retired officer – by the name of Major Dinwiddie.

He must have been about sixty-five, but to me, he seemed much older. I got the feeling he was expecting me. He explained he didn't know much about the consultancy, but it was important work which could save lives. That appealed to me. I'd never relished the prospect of killing people, and fortunately, in my career, I'd never been required to do so.

He said the consultancy would start the following morning and be over by Friday evening, just the four days. I would be paid through Service channels at a rate I would be happy with – if the job went well. He asked me to sign a statement saying I'd be subject to the Official Secrets Act, which of course I was happy to do. I was comfortable with secrets having worked on top-secret projects during my service.

He said "good chap" and told me a taxi would pick me up from my house at six. Actually, he said oh six hundred hours; a habit of a lifetime for him but one I was trying to shed as I struggled to become a civilian. He shook my hand warmly and I left his office.

As I was closing the door behind me, he called, "Major Rayner? Just a little word. You will be working with some really good people, and they'll take good care of you. But they do have their, shall we say, 'procedures'. Just go along with them and you'll be fine."

Life at home was not going well. Our marriage had been under strain for years, and the absence of the longed-for offspring caused us to drift apart. Neither of us blamed the other; we both pretended we didn't mind. The unsure future ahead on a modest army pension was of concern, and I suspected there might be someone else on the scene.

My last posting had been unaccompanied. By that time Mandy

had enough of Army life. She'd found it hard, not coming from an army family, and without children, she felt she was unable to relate to the majority of the other wives. I managed to get home most weekends, but by the time Sunday evening came round I felt she was looking forward to me going off again.

When I came home for good, I decided to prove to myself there was nothing going on, so I bought one of those voice-activated recorders and hid it under the phone table. It was the worst thing I'd ever done because it revealed there *was* somebody else in her life, and it was serious. I hoped to win her back, now I was on the scene full time, and I had great ambitions to do well as a civilian and give her the sort of life she wished for.

So, with a happy heart, I returned to our semi in Tenterden with the good news about the consultancy. Mandy was pleased. She said she might visit her sister while I was away, rather than be alone in the house, and that seemed like a good idea.

I rose the following morning, being careful not to wake her, showered and dressed in my new business suit (ready-to-wear, reduced in a sale). I wore my Parachute Brigade tie as it would show them I was a tough nut who was not going to be messed around or have my time wasted.

I fed the cat, packed my bag, downed my shredded wheat and grabbed a coffee.

The taxi arrived on time and, as it was well before the rush hour, we sped along. After about an hour and a half, we pulled into a multi-storey car park attached to a shopping centre. I didn't recognise it, nor the town. The taxi driver had been chatting. Nice fellow, a bit older than myself, but I reckoned he was ex-military.

He pulled up next to a white van, and as he did so, the driver got out. Seemed to be a nice young man, and smiled when he came round to introduce himself. John apologised about the van but asked if I would go with him. I guessed he knew the taxi driver because they shook hands. He 'asked' me if I would mind travelling in the back of the van, as it would be more comfortable.

And indeed it was. There were two seats side by side, rather like those on a cheap airline, plastic covered but reclinable, complete with seat belts. In front of the seats was a little table with the morning papers, a plastic glass and a bottle of fizzy water.

There was a bulkhead blocking my view forward, and no windows. I asked John about this, and he just said, "It's just how we do things, sir". And he added that if I needed more air just move this lever to the right, and here is the light switch if I wanted a little snooze.

Wow. I thought, how strange. Then I remembered Dinwiddie's words and relaxed with *The Times*.

After about an hour, I put the paper down and inspected the inside of my eyelids. I only came to when the van slowed up, took a tight right turning and stopped. The engine was cut, the back doors opened and I stepped out into a well-lit garage, just as the automatic door reached the end of its closing cycle.

John led me through a door at the back of the garage and down a corridor to a changing room. He asked me if I would don the tracksuit folded neatly on the bench and put on the socks and trainers. He suggested I put all my valuables – watch, wallet, house keys, cash – in the locker, along with my clothes and shoes, as I wouldn't be needing them during my stay. All the kit for my stay, including changes of clothes, washing bag etc. would be in my 'cabin'. Fortunately, the trainers were my size.

I thought this was going to be fun. Maybe one of those corporate team building seminars with some assault course training thrown in. Sure, let's go for it. After all, I had passed P Company, the gruelling entry test into the Paras.

As I emerged thus 'donned' in my clean white tracksuit, John said he'd look after the locker key for me in case it dropped out of my pocket during my stay, and would I mind following him.

The corridor was also well lit but had no windows. Maybe they don't want me to see the test paraphernalia, the scramble nets, the wobbly parallel bars and the ten-foot wall or whatever. I felt qualified to give advice if they needed to improve it.

We went up some stairs, turned left then right along a corridor. Finally, John showed me into my cabin that would be home for the next four days.

"Take your time, sir. When you're ready, the conference room is the first door on your left. Left out of here and left again. Thank you, sir."

All very proper.

3

I did a quick recce of my room: slight smell of bleach, clean and tidy – and it had an en-suite with shower, basin and loo. There was a bed, a bedside table with an alarm clock on it, a writing table with tea-making equipment, a couple of chairs and a wardrobe with shelves with kit on them. And above the bed, on the ceiling, was a great big window, one of those bubble things made of clear plastic.

It was a lovely morning, and I could see a blue sky above me, clear except for a couple of vapour trails. On one of the shelves, I noticed a compact disc player. I'd never seen one in real life before, let alone used one, but I'd heard they were brilliant. Wonderful, I thought. I could be comfortable here.

I popped into the bathroom to 'ease springs', then made my way to the conference room. It had no windows, but two large clear plastic domes in the ceiling letting in the morning sunshine. Three people sat at the large table in the middle of the room, all in tracksuits like mine. A man in a black one at the end of the table rose to his feet.

"Good morning, sir. Do please take a seat." An ageing man, perhaps a retread; possibly even older. Average height and build, nothing remarkable about him – other than the tracksuit. On a man of his age? Really!

He continued. "This may seem a little strange, but for security reasons, I would like to call you Mr White. My name is Mr Black."

Hilarious, I thought. He was in no state for physical activity. He introduced me to 'Mr Green', a youth in comparison sitting to his right. Again, a nondescript character, but with longish brown hair thinning on the top. Not of a military bearing. Small, unimpressive and had that look of someone in a world of his own, in his green tracksuit that had, I guessed, never seen a track.

And before Mr Black could continue I said, turning to the much younger but rather dowdy, frumpy looking thing in the grey tracksuit sitting opposite me, "And I suppose you are Miss Grey?"

Not a flicker of a smile from her; not a word. Mr Black merely said, in a rather huffy way, "Actually, it's Mrs Grey.

"Now, before we start may I offer you a coffee? Or tea, Mr White? Whatever you prefer. You're our guest until Friday, and we'll make every effort to make your stay here as comfortable as possible. If there is anything you need, please ask Mrs Grey and she'll see to it.

"Of course, you must be wondering what all this is about, so let me explain without further ado. We're a think tank, part of a risk management organisation which undertakes studies for corporations and government bodies and other institutions. Our job, in this room, is to think!" He chuckled briefly and carried on.

"Actually, we scope. S C O P E – that stands for 'Strategic Concepts, Options and Probabilities Evaluation'." He seemed proud of the acronym and was warming to his task of describing his organisation, which clearly he'd done several times. "To be precise, probabilities is handled by Probs – our probabilities department."

You don't say, I thought, getting slightly impatient, as I sipped my coffee.

"And while I'm on the subject of departments, I should mention the 'engine room' of our outfit, the Admin and Logistics department – we refer to it as A and L – who look after all the, er, other things, leaving us, here in this room, free to *think*. Which is wonderful, as we don't have any beastly paperwork to worry about.

"But the thinking we do here is a special kind of thinking. Risk management is about weighing up the probabilities of some event, like an earthquake, against the consequences if it did actually happen. Some events, you see, may have a high probability of happening but trivial consequences, while others may have an extremely low probability of occurring – like London flooding – but if they did happen the consequences could be disastrous. We specialise in the latter."

I looked at Mrs Grey. Grey by name, grey by nature. Heavy black-plastic-rimmed glasses, no makeup, and no jewellery except for a wedding ring. Someone must have loved her at some time.

"Probs works out the probability, and we focus our minds on the consequences. We do this by pretending the event has happened. We work out A, what we could've done before the event to mitigate the consequences, and B, what should be done to mitigate the consequences afterwards."

Yeah, whatever. I stifled a yawn.

"Let me give you an example. These days we rarely experience a blowout. I don't mean a good meal." He chuckled. "I mean a puncture. But the *consequences* of having a puncture if, say, we're on our way to the airport might be missing our flight. Now, here in the think tank, or as we sometimes call it the 'brink tank'!" He chuckled again. "We'd *pretend* we were driving to the airport and we'd *pretend* – BANG! We have a puncture. What do we do?"

I got the feeling he was waiting for me to respond, but I just sat there waiting for him to finish and tell me why I was there, wasting my time with some third-rate deadbeats in a crummy room with no windows, sitting in tracksuits listening to Old Father William droning on about punctures.

He continued by answering his own question, then said, "And

what would we wish we had done at some time in the past? We wish we had read the manual which came with the car, found out where the jack and jack handle was stowed, located the jacking points, made sure they weren't blocked with mud, found the wheel brace – and a screwdriver to lever off the hubcap. What else would we need?

"Let's imagine you got safely to the side of the road. You go to the boot, you get out the tools, you roll out the spare wheel – and– "

He paused for effect. "It's under-inflated! You wish you had a pump! You go to kneel beside the wheel, but you notice the side of the road is muddy and stony. You need a mat. You manage to jack the car up and remove the wheel nuts. One drops on the ground. You can't find it. It's dark! We need a torch. Is there one in the toolkit?"

He paused and looked around the room. "And so you see, Mr White, by *pretending* we had a puncture, we can actually come up with some jolly good ways to mitigate the consequences of having one. We might just catch our plane!"

He then proceeded to give me another example of 'scoping'. To be honest, I didn't find it interesting. I wanted to know how I might make a useful contribution, like saving lives.

He came – finally – to a triumphant stop. But no-one clapped, certainly not me. With the air of an ageing actor acknowledging the applause of his dear, dear audience, he turned to his co-star, in this case, Mr Green, and with a flourish of his hand said something like, 'The Floor is Yours!'

Mr Green began. "Mr White, my job this morning is to inform you of how you can help us with the 'scope' we are currently working on. Before I begin, I should just mention that it is very secret."

Yeah, like where the fucking jack handle is hidden.

"In fact, it's supersecret, as we say here, and we'll only tell you what you need to know in order for you to do what we ask of you.

You'll find we often use the word 'dinntik', which is an acronym for 'do not need to know'. Please be patient with us when you hear that. It's not that we don't trust you, it's just that there are some things you do not – er – need to know. Anyway, to come to the point, we want you to help us find a way of blowing up a building."

At that point, I became rather interested. I'd planned and carried out various demolitions including a large derelict building which earned me the Gelignite Gerry title. I'd used cutting charges on steel and crater charges on bridge abutments, and carried out trials with improvised explosives. I told Mr Green and he listened politely.

When I'd finished, he replied, "Really? Well, that's a lucky coincidence."

I heard a stifled snort from Mrs Grey sitting opposite me, and I noticed she had her hand in front of her mouth. I wondered if she was smiling. Then the penny dropped. That's why I was there. I could feel my neck going red.

Mr Green's face was blank and he continued. "Yes Mr White, that could be helpful."

He said he would provide me with some basic information on the building, but Mrs Grey would work with me as my 'research assistant'. The prospect of being with Mrs Grey for four days didn't delight me, but then I thought if I got bored I could take on the bigger challenge of making her smile – without covering her face with her hand.

Mr Green continued. "One thing I should mention about the building we want you to, er, hypothetically blow up is that it's a large building, in a built-up area and it's not derelict. It is, in fact, occupied."

4

"Occupied?" I said. "What *is* this building? Where the hell is it? Why the f–" and my eye caught Mrs Grey, "flaming hell do you want to blow it up?"

Then it came. My first dinntik. At which point I'd had enough. Having been bored out of my tiny mind by Black's blowout, then humiliated by Mister Clever-Clogs Green, I felt it time to show my colours.

I stood up and put my hands on my hips, just as I used to do when addressing my soldiers, gathered around me on the parade square, or on some river bank. I remembered to clench my fists, as my godfather had once quietly told me to do. 'Coppernob, my dear boy, if you must have your arms akimbo, make sure you close your hands. Open hands on hips for a man does not look good. And never just one arm. Please.'

I put on my tough, addressing-soldiers-voice: "I'm here today to help save lives, not to take part in some cloak-and-dagger plot that could kill hundreds of innocent people. Before we go on, I need to know who is your client, where the building is, what the building is for, and why in heaven's name you want to demolish it!"

Mr Black glanced at Mr Green and gave him a slight nod, then slowly got to his feet. Thankfully I was taller than him.

"Mr White, you may want to sit down." He said it quietly and politely with no hint of disapproval or reprimand. No frown of exasperation. No clenched fists.

I replied, "I will NOT sit down, and if you don't tell me what I NEED to KNOW, I will walk out of here, and you can STUFF this tracksuit up your. . . A and L department."

I had always found it went down well with the troops to use a bit of coarse language, but my last-minute attempt to spare the blushes of Mrs Grey failed as I rattled off the abbreviated departmental name too quickly; A'n'L. Her hand went to her face again. My neck went red again. I remained standing, doing my best to look defiant.

I expected Mr Black to say my behaviour was unacceptable and arrangements would be made forthwith to return me home. Instead, in the same quiet tone, as if he were explaining to a child of five he should eat up his spaghetti rings rather than throw them across the room, he said this. "Mr White. Cloaks yes. But daggers, no." He paused, drew breath and continued.

"Our client is a branch of the Government of the United States. The building could be any of half a dozen in as many American cities, all with populations exceeding five million. The building is assumed to be mainly office space with a shopping mall, restaurants and related facilities. It is a skyscraper, and on the roof sits a man with a radiotelephone in one hand–"

I couldn't believe what I was hearing, but I felt some bravado was called for. So, thinking back to Dallas 1963, I injected "And a sniper's rifle in the other?" I thought it quite clever, showing I was up to speed and had anticipated the problem we were 'scoping'.

"No, Mr White. A suitcase, containing–"

"A violin?" A stupid remark. It just slipped out.

Again the quiet, steady voice and raised eyebrows. He was back to addressing the five-year-old.

"Mr White. In the suitcase is an RA-115, a neutron bomb with a yield of 0.6 kilotons, manufactured in the Soviet Union and deployed by them to secret caches in the United States as a counter to President Reagan's so-called 'Stars Wars' initiative. In broad terms, the stand-off between the two superpowers had been maintained by the doctrine of mutually assured destruction which simply meant 'if you nuke us, we will nuke you back', leaving both world powers destroyed."

He sounded as if he was telling this to the five-year-old for the hundredth time.

"However, Reagan's idea was to shoot down incoming missiles before they struck their targets in America. Then the US wouldn't need to hold a vast nuclear arsenal to retaliate with. The Soviets saw it differently: if the USA had the capability to defend themselves from a nuclear retaliation, they could launch a first strike against the Soviet Union with impunity. The secret caches were a way for the Soviets to achieve some retaliatory capacity. Are you still with me, Mr White?"

I nodded.

"A neutron bomb is a specialised thermonuclear weapon which produces less blast but releases a large amount of radiation able to penetrate the fabric of most buildings. In a city of five million, the effect of such a bomb detonated at the top of a skyscraper would be considerable. In broad terms, Mr White, our probability department reckon on 100,000 deaths initially, then 500,000 dying of radiation sickness within the following month."

He let this 'bombshell' of information sink in, then carried on. "If the weapon were detonated at ground zero rather than ground plus a thousand feet, these figures would be halved. On the other hand, if the weapon were prevented from being detonated at all, casualties would be limited to those caused by your demolition, possibly a mere 20,000. You see, Mr White, by helping us find a way to bring that hypothetical skyscraper down, you could save something like 300,000 to 500,000 hypothetical lives. Is that enough for you?

"Well, I can do better. A Soviet nuclear bomb detonated in the centre of, let's say, Chicago is probably going to induce not only widespread panic throughout the whole country but also a demand for retaliation. You may think we in the West are all too sensible to start World War 3, simply because half a million American civilians have been killed – men, women and children. If so, let me remind you that a single shot fired at an archduke in Sarajevo triggered a war which killed 17 million people and wounded a further 20 million.

"Think about it, Mr White. A lump of lead, no bigger than the end of your little finger started one of the greatest and most deadly wars of all time. How does that little lump of lead compare with 600 tons of TNT?

"Mr White. What was the largest charge you ever detonated? 60 pounds perhaps? 600 pounds? Imagine 600 TONS, Mr White, being detonated a thousand feet above a city? Thirty lorry loads, if you like. I think you would agree there would be considerable blast damage. Yes?

"But it's not TNT, is it? Remember, it is a neutron bomb, or to give it its proper name, an 'enhanced radiation device'; the blast from it is merely a side effect, a by-product. What do you think that could do to the fragile balance of world power, Mr White? You rolled your eyes when I first called us the brink tank. Don't you think, perhaps, on reflection, that the word 'brink' might, under the present circumstances, be quite apt?"

I sat down, but because my knees started to buckle. The quiet, dispassionate voice continued.

"Mr White, tell me, do you need to know more? No? Well, I am going to tell you more. Last Wednesday, at about two a.m, when you were probably safely tucked up in bed, I received word that a high ranking double agent had reported to his handler in the American embassy in Paris that four of the thirteen RA-115s which had been hidden in caches across America were missing. Gone. Disappeared.

"You see, each one has a little radio in it, and when the battery gets low, this radio transmits a signal to the nearest Russian consulate. Then someone has to go and replace the battery. Last week a man was dispatched for this purpose to a cache of five bombs, but only one was there.

"Our organisation was asked to carry out a risk assessment, and our little 'brink tank' was given the task of scoping one of the five scenarios which had, by morning, been identified. We needed a positively vetted engineer with construction and demolition experience to help us, and you were chosen.

"If you don't want to be part of our modest little team, please do walk out of that door. We won't stop you. Indeed, I will even give you a going away present. It's the name and rank of that double agent. I have it right here, in this old head of mine.

"But don't be surprised if you are woken up early tomorrow morning by your telephone ringing, and you have a terrible headache. You rush down to answer the phone, thinking something might have happened to your wife who is away on holiday, and there on the rug in the hall is the bloodied and very dead body of your cat. You instinctively pick up the phone to dial 999, not realising it's still ringing. As you put it to your ear, a voice says, quite dispassionately, tell us immediately the name you were given yesterday, and your niece – yes, Mr White, Emily, your seven-year-old niece – will not be sold to the Latvian paedophile ring who have already seen her photograph and are looking forward to some serious entertainment before disposing of her dismembered body.

"It's a simple decision for you to make. You either tell them, or you don't, A or B. Fortunately, in our silly little world of pretending things, we can offer you a third outcome, C. Here it is. During that momentary pause, having heard that dreadful message, you receive a single headshot from a silenced Berretta RG9A fired by a British operative who is part of a team that's been watching your house and monitoring your phone from the moment you left this establishment. Which outcome would you wish for, Mr White? A, B or C?"

For the first time, Mr Black raised his voice. "THE MONKEY'S PAW, MR WHITE! The Monkey's Paw. Do you know the story? Let me remind you. Whoever held the paw would have three wishes, all of which would be granted. But the last wish would always be for death.

"I suggest you, too, Mr White, faced with the three options in the scenario we have just looked at, might also wish for death. In fact, you wouldn't really have much choice, would you? But death for whom? You? The brave double agent who is helping us to avoid Armageddon? Or your niece?"

He paused, waiting for me to answer. There was no way I could have said anything. I did have vague memories of the story from my early childhood.

He continued, quietly, as if he was reading a bedtime story. "The Monkey's Paw was a horrific tale written, I believe, in 1902. I have a name for you to remember, Mr White. In a few minutes, I'm going to tell it to you whether you like it or not. It's the name of the principal character in that tale who saves the paw from the fire to exploit its magical powers. His first wish was for £200 to pay off his mortgage. The next day his son Herbert leaves for work at a local factory. Later that day, word comes that Herbert has been killed in a machinery accident. Although denying responsibility, the firm makes a goodwill payment to his father of £200.

"Ten days after the funeral, his wife, stricken with grief, begs her husband to use the second wish to bring Herbert back to life. Reluctantly, he does so. Shortly afterwards there is a knock at the door, but he knows he cannot let his wife see the horribly mutilated and decaying body of their only son. He makes his third wish, and the knocking stops. His wife opens the door to find no one there.

"The name of that distraught father who had to make that agonising decision to murder his own son? A name woven into that dreadful tale written well before you were born? It was – by a remarkable coincidence, may I say – a Mr White." Mr Black slowly sat down, watching me as he did so.

Mr Green was looking down at his hands. Mrs Grey was looking at me slightly open-mouthed as if she'd seen a ghost. She poured out a glass of water from the plastic bottle on the table and gently pushed it towards me. My knees were shaking. My hands were trying to stop them. I knew if I tried to pick up the glass, I'd spill it.

For minutes it seemed, nobody said a word or even moved. Then Mr Black stood up, smiled at me and walked round to the back of my chair. He put his hands on my shoulders and said "Welcome to our world, Mr White. Thanks for coming. And for staying. Mrs Grey? I think it's time for a spot of lunch, if you please?"

Mrs Grey got up and disappeared out of the room. She returned a few minutes later with a trolley laden with a selection of canapés, quiches, various little biscuity things with fish on them and plates of sandwiches. They were probably delicious, but I didn't feel like eating. I was happy with my glass of water that I'd finally managed to hold reasonably steadily using both hands.

5

I was still sitting there when Mrs Grey cleared away the lunch, and Mr Black and Mr Green went their separate ways. Mr Green merely said see you later, but Mr Black said he'd be 'popping in' from time to time. I thought he was being nice because I'd been such a wimp. They couldn't have failed to notice me shaking, and not eating anything was a dead giveaway. I felt there was nothing I could do to impress them, no way I could gain their respect. I'd disgraced myself. I'd shown fear.

Mrs Grey came back with a big smile on her face. I thought she's going to be nice to me too: she feels sorry for me as well. As she approached, she swept off her glasses with her left hand, extended her right hand, and said. "Well done! You've passed!"

"Passed what?" I said as I returned her firm handshake. "The test!" she replied.

"What test?" I said, trying to think if I had filled in a questionnaire or something when I arrived.

She threw back her head and laughed. "Mr Black's briefing!"

"Do you mean all that stuff about neutron bombs and World War 3 was just a test?"

I was hoping she'd say it was, but she sighed and replied, "'Fraid not. I can assure you that's all for real."

She must've seen the blood draining away from my face. I certainly felt it. Then, with a 'poor boy' look she continued. "But what you must remember is he was scoping, what-iffing, if you like. The situation he was describing is very unlikely to happen, but just might. As he said when he gave his example of the flat tyre, by pretending it's actually happened, we are able to scope more effectively. It's scary, I know, but it's a well tried and tested technique that works."

I began to feel a bit better. She looked me in the eye and I felt I was getting some straight talking. I thought of Mrs Thatcher's quote about Gorbachev 'We can do business together'. Then I realised I'd got the sexes the wrong way around. Or had I? There was Mrs Grey, looking comfortable in her oversized tracksuit, feet apart, with her hands on hips. The word butch sprang to mind. Were her fists closed or open? I can't remember. Head Girl at school, I guessed. Not bad looking, actually, without her glasses.

"But the monkey's paw thing?" I said. "I found that sort of scary."

"You were meant to!" she said smiling with a twinkle in her eye.

"I know it's only a story and I've heard it before, but was the father in the story really Mr White?"

"Yep!" she replied, and then put her hand to her mouth as if she was about to laugh.

"That's spooky!" I said.

She threw back her head and laughed. "Do excuse me. You see, all our guests are Mr White. Mr Black often uses that kidnap scenario and the story. He's quite proud of it actually. When I heard you didn't have offspring, I wondered how he'd handle it. But he used your niece instead; I thought it was quite clever."

I didn't like her knowing I had no children. "But why scare people?" I said. "What's the point? Why the 'test'?"

The Head Girl explained. "None of us like fear. It's an uncomfortable emotion. But without it, none of us would be here, on this planet. The human race, or indeed any animal species, wouldn't have survived without it. It saves our lives, almost on a daily basis, and the more a person can imagine danger, the more able they are to anticipate it.

"Here in the brink tank, we need people who can scope well. It's frightening at times, but a good dollop of fear is an essential ingredient in our mix of talents. People think it's a weakness, but it's not. You can't have courage without fear because you can't be brave about a danger you're not aware of. Mr Black wanted to see if he could induce in you the flight-fight response, to see if you would be any good at scoping. He achieved it, but it's nothing to be ashamed of. Remember, it's not just flight. It's fight as well."

I'd never thought of it in those terms. Fight, eh? She paused and looked at me, putting her head slightly on one side, as if she was somehow sizing me up. "Hey, silly boy, you passed with flying colours. Best ever, actually, but don't let Mr Black know I told you."

And with that heartening encouragement still ringing in my ears, the Head Girl turned on her heels and strode out of the room, probably off to her next hockey match. Or with an accent like that, more likely lacrosse.

"Back soon," she shouted, as she closed the door behind her, leaving me feeling I was somewhere between being an ace scoper and a silly schoolboy.

OK, Mrs Hoity-toity Posh-socks, I'll show you I'm the best scoper you have ever had – and a reasonably good engineer.

The afternoon flew by. Mr Green returned clutching a roll of drawings, shortly followed by Head Girl with glasses back on. She and I sat on one side of the table, Mr Green on the other. He began by explaining that from the thirty-two different building types that may be targeted, he'd developed a generic for our hypothetical study, by averaging out footprint and height and choosing the most common type of structure for the third highest buildings.

He explained the statistical logic of this much better than I could, but I did ask him if it wouldn't be more prudent to choose a type of structure which would be harder than the average to demolish, just to be on the safe side.

He looked at me blankly and said, "I was just coming on to that."

I turned my head very slightly towards Mrs Grey and did a toned-down mime of the rather camp comedian Larry Grayson being offended or outraged, a sort of hmmmm! on a high note but without the audio. Hand went up to mouth again. Sadly, the arms of her spectacles half covered those little laughter lines around her eyes.

We got down to work, and Mr Green talked through his generic design. I found it interesting. It was an unusual structure, based purely on steel for load carrying, and the wind loading on such a tall building played a significant role in its design.

I was glad to see it had a basement; get that thing underground, I thought.

To be fair, Mr Green did brighten up during the afternoon, and when I asked the right questions, he was positively animated. He admitted to knowing absolutely nothing about demolition and seemed quite hurt we should even be thinking about bringing his 'generic' to the ground.

He didn't give me a single dinntik, but if he couldn't answer a question, he said he'd get back to me. He'd be based in his own office, but Mrs Grey would be able to contact him by phone if I had further questions, and he'd send back the answers together.

Mr Black did pop in occasionally but didn't seem to have a clue about what we were talking about – Euler loadings, yield strengths, Young's moduli, live loads and static loadings and so on. There was one engineering term which we all steered clear of: dead loads.

During one of his visits, he did remind us about secrecy. I replied, "Don't worry, Mr Black. I understand none of this must ever be revealed."

"Thank you, Mr White. But I trust you do understand that if,

God forbid, the scenario did, let's say, umm, come to life, the world must never know about the bomb, nor the fact that the building was deliberately brought down. It must remain secret."

I was worried. "But surely, after the event, the general public must be told the truth, that the building was demolished to save all those lives? Surely they will understand it was right to save many more lives than those lost."

"I'm afraid not. Most people will focus on the lives actually lost, rather than the many more which might have been lost: the real balanced against the possible; the actual against what might have been."

He had a point. "But in that case, how on earth can we keep the demolition a secret after it's happened?" I asked.

"Ah," he said. "A good question! Now I mustn't detain you." Having thrown that unexpected spanner into the works he left the room. Mrs Grey and I looked at each other, but neither of us spoke.

We had a break for tea, then for a supper of chicken and chips 'in a basket' which was quite chic at the time. We all took leg-stretches, but otherwise, it was full on, serious stuff. We had a job to do, and we got on with it. Head Girl seemed to keep up which impressed me, and I was beginning to enjoy her company.

Finally, Mr Black popped in to say, children, it's time for beddy-byes. He didn't say that, of course. It just felt as if he had. I think 'pipe down' might have been more his style. It was ten to ten by the conference room clock. Was it only that morning that I had joined the brink tank? It felt weeks ago.

If I hadn't been totally exhausted, I wouldn't have slept at all. I did wake a few times, thinking the unthinkable. The only way of getting it out of my mind was to imagine Miss Butch with her lacrosse stick, dashing around some Benenden field shouting encouragement to her team. Definitely the captain.

6

Wednesday morning. The alarm went at oh five hundred hours, as Dinwiddie would have said, and I jumped out of bed, had an SSS (that's a shower and shave) and put on my white tracksuit. Breakfast was delivered as promised, waiting outside my door. I was actually looking forward to getting back to work with my brink-tank friends.

Friend, then. What should I call her today, I wondered. Miss Baggy Tracksuit 1986? Bad choice. Not the name, but the tracksuit. Must be a man's.

It was a good day. I worked at the IBM AT a lot of the time. That's an early PC. I was using Visicalc, a primitive spreadsheet program, and by using a line for each floor of the 'Generic', I was able to calculate loads and strains and generally explore possibilities.

Both Mr Green and Mr Black had stressed they were after concepts only and were not interested in any detail. This was a great relief. Although the AT could have handled more complex routines, it was achingly slow compared with computers of today, and we would never have made the deadline of 10:00 a.m Friday for the presentation.

What I remember most about that Wednesday was not my scoping efforts. Mrs Grey and I were alone much of the time with Mr Black doing his popping in. We had the odd leg-stretch, of course, breaks for coffee and lunch, but the form the day took was that I would give her a list of questions and she would phone Mr Green. He would tell her when to call back, and in the meantime, we would just sit there waiting.

During one of these slack periods, I said to her, "What's a nice girl like you doing in a place like this?" It was then her turn to do the Larry Grayson bit and the oooh! But I thought I saw her cheeks go ever so slightly red.

She looked down and pretended to do the demure young girl bit, and said, "How do you know I'm a nice girl?" I then felt my neck – yes you've guessed – but I was pleased she was ready for a bit of banter, as it made the time pass more quickly. It was fun. She was nice.

During one of these breaks, I asked her, "How do you cope with all this, pretending that something awful is going to happen?"

"Well," she said, "firstly, we have to remind ourselves we are only *pretending* – as Mr Black kept saying in his flat tyre example. You probably weren't listening," she teased, but she was half-right.

"Secondly, we must remind ourselves the probability of the event occurring is very low, otherwise we wouldn't be scoping it. Thirdly, we have Mr Black to look after us. He is very good; he understands."

I waited for her to go on. She sighed, then said, "For a start, he encourages us to relax and laugh and joke amongst ourselves when we can. He enjoys that, and a bit of teasing. He loves his acronyms and his Spoonerisms and all that sort of thing and making up stories. It's all rather childish, I suppose, but reminding us we are children at heart seems to ease the weight of responsibility."

I asked, "Does he allow a bit of flirting once in a while?"

"Er, no," she said. "Mr Black says that sort of thing is bad for the team, divisive and distracting. He says he wants a 'unisex team' and thinks he's being terribly modern."

"Is that what the tracksuits are all about?" I asked.

"Yes and no. He says he likes us to be dressed the same as it unites the team. It's fine for the boys, but I find this one too bulky. He says I look fine, but you know what us girls are like. He also doesn't like me wearing jewellery or makeup at work. He says 'one team, one set of rules'!"

I pointed to the glasses. "And these?" I asked.

"You've noticed, Smartypants. We're going to have to watch you. You're right. I don't need them, but Mr Black says that people will take me more seriously if I wear them. Can you believe it? Also, he makes me do things like pour the tea and fetch the food. He says he is not sexist, but honestly! This is 1986, for heaven's sake!"

From the expression on her face, I could tell she was quite happy to do anything Mr Black asked of her.

"You said 'yes and no'. What's the no?"

"I'll explain later," she replied, quickly putting her glasses back on as Mr Black entered the conference room.

"How's it going?" He smiled at us, rather awkwardly, as though he realised he'd interrupted us. We both replied, almost at the same time that it was going fine. "Well then, I'd better leave you to it." He looked at me for a moment then said, "Mr White, are you quite happy?"

"Yes, perfectly!" I replied. But he continued to look at me, with raised eyebrows, as if he was waiting for me to go on. He knew I was troubled by something. I decided to tell him.

"It's just that I can't get my head around doing something which will kill thousands of people. I know we're only scoping, and that the demolition might save many more lives, but we can't be sure the bomb will explode. I mean, if its battery has run out. . . It just seems wrong."

"Ah!" he said. "The Doctrine of Necessity! It presents the greatest dilemma known to man. To do wrong, in order to prevent a greater wrong, to commit a deadly sin to avoid a greater evil. Or should I say, to do wrong, something which we know is definitely wrong, in the hope that it *might* prevent a greater evil.

"The easy way out, of course, would be to do nothing. But it's not the easy way out, because by doing nothing, you may be allowing that greater evil to happen; and you would be responsible for it. It would not be easy to bear the weight – the guilt – of hundreds of thousands of deaths, perhaps, which you could have prevented."

I understood what he was saying, but it hardly made me feel better. "So how does an individual decide if the greater evil might or might not happen? Surely, if the probability is low enough, there must be a point where the lesser evil is unjustified."

"That's it, Mr White. That's the dilemma. History has given us a few guidelines, but they are sparse. There was the famous case in 1884, Regina v. Dudley and Stephens, of four shipwrecked sailors who were cast adrift in a small boat without food. In order to survive, the three strongest decided to eat the fourth, the 17-year-old cabin boy."

"Eat him? My God!" It was Mrs Grey. "The poor lad!"

Mr Black continued. "At their trial, they pleaded it was necessary for their survival, and that the cabin boy would have died from natural causes anyway.

"The court ruled that cannibalising the boy was not urgently necessary, as at any moment a ship could have sailed over the horizon to save them. In fact, that's what happened. They ruled that two of the sailors, Dudley and Stephens, killed the boy intentionally and were therefore guilty of murder."

"But if he ate the boy, that's cannibalism!" said Mrs Grey.

"You're right. But under English law cannibalism alone is not a crime. Murder is, of course, and Dudley and Stephens were convicted of murder and sentenced to be hanged. Now, this is the interesting part. Their sentence was later reduced to just six months in prison. So while their defence of necessity failed in court, it was in fact acknowledged as valid by the reduction of the sentence.

"Three principles emerged from this case. A, the action to prevent the greater evil must indeed be necessary – in other words, there is no alternative way of preventing it. B, the greater evil must be imminent. And C, the defence of necessity cannot be used in cases of murder."

"But if we demolish the building and kill loads of people, wouldn't that be murder?" I had to ask the question.

"No," was Mr Black's answer, to my great relief. "Murder has to have an element of pre-meditation, of intent to kill. Your intention wasn't to kill the occupants, just bring the building down. Indeed, if the building had been empty, you would have still carried out the action. Your action was necessary to save others."

"So we wouldn't be guilty?" I asked.

Mr Black sighed. Mrs Grey and I waited for his answer. We were in this together.

"The defence of necessity is interesting because it justifies the crime rather than excuses it. In other words, it makes the action just: it makes it not a crime. This is different from the defence of duress, which acknowledges the crime has been committed but pleads mitigation.

"In England, few pleas of necessity have ever reached the courts, principally because prosecutors have recognised the principle of making the action just, and deemed that no crime had been committed: 'Quod est necessarium est licitum'. That which is necessary is lawful.

"So in your situation, the case would never reach a court. The demolition of the building, even with people inside it, would not have been a crime."

This made both of us feel a lot better.

He continued. "In the United States, early federal cases also recognised the defence. But the Americans take a slightly different view from us. Rather than talk about preventing a greater evil, they use the expression 'achieving a higher social value', but it boils down to the same thing. But what is extraordinary is that in 1834, a United States judge gave the opinion that necessity will excuse high treason, or any other of the higher crimes, *including* murder."

"Murder?" I asked. "Is his opinion still accepted in that country? Are there people there that believe that achieving a lesser evil, a higher social value, justifies high treason and murder? Is the Doctrine of Necessity – in effect – a licence to kill? Or to breach the American Constitution?"

Mr Black smiled. "There are really three types of people in this world. Those who would never deliberately do something bad. Then there are those who would do something bad, if it was for a good reason, like demolishing a building to save many more lives. And finally, those who would do something bad, simply because they are evil people.

"Those are the ones you have to watch, the sociopaths and the psychopaths – and those who haven't anything pathologically wrong with them but were 'born under an evil star'. They might use the Doctrine of Necessity as an excuse for their crimes. Or worst still, as a cover for their crimes, which – because of the Doctrine – may never be heard in court.

"Now, I must leave you two to get on with your work."

After he left, I turned to Mrs Grey. "So it would seem that under common law, it's possible for a person – or a state – to get away with almost any crime, any breach of the law if they can show their action prevented an imminent greater harm. But who's to judge where the balance of harm lies? Who's to say if the greater harm was indeed imminent? What does the word imminent mean?"

"I suppose the person who carries out the action must be the judge," she replied, "because his judgement guides his actions. Rather like in a case where someone kills an armed attacker in order to prevent him and, say, his girl-friend from being shot. He's not guilty of murder if he believed the gun being pointed at him was loaded, even though it might not have been.

"'Mens rea', I think it's called. 'Actus non facit reum nisi mens sit rea'. I might have got that wrong. It means an act does not make a person guilty unless the mind is guilty. Something like that."

It was beginning to worry me. "So an evil person can get away with a truly evil action, either by not being found out, or by claiming it was for the greater good – or achieved greater social value?"

"Yep. I'd go along with that," Mrs Grey replied. Then she added, almost in a whisper, "The bastard!" I pretended I hadn't heard.

We sat there in silence for a while. One of us had to change the subject. I asked Mrs Grey if there was a Mr Grey. "I expect so. Somewhere," she said.

"No, no. Is there one that belongs to *you*, Mrs Grey. Do you have a husband?"

I think she nearly gave me a dinntik, but then she added a definite, "No."

"Is the ring – like the glasses – just part of your 'cover'?"

"No," she said quietly, "it's real."

I persisted. "So what's your real status then?"

She frowned slightly. "Work it out, Dumbo." I must've looked puzzled, because she added, "I'm not divorced."

Finally, I clicked. "I'm so sorry," I said.

She smiled and said, "That's okay," and leant towards me. And for a brief, wonderful moment she put her hand on mine.

We had a leg-stretch, then more hard graft which generated lots of questions for Mr Green. Then the bit I liked: the wait for answers.

"So! Cleverboy," she said, easing her chair back, crossing one tracksuited leg over the other and pushing her glasses to the top of her head. "Does the interrogation continue?"

"Tracksuits," I reminded her. "I asked if it was part of Mr B's efforts to build a unisex team. You said yes and no. What's the no?"

She took a deep breath. "You'll have noticed there are no security cabinets around here – and Mr Green's drawings don't have any wording on them. I know it sounds dramatic, but we keep nearly all the information we need in our heads. No paper. No microfilm. No faxes, teleprinters or anything like that. It's safer that way, and as we're dealing with concepts most of the time, it's OK. We have to help each other out sometimes, but we don't mind. It works."

"But what's that got to do with tracksuits?"

That sigh again. "If someone wanted to steal our supersecrets, they'd have to steal us, in a nutshell. It's the one obsession Mr Black doesn't joke about. The first line of defence against such an attack, as he calls it, is not allowing anybody to *know* you are carrying secrets.

"For example, I expect you came here in the windowless van." I nodded. "Which unloaded you in the garage. Hopefully, nobody saw you come here, so nobody knows you're here, so nobody knows you share our secrets. Obviously, we try and maintain a low profile here anyway, but you must 'always assume the worst', as Mr B would say.

"In theory, none of us here know each other, and he thinks it's best if it remains that way. We can have a laugh and a chat, but we mustn't talk about anything too personal that could identify us. For example, you and I could talk about the films we like, or music, or books, but we mustn't say things like 'I love walking my dog on Richmond Common' as it could be a trace. That's a thing that helps to identify you.

"The colours thing is all part of it. We used to give ourselves false names we'd chose ourselves, but we could never remember who we were supposed to be, so Mr B suggested the Cluedo pieces. He said everyone will know the names are false, so why not make them easy to remember. Simple, really. Not knowing who the others are is the important thing, in case one of us 'got caught'."

She indicated the inverted commas with her fingers. "The risk of it leading to the others is diminished. It's called cut-offs. And he's completely obsessive about cut-offs! Look! Look at this!"

She bent forward and turned down the collar of her tracksuit top. I stood up to see what she was pointing at. I saw this rather slender neck, at the top of which emerged some fine Titian hairs which she was holding up with her other hand. I noticed her skin was smooth and slightly tanned, a small mole on the left side. A neck asking to be kissed.

"What do you see?" she asked.

"Nothing," I lied.

"Exactly," she replied. "That man instructed A and L to cut off every label on every garment we wear in this place. We're not allowed jewellery, watches, pens or any personal items."

She smiled. "But we go along with it because we know he's only doing it for our safety. He's doing his best to take care of us, and we love him for it. He once said we're his family."

"But the labels thing, that's a bit extreme, surely?"

"Well, perhaps not. Some years ago, when I was working in another department – dinntik, by the way – we were asked to identify a man from a single, black and white photo. He was emerging from a building, holding up a copy of the Hong Kong Times so his face couldn't be seen. Fortunately, we had two other traces on him – tiny scraps of information – which when cross-linked together give us much more info than they would alone; the sum is greater, much greater, than the parts."

"We were lucky because he was wearing an ooblow. That was the second trace, after the paper."

"What on earth is an ooblow?" I asked.

"That's the point! Few people know what an ooblow is! Anyway, I wouldn't expect a mere mortal like you to know about such things. It's a very expensive Swiss watch. It's spelt H U B L O T – Hublot.

"The other trace was the suit. We guessed he was in the Far East from the paper he was holding. And, as Mr Smartypants here may well know – but we think is unlikely – virtually all cloth for suits sold in the Far East comes from Huddersfield."

She said some of her 'people' visited the Worsted Weavers Association based there. From the pattern of the material seen in the photo, they identified it almost straight away, a lightweight but expensive one. They provided a list of forty-seven, or whatever, tailors in Hong Kong who had bought some in the last five years. A team of 'people' visited each one and obtained a list of customers who had suits made of the material.

I then said, "which you then crosslinked with another list from ooblow!"

"Brilliant!" she said. "We'd never have thought of that!" She then burst out laughing and explained that the Swiss are generally very slow on such matters – perhaps because we cannot persuade them by offering nice favours like calling off the surprise VAT inspection booked for next week. She said Hublot were pretty cagey about their customers, so it was unlikely they would get far.

"What our guys actually did was to phone up every customer on the tailors' list, claiming to be the police. They explained that an ooblow had been handed in and was it theirs. Most of the customers said 'what's that?', or words to that effect, but three said no, it is on my wrist.

"These were checked out by local 'people' and found not to be the 'man', but finally a helpful secretary said she'd ask her boss, coming back a moment later saying he's wearing it. With further checking, he turned out to be the target. One bloke who was phoned up said it was his! Cheeky blighter!"

She said it wasn't always that easy, but the trick was never giving up. Mr B referred to such operations as 'Mission: Possible'. She said in years to come cross-linking would be much easier. Within ten years all the information in the world could be stored electronically in a space the size of a sugar cube, and that computers would do the cross-linking, not people. She said it would then be much harder to carcass.

"What's carcassing, lass? Is it another of Mr B's acroprops?"

She smiled. "Yes, it is. It stands for cut and run, change and stay silent. Change is for change of identity, by the way."

She hesitated, then continued. "That's not just changing one's name. To do it properly, you have to kill yourself off and be 'born again' as a different person. If you don't dead yourself, they'll keep looking and eventually find you."

I felt this was getting kind of serious. "But surely," I said, "things could never get as bad as that. What exactly is the threat?"

"Firstly, the other side." I could sense another of Mr B's briefings was about to emerge. "They might try and extract secrets from you." My stomach churned. "You mean. . . by torture?"

"No, that's very unlikely, and ineffective. You need to get the target *wanting* to tell you the information. It's a much more subtle approach, a psychological one, like in Mr B's story yesterday."

"You mean they would threaten to kill a child?" The idea sickened me. She must've seen the look on my face.

She said, "Don't worry, that's extremely unlikely. They're not psychopaths. They're professionals. We scoped it a few years back. For a start, if anybody actually wanted to kidnap a child and sell it into slavery, they'd just do it. They wouldn't pussyfoot around phoning up relatives. The threat has to be sudden and shocking to evoke an immediate, unthought-through response.

"Following the scope, we were all given a selection of names to learn off by heart – Soviet, Brit and a few others, names of people, operations, that sort of thing. The drill if you got the phone call was to fake utter shock 'n' horror and between sobs and retching keep saying the appropriate name over and over again until they ring off. If you do it well, they can't get a word in edgeways. We actually practised it; great fun. By the time they've found out the name's false, you've called the crash trolley. Before you ask, dinntik."

"And the second threat?" I asked. "The three little pigs," she replied. "Press, PR and Propaganda. The Press and PR are on our side. Propaganda is the term we give to the PR put out by the other side.

"Think what an investigative journalist might make of it if they knew what we'd been discussing yesterday morning. What a story! I'm not saying they would physically threaten you, but they would pry, and pry, phone you, tap your phone, go through your rubbish, bang on your front door, bribe you, befriend your friends – do almost anything to get a story of some sort. They would delude themselves they were doing it because 'the public has a right to know'. But I tell you, they would be doing it for fame and fortune."

"So how the hell do you deal with that?" I asked.

"It's countered in two ways, by not allowing our people to have any corroborating info, like knowledge of this place, where it is, what it looks like. The other is to have a plan to discredit the source. Press announcements saying things like 'It is understood that Mr White did not collect his medication last week. The public are advised not to approach him but to inform their local police station.'

"You've seen all that sort of stuff. Throw in some alleged crime or perversion, say he thinks he's the Messiah, and the press will drop him and his 'fantasy' like a hot brick. They are shit-scared of being taken for a ride and made to look silly. Hits their advertising revenue."

"Any other threats?"

"Yes," she replied, "the last is the most dangerous of them all. While the other two groups are trying to get information out of you, this group don't want the info revealed. They want it buried, shredded. Often they're on your side."

"Shredded?" I asked. She was frowning, but I had to know what she meant.

"Shredded? If you want to get rid of a secret document, you shred it in a shredder – although that's not very secure. If the secrets are in a person's head, like with us, you shred the person. Shredded, deaded. Some say it's Cockney rhyming slang. Shredded wheat."

I started to go through the alphabet. I stopped when I reached M. Shredded meat. Dead meat, I thought. Murder. "How could they ever do that?" I asked. I was stunned by her reply.

"You're planning to demolish a building with people in it, perhaps 10,000, entirely innocent civilians. How do you justify it? Because your action is saving many more lives. The greater good, as Mr B was saying yesterday. If 'one of our people' were to defect, say, carrying secrets which could give away dozens of assets, a shredding could be justified on the grounds of 'the greater good', of saving the lives of those assets.

"Take you, for example. Supposing you'd left when you said you might, and gone to the Press to expose this evil group of people who were planning to do this demolition, d' you think Mr B would allow you to do that? Good people sometimes have to do bad things for good reason."

She was beginning to sound like Mr Black, and she was frightening me. She smiled and said sorry, and her gorgeous smile made me feel better.

"It happens very rarely, and it's tightly controlled. It's classed as a lawful killing of an 'enemy combatant armed with sensitive information which could be dedah dedah dedah'. You'd be classified as a threat to the state and therefore an enemy of the state.

"They say it's not murder because the pre-meditated intention behind the action is not to kill, but to actually save lives. All gobbledygook of course, but it eases the conscience of the poor minister who has to sign it off.

"Mr B calls them Fatwas. Another of his mnemonics: For Assassination, Termination or Whatever Authorisation. They're interesting documents – not that I've ever seen one – but they have to go into sufficient detail to justify the, er, action, yet not give away too much, bearing in mind a politician has to see them. They truly are supersecret! The recommendation is made by an ad hoc committee of three – all named – and the most senior of them signs it before it's passed to the minister.

"Nobody likes getting involved in that sort of op. Often it's passed to another service or one of our allies. It's slightly easier, then. Actually, if one of our own carcasses, i.e. disappears, everyone in the department is quite pleased."

I was amazed. I had no idea about these things. I let her carry on.

"If you are unlucky enough to be on the wrong end of a Fatwa, carcassing is best, but getting rid of yourself is quite hard because there is no body – at least not your body. If you have the time, you wait for something like a train crash, then lay a trail indicating that you were on that train and haven't been seen since. Plane crashes are more difficult, because of passenger manifests and ticket records, things like that, but it can be done."

This sort of conversation took place in fits and starts during the day. A balance between fun and fright, mixed in the weighty task in hand. Mr Black popped in at tea-time to say there would be 'prayers' tomorrow morning at 10:00 a.m. and would we mind awfully coming along? And good news! A and L have their chef back, and he wondered if I would like to try his boef bourguignon followed by his 'bombe surprise' that evening in the comfort of my own cabin. I think 'bombe' was a joke, so I laughed, and then I said something which I'd prepared earlier:

"I'm sorry Mr Black, but I really don't think I can spare the time. Mrs Grey and I have a lot to get through, and. . ."

Tracksuit '86 played her part, looking weary but resigned, and his reply was just what I'd hoped. "Well, why don't the two of you work through over a nice meal, for once. I'll let them know. It'll do you both good. See you tomorrow at ten, then. It's going well, keep it up."

I expected him to say 'children' at the end, but he didn't.

And so it was that Mrs Grey and I found ourselves, still in our tracksuits, sitting opposite each other across the little table in my 'cabin'. She'd brought the food on one of those heated hostess trolleys and had carefully laid the table. "Well," she said, "here we are!"

I replied, "So, did you get those answers out of Mr Green?"

She looked really sad. "Bad news, I'm afraid. Mr Green apologises and says he can't get them to us before tomorrow but he will see us at prayers."

"My goodness, Mrs Grey" I replied. "That's truly terrible." We both burst out laughing and dug into our prawn cocktails.

Between mouthfuls, I said, "Mrs Grey, what's your real name?"

She munched away, swallowed and said, "Dinntik."

"My!" I replied, "that's a pretty name!" I then added the other part of that well-worn remark, "for a pretty girl!"

She did the demure bit again, playing the role beautifully.

"But may I call you Dinny?" I asked.

"Hey," she said, "I like that. As in Dinny Hall. Yes, kind sir, you may call me Dinny." Then added, "But only in this room."

"Sure," I said, "but who, where or what is Dinny Hall?"

"She's a she, shilly boy!"

"You're slurring your words. No more fizzy water for you, young lady!"

More prawn cocktail. Then she asked, "Mr White, what's your real name?"

"Dinntik," I replied.

"Dinntik? That's a pretty ugly name for a pretty ugly fellow. Can I call you Dinny?"

"No."

"Why not?"

"It's a girl's name. You've already told me that."

Stupid, childish fun. But it took our minds off the study.

"Hey," I said. "I tell you what. You can call me Danny."

"Yep, Dinny and Danny! They go well together," she said.

"What? The names? Or the people?" I asked.

"The names, Clotto! We hardly know each other!" I nearly said nonsense, we have known each other for ages. Then I realised we only met the previous day.

"Well, we must put that right, mustn't we?" I said. "Tell me about yourself."

"It's a bit of a saga, really. Not sure where to begin. Left uni and became a sort of civil servant. Loved it, until one day I was told they wanted me to honey-up a target – that's do the, you know, honey-trap thing. I said no way. I'd met my husband in my last year and he was my first proper boyfriend. Really the first man I had that magic feeling for, of wanting to have his baby.

"I suppose that's what love is, really, nature's way of getting us to pro-create. We'd only just returned from our honeymoon – honeymoon! And there I was being asked to do a honey-up.

"Actually, my immediate boss was a decent fellow and said he'd see what he could do. A couple of days later I was summoned to his boss's office. Action Man. That's what we called him." She frowned when she said the name.

"He virtually told me I'd do it. He banged on about being a good soldier, doing what the country needed me to do – all that sort of thing. I just said he'd got the wrong girl. He then lost his rag and said something like 'look lass; we've got to get some dirt on this fellow'.

"Can you imagine how I felt? He was telling me I was dirt! And then he said 'Come on, surely you'd like to be bonked by a lord, all that power! All that dosh! He'll buy you nice things, like new clothes, nice shoes' etc. etc. He was awful." She clenched her jaw and frowned. "Still is."

"But what an awful thing to have to do," I said. "That's terrible!"

"Yes," she said, "and I was only twenty-two at the time." Then after a brief pause, she added, with a twinkle in her eye. "Of course, had I been twenty-three, it would have been fine. . .."

Soldier humour, but it bucked us both up for a moment. I said I thought honey-traps were only for people like Soviet spies.

"No. Anyone you need to control. The target was a judge taking part in an inquiry. In the interests of the Nation – I can't tell you why – it was of great importance the outcome went a certain way. Happens often. Get some dirt and you have control. If the target hasn't got any dirty laundry in his closet – good word, by the way – you make some!

"Of course, these days people aren't so concerned about marital infidelity, or even homosexual affairs. So the honey in the trap is of a stickier, messier kind. Best not to ask."

"So, when you refused, did they just find somebody else to do it?" I had visions of some other poor girl having to 'be a good soldier'.

"Nah. Someone went and saw him – the peer – and explained the situation. And reminded him of his oath of allegiance. He was offered the opportunity of an audience, but said it wouldn't be necessary."

"What do you mean 'an audience'?" I was puzzled.

"With her, the Queen." She must have noticed the amazement on my face. "People don't realise just how powerful she is. But think about it. Every MP, every Privy Counsellor, every lord, members of the Armed Services, they all have to swear allegiance to her. They have to do what she tells them to do. Otherwise, it is a breach of oath. A reminder now and then can work wonders. Audiences are rarely necessary."

"Jesus!" I'd never thought about that. I'd sworn that oath myself when I signed up. "Going back to you and. . . Action Man. What happened then? After you refused?"

"I told my husband – he was in the same line of work – and he went ballistic, as you can imagine. He threatened to blow the whole thing open, apparently."

"And did he?"

She took a deep breath. "No. He didn't have a chance." And then I thought she said 'he was sacked'. But she didn't. In a matter-of-fact way, she simply said he was shredded.

"Fell off a yacht, wasn't wearing a life jacket, drunk, his fault, body never found. Usual stuff. He never drank, by the way. All I have is the ring." She looked down at her wedding ring.

I sensed her mood had changed. I saw she was clenching her fists, her whole body seemed tense, and she was frowning. I wanted to know more about Action Man, whether there were many like him among her 'people'. But I thought I'd let it go.

Then she jumped up, put the Head-Girl smile back on her face and said, "Let's try this boef bourguignon, shall we?"

It was time to move onto another subject, something she might actually enjoy talking about. "Tell me about Mr Black."

Just as I thought, it brought an immediate smile and a kind of faraway look in her eyes.

"Mr B?" she said. "Where can I start?" I felt it was best not to say anything. I let her continue.

"I first met him shortly after, you know, that thing I was talking about. He persuaded me not to leave the Service. It took him about four months. I was on sick leave. He wasn't persistent, he just gently helped me get over the, the anger – trauma, I suppose.

That thing American soldiers got after Vietnam, 'Post traumatic stress disorder'." She said it with an American accent.

"We talked a lot. We got to know each other. He joked and tried to make me laugh. I'd tease him, and he'd pretend to be offended, then he'd laugh and tease me back. Yeah, we got on. We got on really well. He once bought me a necklace. . ." She stopped. I think she must have seen my frown.

"There was never any sort of, you know, that kind of thing. But I did love him, and I still do love him, how you would love a kind old uncle. I assumed he wasn't married – and never had been – and when I asked him one day, he didn't confirm it or deny it. He just said he was married to his work.

"I think I did upset him once, when he offered me a job with his 'people'. He described what I'd be doing – no daggers, only cloaks, no boring stuff, make-a-difference and all that, and he would be my direct boss. I couldn't believe it. I thought no-one would ever want to employ me again. Anyway, I flung my arms around his neck and hugged him, and I told him he was my fairy godfather. He stiffened – no, silly! He backed away. Honestly, you men!. . . He said I wasn't to call him that.

"The job was great – still is. He set the organisation up about twenty years ago, all on his own to begin with. I asked him once why he'd got involved in this scoping thing, and he said that if I'd seen the things he'd seen, I'd understand.

"He'd been involved in something called Op Grapple, the testing of Britain's first H bomb. Anyway, he saw the thing go off, and told me it was his 'Strangelove moment'. Did you see that film?" I nodded but let her continue.

"He showed a video of it shortly after I joined. Great film. Very funny – except the ending which showed all those atomic bombs going off. Do you remember that? To Vera Lynn singing We'll Meet Again? That's what he foresaw, he said, the world being wiped out."

And, looking into the distance above my left shoulder, she stood up and started to sing, in a lovely voice:

"We'll meet again, don't know where, don't know when,
But I'll know we'll meet again some sunny day."

As she sang the second line, she looked at me. I didn't know if it was part of the wartime-nightclub-singer act, or something else.

"Apparently, the nuclear test went very well," she continued, as she sat down. "So well that the yield was much bigger than predicted. As a result, he and his ship got a far greater dose of radiation than they should've done. But he's still here, thank goodness. 'A great success'! Yep. That's what they said about the test.

"I'll never forget my first solo assignment. Can you imagine this? At twenty-three I was sent off to join the ladies at Greenham Common. Well, females, anyway. Actually, I met some really, really nice people there. Okay, there were some horrors.

"I did meet one girl who was very kind and funny. We got on really well, and she introduced me to lots of others. Then one evening she asked me back to her bivvy for hot chocolate, but she wanted more than I could offer her. I said I was sorry, but I really wasn't up for it as I sat there letting the enamelled cup warm my hands. She cried, and I tried to comfort her. But I just couldn't. Me? Can you imagine?"

No, I thought. *Not anymore.*

"My brief was broad. Go and talk to them. Get to know them. Find out what makes them tick. He explained they were very anti-men and that I was the best 'man' for the job! He's so funny sometimes, and he doesn't notice!

"So off I went. I was there, on and off, for about two months. When I was recalled – now this was the exciting part and is still very hush-hush – Mr B asked if I'd mind awfully going to London with him to meet the client."

"Let me guess," I said. "You went up to London to visit the–?"

"Nah, not the big 'ouse. Just a terraced job in a side street. Anyway, Mr B told me there was no need for any preparatory work, just go. He hates reports and all that sort of thing. Anyway, off we went in one of the cars, and as we turned into the street, I thought 'OH MY GOD!!!!'. But the Prime Minister was fantastic.

"As I walked into her office, she got up and came around her desk towards me and, extending her hand, said something like 'thank you so much for coming, my dear, it is really such a pleasure to meet you, and what a lovely necklace that is! You must tell me where it came from, but I would imagine it was very expensive and surely must have been a present from a very special person but I mustn't pry. . .'

"Up to then, I hadn't said a word except a mumbled 'ma'am'. But soon we were nattering away. I told her the necklace was a Dinny Hall, and she said I was very lucky but deserved to be lucky and so on. It was the one Mr B had given me two weeks earlier, and I was wearing it for the first time. Anyway, his stage cough broke the spell, and we got down to business over a cup of tea which she poured herself.

"She asked me lots of questions, not in an interrogation style, but in a kind of 'can you possibly help me' way. Rather like Mr B would. I had a feeling they'd met before. Mr B was good too. He 'reminded' us of how Lyndon Johnson, when running for president in 1964 had countered the Goldwater campaign slogan 'in your heart you know he's right', with 'in your heart you know he might', meaning he might use nuclear weapons in a first strike against Soviet Russia.

"Mr B said if you happen to be a Russian, that's quite scary, and went on to say we don't want the Russians to be scared. Quite the opposite. We want to show them we're not about to unleash our nuclear weapons, and what better way of doing this than to have a women's movement in UK demonstrating against them. If the Soviets wanted to fund this, why not let'em? Or words to that effect. I thought it was very clever. . ."

A happier time for Dinny. It was good to see her smile, and I loved her stories. I said, "Hey, you've got a voice! Where did you learn to sing like that?"

"Oh," she replied, "I've always been keen on dance and drama, singing, that sort of thing. I wanted to be an actress when I was at school."

"Sing me something else," I asked.

"OK. . . " She paused, obviously thinking of something suitable. "How about this then?"

At which point she got up and started humming and swinging her hips to that Beatles song.

> "Listen, do you want to know a secret
> Do you promise not to tell, whoa oh, oh,"

As she started to sing the words, she danced, and she smiled when she flashed her eyes in my direction. I was struck dumb. Then I managed to say "Wow! Were you ever one of Pan's People?"

She stopped and said "Nah! But we used to dance along with them in our drawing room – me and my friend – when they were on the box. I was probably about eight at the time, but it was fun."

"Sing some more," I urged, "you're great!"

She began again, humming, dancing.

> "Closer, let me whisper in your ear,
> Say the words you long to hear. . ."

And then she stopped suddenly and said "Hey, have you seen *Temple of Doom*? That opening sequence?" I had, actually. It had come out a couple of years previously, great film with a great beginning with Kate Capshaw singing in Chinese and dancing to Cole Porter's 'Anything Goes'.

Before I could reply, Dinny was off, strutting her stuff like a Busby Berkeley babe, singing in English – thank God – and tap-dancing around my room in her trainers on the soft synthetic carpet. A sort of silent tap dance. It didn't matter. She was wonderful.

"In olden days, a glimpse of stocking
Was looked on as something shocking.
But now, God knows,
Anything goes.
   "Good authors too who once knew better words
Now only use four-letter words
Writing prose.
Anything goes!"

As she got to the next verse, she fixed her eyes on mine and started to dance towards me.

"If driving fast cars you like,
If low bars you like,
If old hymns you like,
If bare limbs you like,
If Mae West you like,
Or me *undressed* you like,
Why, nobody will oppose.
Anything goes!"

And then she stopped. "Phew, it's hot in here," she said, puffing gently. "I must take this wretched thing off."

And she started to pull up her grey tracksuit top. As she did so, the white tennis shirt she was wearing underneath rode up a little, revealing for a few delicious moments a bare midriff, flat, tanned and simply beautiful. My pulse rate quickened, and I could feel myself going red again. I thought I must say something, do something. So I got up and said, "Well, in that case, I think I'll turn the central heating up."

Always ahead of me, she laughed and said, "In your dreams, sonny!" I had expected something similar, but it was a put-down. In both ways.

She said she'd better be going; then she noticed we had hardly touched the boef bourguignon on our plates and hadn't even started our meringuey things. "Hey, we can't leave all this!" she said. "The chef will be mortified!"

"Well, I'm sorry," I said. "I'm stuffed." In fact, the last thing on my mind was food.

"Me too. We'll have to put it down the loo. Hey, pass your plates over." And before I knew it she'd disappeared into the bathroom and flushed away the evidence.

As she loaded the empty plates onto the trolley, she looked at the clock and said, "Time for me to go!"

Before I could recover, she came around to where I was sitting, ruffled my hair, grabbed her tracksuit top then marched out of the room saying, "See you tomorrow!"

Head girl again. I didn't want her to go. I quickly finished putting everything back on the trolley, opened the door, and wheeled it through. But there was no sign of her.

In my dreams, I thought. That's better than nothing. But I didn't dream and slept soundly until the alarm went off the following morning.

9

On the Thursday morning, we managed to fit in two solid hours of work before we had to shut down the computer and clear the table for 'prayers' – a service term for a briefing. Mr B arrived precisely at ten followed by Mr Green five minutes later. It reminded me of my university days: the 'academic five minutes'.

Mr B went through the pleasantries. He hoped I'd slept well and that the food last night 'had been up to muster'. I said it was delicious, and I was careful not to look across the table to Mrs Grey. He then began the proceedings by saying some further information had come to light which we might find helpful – good news and bad news.

Looking in my direction he explained he always started with the good news because if the bad news came first, it would be more likely to be forgotten. In scoping, he said, one must focus on the worst, the puncture on a wet muddy road in the middle of the night.

Spare us that, please, I thought.

"So, the good news is that RA-115s are actually quite safe bits of kit. The guts of them are based on a 105mm howitzer nuclear shell. As you can imagine, these things have to be strong and stable, A, to be fired out of a gun, and B to survive a counter bombardment on one's gun lines."

Mr Black continued. "Now what does that mean for us here? It means this." And he bent forward leaning on his knuckles. "If you, Mr White, can get that building down, no matter how violently you have to do it, the probability of that device detonating as a result of your demolition is virtually nil. However, it could become a serious rad haz at Ground Zero. So the message is, Mr White, get that thing down as low as you can, as quickly as you can, with as much debris on top of it as you can: bury it!"

He sounded as if he was briefing his band of commandos the night before their raid on the German heavy water plant at Telemark. *Yessir, it'll be done sir, just the way you want it.*

My tendency to be on the border of insolence with my superiors was probably one of the many I failed to achieve further promotion. I remember being briefed on some task or other and I said to my commanding officer 'I'll do my best, sir'. He looked down his nose at me and said 'Rayner, it's not good enough merely to do one's best. One must do what is necessary'. At least he admitted it was a quote from an even greater man than himself: Churchill.

Mr B continued in this vein, warming to his task – and frankly frightening the life out of me. I was responsible for the demolition of this building and therefore saving the world, yet in the course of this achievement, I would kill tens of thousands of men, women and children.

His earlier assurance that I wouldn't be tried for murder was of little comfort. Then I remembered what Dinny had said: it was all pretend.

"Now the bad news," Mr B beamed. "Word has it a price has been put on these things. I'm not suggesting you will see them being advertised in Exchange and Mart!" He chuckled. "No, what I am saying is there are indications that someone is trying to sell – or buy – a device. We don't know which. We must, therefore, assume that knowledge of the missing bombs is out there. The price indication rules out the lone-wolf as our perp, so we can assume the perps are a hostile state or a state-sponsored organisation. If so, the ransom scenario must be evaluated."

Mr B must have noticed the puzzled look on my face, as he went on to explain. "Imagine, Mr White, the man on the roof with his radiotelephone. He dials 911 – that's equivalent to our 999 – and says he is at the top of a building with an RA-115, serial number so-and-so, and could he please talk to the President."

He must have read my mind. He said, "Please don't concern yourself with how that situation could develop – we have another team working on that. Just bear in mind we need to remain in full control of the demolition, yet be able to proceed at a moment's notice. Talking of timings, another team has evaluated the 'prior knowledge' probability. They reckon there's a high chance one of the intelligence services we are work with will get a whiff of something."

I asked how long such a warning was likely to be. He looked up at the ceiling. "Imagine a four-dimensional matrix of probabilities: time, quality and reliability of info. . ."

He must have heard my sigh because he looked at me and said, "Mr White, assume you have two weeks to prepare your demolition, but it must be done with absolute secrecy."

He then ended on a much brighter note. "Aren't we lucky we're not dealing with a psychopath! Coffee now, d'you think, Mrs Grey?"

Yeah, really lucky. And we've got all that time, too. Then I reminded myself we were only scoping, pretending. Tomorrow, I would walk out of this damn place, whatever, wherever it was. And hopefully, get paid a major's daily rate for my trouble.

Over coffee, Mr B came up to me. "Mr White, it's good to have you on the team, and we're really grateful for your efforts. If there's anything I can do for you while you're here, any help I can give you, do please let me know."

I wanted to ask him about Dinny, about Action Man and what had really gone on. I wanted to talk about her, not the study.

"Thanks, Mr Black," I replied. "I was thinking about the man on the roof. Surely there must be another way to deal with the situation. I mean pulling the whole building down seems a bit drastic."

"I agree," he reassured me. Was he just being nice?

He then went on. "When you arrived here, I gave you an outline of what we do. I think perhaps you're ready for the bigger picture. Scoping isn't a single study. It is rather like a tree. The base scope, the trunk, identifies the current situation. In our case this week, the missing bombs. Sorry. I should explain something else. They may be missing. Just because a double agent tells us they are, doesn't mean they definitely are.

"So the first evaluation is of the raw information. If the probability and possible consequence calculation produces a figure above a certain threshold, we 'pretend' the situation is real. This might then generate a number of simultaneous scopes which in turn lead to further ones and so on and so forth. It becomes like a tree.

"Your scope, I can assure you, is on one of the outer branches. An important one, yes, but don't let it get to you. And when you leave us tomorrow, just forget all about it, and forget about us, this place. Everything. All this. . .It's best all round – if you see what I mean."

This prompted me to ask another question. "The presentation tomorrow, how long have I got?"

"As long as it takes," he replied.

"What form of presentation should I give? I don't know what you're expecting."

"Well," he said as if he was giving it a lot of thought. "I'll get A and L to set up our overhead projector here, and I'll ask Mrs Grey to bring you some view-foils and china-graphs after close of play."

I was beginning to like Mr Black, but 'china-graphs'? Those pens used for writing on plastic? View-foils? *We are in the dark ages here.*

Coffee came and went, as did lunch. More of the same intense work, questions for Mr Green and breaks for leg-stretches and chats. And it was the chats I enjoyed most. Just me and Mrs Grey – or as I preferred to think of her, Dinny, my research assistant.

During one of our breaks, I said to her, "Tell me something. Mr B said I must forget everything when I leave here, but how on earth can one get super-secrets out of your mind?"

She gave me a couple of tips which she'd been taught in training. One was to imagine writing down all the secrets and locking them away in a wooden box – like a tuck-box at school, she said – then floating the box down a long, wide river. You watch it till it's a tiny speck on the horizon until it finally disappears, out to sea perhaps. Best done at night, when you are really tired.

"Does that *really* work?" I asked.

"Work?" she replied. "Of course not!" She then admitted the technique works to a certain extent but explained about flashbacks: how some trivial thing, a piece of music, a smell, how any sort of trigger like that can bring it all back.

Retros, she called them. She said the syndrome was like retrograde amnesia, but instead of forgetting something you are trying to remember, retros made you remember something you're trying to forget.

"But don't worry," she reassured me. "Secrets are usually volatile. I don't mean they explode in your face – although sometimes they can do that. I mean they evaporate over time; they lose their power and pass their sell-by date. They cease to be secrets, or at least not be secrets anyone cares about or have any consequences.

"Like the Lusitania, you know? That sailed from New York with all those munitions on board, and got torpedoed by a German sub? It was a real super-duper secret at the time, for very good reason. It was a set-up. It was plain, old-fashioned murder. Believe you me, I know about the Lusitania."

"Murder? Surely not. It was an act of war. As you say, she was carrying ammunition. You can't blame the Germans."

"The Germans? No. I'm not blaming the Germans; I'm blaming Churchill!" She was getting angry.

"Listen. A week before the sinking, Churchill wrote to the President of the Board of Trade saying it was most important to attract neutral shipping to our shores in the hope of embroiling the United States with Germany. Then, lo and behold, a week later the Lusitania sails into an area patrolled by German U-boats without a destroyer escort. I'm not saying he organised the whole thing, just that he let it happen."

"But isn't it rather like what Mr B was saying, that by letting it happen it might have stopped Britain being beaten by the Kaiser – a small wrong to prevent a great evil? Or like us demolishing a skyscraper to prevent World War 3?" I thought I was making sense, but apparently not.

"No. It's NOT like us at all. The Lusit– Look, there's no point in looking at me like that!"

It was our first row. I thought I'd better shut up and let her continue.

She did. "Anyway, after the sinking Churchill wrote – actually wrote it down – that we should regard the sinking as 'an event most important and favourable to the Allies'. He said the poor babies who perished in the ocean struck a blow at German power more deadly than could have been achieved by the sacrifice of 100,000 men. For him, it was a balance of two evils: the sacrifice of 1198 passengers and crew or the sacrifice of 100,000 soldiers!"

It was strange to see her angry, and it made me feel uncomfortable. But I thought I ought to put her right. "Yes!" I said. "That's my point! The Doctrine of Necessity! It wasn't murder. It was to prevent a greater evil."

She calmed down, then replied: "Danny. Remember Mr B saying our thingy – demolishing the skyscraper – wouldn't be murder because our intention was not to kill the people inside, just to bring the building down?"

"Yes. Go on," I said.

"Well, for Churchill, whether he made it happen or let it happen, the intention was not the sinking of some old ship, it was the killing of the babies. And the other civilians, especially the American ones. That's what persuaded the Americans to join the war. It was the killing, not the sinking. The killing was intended. It was murder. In our case, it's the opposite. We don't want the killing; we just want to sink the building."

She had a point, I suppose. I said nothing.

She continued, looking into the distance. "But what does it matter, today, if the truth about that ship and her last voyage were widely known? Populations are not going to be thrown into panic. No-one's going to declare war on anyone. People aren't going to die if the truth is disclosed. . ."

Then she was back to her normal, lovely self. Two subjects I need to steer well clear of, I thought. The Lusitania, and Action Man.

10

It was ten to seven that Thursday evening when we called it a day. I knew I had a lot of work ahead of me, preparing my presentation and doing all those view-foils. No numbers, mind, just concepts. That was a great relief. I just hoped Dinny would stay and help. She said she'd bring the supper round – and I just hoped Mr B hadn't forgotten about the china-graphs and things.

I went back to my accommodation, showered – and shaved – and cleaned my teeth. Ever the hopeful. And no sooner had I put my feet up when there was a knock at the door. As I opened it, I could hardly believe my eyes. It wasn't Mrs Grey. It wasn't Dinny. It was Julie Christie, Jean Shrimpton, Ursula Andreas, Audrey Hepburn and a few others, all rolled into one.

The apparition giggled, pushed past me with the trolley, then turned towards me. "Do you like it?" she asked.

Here was Dinny, wearing an exquisite dress, pale cream, sleeveless, tailored around a delightfully slender waist, one of those light silk scarves around her neck. Hem breaking midway between knee and. . . I dare not imagine. Legs that went on forever, tanned, slim and finally disappearing into a pair of what would now be called killer heels.

Her Titian locks, normally bobbing around her shoulders in a rather unkempt bob in need of a trim, were held up in what I suppose today would be called a crunchy. Her eyes looked beautiful, just a touch of shadow, no mascara, and I guessed that she'd put just a little something on her cheeks which added contour to her face.

"H-hey!" I said. "You look absolutely f-fantastic! I'm sure Mr B would not approve of, of. . ." I didn't quite know where to start.

"Actually, it was his idea," she said, "as it was your last evening with us. He didn't want you to go away with the impression we slopped around in baggy tracksuits all the time. He said he wants you to realise we are just normal people. He really likes you."

Normal people, I thought. *Yeah. Just a normal, run-of-the-mill English Rose you pick up from any old garage forecourt.*

The emotion I felt was strange. My pulse was racing, but she hadn't gone to all this trouble on my behalf; she was just following the instructions of her superior spy-master.

It was also strange because I felt an element of relief it wasn't for me. I treasured the relationship that had gradually grown during those days which felt like weeks. I didn't want anything to happen which might endanger it. It was something special.

It was a kind of love uncomplicated by sex and built on respect; between two friends on the same wavelength having a shared sense of humour – and a shared mission: soldiers fighting to save the world. I didn't want to jeopardise that bond, that unity of purpose and spirit, by a fuddled, muddled attempt at romance, let alone seduction; that sort of thing was never one of my greatest skills. And the last thing I could do with right now in my life was an emotional involvement with someone I'd never see again.

My pulse eventually slowed right down to a running pace, and I thought it wise to start work before we dined. I asked her if she'd brought the china-graphs and she collapsed into laughter, bending forward with her hands on her thighs to support her.

"Oh," she said as she recovered herself, "I am so sorry. It was Mr B! It was one of his little jokes! You don't need those for tomorrow, no view-foils, no overhead projector, no nuffink!"

"What?" I said, not quite able to work out what the joke was. "Is the presentation still on?"

"It most certainly is," she replied, "but Mr Blue will be there."

Oh, right, I wanted to say. Another Cluedo piece. That makes it all so easy.

She continued. "At 10 o'clock you'll go into the conference room. Mr Black will introduce Mr Blue and then say something like 'do please Mr White if you would be so good as to please carry on'. You then say anything you want. Anything – isn't it a lovely day, for example. Mr Blue will then politely agree with you and say, er, after a few pleasantries, something like 'and do you find that weather is an important factor when it comes to demolition, Mr White?'. You'll be off!

"His job tomorrow," she continued, "is to draw out of you everything you know about demolition and everything you have thought about over the last few days about this scope. He's trained to do it. I've seen him. He's brilliant."

My mind was working slowly. "So does that mean we have no work to do tonight, nothing to prepare, nothing to rehearse?"

"Yep. Sorry about that. Mr B's orders. He wants you to be fresh in the morning. So I'm afraid after we've finished this meal we'll have to just sit around and twiddle our thumbs until bedtime."

As she said bedtime, she gave me that look of hers. *Shit*, I thought. *I hope she doesn't keep doing that.*

"No work of any kind." She looked sad. I hoped it was the actress in her.

Then she said "Hey! I've got something to show you!" and she started untying the scarf around her neck. I was up to a sprint again. Time slowed right down as I watched and waited. "DaDah!" she exclaimed, waving her scarf high above her head. For me, it could have been the seventh veil. Then she threw it on the bed and walked right up to me and said, "Have a look at this, Danny boy! It's my Dinny Hall!"

I was within six inches of her plunging neckline.

"The one Mr B gave me. The one Mrs T admired, you know. The necklace! I told you about it."

"Really beautiful!" I said. I can't remember what it looked like. The necklace, I mean.

"And that's not all!" she said with a wicked smile, and she bent down and lifted up from the bottom shelf of the trolley an ice-bucket containing a bottle which was certainly not cava from Tesco's. "It's from the chef!" she exclaimed, "he said we've got to have it with the oysters."

It was a strange evening. I cannot recall the rest of the meal. I suppose we ate it. We drank the champagne, all of it, because I can remember seeing the upturned bottle in the bucket. We talked about music and films. *Dr Strangelove* came up again, and we discussed Peter Sellers in his three roles – or was it four?

We sang 'We'll meet again' together, looking into each other's eyes, pretending we were Charles and Cynthia, saying goodbye – or is it au revoir – on Waterloo Station in wartime London. When that got a little bit over-sad, I told her about the Goons and sung for her their version of We'll Meet Again.

You may never have heard the Goons. It was a weekly radio show when I was a lad. It had some stupid characters in it like Bluebottle and Neddy Seagoon, and each week they had some wacky adventure. In one episode they were stranded on an island somewhere in the Antarctic and were running out of supplies. 'Oh no!' they said, as they looked at the scraps of food on their plates, and then they broke into song: 'Whale meat again, don't know where...'. It made her laugh.

Then we got onto *Where Eagles Dare*, a great World War 2 film. Now you will have seen this one. It's the one where a special forces team rescues an American general from a castle in the Bavarian Alps. It's Richard Burton who says the immortal words, which I'm sure you and every Dan, Daniel or Danny knows so well:

'Broadsword calling Danny Boy, this is Broadsword calling Danny Boy'.

Dinny started it. She did a really good Richard Burton impression, lowering her voice and putting on a very slight Welsh accent: "Broadsword calling Danny Boyee. Come in, Danny Boyee."

It had a certain credence to it, tension, excitement. I said I'd call her Broadsword from then on, and she said it was a bit long, so I suggested 'Mrs Broad'. She said it was the name of a rather plump dinner lady at her school, so for that evening, the last evening we'd ever spend together she was, for me, Broadsword.

"And Broadsword has another surprise for Danny Boy." Oh no, I thought. She then fished from the trolley shelf a packet with a CD in it. "It's from Mr B. He wondered if you might like to try out the new machine. We don't have any proper discs here, but he got A and L to copy some of his 'records' onto a blank. I expect they're old 78s, knowing him."

We put the disc in the player and pressed play, and we let the machine take us through the selection. We had a good laugh. 'Some Enchanted Evening', from South Pacific, was the first one we heard. Then 'Catch a Falling Star', would you believe it. Some of them were so dated. Almost wartime stuff.

We were sitting at the table opposite each other. We must have finished eating by then, and our glasses were practically empty. We hummed to the tunes we recognised and with the romantic ones we would pretend to be Charles and Cynthia again, looking into each other's eyes knowing it was our last night together, but being brave about it. Pretending! For the first time since arriving at that place, I wished we were only pretending that tomorrow it would be goodbye for ever.

The song changed. It was Bing Crosby. Pre-war! But a captivating melody. I think Dinny – Broadsword – sensed a change of mood in me, or maybe in both of us. She got up and started swaying to the music, eyes closed, mouthing the words.

"When the blue of the night meets the gold of the day,
Someone. . .waits for. . .me."

At the end of the second verse, when it was just the accompaniment playing, she opened her eyes and looked at me and said, "Broadsword for Danny Boy".

I said no, that's not right. It's Broadsword *calling* Danny boy.

She said, "It feels right. Broadsword for Danny. Dance with me, Danny."

One bottle of champagne is not a great deal between two, but I was utterly intoxicated. I got up and moved towards her. She held out her arms, slightly bent at the elbows. She continued to sway to the music as we eased our bodies towards each other, my hands around her waist, hers around my neck. We kissed.

I don't suppose you've ever heard the end of one of those 78 records when the needle reaches the middle. Anyway, it wasn't until the faint tsshhh-tishh came that the spell was broken. We sort of looked at each other, not sure what to do. Not sure what had happened. The Head Girl had gone, just a rather bewildered and vulnerable-looking young lady. I didn't look at the clock to see what time it was. It must have been late, as I noticed the moon through the plastic dome in the ceiling.

I turned away and put the plates and things back on the trolley. I needed something to do. The tisshh-tishh stopped. It was the last track on the CD.

The Head Girl returned. She looked around the room, then straight at me and suddenly said "Hey! Do you want to do something exciting, really, *really* exciting? Yes? In that case, you must do EXACTLY what I say."

It wasn't really a question – but I would have done anything she told me to. "Get rid of that tracksuit and shirt and take off your socks and shoes."

As she was saying this, she kicked off her killers, flicked off the light, and in the light of the moon shining through the ceiling dome I saw her reach behind her back and fiddle with something, then step out of her dress. Panties yes, bra no.

"Quick!" she said, "follow me!" and she dashed out of the door and sprinted down the corridor. I followed as fast as I could, worried that I might lose her. She darted through a side door, then down a metal spiral staircase. "Come on, Danny boy," she cried, as she looked up briefly to make sure I was keeping up. I almost threw myself down the stairs in my efforts not to lose her.

At the bottom, she took a right through another door and ran into what seemed to be a large hall, illuminated solely by moonlight coming through domes in the ceiling. As she dived into the swimming pool, the surface of the water broke into ripples that scattered the reflected light into a kaleidoscope of soft sprites, dancing around the walls and ceiling, and illuminating the figure of this goddess of a creature, powering her way through the water to the far end.

I was never a strong swimmer, but I could jump into a pool in full battle order and swim a length – it was a test we had to pass at Sandhurst. I dived in and swam towards her. We met in the middle while she was already on her way back. It was just deep enough to make me tread water.

"Wow!" I said as she swam around me catching her breath and grinning broadly. "You are some swimmer!"

"Thank you, kind sir," she said, "I was thrown into the deep end at an early age. And I'm a fully trained life-saver. Hey, let me show you."

With a powerful arm-stroke and kick of her legs, she was there beside me, putting her arm around my neck, deftly turning me on my back and dragging me to the side of the pool, before I knew what was happening. Just as well. I could feel the firmness of her young, naked breasts on my back, the strong forearm, the inside of her thighs gently brushing my buttocks. The tepid water had not cooled my ardour as much as I would've liked.

We swam some more and splashed each other, shrieking and

yelling in the pretence we wanted it to stop. But sadly, it did, as Broadsword swam to the steps, got out and said, "Come on, Danny boy! Time to go. Wring out your knick-knacks, or they'll drip everywhere."

And as she was saying this she whipped off hers and ran towards the door whirling them above her head. I jumped out of the pool, did what she told me to do and chased after her. I was hoping she would slow down because I didn't want the moment to end.

———

And so it was that I found myself totally nude, chasing a likewise attired young epitome of beauty, along a dark corridor illuminated only by two or three pools of moonlight that managed to find their way through the domes above us. I had a fleeting recollection of Keats's Ode on a Grecian Urn. Of maidens loth, of mad pursuit, wild ecstasy.

That athletic, naked form running ahead of me, and an almost primaeval urge to chase and catch, to hold her in my arms. But then we reached the door of my cabin. She stood aside, hands on hips, catching her breath, smiling broadly. I went in first, to the bathroom and threw out the bath towel to her. I stayed in the bathroom, had a quick dip under the shower, dried myself and put the hand towel around my waist as best as I could then went out of the bathroom to get my tracksuit.

She'd gone. I was stunned. There was the bath towel draped neatly over a chair. Then I heard it, quietly at first then getting louder. "Broadsword calling Danny Boyee! Broadsword calling Danny Boyee! Come in Danny Boyee!"

And with that, she threw off the duvet. I was 'inescapably drawn towards her by some hidden force' as a Barbara Cartland novel might say. When I reached the bed she was kneeling, facing me, with her knees apart, and the only things she was wearing were her necklace and a broad, naughty grin. We embraced, and from that moment onwards we were on autopilot, doing what our instincts were telling us to do and had been for millions of years.

But it wasn't a silent passion. We talked and laughed, cuddled and cried, kissed and hugged. After the first time, I said, "And how was that for you, madam?"

She laughed. "The best!" she said, and we kissed again. Her remark gave me confidence, something which had always been in short supply with me and girls.

I said, "The best, eh? Have there have been others? Indeed, madam, there must have been at least two. Otherwise, this time would simply have been 'better'." She laughed and said there had only been two – this week. And we laughed some more.

It was not all laughs. As we lay there quietly lying in each other's arms, she said, "Danny, you do know we will never. . ."

She paused, and I thought I knew what she was going to say next. "Danny, we will never eat whale meat again". We laughed briefly. She composed herself, then said it. Those dreadful words I didn't want to hear: we'll never meet again.

She broke the sombre mood by suddenly saying "Write something on my back, Danny!"

"But you forgot the china-graphs," I replied.

"No, silly boy, with your finger! I have to guess what you're writing." First, I wrote HG. "Give me a clue", she said.

"School," I replied.

"How did you know I was head girl?" Too easy. I then wrote the letters I O U.

"I owe you?" she said, "What do you owe me – or what do I owe you?"

I told her she was wrong. I said they might not all be letters. She said tell me. I said, "Work it out, Dumbo!"

After a pause, she suddenly announced, "I've got it! The O is a zero, nil, love! 'I love you'!"

I replied, "I knew you'd admit it in the end."

She said "No, no no. The message you wrote."

"What was it?" I sleepily asked.

"I love you," she repeated.

"There you are! You've said it again!"

She had asked me if I would write it again. I said "What? I love you?"

"Now you've said it too!" she replied. We laughed and hugged, but I think we both knew how we felt. Yet we had to pretend it was just a silly game. Communications were good that night. Danny boy came in quite a few times.

Our love-making was quite different from anything I'd experienced. It wasn't the embarrassing ritual I'd gone through in recent years. There was no pressure to produce that longed-for family, no dread of not getting it right. With Dinny it was fun. I said this to her, and she replied "Of course it is! It was meant to be fun! When God gave us the emotion of fear, she felt sorry for us-"

"Hang on," I interrupted. "Who said God was a 'she'?"

"God? Mother Nature. Call her what you want. Anyway, she realised fear was important, and it had to be unpleasant. So when she programmed us with the other emotion to guarantee our survival, the urge to procreate, she decided to make it a pleasure for us; enjoyable, fun. It was only humankind who made it sinful and dirty and shameful and all those other things because it was a primitive form of birth control. Now we have the pill, we don't have to pretend it's wicked any longer. Aren't we lucky!

"Hey, have you ever been to the Isle of Wight?"

"No", I said, wondering what line of thought had prompted that question.

"Well, one of the ferries that does the crossing is run by the Red Funnel Line. It's known locally as the Red Fun-hole Line." I sniggered, and she continued. "And did you know the Queen Elizabeth has two red fun-holes?" I giggled at her silly joke. She carried on "And. And – be quiet for a moment – and did you know the Queen Mary had three?" So it went on. Sex and silliness with the odd bit of sleep in between.

When I awoke in the morning, it was one of those slow awakenings, when you're not quite sure where you are. There was sunlight. I was alone on a bed covered by a duvet. Someone was whispering. It sounded like "Broadsword calling Danny Boyee. . .Broadsword calling Danny Boyee." I thought this must be a dream, but as I turned over, slowly, careful not to wake up too much, I saw Mrs Grey in her tracksuit smiling down at me. No make-up, no jewellery. She had brought me a cup of tea, which she carefully put on the little table by my bedside.

"Thanks, Mrs Grey," I mumbled. Before I had the chance to wake up properly, she turned and walked out of the cabin, shutting the door quietly behind her.

11

Friday morning. I walked into the conference room and it was as Mrs Grey described. With introductions over, we got down to business. It was great she was there. While I found it hard to believe what happened in the night, it felt quite different with her in the room.

It was as if there was a kind of secret understanding between us – which in a way I suppose there was. I felt she was supporting me, watching my back for me. Like an actor on stage, confident in the knowledge if I forgot my lines, a quiet prompt from the wings would put me back on track.

We got off to a good start. I began by saying that controlled demolitions don't always involve explosives. I described how chimney stacks used to be brought down chopping out a vertical slot in the brickwork at the base of the chimney on the side facing the direction you want the structure to fall. A stout piece of timber would be wedged in this vertical slot, then the bricks on either side removed until it was evident the thing would fall without the timber strut there. A fire would be lit around the strut which would eventuality burn through, and down would come the chimney.

I explained the techniques of pulling a building down using steel cables, and perhaps the more familiar one we often see on our streets, of swinging a heavy iron ball – a wrecking ball. In

all cases, the trick was to use the gravitational energy of the
structure to do most of the breaking and the crushing, the
bending and buckling. I said this was also true when using
explosives.

Apart from using gravity, the key was to exploit any weakness
in the structure. If there wasn't a weakness, you'd make one –
for example by removing redundant structural members first, so
there were fewer to deal with at the time of the main demolition.

This preparatory work needn't be done by conventional
explosives, as there were other methods of cutting steel and
concrete using things like plasma cutters, thermic lances, and
even the humble angle grinder.

And not just tools, but chemicals too. For example, the one
we give to our children to play with at Christmas – that stuff on
sparklers, otherwise known as thermite. It burns at a high enough
temperature to melt steel. As does magnesium, once you get it
started. And molten aluminium, which can be highly explosive if
it comes into contact with water; weight for weight, it has four
times the explosive power of TNT.

Finally, I mentioned ADMs. One advantage of not reading from
a script or notes is that you can watch your audience: their body
language, their eyes. When I said ADMs, I noticed Mr Blue and
Mr Black looked at each other; just for a moment. I realised
they might not be familiar with the term. It's not surprising we
engineers use the acronym because the full name is a bit of a
mouthful: atomic demolition munitions. I explained an ADM was
an example of how a nuclear explosion could be used for peaceful
purposes, although its high cost would prevent its use except in
exceptional circumstances.

I said other preparatory work might well include the removal
of window glass to let the air out as the building collapsed.
Otherwise, the squeezing of the air would slow the collapse down.
Rather like when you use a bicycle pump, you have to put some
effort into it in order to squeeze the air through the valve.

The tricky part of explosive demolitions was using as little as possible to avoid damage to the surroundings, yet sufficient so you can guarantee progressive collapse under gravity. The nightmare with such demolitions is a building that starts to fall, then slows down and stops before collapse is complete leaving a highly unstable and dangerous structure to deal with – and a lot of red faces.

I explained that tall steel buildings, like Mr Green's 'Generic', were particularly tricky, as steel was both springy and ductile, springy at first until it reached its elastic limit then as you applied even more force, it would become plastic, like plasticine, until eventually it would fail.

On the other hand, concrete and brick are not springy and ductile; when they reach the limit of their strength, they simply crack and crumble. I suggested it's a lot easier to crush a block of concrete with a sledgehammer, than an equivalent block of steel. But steel did have a weakness. In a normal fire, it could soften and lose much of its strength – which is handy if you are a blacksmith.

Without fire, the forces required to make steel fail are much higher than those it was designed to bear in normal use. One way of producing these high forces was to use gravity to accelerate the upper part of the building, so it crashed into the ground, storey by storey. In other words, it was a succession of impacts, like hammer blows.

This seemed to go down well, and Mr Blue asked a few questions, nodding toward me to carry on if his questions didn't get me going again. At some stage, Mr B rose to his feet and said it was, perhaps, d'you think, time for coffee, if you please, Mrs Grey, if you would be so kind. It made me smile. As I looked across at her, I noticed it had made her smile too.

During the break, I quietly told Mr B I hadn't given much thought to how the demolition could be kept secret. I didn't have a clue to how you disguise the taking down of a skyscraper.

"Mr White. There is no need for you to concern yourself about that. Your speciality is the demolition. Others will attend to the difficulty of protecting the general public from the reality of the situation."

You mean from the truth, I thought. I also said I found it worrying that Mr Blue was using terms like 'can we do this' and 'will this happen', as if he was going to knock the Generic down next week.

Mr B reassured me. "I know you would prefer all this to be discussed in hypothetical terms – woulds and coulds rather than wills and cans – but Mr Blue needs to pretend it's going to happen. That little element of pretence makes it more real for him."

I don't think Mr Black realised the contradiction in terms he had just stated.

He continued. "Fear can help us remember things as if it were yesterday. The emotion of fear writes it all down in indelible ink in the log-book of our brains; it is there forever. Happiness, divine happiness – bliss – has the same effect."

I hoped he was right as my mind wandered back to the night's activities.

He continued. "Mr Blue needs to think it is going to happen next week. Otherwise, he might forget some of the detail. He's only human."

We carried on after coffee and through a working lunch. We all agreed on some basic principles: that preparation can – could – only be done when there's clear evidence the detonation of the suitcase bomb is imminent, and then in secret; the main demolition was to take no longer than thirty seconds; the bomb must be brought down to Ground Zero or below.

I was pleased we agreed that any plan must reduce the risk to human life, as well as limit damage to the surrounding area.

I explained we'd have a debris problem. With a normal demolition, you'd end up with a pile of debris which could be, disappointingly, as much as a third the height of the original building. And with a normal demolition, you'd clear the building of everything: furniture, floor coverings, doors, ducts, pipes and wires. If not, the debris pile would be even higher. Worse still, the crushing of all that furniture and things would absorb a significant portion of the gravitational energy we needed to bring the building down.

I reminded those present about the sledgehammer and concrete block and asked them to imagine using a sledgehammer to crush a steel filing cabinet. It would take quite a few swings.

I had to stop myself smiling went Mr Blue mentioned the weather, and asked if there were any related implications we should take into account. This led me nicely into wind loads, and I explained how the Generic was designed to withstand a wind of 200 mph, which would exert a horizontal force of about 4000 tons on the building. I noticed Mr Green nodding. I presumed he was the man who'd done those calculations for me earlier in the week.

I said the building was in effect a solid core within a hollow steel box, and that this outside steel box acted like guy ropes around a radio mast keeping it vertical. In a strong wind, the windward side of this outside shell would actually go into tension. Then I mentioned the roof structure. This had worried me, and I think also Mr Green. Its job, apart from supporting the roof, was to transfer the tension forces created by a high wind into compressive forces on the central core.

The roof truss was so massive that if you cut all the columns of the central core at ground level, the central core would remain there hanging from the roof truss with the outer shell taking all the weight of the whole building.

At that stage, Mr Blue said "Excuse me, Mr White. Could you just run that past me again?"

Which I did, with Mr Green kindly helping me out. We had an interesting discussion, with me explaining that we couldn't bring the building down merely by cutting the core at basement level.

Mr Blue asked if we could cut it at the top as well – which was something I had looked at, thank goodness – and I said I could not guarantee the outer shell would collapse. Even if it did, an outside shell with all the floors ripped out by a collapsing core would be unstable and likely to buckle.

Mr Blue was starting to look worried. "But don't we want it to buckle and collapse?"

"Yes," I replied, "if we could guarantee equal buckling all around the building, which we can't. There is a risk the shell would fall sideways, rather like a chimney stack. We need to use the core as a stabiliser, like the keel of a ship, so the outside shell falls vertically."

At that point, I paused to allow it to sink in. I took the opportunity to glance at Mrs Grey. She gave me a faint smile and a very slight nod. It was equivalent to my mum, jumping up and down on the touchline whooping and screaming when I scored my first try. Just a dream. My mum was never on the touchline. And I never scored a try.

I was jolted back to the conference room by a simple question. "So, Mr White. How are we going to get the bomb down to ground zero?" Simple, really, and I explained.

―――――――――――

It was over. Mr Blue came round and thanked me and shook my hand. Mr Green smiled and said well done. I thanked him for all his help. Mr Black said it went really well and that I could feel quite proud of what I'd done. He apologised it had taken so long – the clock showed it was ten past six. He said they had to get me back home.

When I entered the garage in my cheap suit and tie rolled up in a pocket, Mr Black led me to the back of the van and handed me my bag. His last words to me were, "Remember what I said, old chap. Just forget us. All of us. It's for the best."

The back door slammed, a slight crunch of gears, the revving of an engine and I was speeding away from where I knew not. It was only then I realised I hadn't said goodbye to Mrs Grey, Dinny and Broadsword. Just the one person of course, but she was my sword and my shield, my rock and my staff, my love. But not my life nor any part of it from now on. Yet I wanted to be there for her, to help her, to protect her.

Is that just part of loving someone, part of the instinct written into the programme? Or did I fear for her safety? What if she was in danger? Of course, she had Mr B to look after her, but one day he would retire or just not be around.

I was grateful to Mr Black for sparing me the pain of a dreadful goodbye, rather than the cheery 'au revoir' I'd dreamt of yet knew was impossible. I slept all the way to the car-park. Then it was goodbye and thanks to John. Soon, it seemed, I was thanking the taxi driver – same one, by the way – outside my little home in Tenterden.

12

It wasn't a happy return. In the 'Dear John' letter on the kitchen table, Mandy explained with remarkable tenderness that the time had come for us to part. She'd met a friend at a college reunion. While her pregnancy had come as a complete shock, she felt her destiny was to go ahead and have the child and allow it to grow up with its true father as her partner. It would have a proper mummy and daddy.

Our original dream, but without me. It was not a great shock. Somehow you can sense these things. But in a way, I felt happy for her. It was probably her last chance. And, selfishly I suppose, it took away any feeling of guilt I had about Broadsword.

I slept surprisingly well until I heard the postman putting something through the letterbox. I wandered down and picked up the buff envelope. It was a payslip from the Army Pay Office. *Quick work*, I thought. Then I had a surprise. The amount was for £27,542.52.

Obviously a computer error, which I'd have to sort out pretty damn quick. My "ex", as she was now, would expect us to share our assets, but if I then had to give her half of something I hadn't got, I'd be in a right fix.

Sunday was a busy day sorting out the attic. I needed to do something physical to take my mind off things. But on Monday I decided to go up to London and drop in on Dinwiddie in Room

109 at the Old War Office. I'd take the pay slip and ask him to look into it. And at the same time, I'd offer my services, if ever they were required again, to the same organisation with the intention of meeting Mrs Grey again.

I got to the Old War Office about mid-day and reported to the reception desk. The lady looked up Major Dinwiddie in her lists.

"I'm sorry dear, but Major Dinwiddie is no longer with us." Her voice dropped as she said the words. "He passed away."

I could hardly believe it. He was elderly, but seemed fit and well a week previously. "When did he die?" I asked.

"During the Christmas break, dear," she replied, "the year before last."

I must have the wrong name, I thought.

"Major Dinwiddie, Room 109?" I said. She picked up another millboard and looked down another list.

"Room 109, dear?" I nodded. "I'm sorry. That's a storeroom."

Cut-offs!

Mike wasn't much help either. After leaving the Old War Office, I walked the few miles to his office and luckily he was in. But he seemed to know less than I did. Dinwiddie had called him on the Sunday and merely asked him to pass me the message.

I told Mike about the payslip. He thought I should let the Pay Office find the error. The money wasn't due to be paid until the end of the month, so there was plenty of time. He then gave me the number of a Pay Corps friend of his and suggested I ring him if I was concerned.

I told Mike about Mandy, and he said he'd heard it on the grapevine. He was kind of sympathetic, but I think he felt I was punching above my weight when I married her. He promised to get me up to Norfolk for a weekend. I said yes that would be great. He wished me well and I departed.

Back at an empty house that evening I poured myself a beer and tried the box trick Broadsword told me about. I closed my eyes and pictured the taxi, the van, my cabin and the conference room

– and to each mental picture I added the faces of the people: Mr Black mending a puncture, Mr Green and his Generic, and Mr Blue with his black curly hair pushing the button which would bring the building down.

I took each picture and put them in the box, locked it, threw away the key and launched the box into the swirling river at my feet. It floated away downstream until it was out of sight, away to the open sea and gone forever.

Broadsword? No, I wasn't going to commit her to a watery grave. I wrote her name on the back of a business card and I put it in my wallet – rather like one might do with a photo of a loved one. And that's all I had. A name. Not her real name, but one I'd given her. I knew by looking at her name I'd be able to recall not only an image but also the sound of her voice, her singing and dancing and our midnight swim in the moonlight.

The following morning I rose early, made some coffee and tidied the place up. I threw away the half-empty shredded wheat carton, and to this day I have never eaten another of those dreadful things. At nine o'clock sharp I phoned Mike's Pay Office contact. I gave him the coding on the pay slip, and he said he'd get back to me.

Just before lunch, he did so, and to my surprise, he said all was in order. There'd been no mistake. The code was an unusual one rarely used in peacetime. It was a payment made in special cases, an example being when a service person had operated in extreme conditions behind enemy lines for an extended period. He asked me what I'd been up to.

"Oh, saving the world," I replied, "shagging Mata Hari, the usual stuff you know. Can't say any more. Top secret."

He said the payment wasn't taxable as it was classed as compensation.

The money was a Godsend – or should I say a Mr Black-send. For I am sure it was he who decided on such things. It allowed me to kick-start my business, and by ploughing back profits, I slowly expanded.

Then I had another piece of good fortune. Mike phoned to asked me up for the promised weekend with him and his wife, Sue. I thought a break from Kent would be good, so I accepted his kind invitation.

It was a great weekend, a bit of walking and bird-watching, and bridge on the Saturday evening. He'd asked a neighbour to make up the four, and I am glad to say we wiped the pants off Mike and Sue.

My bridge partner was Julie whom you've met. She'd been recently widowed and had two teenage daughters, Frances and Fiona. She was planning to move to Sevenoaks to be nearer her mum, once Fiona had left school the following summer. I was working on a restoration project near Sevenoaks, so I offered to introduce her to some local estate agents.

Over the next year, we met quite often, just as friends at first, but I think we both felt our future was to be more than that as if the gods had conspired to bring us together. She found a house on the outskirts of Sevenoaks, and I helped her with a bit of restoration.

I had to move out of Tenterden because Mandy and I finally managed to find a buyer at a reasonable price. Julie suggested I rented the stable block at her place. It was more like a derelict garage, but I cleaned it up and sorted it out. The loft became my home and downstairs I had my workshop. She never charged me any rent saying it was worth much more to her to have a handyman around the place.

Then I began to sleep in the main house during the winter months, and the loft became my office. Finally, in 1997 we tied the knot officially. Of course, you know her and her wonderful daughters, now mums themselves with their little ones. They all call me G-pa and I regard them as family.

Did I ever take that business card out of my wallet? Yes. Once.

I wanted to thank Broadsword for getting Julie and me together because it was the hope of working with her again that prompted me to phone Mike after the consultancy. I hoped one day I'd meet her again and would be able to introduce her to Julie.

I'd told Julie about Broadsword when we first became 'an item'. Someone I met at an engineering conference, I said. Didn't know her name. Never saw her again. Was it a success? Yeah, we made love all night long, and the following day we blew up the Empire State building. Julie said 'whatever' and changed the subject to something more interesting.

Did I have any other 'retros'? Sure. I was reminded of Broadsword whenever I heard or read the name of that ill-fated ship, The Lusitania. We agreed to disagree on that one, and I never brought the subject up again. It was too sensitive an issue. It made her angry.

Rather like the guy she referred to as Action Man – although I was right behind her on that one. To try to force a newly married young woman to do that kind of thing was dreadful, and for her to lose her husband because she refused. She must've blamed Action Man for that, but knowing her, I guess she also shared some of the guilt herself. Not for disobeying an order, but for telling her husband about it and the awful consequences. But surely you don't hold secrets from your new husband.

No wonder she suffered from post-traumatic stress disorder. Under the circumstances, I think Mr B did a pretty good job of sorting her out. I just hoped her path and Action Man's would never cross again.

I was also reminded of her whenever I heard any of those corny songs provided so kindly for us by Mr B. I was – and still am – taken back to my cabin, to that amazing evening, our last ever. We laughed at those songs at the time and thought they were rather soppy, but somehow they struck a chord, stirred an emotion and reminded us of the sad situation we were in.

Mocking their sentiment was our way of handling it. When I do hear them, I try to listen to the words, and despite having been written so long ago, they echo my feelings of that night so well.

> And the gold of her hair
> Crowns the blue of her eyes
> Like a halo tenderly
> If only I could see her
> Oh, how happy I would be
> Where the blue of the night
> Meets the gold of the day
> Someone. . . waits for. . .me.

And I like to feel that her feelings are echoed in the words of that wonderful song, Danny Boy.

> And if you come, when all the flowers are dying
> And I am dead, as dead I well may be
> You'll come and find the place where I am lying
> And kneel and say an "Ave" there for me.
> And I shall hear, tho' soft you tread above me
> And all my dreams will warm and sweeter be
> If you'll not fail to tell me that you love me
> I'll simply sleep in peace until you come to me.

I must admit it's the tune that appeals to me most when I hear such songs; I don't listen carefully to the words. Now with the Internet, you can google almost any song and read the lyrics. Sometimes you can discover some beautiful poetry.

Since that night I haven't seen the films we discussed – *Dr Strangelove, Where Eagles Dare,* and *Indiana Jones and the Temple of Doom* – but they too would evoke fond memories. Treasured ones. As does that simple phrase, 'Come on Danny boy', which Helen uttered on that evening when we first met. When I heard it, I was – for a moment – chasing Broadsword down the spiral staircase, jumping into the pool after her, then trying to keep up as she ran back to my room. When I was young, all this would have been sentimental twaddle, but as an old man, I no longer mind if it is.

But the biggest retro for me was not sentimental at all. In fact, it blew the padlock off my wooden box and tipped out its contents at my feet. It happened at about two o'clock in the afternoon on 11th September 2001.

13

For me, 9/11 was an amazing, terrible thing. The scenario we'd scoped, with its extremely low probability, seemed to be coming to life before my eyes on our TV screen. Not just one skyscraper, but two. Then a third.

It was a strange mix of emotions. When I watched the first one go down, my first thought was wow! They've done it! I felt quite proud the plan succeeded, the one Broadsword and I had worked on fifteen years previously. I wanted to give her a call, but of course, I didn't know her number or her name, or anything about her.

Then the other one collapsed. Again, a perfect result. Must have been two bombs. I thought of the casualties; then I remembered the consequences had one or both those bombs exploded a quarter of a mile above Manhattan.

For the next few weeks I watched any TV programme I could find about the event – news, chat shows – and I read every relevant newspaper article I could put my hands on. I was pleased the casualties were much less than we had scoped. Ironically, those dreadful fires had got most occupants out of those buildings and cleared much of the area around them before they collapsed.

In those days following I half expected to hear an announcement from the White House saying that two Soviet enhanced radiation devices had been located in the debris of the World Trade Centre and had now been disarmed:

> 'We are indebted to Major Rayner of the British Royal Engineers for helping us demolish the Twin Towers, thus avoiding lots of mega-deaths and a possible nuclear exchange. Our sincerest condolences are extended to the families of those whom we killed in the process. A search is on for two more neutron bombs hidden somewhere in the Country some years ago but have now gone missing. If you see an unattended suitcase, particularly on the roof of a skyscraper, you are advised not to approach it but to report it to your nearest police station'.

What rubbish. What could they possibly say? Fortunately, we were told the planes alone caused the towers to collapse, thus dumping all the blame for all the deaths on the terrorists. I hoped and still hope that was the case. But having studied in some detail Mr.Green's Generic, I knew that imploding it onto its own footprint wouldn't have been an easy task. Doing it by flying a plane into the top of it? Almost impossible. Doing twice in one day? Broadsword's put-down sprang to mind: in your dreams.

But the Twin Towers were not the Generic, neither in size nor construction, and perhaps the real ones did suffer from some undetected design or construction defect, even though they were supposed to have been able to withstand a plane flying into them. One thing though is certain. The 'perps', as Mr B called them, couldn't have imagined in their wildest dreams that both towers would collapse to the ground so perfectly, let alone planned it.

Nor could they have guessed that falling debris from one of the towers would strike a third, causing a fire which would make it, too, collapse completely into its own footprint. The 'perps' were extremely lucky that day.

Another thought that crossed my mind was this. Mr B said it was likely that the collective intelligence services of the Western World would get some warning of the attack, so some people, somewhere, would have prior knowledge of it. Did the head of our intelligence services know in advance? If so, did he tell Tony Blair, our Prime Minister of the day?

And likewise, across the pond, did Mr President know it was about to happen when he started to read My Pet Goat? He sure got his knickers in a twist on how he heard about the attacks. According to him, he saw the first plane attack on television, when he was waiting to go into the classroom. But it wasn't televised. And then he said he thought it was pilot error. Yet in his Address to the Nation that evening, he said: "Immediately following the first attack, I implemented our government's emergency response plans." One of those statements must have been wrong.

Even after the second plane went in, some broadcasters were speculating on the cause being equipment failure either on the aircraft or in air traffic control systems.

Years later I downloaded the report on the Twin Towers produced by the US National Institute for Standards and Technology, commonly called NIST. I thought I'd find the answers I was seeking. It was a good report and I would've been happy to accept their conclusion that the planes alone had caused the collapses, but for three things.

Firstly, as Mr B might have said, NIST stated in the small print of their report that the threat of court action prevented them from revealing a large amount of evidence which they had gathered as part of their study. Or to put it in their words: 'A substantial portion of evidence collected by NIST in the course of the investigation has been provided to NIST under non-disclosure agreements'.

Secondly, their investigations stopped short at the beginning of the collapse and did not examine how the collapse actually happened.

And thirdly, NIST tells us the top blocks of the towers that crushed the undamaged storeys below were 'essentially in free fall, as seen in videos'. For a block of twelve storeys to fall through ninety undamaged storeys below it at 'essentially free-fall speed' is, dare I say it, a mathematical impossibility.

Another approach I took was to assume it was a terrorist attack but to try and understand the motives of the terrorists. If it all made sense, the likelihood of the official account being correct would have been much greater. But a terrorist attack didn't make a great deal of sense. Not to me.

For a start, nobody seemed to know why the terrorists did all those things: two planes flying into the twin towers; one into the side of the Pentagon; the fourth destined for the White House – or was it the Capitol?. And the anthrax attacks. Perhaps the terrorists had never heard of the acronym KISS: keep it simple, stupid.

Bush said it was because they hated our freedoms. Blair said it was because the 'madmen', as he called the attackers, wanted to kill as many people as possible. Bin Laden said it was because US forces were occupying holy sites in Saudi Arabia, his home country. Benjamin Netanyahu, the former prime minister of Israel, said 'It's very good... Well, not very good, but it will generate immediate sympathy'. He added that the attack would 'strengthen the bond between our two peoples because we've experienced terror over so many decades, but the United States has now experienced a massive haemorrhaging of terror'.

If you want to kill lots of people, why fly into the tops of buildings rather than into the bottom of them, or along a densely packed street? Why fly into the hardened side of the Pentagon rather than go for the soft centre? Why the Pentagon and not Broadway? Why not Three Mile Island?

Lots of questions, but nobody seemed to want to address them. If the attack was to terrorise, Blair certainly helped the terrorists along. This is what he said in a speech to the TUC a month after the event:

"Within a few hours, up to 7,000 people were annihilated, the commercial centre of New York was reduced to rubble and in

Washington and Pennsylvania further death and horror on an unimaginable scale. Listen to the calls of those passengers on the planes. Think of the children on them, told they were going to die...

"Think of the cruelty beyond our comprehension as amongst the screams and the anguish of the innocent, those hijackers drove at full throttle planes laden with fuel into buildings where tens of thousands worked...

"They have no moral inhibition on the slaughter of the innocent. If they could have murdered not 7,000 but 70,000 does anyone doubt they would have done so and rejoiced in it?"

Nice one, Tony. I bet they liked the bit about the children being told they were going to die. Where did you drag that up from? No parent tells a child they are going to die in such circumstances. Why do the terrorists' job for them? Why did you exaggerate the number of casualties? Why say the commercial centre of New York was reduced to rubble when it wasn't?

It's as if you wanted there to be more deaths, more terror. Did you want your nation terrorised? Did you seize the opportunity presented by the terrorists' attack to manipulate public opinion, or were you in on some master plan right from the start? Or were you yourself terrified and couldn't think straight?

If the enemy's objective was to terrorise, Tony Blair helped them. That's high treason.

It's hardly surprising that people looked behind the ridiculous rhetoric and theorised about what might have happened. All those conspiracy theories, and films like Fahrenheit 911, Loose Change and In Plane Site. While many of them had obvious flaws in them, so did the official account, and these weaknesses in the official version spurned further counter-theories which are still going on to this day.

It's hard to rubbish them all. They're only theories, suppositions. So I still can't say if my scoping efforts fifteen years previously had anything to do with the events of that terrible day.

Am I a conspiracy theorist? Certainly not, if the term applies to someone who accuses governments of planning and carrying out in secret unlawful or harmful acts. I don't accuse anybody of anything.

But the label has changed its meaning over the last two decades and is now applied in a derogatory sense to anybody who does not swallow the government version of an event, hook line and sinker. If that is how you define a conspiracy theorist, yes I am one.

To be fair, there're many good and perfectly normal people who regard it as disloyal to question their government. In some cases, they see it as a form of treason, and they regard conspiracy theorists as traitors. They are reluctant to do any serious investigations themselves – perhaps they feel that to do so would in itself be disloyal.

Do I believe 9/11 was a conspiracy? Of course it was. A conspiracy is a secret plan by two or more persons to do something unlawful or harmful. Nobody can doubt the plan for 9/11 was secret, and that it involved a group of people, and the act perpetrated was unlawful or harmful. The only doubt is who made up the group.

Do I believe there was a cover-up? The NIST reports says there was. What we don't know is what was covered up, why it was covered up and by whom. Why don't we know? Because the cover-up was – how can I put this – covered up.

14

In 2005 I sold my business and retired so I could enjoy time with Julie and my adopted family. Being keen skiers – as you well know – we were able to get away in those dull winter months and enjoy the snow and sunshine of the Alps. Then in 2012, we bought the chalet in Samoens next to yours.

As the years went by, I often thought about what Mr B said about the Doctrine of Necessity and how it could annul a crime. I wondered if necessity could also annul a moral obligation. Can it, for example, justify dishonesty? Is it OK for a democratic government to lie to its people, merely because it thinks it's necessary? Is it OK for a civil servant to produce a dodgy dossier because he has been told it's necessary? Is it right for a democratic government to dupe its own people?

On the other side of the fence, is an individual entitled to use the defence of necessity against their own government. This is what happened in the interesting case of Katherine Gun, a translator at GCHQ in Cheltenham. In January 2003 she came across an email from an American intelligence agency requesting aid from GCHQ in an illegal operation to bug the offices of the UN Security Council which could determine whether the UN approved the invasion of Iraq.

She believed the operation would be against the Vienna Conventions, which regulate global diplomacy. She gave a copy of the email to a friend who passed it to The Observer newspaper. Less than a week after the story broke, she confessed she'd leaked the email and was arrested and charged with an offence under the Official Secrets Act.

She planned to plead not guilty on the basis she acted to prevent imminent loss of life in a war she considered illegal. It was a classic example of the defence of necessity. Nevertheless, the case went to court, but within half an hour it was dropped because the prosecution declined to offer evidence.

The defence were expected to argue that trying to stop an illegal act 'trumped' her obligations under the Official Secrets Act. So perhaps the Prosecution Service accepted the defence of necessity, that under the circumstances her action was just and therefore no crime had been committed. On the day of the court case, this 30-year old girl was quoted as saying: "I'm just baffled that in the 21st century we as human beings are still dropping bombs on each other as a means to resolve issues." I kind of like that.

Coming back 9/11, I think I would have a clear conscience if my action had saved many more lives. But what if there was no bomb? How could I argue I chose the lesser of two evils? Supposing some elements of the US Government had deliberately demolished those buildings to deceive their population into supporting a long-planned invasion of Iraq? Could I accept my involvement was justified and therefore legal, as the 'social value' of securing oil supplies or whatever for the nation was greater than the 'social harm'? How many deaths would be justified to achieve a strategic foreign policy objective vital to the nation's future?

These are not matters for a simple soldier like me. My concern is this: leaving aside the law, was I wrong to propose a way of demolishing Mr.Green's Generic? Probably not, but how would I feel if someone I knew, someone I loved, had been sacrificed for a 'higher social value'? Does my instinctive obligation to protect those I love override my duty to seek less social harm?

If Churchill's dearly beloved wife had been aboard the Lusitania on that fateful voyage, would the warning of the enemy submarine have got through? Would the destroyer escort have been provided?

I became a bit of a cynic on 9/11. I hadn't developed any theories of my own, but some of the explanations supporting the official version of events were invented to do just that. For example, the sound of an explosion heard coming from the basement of one of the towers was a lift crashing down because its cable had been severed by the aircraft impact. All lifts in modern buildings have brakes which automatically lock the car in place if the cable is cut.

And I was suspicious of Larry Silverstein's famous use of the demolition term 'pull it' while on the phone to a fire chief about Building Seven, the third skyscraper. Larry was the owner of the World Trade Centre. It was claimed he wasn't talking about pulling the building down but to pulling the firemen out. I have never heard a group of people, be they a platoon, a squad, a football team, a family or a married couple being referred to as 'it'. We invariably use the plural pronoun, they or them, if we do not use the actual noun.

And the report of the collapse of that building by a BBC newsreader, while it was still standing, being just a 'mistake on her part', is not correct. News readers don't ad lib to that extent; they read the news from a script.

I don't think 9/11 was a crime committed by an evil cabal within the United States Government to manipulate the minds of the populace into supporting a profitable war on terror, and I doubt it was a secret operation to polarise the West against the Muslim World.

But whenever I read about acts of terror, I do find myself

looking for certain signs that suggest things may not be quite as they seem: the fireproof passport; the alleged perpetrators dying at the scene, or killed shortly afterwards by pursuing police; the lack of a proper forensic investigation; the rapid production of video footage and photos of carnage, some obviously false; the combining of totally separate acts of terrorism on the same day, rather than a single, well planned and supported act with a clear aim; the apparent lack of understanding of why the alleged perpetrators did what they were alleged to have done.

Then there are the mistakes, like the London bombers who caught the train to London which didn't run on that day. This isn't a wacky claim by some crackpot on a conspiracy theory website. It was admitted in Parliament by the then Home Secretary and is recorded in Hansard.

The Charlie Hebdo attack footage of the shooting of the policeman on the pavement went awfully wrong. Someone forgot to top and tail it, so we saw the 'terrorists' car' stopping at the marker – a trainer shoe on the road – then the bloodless attack on the policeman conveniently lying on the ground so he couldn't run away.

We were told the terrorists had shot and injured him. But he was lying on the ground when the terrorists got out of their car, so who had shot him? And having killed the cartoonists to avenge their prophet, why did they stop their car, get out of it, run along the street to kill an injured policemen? It makes no sense.

After the two 'brothers' returned to their car, one of them gave the "it's a wrap" hand-signal to the cameraman on the roof, and the other – the one that looks like a woman, runs like a woman and doesn't like untidiness – picked up the shoe and popped it in the car. We weren't meant to see that.

I'm not suggesting that these events were all engineered by nefarious forces, but my brief brush with Broadsword's sort of 'people' prevents me from blindly accepting what I see on television and read in newspapers.

I don't accuse anybody of carrying out such acts, but democratic governments might stage false flag attacks or use genuine ones to influence public opinion either in their own country or others.

That's one of the weaknesses of democracies: their governments need popular support. In some circumstances this may require a bit of persuading, especially when they want to drop bombs on another country as a means to resolve issues, to use Katherine Gun's words.

It helps if we don't like the people they want to drop bombs on. So, if politicians and the mainstream media start demonising the leader or leadership of a foreign power, or their subjects, you can be pretty sure it's a prelude to some sort of hostile action against them by our government, either directly or by proxy, on our own or with our allies.

Have you ever noticed that our enemies are always mad, evil, fanatical, cowardly, cruel, uncivilised demonic monsters? Maybe they no longer eat babies for breakfast – but they do terrible things to them like throw them out of incubators or shoot unborn babies in their mothers' wombs. Or they chop people's heads off, throw people off tall buildings and deliberately shoot down airliners.

In comparison, we in the civilised West are compassionate, and if we have to exert force against anybody, we do not resort to barbaric and mediaeval methods. We use the more humane technology kindly provided by our armaments industries. We rip their bodies apart with jagged fragments of steel from a bomb dropped from a B52, or inflict the most horrific injuries by propelling lumps of metal at high speed through their flesh and bones from an Apache-mounted cannon at a rate of 600 lumps per minute, or blast their limbs off with a drone-launched Hell-Fire missile.

Of course, we do this at a distance which makes it OK, and we truly regret the 'collateral damage' suffered by wedding parties and picnics which is sometimes the consequence of our carefully planned surgical strikes. Surgical! What a word to use. Dan, there is a video on YouTube called 'Collateral Murder'. If it is still there when you get this, I urge you to watch it.

When *we* drop bombs on people and kill them, it's not murder because we don't intend to kill them. Unlike the evil jihadists who deliberately kill their victims, we merely want to neutralise our enemy or incapacitate them (as long as the word has three or more syllables, it doesn't sound so bad). If they die as a result, slowly in agony from the injuries we inflict on them, or live on for a few days and starve to death perhaps because their jaw has been blown off or their guts torn out, or survive for a week or two then die of septicaemia, or remain horribly crippled and unable to do any kind of work for the rest of their short lives, that isn't our concern.

And unlike our evil enemies, we do not use terror to frighten civilian populations. We do not send suicide bombers into shopping centres or fly planes into buildings. We just carpet-bomb the rag-heads to create 'shock and awe' which is fine. After all, we are fighting a war, 'a war on terror', and that's the sort of thing you do when you go to war. We're told that if we are ever to sleep soundly in our beds again and preserve our freedoms, we must 'win' this war. To 'keep our streets safer', they tell us.

What a ridiculous concept. But our governments tell us what they need to tell us to gain our support for their policies. We believe what they tell us, and we rally around the flag.

History is full of examples of governments manipulating popular opinion by one means or another. In most cases such deceptions were orchestrated by good people, doing for their country what they thought was right at the time – although you can argue that nobody does what they thought was wrong at the time.

Patriots with a sense of duty, not greedy, evil megalomaniacs with a secret plan for a new world order. Just policymakers who needed the support of the masses, either in their country or another. Sometimes their policies don't work out quite as they imagined, like in Afghanistan, Iraq, Libya and Syria. But someone's got to make the decisions. Someone's got to look after us and our best interests.

We, the public, are like a herd of cows. We are happy to eat grass, be milked, enjoy the little luxuries in life like salt licks and one of those rectangular things in the corner of our field which is always full of clean water – and a nice dry cowshed in winter with lovely warm straw which gets changed every day, fresh hay to eat and – if we are good – some tasty cow cake. But would we support the killing of the cows in the farm up the road to get these things? Nothing could be further from our tiny little minds. Unless we were persuaded that they weren't cows at all but evil monsters with claws and big teeth who wanted to kill all the cows in all the farms and steal our grass. Sometimes words aren't enough to convince us. A picture is a thousand words; a video is worth a million.

But who cares? As for 9/11, here we are, fourteen years later and memories are beginning to fade. Nobody wants to talk about these things, let alone the mainstream media. Which is probably just as well. The last thing we need in the West is for our governments to be facing a Nuremberg-style investigation.

15

I think it was about five years ago that another incident occurred. Strictly speaking, it's not part of your story, but I think you should be aware of it.

Julie and I were at home one evening and the phone rang. She answered it, and with her hand over the mouthpiece, she said it was a Mr Dinwiddie, for me. At the mention of the name I nearly had a retro, but as calmly as I could, I took the phone.

He was very polite, saying I'd met his elder brother many years ago and could we meet at his club for lunch one day this week; he'd like to discuss something with me. It was a clever way of telling me a little bit about himself and the purpose of the meeting without revealing anything.

For a moment I wondered if they were going to offer me another consultancy, then I thought it unlikely he would invite me to lunch just to say that. Anyway, I agreed, and we fixed it for the following day at 12:30 p.m.

I wondered if Dinwiddie junior would have news of Broadsword – or maybe a contact number – and I did think what fun it would be to meet up and recall old times. Julie and I were very close, but I was still bound by the Official Secrets Act and couldn't have told her anything about Broadsword. To have met her in secret would have been dishonest, unfair and probably unwise.

Off I set next morning wearing my best suit and Parachute

Brigade tie. I walked from Charing Cross to Dinwiddie's club in St. James arriving about ten minutes early having much enjoyed the stroll. I thought about doing a timing loop, as the RAF would say but instead, I made sure my tie was straight and strode straight into reception.

I said who I was and that I was meeting a Mr Dinwiddie. I was asked to take a seat in the hall in one of those large armchairs you find in gentlemen's clubs covered in worn brown leather. There were magazines on the coffee table in front of me, and I picked up Country Life. I always enjoy looking at it, all those beautiful houses for sale – and Tottering-By-Gently, of course, on the last page. While I could never describe myself as a country gentleman, I do identify with the male character in those drawings because I think we share similar problems in the autumn of our lives. But I'm proud to say Julie is nothing like his wife. Julie is slim, elegant and much younger; I'm a lucky man.

On the dot of 12:30, a youngish man with blonde hair came up to me and introduced himself as Andrew Dinwiddie. Was he the brother of the man I met in Room 109 at The Old War Office in 1986? No way. Public school, smartly dressed, highly polished shoes, strong handshake.

"Call me Andy, Mr.Rayner." He was confident and polite, relaxed and friendly. Rather like you are.

He guided me into the inner sanctum where we sat down side by side on a sofa. As we did so, a waiter appeared and asked us if there was anything we would like from the bar. My surroundings nearly inspired me to ask for a dry sherry – something I haven't had for years – but then I decided a G and T would be better.

Andy was affable, smiley and had the time of day to chat. We talked about the weather, football, opera, and Afghanistan and Libya. We touched on the Chilcot Inquiry, and why we went into Iraq, and eventually we got round to 9/11. Andy said it was time we went into lunch and he ushered me into the dining room.

He led me to a table for two in a corner where we sat down.

We had a look at the menu and I said I'd be happy to follow his recommendation. The waiter came and took our order of pate de foie gras followed by Dover sole accompanied by a bottle of Pinot Grigio.

While we were waiting for our first course, Andy said his research department took a particular interest in the tragedy of 9/11, not on the technical side of things but on the impact on public opinion and the effect on international relations. I replied I was interested in it mainly from an engineering point of view and in particular how the towers at the World Trade Centre collapsed.

I was careful not to let on about the scope. He seemed fascinated by what I had to say, but I didn't feel he was pressing me. Perhaps he knew about the scope anyway, even though he would've only been a schoolboy at the time.

I wanted to ask him about Broadsword: how she was, where she was living and if she was still working for whoever she had been working for. I realised I knew nothing about her. Nobody except me knew her as Broadsword. Mrs Grey? Perhaps she wore a different tracksuit for each scope. I could try other colours. 'I say, Andy, whatever happened to Mrs Grey/Black/Cerise/Magenta?'. He'd think I was potty. Then I realised there was a name I remembered from the scope. Not a colour, not a proper name. A nickname. Action Man.

I hadn't realised Andy was still talking about 9/11 and its effect on the Special Relationship with the USA. I mumbled something about there being many unanswered questions, and Andy agreed. He said it was a pity because much effort was going into quelling any public disquiet, but the internet was being used to spread rumour and suspicion – and this was undermining confidence in the official account.

I said I wasn't surprised, and that I myself found it hard to believe some aspects of the US Government's investigations. He nodded his head in agreement, then said something like this.

"Mr.Rayner, you have a background in engineering, and I'd

guess you've given much thought to how those buildings were destroyed. I'm not an engineer but I've looked at other aspects of those events and I personally believe there was undue haste in putting out the official account. In my opinion, this resulted in some anomalies which in turn have generated much speculation."

He paused to sip his wine. "We in government believe this speculation is harmful, and we think it's in the best interests of the UK, and our allies of course, for it to cease."

He looked at me as if he were telling me off. And I remembered the comment I had recently posted on a website. The site implied that a some minor celebrity was a 'truther' and thus a nutter because he reckoned there'd been some sort of cover-up. I signed into the website as a guest and simply pointed out that NIST had said as much.

I picked at my food trying to work out how to respond. "Surely, though, it's important we get to the truth?"

"Normally, I would agree," he said, "but sometimes there are more important things than the truth to take into account."

I must have rolled my eyes or made some other gesture to reveal I didn't agree with him.

"Look at it like this. None of us knows exactly what happened. The official account could be right, apart from one or two minor errors which can be explained away. Or, as some people believe, the whole thing could have been a massive deception planned to justify the war on terror. Between these two extremes is every shade of grey.

"Let's assume for the moment the official account is correct. Any theories which contradict it are dangerous, as they'd imply the US Government is lying, even though it's telling the truth. It's not in the best interests of that country – or any country – to have its subjects mistrusting their elected government." I nodded in agreement, and he continued.

"Now, let us go to the other end of the scale. Let's suppose it was a massive cover-up, a false-flag attack, a deception, and that irrefutable evidence came to light to that effect. There would be a public outcry and a demand that those responsible be brought to justice and punished accordingly.

"Where would it all end? Who would be charged and for what? How would the investigation be carried out? Who would try the accused and what agency would carry out the sentences? Mr.Rayner, may I suggest there could be anarchy? Do we need our superpower ally to be reduced into a state of chaos? Can we afford to take that risk?"

I raised my eyebrows, admitting he had a good point.

"You see," he continued, "in both scenarios – the 'inside job' one, and the one described by the US Government– it would *not* be helpful to make any accusation against them. So whatever happened on that day, whatever the shade of grey, it's in our interests to support the official version. It makes no sense to do otherwise. Wouldn't you agree?"

I found myself pecking at my Dover sole, not concentrating on what I was doing. I was trying to think of a reply.

"'Oh, what a tangled web we weave when first we practice to deceive'," I said. "Surely the truth will come out sometime. I mean the deception – if there was one – couldn't go on forever, could it?"

"Who knows?" Andy said. "But what is important to us at the moment is to reduce the accusatory speculation; it's dangerous. And I would request on behalf of Her Majesty's Government that you, as an expert engineer with relevant experience, help us reduce such speculation. Would you be willing to do this?"

I seized the moment. "Well, I'm afraid you might be disappointed in me. I'm no Action Man!"

I watched him carefully. His fork, with a bit of Dover sole on it, was on its way up to his mouth. When I said the nickname it stopped, halfway there. He looked me in the eye, but for no more than a few milliseconds, then continued eating.

"What sort of help have you in mind?" I asked.

"Nothing onerous." He was back to being affable Andy. "In fact, it's quite simple. We would like you to be, perhaps, a little bit more discreet with your ideas."

The old saying came back to me 'there's no such thing as a free lunch'. I had been reprimanded, politely but in no uncertain terms, and told to keep my mouth shut. But I got what Andy was saying.

I enjoyed the lemon sorbet laced with a dash of vodka, followed by coffee. Andy, having done the business, moved on to talk about other things, and – free or not – I enjoyed the lunch and his company. I felt he was an honest guy doing his job, and when the time came to part, I said I'd not be joining the speculators on the internet. He thanked me for my understanding, and we shook hands and said goodbye.

On the way home in the train, I thought about what he said. And about what he didn't say but told me by his body language. That Action Man was still around somewhere in the organisation, probably climbing up the promotion ladder; or climbing on the backs of others, shredding people who threatened the Service or who threatened him because it was necessary and therefore justified, for some warped reason or other.

I thought about Broadsword and that poor husband of hers. And I worried for her. I remembered her reaction in the think-tank. At the time, I thought it was anger, but I wondered if it could also have been fear. I remembered Mr B saying some people do evil for evil's sake, and those were the ones you had to watch. And then I realised Mr B must have retired, and I wondered who – if anyone – was watching over her.

My thoughts then returned to the meeting. I realised Andy must've known about the comment I had posted. That's what started my fear of email and any communication over the ether. You never know who is listening and watching. May I suggest you, Dan, exercise the same caution with this story.

Now, back to happier times: our skiing trip in April last year.

16

How lucky we were with those wonderful conditions just after Easter! The endless sunshine, the lingering snow, the lack of people – and the company of you and Helen and the children on those great trips we did together.

I particularly enjoyed those early forays we went on, just you and me, catching the first lift up and dashing around the mountains and meeting up with Julie, Helen and the kids for coffee. Then Helen and I would take either Josh or Lucy for a lesson, while you disappeared off with Julie and Lucy or Josh, meeting up again at some delightful mountain restaurant for a long and relaxing lunch.

On one of these days, Helen and I arrived at the restaurant ahead of you and the others. Josh was playing in the snow next to the terrace where we'd based ourselves, so we had the opportunity to chat away, as one does on such occasions, over a cool beer. Helen and I hadn't talked much, so it was good to get to know her better.

I asked her why you didn't like to be called Danny. I had noticed you saying to people you met, 'the name's Dan' if they called you Danny.

Helen provided the answer. "It reminds him of his mother. She always called him Danny."

"So, didn't he get on well with his mum?" I asked.

"What? The exact opposite, if you ask me! He was a mummy's boy. There were just the two of them, you see. No dad. Danny told me his mother used to say how lucky she was that she didn't have to share him with anyone else."

"That was a nice thing to say to him. But that must have been terrible for her. Was there anyone else on the scene?"

"She never got married, but there was an uncle – Uncle Dick – who was very good to them. He's still around. He lived near them when Danny was a boy, and he'd see them a couple of times a week. Take them out on high days and holidays, that sort of thing. And he arranged – and paid for – Danny's schooling when she died."

"Died?" I asked. "That's tragic!"

"Yes. He became an orphan, just before going off to boarding school. Poor chap! It was just as well he changed school, as he had a spot of bother at his old one. You know what boys are like at that age. They used to tease him about not having a dad, making out that his mum was some kind of whore. And when his mum visited the school on sports day, he overheard a boy saying something like 'gingernut's mum's a gingerslut'.

"There was a fight. Can you imagine it, in front of all those parents? Anyway, Danny reckons he would've been expelled if it hadn't have been his last term. What was even worse for him was his best friend tried to comfort him by saying that it might not have been his mum's fault she got pregnant and she could have been raped. So I'm afraid Danny does not have a high opinion of his father."

"I'm not surprised," I said. "Did his mother ever talk to Danny about him?"

"I gather not. Obviously, I never met her, but I feel I know her because Danny talks about her a lot. Little stories about her, things she used to say. I wish I'd met her. She sounds as if she was such a fun person, and kind. He was devoted to her. He once asked her about his dad, and apparently, she danced around the room reciting those famous lines 'Beauty is truth, Truth beauty, That is all ye know on earth, And all– "

"All ye need to know," I interrupted. Ode on a Grecian Urn. I felt a retro coming on.

Fortunately, at that moment Josh cried out, "Daddy Daddy!", pointing to you and Julie walking up to the ski racks by the entrance to the restaurant, leaving little Lucy with Josh playing in the snow hole he'd made. By the time you'd dumped your skis in the rack and walked up the steps to join us, I was back to normal. Or normal for me. We had a great lunch; then we skied together like a family would. Three generations. Six of us. Great fun.

My next retro came later on during that holiday, and it also involved Helen. It was our last night. We'd gone out to a restaurant together, the girls wearing dresses and us boys shirts with collars. The evening was clear and cool so we'd wrapped up for the ten-minute walk.

I found myself sitting opposite Helen. She'd taken off her ski jacket but still had her scarf around her bare neck. After a few minutes in that cosy little room, she took the scarf off revealing a necklace similar to the one Broadsword was wearing on that special night all those years ago. I was back in my cabin.

Julie looked at me with that look of hers. "Darling, are you OK?"

"Yes, I'm fine, " I said.

Then Lucy, ever the one to pick up on a change of mood, said, "Gewald, you look sad."

"Of course I am," I roared "because Julie and I are going home tomorrow and I won't be able to ski with you again."

"You mean until next year," she reassured me. At my time of life, it was nice to know someone thought I might just be able to get on those planks again.

As we walked back to the chalets after a delicious meal accompanied by slightly too much wine, I said to Helen, "That's a lovely necklace you're wearing. Is it a Dinny Hall by any chance?"

"Hey, that's very clever of you!"

I wanted to tell her all about Broadsword, how I got to know her, why I called her that, and how I lost her. But as you must have realised by now, that would have been impossible.

"Was it a present from Dan?" I asked.

"Ye, it was. Do you like it?"

"Er, yes," I said. "It's beautiful."

17

I'm glad to say Lucy was right. One year later, this year, Julie and I were back in the Alps staying in our chalet next to yours, enjoying the snow and the sunshine, the mountain air, the excellent restaurants and, of course, your company. At the time I didn't know it would be my last time skiing, or that I'd never see you and Helen and the children again.

Both my step-daughters came out with their families during the season, and there was one occasion when all fourteen of us overlapped for a couple of days. It was over your birthday. Do you remember the trouble we had reserving a table for your birthday meal? But we managed, at that place in the forest beyond the main lift station. Quite a walk through the trees and up that little track.

We booked the table for seven so the kiddies wouldn't be too late to bed, but it was getting dark when we set off. It was a clear sky, and as we entered the forest, we could just make out the diminishing glow of the sun as it sank beyond the western horizon.

It was getting cold as we trudged through the forest, and what had been slush on the path that afternoon was beginning to freeze. But the uphill walk kept us warm. There was enough ambient light from the village to allow us to see where we were going, but the children found it a bit spooky, especially when the older ones pretended the forest was haunted and frightened the others – and themselves – with tales of ghouls and trees that moved and vampire bats.

It made us grown-ups smile – but I would *not* have liked to walk through that forest alone, in the dead of night. Soon, we saw through the trees the lights of the restaurant guiding us to our destination. By the time we arrived, we'd worked up a good appetite.

It was a welcoming sight inside, very much a traditional mountain chalet complete with log fire, cowbells hanging from the ceilings and spring flowers in little vases on the tables. Ours was a long one, all laid up ready for us with candles lit, jugs of iced water and baskets of freshly baked bread.

I sat at the head of the table, and the little ones were all down the other end so they could have fun without having to be too polite to the rest of us. You were on my left, and this gave us a chance to chat. We ordered our meal, and some local wine to go with it – cokes for the kids – and settled in for a good evening.

The waitress who'd taken our order – a pretty young girl in traditional costume – came back to say your choice and mine for dessert, the crème brulee, was off. I said, "Well, there we are, as my mother would say." It was one of her favourite expressions.

This got us talking about parents, and I told you my dad had died when I was in my teens. I added that I was sorry to hear about your father.

You replied, "Who? The bastard who knocked up my mother and buggered off?"

I'd never seen you look angry before. But I was angry too. Didn't the man realise what he'd done? Abandoning a young woman carrying his child? Giving up a fine son any father would have loved and been proud of? I didn't know what to say.

Our main course soon came, and we tucked into the various things we'd ordered, all looking at each other's dishes to see what we might have had.

When the waitress came to clear the plates away, she said there was, after all, one crème brulee left. We decided the birthday boy should have it, and when it arrived we saw it had been specially made with happy birthday written in white caster sugar on the brown crust.

By then the restaurant was beginning to fill up, and when we sang Happy Birthday, everybody in the room joined in. You made a little speech which made us all laugh. The free 'digestifs' went down well, and before we realised it, it was nine o'clock. The walk back – down hill – didn't take nearly as long. We were under a starry sky guided by the twinkling lights of the village ahead of us. It had been a special evening.

The following morning we all had a bit of a lie-in, as we'd agreed on the way home from the restaurant to meet at the lift at eleven, after the first rush. Julie's girls and their families were off back to England after breakfast, and I was feeling a bit 'fatigued', as they say. But after the medicinal coffee and a croissant, I was ready for what lay ahead: a wonderful day's skiing in bright sunshine under a cloudless sky.

We did some great runs. Josh and Lucy were making brilliant progress, and Julie and Helen were enjoying their skiing together, being of similar standard cruising the blues and sensibly avoiding the blacks. We decided to stop for lunch, but you and I eventually succumbed to pressure from Lucy and Josh to take them down their first ever black run.

The one we chose was more of a red, and in good viz it was no problem for them. We selected an easy route, taking the corners wide so they wouldn't go too fast. Wasn't it great to have the run to ourselves! So 'moving obstacles' – in other words people – was one thing we didn't have to worry about. It went well with no falls, and when we reached the bottom, there were whoops of delight and congratulations all round.

There was no queue at the four-man chairlift, and up the slope we went. You may remember I had Lucy on my right, and you were on my left with Josh on your left.

About two-thirds of the way up the lift stopped. Lucy said, "Gewald, what do we do now?"

I took off my sunglasses so she could see my eyes and replied we just had to sit there and wait for the lift to start again. I said it was a good opportunity to enjoy the view and have a chat.

"Gewald, can we have a chat?"

I was just about to answer, of course, my dear girl, when Josh leant across you and me and said to Lucy "His name is Gerald, you smelly little pooh!"

I was just about to say something like hey, young man, that's no way to talk to a lady, when Lucy replied in quite a loud voice for a little girl, "If I'm a little pooh, you're a BIG pooh, and BIG poohs are more smellier than little poohs!"

Wow, I thought. Not bad for a five-year-old. Then I explained to her that I, too, couldn't say my 'Rs' properly until I was about ten, so if anyone asked me my name I'd say it was Gewald Wayner.

This made her laugh. Then she asked, "Gewald, will you be my other grandpa? My best fwiend Alison has two, but I only have one at the moment."

"Well," I replied, "I can't really be your grandpa, but I could be your pretend grandpa – and you could call be G-pa. How about that?"

"Mr Bee said it's good to pwetend sometimes, if you please. He's vewy old, though, even older than you, actually."

I nearly said I knew a Mr B once who also liked to pretend. But I turned to you instead. "Dan, who's Mr B?"

"Mr B? Lucy's Mr Bee? That's Uncle Dick, my mother's boss at the leisure centre. He was Mum's uncle – or sort of uncle – and she used to tease him and call him Mr Brittas, then Mr B. There was a television series called The Brittas Empire, all about a leisure centre– "

I stopped you. "How did your mother die?" I asked.

You frowned, obviously trying to follow my train of thought – or lack of it.

"What? Oh, she'd gone to a seminar run by the ILS – the International Life-Saving Federation – in Washington DC. Had to go. Didn't want to leave me. I said I'd be fine. It wasn't the first time she'd been away on such things. After the conference, she went to New York for some reason. Meeting someone, I think. At The World Trade Centre to be precise. You know? Those planes? 9/11? Nothing– "

"Whoohee, off we go!" cried Lucy.

I hadn't noticed the chairlift had jolted back into life. I was confused. I tried to work out some numbers – dates, ages, that sort of thing. I couldn't quite grasp what was happening. Then you and the kids were shouting at me. The bar must have gone up, I dropped one of my sticks, then my glasses fell off my lap.

The next thing I remember was sprawling on the hard snow at the top of the lift, with Lucy bending over me. I remember her eyes full of concern, compassion. I'd seen that look before. Windows to the soul.

She said something like, "Don't die, G-pa. Will you still be my pwetend grandpa?" I shook my head.

Josh was asking me where it hurt. He must have seen the tears in my eyes. The lift had been stopped. You – I think it was you – had taken off my skis. Someone had called the blood-wagon. I couldn't speak, but I cried in pain. Terrible pain. I started to shiver. I was shaking. My mouth had gone dry, so much so that I couldn't say anything that made any sense.

The blood-wagon took me down the slope at an alarming pace. I was facing backwards which made it seem faster than it probably was. I didn't really mind what happened to me, but I was concerned for the others. Had someone told Julie? She was already at the bottom when I arrived. God knows how she got down before me.

When we arrived in the hospital bay, I was whisked inside.

After a short wait, I was seen by a doctor who asked me where it hurt. I couldn't really answer because it hurt everywhere. I pointed to my knee. I was then wheeled off to have some CT scans.

Julie told me afterwards that the doctor said nothing was broken, but I should remain in hospital overnight for observation. They were concerned about my shivering. I can't remember much more. I think they'd given me painkillers – and maybe something to help me sleep.

I kept thinking of Broadsword and those towers, of what I'd done, what they'd done. Of how I'd abandoned her. What a bastard! Then I would tell myself I was subject to the Official Secret Act and it wasn't in my power to do anything else. It hardly consoled me.

I do remember waking up at one stage in the night when it was pitch dark. It seemed the whole hospital was utterly silent. I did hear the odd car go past, but a long way off, probably on the autoroute. Then I heard voices. A man's, followed by what sounded like those of two women – all in French, of course. They were not nearby, so I couldn't make out the words. Faint mutters at first, then I heard one of the women scream – a chilling scream. Then silence, then the man talking. A woman's voice again. Another scream and a moan of someone in pain. Raised voices, all three seemed to be shouting.

Then I heard it. The unmistakable cry of a newborn baby. Some brief laughter, then more crying, but I could tell this time it was for joy. More chatter; in relief perhaps, maybe pride. It was the nearest I'd come to being present at a birth – apart from mine, of course. And I felt it was a huge privilege. For a few precious moments I stopped grieving for Broadsword and myself, and I thought of that new life.

As I lay there in the darkness, I was reminded of what she had said about starting a new life, of being born again, of escaping from a threat. And I wondered if she really did die in the collapse of those towers. Perhaps it was my way of handling bereavement. Maybe I just couldn't accept she'd gone, even though I'd accepted the fact that I'd never see her again.

The following morning I was in better shape. I was tired – probably the morphine – but I was no longer shaking. I'd eaten nothing since breakfast the previous day, so the coffee, fruit juice and cold toast brought to me by a cheerful auxiliary were most welcome.

Julie came early and patiently sat by my bedside, but I felt I couldn't tell her what had happened. But she seemed to understand. She had her own box of memories, which sometimes she wished to revisit but at other times to lock away. She knew there was something wrong and that I couldn't share it with her. So we talked about other things, pleasant things like the family, of home in England and our plans for the summer.

At about eleven the consultant came in, a man of about fifty with grey frizzy hair wearing the statutory white coat with a stethoscope around his neck. He asked me in good English how I was and where it hurt. He looked at my notes then into my eyes.

He turned to Julie and said that I'd had a great shock. A fall at my age could cause many different effects, some of which we do not fully understand. He said he'd discharge me that afternoon, on the condition I went straight back to England. I could drive but for no longer than an hour at a time, and once home I should rest for three days, then take light exercise.

He suggested it might be sensible if I gave up skiing.

18

I hope this story has led you along a gentle path to the truth without shocks or surprises – or the wallop of emotion which literally knocked me off my feet on that dreadful day. I hope it's shown you your father didn't abandon your mother; they were torn apart by cruel circumstance.

He was *not* a serial seducer, not a date-rapist who drugged your mother into submission, nor some psychopath who by threat or by violence forced his seed inside her. She was no slut; a fine, kind, brave lady. You were conceived in love and – had the situation allowed it – you would've been brought up by loving and caring parents who would've been very proud of their son.

I loved your mother, yet it seemed I'd had a hand in her murder. How could I ever face you? I just hope this story – your story – goes some way to achieve what I could never have explained to you in my lifetime. And I hope during my remaining years I might be able to add the final chapter, and that it might allow you to forgive me, even though it will be after I'm gone.

I also hope the story also tells you something about me, your dad. Some of the things I've done in my life, what I've been through, why I did what I did and where I have failed and succeeded. And about some of my views on things, for what they're worth. It may not be of any great value, but one day it could be of interest to my grandchildren, and their children. When the time is right.

Don't grieve for me. It's a great privilege for me to know that a small part of me will live on in you, and in those wonderful children of yours. My own flesh and blood. A kind of immortality, thanks to you. And thanks to your mum, my Broadsword. I just hope she's OK.

PART 2

The Diary

1

From: *Gerald Rayner*
To: *Daniel Braithwaite*
Subject: *Gerald Rayner*
Date: *1 February 2017 11.39*

Hi Dan – it's me, Frances, on G-pa's new computer!! I found the attached letter in his drafts folder. As it's addressed to you I thought I'd better forward it on. I haven't read it but it seems to have various dates on it.

We 're doing OK here. G-pa left his body to medical science, so there's no awful funeral to go through. We plan to have a memorial service for him, probably in the spring. If you and Helen could get over, you'd be most welcome.

Love to all
Frances xxx

---

22 Oct 15

Dear Dan – by the time you read this, you'll have read the letter I wrote to you four months or so ago. And I trust you'll have managed to digest the story which goes with it. Both are sitting in their Jiffy bag on my desk at the moment, as I am still here. But I'm sure the package will be sent out to you when my time comes.

How long I've got is anybody's guess, but at the moment I'm reasonably fit and well as I approach my 73rd birthday next week.

I've changed my computer since I produced the letter and story and I didn't keep a copy of either. So yours is the only copy. I was quite emotional when I wrote the covering letter which was more of a lament than anything else. I was saying goodbye, as I knew we wouldn't meet again. You probably thought I was being a sentimental old fool – but at least I avoided the words 'Goodnight sweet prince'!

I'm glad to report I've fully recovered from my accident and the shock that caused it. So why am I writing this now? As I said in that first letter, there's a final part to the story which hadn't yet been written because it hadn't happened. I'm going to attempt to write it as it unfolds.

I hope I can finish it and add it to the Jiffy bag. As you can see, it's like a diary, recording my thoughts and events which I think are relevant as and when they happen.

***

14 Nov 15

Attacks in Paris last night. Terrible. No doubt they'll find the perps' passports.

Sorry, I'm being cynical. I wish our leaders would try harder to understand so-called terrorism. It's not because they hate us or any of that rubbish, it's merely them hitting us back. The so-called radicalised Muslims see terrorism as a form of self-defence – the only form of defence they have against the myriad of killing devices available to those nations competing for their oil.

To hit us back somehow, to avenge. If they had drones with Hellfire missiles or B52s with bunker-busting bombs, maybe they'd attack military targets. But if you've only got a handful of Kalashnikovs and a few home-made suicide vests, you're limited in your choice of target.

Rant over.

Mustn't get distracted.

17 Nov 15

I am, I believe, getting over my bereavement. I loved your mum very much, and I was devastated to hear about her death, but the truth of the matter – I keep telling myself – is I did only know her for three and a half days, and while we got to know each other pretty well in that time, it was hardly a life-long relationship.

I didn't expect to see her again, and I made no serious attempt to do so, principally because I didn't know where to start. And her boss at the think-tank-cum-leisure-centre, Mr B, made it quite clear to me it wouldn't be a good thing, if you please. It had never occurred to me on that one night together a child could have been conceived. When I read in Mandy's letter she was expecting, I rather assumed that I'd been the one firing blanks all those years.

The fact that 9/11 had robbed you of your only known parent does weigh heavily on my mind. And the possibility I could have in some way been responsible does encourage me to make amends. I want to establish if she did die at the World Trade Centre in 2001, and that it wasn't a "carcass job" as she would have called it.

Bearing in mind her employment, it is possible she was under some kind of threat. Certainly, she was a bearer of super secrets when I knew her in 1986, and I guess she continued in that line of work. Mr B was careful in looking after her, and she was sensible about all matters of security, but I wouldn't rule out the possibility she held some important information in her head and might have been regarded as a risk. Perhaps she 'knew where the bodies were buried'.

Perhaps they were concerned she might make it public or release it to 'the other side', as Mr B would have said.

I would not put it past her to be a whistleblower. She was a woman of integrity, and I think she would not stand by and say nothing if she felt a great wrong were being done or were about to be done. Rather like Katherine Gun some years later; I believe I mentioned her in the first part of your story.

If your mum did blow the whistle on something really big, she'd have two choices. To blow it and fake her death and stay silent – or blow it and spend the rest of her life in exile somewhere as Snowden and others have done, living in constant fear that one day 'they' will get you. As she said to me, they have to get you in the end if you remain alive, in order to deter others. I think she would've chosen the 'carcass' option.

Also, there was that business with Action Man when she refused to take part in a honey-trap operation. You may recall her husband of a few months died in an accident shortly afterwards, and she thought he'd been 'shredded'. Maybe she thought she was next. If I'm to find out the truth, where the hell do I start? I must remember: Mission Possible.

---

18 Nov 15

I had a thought in the night, which was to find out who she was. At least it would be a start. I could email you and ask you all sorts of questions, which I am sure you could answer, but I don't want to contact you at this stage, as it would be wrong for me to raise any possibilities which might be totally unfounded. Anyway, I don't think I could get in touch with you until you've read the story.

I thought I'd start by listing all the things about her which I can remember. Helen mentioned her first name was Eleanor, and I guessed she was born around 1960 and married in 1981 or 82. Her husband died about a year later in 'a boating accident'. I assume he was born in the late 50s.

Eleanor probably went to a private school and was a boarder. She said she'd been Head Girl. At her school was a dinner lady known to the girls as Mrs Broad. Eleanor was keen on dance and drama, had a good voice and wanted to be an actress. She was sporty, a good swimmer and worked at Mr B's leisure centre as a swimming coach and life-saver. She had reddish hair, a lovely smile, was very beautiful and not easily forgotten.

---

21 Nov 15

I've just read that last sentence! I must watch the retros. Today I'm going to do some serious googling – girls boarding schools, leisure centres in the South East, births marriages and deaths. The dinner lady is probably no longer with us, but she might live on in someone's memory. Talking of memory, I recall Broadsword – or should I now call her Eleanor – telling me about traces, getting them to intersect like bearings on a map, in order to identify a person.

There can't be many Eleanors around, so that's a good trace to start with. I know your surname is Braithwaite, but I don't know if that was her maiden name or her married name, or indeed her name at all.

---

25 Nov 15

Just had an amazing couple of days looking up all sorts of things. I had to sign on for some of the services, but if I cancel within a month, there's no charge. The detail is astonishing, and a bit worrying. And you don't need to have much information to get an awfully long way.

For example, I didn't know when her husband was born, which on the Government Archives site is a required item. So I simply searched each year from 1955 to 1958. I didn't need to go further than 1958 because I found him! Poor chap. Not many born around that time died in the early eighties. And only one Braithwaite. Trevor. And his spouse? Eleanor Lucille Titania Braithwaite.

But you knew that. For me though, it was an encouraging start, and it wasn't long before I found her maiden name, Wilkinson. I then searched for and eventually found the record of her death, which was a bit sad. As expected, it showed she'd died in New York on 11th September 2001.

I never did find Mrs Broad, but my email to 27 girls' boarding schools asking for news of Head Girl E. L. T. Wilkinson was enough to produce the required result. I felt slightly guilty pretending to be her old forgotten best friend Susan Smythe, but there we are. I suppose on the scale of guilt I'm experiencing at this late stage of my life, it's fairly minor.

Her obituary appeared in the newsletter of her school's old-girls association. She was indeed Head Girl at West Heath from September 1978 to July 1979.

---

28 Nov

West Heath. I should have explained. It's up the road from here. Most of us locals know about it because of its famous pupil, a certain Lady Diana Spencer. I wonder if they knew each other.

Just googled her. Lo and behold, they overlapped! At least for three years, before Di went off to Switzerland to be finished. In fact, they might have been in the same class, as they were about the same age, Di having been born in July '61. They might have even been friends, as the website said that Di was a good pianist and dancer. And Eleanor loved to dance (am fighting off a retro!).

They had a lot in common – good looks, charisma, a sense of fun – including the fact that they got married at about the same time. Perhaps they went to each other's weddings. Perhaps my Broadsword knew Prince Charles!

Typical.

---

3 Dec 15

So, the Prime Minister got his way last night. Our boys in blue are striking ISIS in Syria as I write this. Not happy. Dan, do skip the next few paragraphs if you want, but here are my thoughts.

There may well be good reasons for these air strikes, but

'making our streets safer' is not one of them. Indeed, the likelihood of terrorist action in this country has overnight become greater. There are two reasons why this is so.

The logistics required to mount a terrorist attack in, say, London, are not dependent on ISIS in Syria or on any other of their overseas bases. The perpetrators and their armaments are most likely already in this country. The defeat of ISIS in Syria would do nothing to prevent a terrorist attack in London. It would encourage it.

The motivation for jihadist terror attacks is not because they hate us or want to terrorise us or destroy our way of life, nor do they do it because they are mad, evil, brainwashed or radicalised. The attacks are simply in retribution for perceived wrongs against them, as demanded by their religion. They are a form of defence: if you invade our lands and bomb the shit out of us, we'll kill a few of your civilians.

Our launching air-strikes against them is like somebody bombing Canterbury Cathedral to stop the spread of Christianity. It's irrelevant. The enemy is an idea, a culture, a religion, not a task force you can attack with weapons. If ISIS were wiped off the face of the earth, other groups urging jihad against perceived enemies of Islam would emerge. All the strikes will do is to help ISIS recruit more people and incentivise their followers to launch more attacks against us.

It was dishonest for the politicians to say the strikes will 'make our streets safer', or to imply that a 70,000-strong army of lovely people was waiting to sort Syria out once we had screwed it up even more. Surely, a lesson from the Iraq intervention is that if a leader has to lie to garner support, they are probably about to make a terrible mistake.

Let's hope not.

1 Jan 16

Happy New Year to one and all! Let's hope it's a good one, mission-wise.

———————

8 Jan 16

I was so sorry to hear 'our' Mr B passed away. I know Julie sent you a note of our condolences, and I trust you, Helen and the children will be comforted in the knowledge that he had a long and fruitful life. Julie never met him, but we knew he was a sort of dad to you. I just wish I'd known him better – and for longer. He was a kind and modest man with high principles, and from what Eleanor told me about him, I gather he was an important figure in the world of national security.

I still don't know who he is – sorry, was. And perhaps I don't need to know. Eleanor's uncle? Or just her boss at the leisure-centre-cum-think-tank. Anyway, he must have retired from that job a long time ago.

Obviously, you knew him much better than I did, but I sometimes wonder about that evening I spent with Eleanor, my last evening at the think-tank nearly 30 years ago. Did Mr B hope it would work out the way it did? That CD of romantic oldies he produced, the oysters and champagne, Mrs Grey looking a million dollars – on his instructions! Did he want 'love to come and tap us on the shoulder'? Who was he doing it for? Did he ever consider the outcome, a baby boy nine months later?

Or was it an affair by proxy? You might have seen that film with Cate Blanchet. I think it was '*Elizabeth, the Golden Age*', or something like that. It claimed Queen Elizabeth loved Raleigh and wanted a physical relationship with him, but she was worried this might end up with her losing her crown. Instead, she engineered a relationship between Raleigh and her close lady-in-waiting Bess Throckmorton so she could enjoy a love affair by proxy.

I know the sexes are the wrong way round, but Mr B certainly loved Eleanor, and she was devoted to him. Big age gap, of course. Maybe his exposure to radiation at that nuclear test site had something to do with it. Perhaps it had made him impotent – or at least caused him to worry that any child spawned by him might be affected by it. Perhaps, like me, he wanted to be a dad and the only way he could do it was by proxy. Only a thought.

It's such a shame he's gone. If your mum's still alive, who's going to look after her now? Perhaps I should also be trying to find out about Action Man. Not that I could do much about him. Warn her, maybe.

———————

15 Apr 16

Just got back from a fantastic holiday in Laos and Cambodia. No doubt you've just had a wonderful week's skiing, you lucky chap!

I have been thinking a lot about Mission Possible, but I'm afraid to say little progress has been made. I still cannot say Eleanor definitely died on that dreadful day, or if she used it somehow to fake her death and start a new life under another identity. If she's still alive, she has certainly stayed silent, which in one way is extraordinary. What mother would abandon a child of fourteen? Certainly not Eleanor. If she did 'carcass', it must have been for a very good reason.

So, there are still lots of questions, but not much in the way of answers, I'm afraid. Yet. 'Mission Possible', I keep saying to myself.

---

21 May 16

If only I could talk this over with Mr B. Sadly I can't. But what I can do is to follow his technique and do some pretending. I'm going to pretend she did carcass – cut and run, change her identity and stay silent – to protect herself, or Mr B, or possibly you. Furthermore, I'm going to pretend she was under threat because of something she knew which, if revealed, would have cataclysmic consequences for someone or some others. Perhaps 'they', whoever 'they' were, needed her shredded.

Deaded. The way my mind is working is this. If that information has found its way into public knowledge during the last 15 years, she no longer has a reason to stay silent and is no longer under threat. My dream – and I'm still pretending – is that she is alive and that I'll find her and make it safe for her come back so she can be re-united with you and your family. Grandmas are useful.

---

22 May 16

And mums are too, of course! But heaven knows how I could achieve it. Finding her is going to be difficult, as I have no doubt she would have done a pretty good job. False passport and other documents, perhaps a change of nationality and possibly a change of looks. And cut-offs; all the way along her escape route, no doubt. But before I think about the how, I'm going to find out why she went.

I think my first step is to imagine what sort of information she possessed, the release of which could have posed a danger. It must have been true and factual, as there is no point in silencing someone for having just a fanciful view or theory. Also, knowing she was unlikely to betray her country or her colleagues, I am going to rule out things like names of agents, techniques and strategies, military secrets and so on.

As for the threat which she might have perceived she was under, I think I can assume it was not from a rogue or criminal element, but that of a lawful killing 'for the greater good'. In other words, someone somewhere might have made the judgement that the lesser evil of killing her was justified because it prevented the greater evil which would be inflicted on their organisation, their nation, or even the world if she divulged the sensitive information she held.

Maybe someone within her organisation. Someone like Action Man, perhaps. Wretched man. Why do I keep thinking of him? I suppose it was her reaction when she first mentioned his name in the think tank all those years ago.

Would she want to divulge sensitive information? Supposing she herself saw the balance the other way around, like Katherine Gun, that by breaching the Official Secrets Act – a crime – and telling the world, she was preventing an even greater crime against humankind. Hmm.

---

4 Jun 16

A funny thing happened today. A parcel arrived, and in it was a school tuck box. You'd be more familiar with these things than I am. Obviously, it was quite old, and I would imagine it had seen good service in more than one boarding school. The four initials, RGDB in black paint on the lid were just about readable, but they meant nothing to me. It reminded me of Eleanor's technique for forgetting super secrets – to imagine stuffing them all in a box and floating it down a river.

Anyway, I was able to pick it up by its handles and carry it in from the porch, so I knew there wasn't much in it. Attached to the wrapping was an envelope, and inside it was a typed letter from some firm of solicitors, saying it had been in the estate of a Lt.

Comd. Sir Richard Bentley KCB, RN, deceased, and had been left to me in his will. The letter said the value of the box was 'nil', so I didn't get too excited.

Apart from not knowing who the hell this guy was, there was no key for the padlock, so there was some frustration there.

Julie said, "What on earth are you going to do with that?"

"Oh, I'll find a use for it. I might keep my camera equipment in it – tripods, spare batteries and that sort of thing." I could tell she disapproved of yet more clutter in my office.

―――――――――

20 Jun 16

Now, this is interesting. I have managed to angle-grind the padlock off the mysterious tuck box, and you will never guess what was inside. A CD! No label, just a blank disc in a white sleeve. And when I put it in my new computer, guess what I heard! 'Some Enchanted Evening', 'When the Blue of the Night...'. Of course, I realised what it was, and whom it was from. Mr B. Our Mr B.

And, a knight of the realm! Not surprised, though. He was quite a man. It was kind of him to think of me in his will, and I said a thank you to him for a useful little present. But I think he was telling me something, that I should metaphorically put any secrets I have and lock them in the box. Or maybe it was his box of secrets.

Listening to that CD was, of course, another retro for me. Those old-fashioned tunes. That night when Eleanor and I swam in the pool. But I think I've reached the stage where I can look back to those times without feeling too weird, now I know what happened. The night I became a dad-to-be. Your dad-to-be.

―――――――――

21 Jun 16

I woke early today, Mid-Summer's Day. Perhaps it's these light mornings. I was there in bed, lying on my back, next to Julie who was still fast asleep. And I thought more about Mr B's box. What if he were telling me something else? If it were just the CD that he wanted me to have, why didn't he just send it through the post? If it were just a box, why put a padlock on it?

I was careful not to wake Julie, as I put on my dressing gown and went across to my office. I lifted the tuck box onto my desk, and using the desk lamp as a torch, I inspected the box thoroughly. I didn't really expect to find a hidden compartment in the floor of the box, so you can imagine my surprise when I did.

I noticed that the plywood inside base of the box was relatively new and had no markings at all, yet on the outside, there were rivets of some sort. So the plywood sheet lying in the bottom was like a lining.

I imagined that between this and the bottom of the box itself there would be a layer of sovereigns, perhaps, or some other great treasure Mr B wanted me to have. Or some other memento of our brief time together working on the neutron bomb scope. Or a letter, revealing some great truth which I alone would be privileged to be burdened with. Maybe his life story? Now that would be interesting.

<hr/>

22 Jun 16

Disappointment, I am sorry to report. Yesterday after breakfast, I took the box into my workshop, and I started by screwing four small screws into the plywood lining at their four corners, leaving a couple of millimetres of each screw head proud of the plywood. To each of these screw heads, I attached a length of thin nylon cord roughly double the height of the box. I tied the other end of each cord to form a loop, and by using a large screwdriver as a lever resting on top of the side of the open box, I was able to exert a considerable upward force on each screw in turn.

By going from one to another, I was eventually able to lift the plywood lining. It had been glued in position, but only around its edges, so once it started to come up, it came away quite easily. It wasn't long before I was able to get my fingers behind one side of the sheet and pull it free of the box.

As you can imagine, I felt quite pleased with myself and excited at the thought of revealing the secret of the box. But when I looked inside there was nothing. I put the lining down and tipped the box towards the window so I could get a good look inside. It was bare. Nothing but the ends of the rivets showing which attached the base to the side-wall brackets.

Mission possible. Mission possible.

―――――――――――

4 Jul 16

US Independence Day. But it's a good day! Julie, bless her heart, said it might be a good idea if 'we' tidied my workshop. It was the opposite of the Royal We, and over the twenty odd years we'd been together I'd got to know and love it. When Queen Victoria said 'we are not amused' she meant 'I am not amused'. When Julie says something like 'we must tidy up my workshop', she means I must do it. It's her way of gently nudging me to do things I ought to be doing rather than dreaming about the mission I've set myself.

She isn't against my 'Mission Possible'. In fact, she encourages it because she knows I like puzzles and challenges, and she likes to see me happy and occupied and not hanging around the kitchen and stealing the odd biscuit from the biscuit tin in the larder. But she has never asked what the mission is, and I've never told her.

Back to my workshop. On the bench was the false plywood floor of the box, still with its four screws and the bits of cord. I removed these, as I reckoned the rectangular sheet would come in handy for something. I turned it over, and to my disappointment, I saw it had been covered with that sticky plastic sheet you can get for covering shelves or whatever. Messy stuff to get off.

Anyway, I started peeling the plastic back and found a blank sheet of A4 paper – wait for it – folded around a microfiche!

I'd come across these when I was serving in Germany. Basically, they are a plastic film – like an old negative but thicker – about a hundred mill by one-fifty containing seven rows of tiny photographs. Each row has fourteen photos, so the whole sheet contains ninety-eight. The photos can be of anything – proper photographs, drawings or pages of text.

Normally, at the top of the sheet there is a title, but on the sheet that I rescued from the box lining there was nothing to indicate what was on it. The photos themselves are so small that you can't read them with the naked eye, so you need a fiche reader, a special machine, to see what's on each photo.

So, Mr B has given me some information! Do I really want to know what it is, I ask myself, remembering his horror story of me lifting up my phone and being asked to provide the name of the double agent. But I knew he would've given me the sheet for some good reason, so I thought, right! I'm going to get to the bottom of this. Tomorrow, I'm going to find a reader.

Yes, I did tidy up my workshop. And I did throw out a lot of important and valuable junk which might well have come in handy one day – but Julie doesn't do junk. She was thrilled to see the four large plastic refuse sacks which I had filled with the precious stuff.

She wanted me to get rid of the tuck box, but I said it might come in handy one day. And it did. Today. Because I put the fiche in the bottom and replaced the lining on top of it. I closed the lid and locked it with an old Yale padlock I had been keeping – in case it came in handy.

It's now on my desk in my office, next to me as I write this. Somehow, I've got to get hold of a reader.

3

20 Jul 16

Had a brilliant idea this morning. I phoned up our local library and asked them if they had a reader I could use. They didn't, but told me the reference library in Tunbridge Wells had one. I decided I'd just go there and ask them face to face if I could use it. It took me about twenty minutes to reach Tunbridge Wells, then another fifteen to find a place to park. But I found a space near the library and soon I was standing in front of the head librarian's desk.

She agreed to my request and guided me to where their machine sat. She removed the dust cover and offered to show me how to work the thing; I said I had used them before and should be able to manage it. She left me to it, saying if I had a problem to come and see her. I sat down at the table, switched it on and fed in the fiche.

It's quite difficult to use as you have two knobs to twiddle; they move the fiche around so you can see on the screen above an enlarged image of each photo. I started in the top left-hand corner and was disappointed to see it was just a newspaper cutting. No date, no headline, and a quick scan down the page showed me it was just some article out of the travel section of a newspaper.

So I just had to work my way through the photos. I didn't know what to expect, but I was on the lookout for anything that might be relevant to me or to Mission Possible, or to anything which Mr B may have wanted me to know about.

Only another 97 to go, I thought. More copies of the same newspaper page. I had made my way to the fifth or sixth photo when I saw the heading – and it stopped me in my tracks. It said TOP SECRET. I looked around me, to see if anyone was watching me.

Fortunately, there was only one other person in the room, and he was fast asleep. But I quickly twiddled the knob to bring me back to another newspaper cutting, just in case someone walked into the room and saw me. I decided I couldn't go on like this. I would have to find another way to view Mr B's treasure.

—————————

22 Jul 16

I've found it. Some time ago I bought online a USB microscope. It's rather like a pen in size and shape, perhaps a bit fatter. It's on the end of a cable which you plug it into a computer's USB port. If I hold the microfiche against a window and put the microscope's head against the fiche, I can then get an image of the photo on my computer screen. The important thing is I can then press a button on the microscope, and the picture is captured and saved onto my hard drive. Brilliant.

In the next couple of days, I'm going to copy the whole thing onto my computer, then lock the fiche away. At my leisure, I can then examine each photo on my screen and extract to a separate file any which look as if they could be important, like the Top Secret one I saw in the library.

—————————

1 Aug 16

School holidays, and it's been a bit busy here. Despite that, I'm about a third of the way through my task of scanning into my computer all the photos. I haven't looked at any yet, except those

I saw in the library, but I am concerned about the security issues. If there's one Top Secret one there, there could be others. I have therefore decided to take my computer offline. As Mr B. would say, you can't be too careful.

It's a long, fiddly task, and you have to have steady hands. But until I know what I'm dealing with, I don't want anyone else involved. I feel I have got in my possession something I shouldn't have. In a way, I feel guilty. Stupid idiot.

---

2 Aug 16

This is serious. I've just had a sneaky look at that Top Secret document on my screen. Below the security classification is the Crown crest, the one with the lion and the unicorn. Below that is a title: Application for Authorisation under Section 7 of Chapter 13 of the Intelligence Services Act 1994'. Below that are the words:-

> 'Authorisation is hereby sought for an act or acts against the person described hereunder in order to achieve the purposes and for the reasons specified below'.

It then gives a name: Eleanor Lucille Titania Braithwaite nee Wilkinson. The act or acts are described as:-

> 'measures necessary to prevent the unauthorised release of information which if released would not be in the interests of national security with particular reference to the defence and foreign policies of Her Majesty's Government, nor in the interests of the economic well-being of the United Kingdom'.

Below that, it says:-

> 'The undersigned do hereby certify that nothing will be done in reliance on the authorisation beyond what is necessary for the proper discharge of a function of the Intelligence Service; and that, in so far as any acts may be done in reliance on the authorisation, their nature and likely consequences will be reasonable, having regard to the purposes for which they are carried out'.

There follow three signatures, but I don't recognise the names. Perhaps one of them is Action Man's. Underneath them, there is a signature I do recognise – or at least I know the name typed below it. Then below that is the person's appointment: Secretary of State for Foreign and Commonwealth Affairs. And the date: 29th July 2001. A licence to kill?

---

4 Aug 16

It was quite a shock seeing that document. It confirmed my worst fears, that Eleanor knew something which, if disclosed, would not be in the interests of the Nation – in the view of whoever signed the application. The measures necessary reminds me of the Doctrine of Necessity, that if a measure is necessary to prevent greater 'social value', it is lawful.

I suppose killing one person is fairly insignificant compared to the interests of national security and economic well-being. If you are the Nation's leader.

But then I had a thought. It is extremely unlikely she'd been killed accidentally at the World Trade Centre, just a few weeks after the Class Seven had been issued. Far too much of a coincidence. It is much more likely that she found out about the Class Seven and that her trip to America was to escape the 'measures necessary' before they could be enacted.

So she might still be alive. This is wonderful news. Thank you, Mr B for that vital bit of information.

I wonder if the information she was carrying in her head concerned 9/11. Maybe she knew those towers were going to be taken down, bomb or no bomb. There were rumours our intelligent services had prior knowledge of the attacks, and maybe she got wind of that.

---

6 Aug 16

Perhaps she went to New York with the intention of warning

people; I wouldn't put it past her. Perhaps someone in the Intelligence Services thought she would spill the beans – whatever the beans were – or maybe our allies thought as much and 'requested' that she be silenced. Who knows?.

Then there was the first Gulf War and those crippling sanctions on Iraq that followed. They were causing so much misery to the ordinary people of that country. Perhaps she felt she should tell the world how the US Government had indicated to Saddam Hussein that they wouldn't interfere if he invaded Kuwait. How they set Saddam to provide a reason for the Coalition's invasion of his country.

By the end of the 90s, at least well before 9/11, the plans for the second invasion of Iraq had already been drawn up. Perhaps she knew this and felt the world should know. Whatever the reason for her cutting and running, I see my mission is to find her and get her back safely. Impossible? I hope not.

4

20 Aug 16

I have been racking my brains over the past week trying to work out how you find someone who has deliberately changed their identity and started a new life. No success, I'm afraid. I have no idea where to start. She could be anywhere in the world. She could have changed her looks. Anything from dyeing her hair black to having plastic surgery. So what I am going to do today is to phone up a few private investigators and see if they can give me any ideas; any techniques or tips.

Good news! I have just arranged to meet a guy in Tonbridge tomorrow. Not far from here, fortunately, as driving is not one of my favourite pastimes these days. I explained to him over the phone roughly what I was after and he said he would give me an hour of his time, in his office, for £100. Cash only, mate.

21 Aug 16

Just returned from my meeting with Stan. Very interesting, and worth the £100 just for the entertainment value. But he did set some thoughts going in my head which are worth further consideration.

His office was unimpressive. It was on the outskirts of the town in a Victorian semi which – like its neighbours – had been rezoned for commercial use. His office was upstairs, above an undertaker's.

There were just the two of them, Stan, a rather rotund man in his late fifties, and his secretary, Sandra, about half his age. Each had their own office, linked by an intercom. Stan's was modestly furnished with a partners desk, behind which he sat on big swivel chair which reclined and squeaked when he leant back on it.

On my side of his desk was a cheap office chair and beside it was a coffee table. Sandra showed me in, having answered my knock on the main door. As she did so, she asked if I would like tea or coffee. I chose coffee. Stan greeted me unenthusiastically and waved me to take a seat, then sat down and said, "Fire away!"

My first thought was that I was probably going to get my money's worth, as he wasn't going to waste time talking about the weather. I thought how on earth can I start? Obviously, I wanted him to know as much as possible about my mission, but I couldn't divulge any classified information. I couldn't say anything about the scope – and certainly not about the top secret Class Seven.

"I am trying to trace someone who might have deliberately disappeared," I said.

"Male or female?"

"Er, female. Must be aged about 57," I replied.

He sighed. "Your relationship?"

"A friend," I said. His eyebrows went up.

"Last seen?"

"1986." He leaned forward in his chair, resting his elbows on the desk.

"Thirty years ago, eh? What did she look like?"

I said she was about five foot six – I was guessing – had a slim, athletic body; very beautiful, blue eyes, Titian hair, a gorgeous smile. Laughter lines. . . He held up his hand to stop me.

"So you want to trace a middle-aged Caucasian lady with grey hair, facial wrinkles and probably weighs about ten stone. Where do you think she might be?"

"I really don't know. Anywhere in the world, I suppose." He pursed his lips and shook his head.

"Look, mate. Most of the blokes who walk through that door want to find out who's bonking their wife. Often, the only thing they can give me is a brief description of the sod's car – seen by a neighbour perhaps – and half a number plate.

"Easy! One phone call and it's done. I shell out two hundred quid to my contact, the bloke gives me five hundred and the job's done. He's happy, I'm happy! What you're trying to do is impossible."

He must have seen the expression on my face, as I looked down at my hands in my lap. At that moment, Sandra came in with my coffee – and tea for Stan. She put my cup – a big china thing – on the table beside me, gave me a smile and walked out of the room. Stan took a sip of his tea, then leant back in his chair and said "What's this all about, mate? I've heard it all before, y' know. So you won't shock me."

Here goes, I thought, and I told him. "The middle-aged lady is the mother of my only son. I abandoned her before he was born. She disappeared when he was fourteen, believed to have died in the 9/11 attacks in New York. I believe she is alive."

Stan breathed out slowly and looked up at the ceiling. For a few minutes, he said nothing, then said, "Why?"

"I'm sorry," I said, not following his train of thought. "Why what?"

"Why did she disappear, leaving a fourteen-year-old son? D'you think she chose to do that?"

"No. She was under pressure. Great pressure. Her life was in danger. She was very close to her son – our son, and possibly his life was in danger as well. I can't tell you any more."

"Okay-zee, I get the drift. Look, mate. I can see why you are doing this, but I would advise you to stop. Right now."

I didn't stand up and put my hands on my hips, but I did say in a quiet but determined tone that I was seventy-three years old,

I had set myself this task, and I wouldn't give up until it was completed.

"I take it she wasn't involved in any sort of crime, not a 'gangster's moll', anything like that?"

I shook my head.

"Look, most of my work is done here, right here in this office. On the phone. On the computer. We do trace people and, yes, it can be difficult, and sometimes we need to use other resources, and then it gets expensive. To trace someone who is deliberately in hiding – if they are any good – takes a lot of resources and a lot of time. I'm sorry, but you aren't going to succeed."

He must have seen the look on my face, as he didn't stand up and shake my hand and show me the door. Instead, he looked at me as if he'd suddenly had an idea. "Do you know who would have been threatening her? Who was she running away from?"

There was no need for me to answer the question. He looked at me and just said, "It's the security services, isn't it?" I nodded. "Do you think she defected?"

"No," I answered. "Nothing like that. She's a patriot through and through. And she must have had the highest security clearance, as she worked with really secret stuff."

"Have you any proof they were after her – and I just want a yes or no?" Again I nodded.

He smiled. "Okay-zee. Give me a couple of days. I'll sleep on it. No promises, mind. I'll give you a ring."

I thanked him and stood up to leave. I said I'd better give him my phone number. "Nah, mate. Already got it."

---

23 Aug 16

Stan rang back today. Said it would be best if I came into his office. We agreed at ten tomorrow. I found this encouraging, as he wouldn't want me to visit him again if he had nothing important to say. We shall see!

---

24 Aug 16

Just got back from Stan's. Very interesting. Sandra greeted me and showed me into Stan's office – and a couple of minutes later she came back with my coffee. Same cup, same stains. Stan was behind his desk sipping his tea.

"Ever done judo?" he asked. No chat about the weather.

"Yes, a bit" I replied.

"In that case, you know that one of the principles is to use your opponent's weight to your advantage. That's what you've got to do. The only organisation capable of finding your lady, the only one which has the resources worldwide to carry out such a search is SIS, the Secret Intelligence Service. MI6. They can, of course, call on their friends – GCHQ, other security services – if they need to. The trick is to get them to do it."

"How on earth could I persuade them to do that?"

"You don't. You get them to want to do it. You get them DESPERATE to do it. High priority job. Right from the top. Look, if her line of country was what I think it was, she would've only gone into hiding and left her son – your son – because of a Class Seven job. That's an authorisation to chop someone, including someone on your side who's a huge danger to national security."

I resisted the temptation to say yes, I know about those, I've got one at home.

"They hate doing those things to their own people, you know. They always try and find a better way. If they can outsource it, they will, but sometimes they just have to get on with it. But give them an excuse not to, and they'll take it.

"Like your lady's disappearance at the World Trade Centre. Why chase around if the target's dead? They're also very twitchy about issuing Class Sevens, because of blowback, of getting rumbled.

"The general public can't accept that sort of thing, governments going around killing people. Unless they've been a squaddie or a spook, they can't get their head around the idea of knocking someone off to protect the nation – or the national

interest. Class Sevens are very, very secret. The funny thing is –
sorry, funny is not a good word to use – the interesting thing is
they have to keep hold of the paperwork to prove the action was
authorised, should it ever be questioned."

I sat there listening. My untouched cup of coffee getting cold
on the table next to me. When Stan stopped to sip his tea, I
remembered the arguments, the Doctrine of Necessity, 'the
greater good', lesser of two evils, and that Latin quote: 'Quod est
necessarium est licitum'. That which is necessary is lawful.

"Now, this is where you come in," he continued. "If you do have
evidence that one of these Class Seven things was issued which
named your lady as the target, you're home and dry!"

I didn't get it. Had I missed something? He must have seen my
puzzled look because he went on to explain.

"Look, mate. Supposing you presented them with evidence that
the Foreign Secretary – the guy that signs these things – had
authorised an action designed to shut your lady up, how do you
think they would react? And supposing you also presented them
with a death certificate showing she disappeared some weeks
later, no positive ID? It wouldn't look too good, would it? If you
were Foreign Secretary, what would you do?"

Back to pretending. "Firstly", I said, noting that Mr B's training
was still evident in my approach to such situations, "I would want
to keep the whole thing under wraps. Secondly, I would deny it
and claim it was an absurd accusation that couldn't possibly have
any truth in it."

"And, my friend, how would you do that? How could you, as
Foreign Secretary, prove BEYOND DOUBT you hadn't murdered
her?"

Then, of course, it struck me. "Find the lady. Bring her back
alive."

"Well done, mate! You don't need me to help you after all, do
you!"

He got up and came round his desk and joined me. He showed

me to the main door, shook my hand and wished me good luck. I thanked him, as I fished out my wallet with the two hundred pounds in cash which I had withdrawn from an ATM on the way there. I assumed he would charge me double, for the two sessions.

He held up a hand. "No mate, no charge. Always happy to help a fellow red-job."

He was referring to the red beret, worn by us 'paras'. How did he know I was one? On that particular occasion, I had not been wearing my Brigade tie.

---

25 Aug 16

Should have asked Stan about Action Man. He seemed to know a lot about the intelligence services and that sort of thing. And about being a soldier. Ex-SAS perhaps? Then a thought struck me. My old mate Mike was SAS, then in the security industry before he retired. I'll give him a ring.

Just come off the phone to Mike. After the pleasantries, it went something like this.

"Mike, can I ask you to do me a favour."

"Sure, you can ask. Whether I can help you I don't know. If it's money you want, remember you still owe me a fiver from that bet we had at Abingdon."

"No, nothing like that. Action Man. Does the name mean anything to you?"

"Sure does, I've got one in my toy box."

"I'm being serious. It's important. I believe it's the nickname of a bloke in the security services."

There was a long sigh at the other end of the phone. "Means nothing to me, I'm afraid – but I could ask around. What about him? What do you want to know?"

At that point, I realised I didn't have a clue about what I wanted from Mike, or what I would do with any information he gave me. So I just said "anything would be really helpful. Please?"

Another sigh. "I'll see what I can do."

1 Sep 16

It's been a while since my meetings with Stan, and it's only now that it's beginning to sink in, that my mission is possible. All I need to do is to write to the Foreign Secretary and explain the situation, enclosing a copy of the Class Seven authorisation, as I have now learned to call it. I could threaten to go to the papers if they didn't agree to my terms.

Then I considered the difficulties. A, the current Foreign Secretary is not the one who signed the document. B, my letter would never reach the Foreign Secretary, and would probably be tossed into the bin by a minion, specially assigned to fend off nutters.

Or would someone come round to my house, be very polite and say that it was not helpful to pursue a matter such as this, a matter which was alleged to have happened many years ago. Any embarrassment arising would not be welcomed by Her Majesty's Government, and it would be in the Nation's best interests if I forgot about the matter and handed the forged authorisation over to them.

They might offer to do me a great favour, like cancelling the surprise VAT inspection planned for next week – except I was no longer in business. But I did wonder if they would make life uncomfortable in any way for my step-daughters and their families. That, I would not want.

So, it needs more thought.

Just about to go to bed, having fallen asleep in front of the telly again. Some legal drama. But it did give me an idea. As I didn't have to pay Stan for his help, perhaps I could buy an hour's worth of advice from a solicitor. Again, I would have to be very careful about what I told them, but they might just be able to steer me in the right direction, rather like Stan did. Tomorrow, I'll phone around.

5

Had a good meeting at the solicitors' today. I'd arranged it for 10.30 a.m, but by a quarter to eleven, I was still hanging around in reception reading the papers and drinking their coffee. Eventually, he appeared, a Mr Brian Bolding, tall, bald as a coot and about forty-five years old. Smart suit, firm handshake and an air of expensive after-shave about him.

He led me into a small, oak panelled conference room with a tall ceiling and oil portraits on the walls of past partners. Between them were shelves of books. Impressive, but I did wonder if the books were ever taken down and read. These days it must be so much quicker to look up things like case law on a computer.

Mr Bolding was a time-of-day person. We sat opposite each other across a large, highly polished mahogany table, and talked about the weather, the traffic in Sevenoaks and the magnificent listed building we were in that had been their offices for a hundred and ten years. I hadn't worked out beforehand what I was going to say. I thought I would just pretend he was Mr Blue and wait for him to drag it out of me when he was ready.

Finally, the moment came. "Now, Mr Rayner, what can we do for you today?" I said I wished to sue the Secret Intelligence Service under the Corporate Manslaughter and Corporate

Homicide Act of 2007 because they'd authorised the murder of my son's mother.

I then passed across the desk to him a copy of the Class Seven authorisation Mr B had kindly given me via the microfiche. I told him I wished to claim damages for myself of £1m and £5m on behalf of a second victim, closely related, my son.

He looked as if he'd seen a ghost. He picked up the document and examined it closely, frowning at first, then his jaw slackened and his eyebrows went up as he read the text. With a shaky hand, he placed the document back on the table as if it was a bomb that might explode at any second.

"I'm most awfully sorry, Mr Rayner, but the partnership doesn't undertake work of that, umm, nature, and even if we did, I fear there would be no possibility it would ever succeed." He stood up, I think as a signal to me that the meeting was over, but I just sat there. He looked uncomfortable, not sure whether to remain standing or to sit down.

My turn to speak. "Mr Bolding. I do not want the action to succeed. Indeed I want it to fail. I simply want the Secret Intelligence Service to prove what I believe is the truth, that the woman is alive and well, and I want them to prove that by finding her and presenting her to the court."

He wouldn't meet my gaze as he jerkily found the comfort of his chair.

"Mr Rayner, we couldn't possibly contemplate taking on such a bizarre case. No hope of winning? We have our *reputation* to think about!"

Then I had an idea which I thought might put him out of his discomfort.

"When I phoned up a couple of days ago, I said I'd like to have an hour's worth of advice from a senior partner. And that's all I need, advice.

"You see, I'm an author, and I'm writing a story about a man who is trying to locate a woman. She's disappeared in mysterious circumstances following a Class Seven authorisation. That document in front of you is something I cut-and-pasted last night. I couldn't tell you at first because I wanted to get your reaction to the proposal I put to you, and I must say your reaction was, er, invaluable. You would, of course, get an acknowledgement in the book, and I dare say it might make an interesting dinner party story for you. And there would be no liability issues for you."

He relaxed and looked me straight in the eye. A smile began to form on his lips. "How *exciting*!" he said. "What can I do to help you further?"

"What I would ask is that we proceed on a solicitor-client basis at this stage and keep it utterly confidential because it's important the plot remains secret. Naturally, I would pay you your hourly rate for this meeting and any subsequent ones. What I need to know is how might such an action proceed."

"I see, I see!" he said, reaching for his notepad and preparing himself for the thrilling task ahead. "But my first thoughts are that your character should not be contemplating a *civil* action at all. Your character should–"

"Mr Bolding, to make things easier, why don't we pretend the character is me, Gerald Rayner, and we pretend the woman who has disappeared is. . .is Martha."

He agreed. He said that under the circumstances he would *not* advise me to go down the civil action route, as it could take an awfully long time. He said a civil action does have the advantage that proof of wrongdoing is based on a balance of probability rather than 'beyond reasonable doubt' which is required in a criminal case. But as I have documentary evidence that a minister of the crown authorised a termination of Martha it would seem beyond reasonable doubt that the Intelligence Services were responsible.

"I think you could get them to find Martha without actually going to court. I would imagine the 'powers that be' would prefer a swift solution, *under the media radar*, rather than a challenge in the High Court. And what better way of having the case dismissed than producing Martha alive and well!

"My recommendation is that you get the ball rolling by taking out a *private* prosecution. Now that may seem a bit strange, but the right of the *individual* to institute criminal proceedings is of great antiquity!"

I tried to look interested. He continued.

"When the post of Director of Public Prosecutions was created in 1879, the Act of Parliament expressly preserved this right, and it remains *to this day*. In fact, the police and public officials have no more powers to initiate prosecutions than you do."

I asked what was involved. He said he needed to check the latest legislation, and that he would send me some notes when he'd done this. I suggested it might be better if I collected them from reception, rather than him email them to me or sending them by post, if he could just get someone to ring me when they are ready.

And so our meeting ended. Not a great deal of progress, but in Mr Bolding, I think I have found an enthusiast: a legal eagle unfettered by concerns which a real-world case of this nature would inevitably raise. Ready and willing to immerse himself in a *pretend* world where nobody gets hurt but he still gets paid.

I await his comments.

------

13 Sep 16

I had a call from Mr Bolding's secretary to say his notes were ready for me. I was able to pick them up this afternoon and I've just read them through. Quite helpful, actually.

The first thing he pointed out was that the security services were not on the list of those government departments which one can sue, and he still thinks the private prosecution is the best route. Furthermore, he feels the target should be the Foreign Secretary, or his office, as they signed off the authorisation.

Launching a private prosecution is relatively simple and quick, and it could produce the result we are after. There is a snag, though. Although the Crown Prosecution Service has the power to take over a private prosecution, they also have the power to discontinue it.

However, the CPS has always adopted the policy to stop private prosecutions only if they represented a genuine injustice to the defendant. But by 1998, two other factors had been added: a case would be stopped if 'the public interest factors tending against prosecution outweigh those factors tending in favour' or there was 'clearly no case to answer'.

He believes there *is* a case to answer with our Class Seven authorisation as evidence. He cited the statement made ten years ago at Princess Diana's inquest by the head of Secret Intelligence Service that any proposal to use 'lethal force' would require a Class Seven authorisation signed by the Foreign Secretary. So it follows that the Class Seven document of which I have a copy could well have initiated the murder of Martha.

What worried him most were the public interest factors which might weigh against allowing the case to continue, but as this argument is rarely used, to do so would probably attract undue attention from the media. Finally, he did mention the Doctrine of Necessity: the disclosure of information by Martha would have caused a greater evil than that of disposing of her. On the other hand, for the defence of necessity to be valid, the greater evil has to be imminent.

Then he mentioned what I thought was quite a clever point. If Martha is still alive, sixteen years after the Class Seven was issued, any greater evil envisaged when the thing was signed was not imminent. Therefore a defence of necessity would fail. So too would a charge of murder as she was still alive, but one of attempted murder or conspiracy to murder would stand.

He then explained what I had to do to start things off. Simple, really. I have to 'lay an information' before a magistrate. The information must contain a statement of the offence and identify the legislation which created it, along with the particulars of the offence so it's clear what the prosecutor alleges the defendant has done. The magistrate then issues a warrant or summons.

His conclusion is that the process would put the security services in a difficult position, and could be persuaded it would be in their best interest to find Martha – or produce rock-solid evidence to the court that she was alive and well.

At last. We have a way ahead.

6

14 Sep 16

Had a nice supper with Julie, just the two of us which is always a treat. I wanted to tell her about progress, but it's such a long and complicated story. After the meal and a scotch I slipped away to my office and googled 'Class Seven authorisation'. Interesting. I found a couple of reports covering the appearance at Princess Di's inquest of the Chief of the Secret Intelligence Service, otherwise known as 'C'. Then I read through the actual transcript of him in the witness box being questioned. As Mr Bolding had said in his notes, C admitted there is a procedure for authorising lethal force – a euphemism for killing someone – but it's tightly controlled.

C said this at the inquest:

'There would be a plan written and described from the appropriate section. It would come up through several managerial filters as to whether the proposal was viable. That proposal would also have to include a passage of legal compliance. So there would be a reference as to whether the proposed act would be lawful under an ISA authorisation [ISA is Intelligence Services Act 1994]. When the paperwork was completed – and this would apply to an initiative overseas as much as to one developed within head office – it would be signed off by, let's say, the senior regional official. It would come to me for further signature and then it would go down restricted channels to the Foreign Secretary.'

He also said he'd never known a Class Seven authorisation being issued for an assassination in his thirty-eight years with SIS. He confirmed it included using 'lethal force' but insisted it 'played no part in the policy of Her Majesty's government'.

Yeah, a very carefully thought-through and amazingly complicated procedure, involving judges, C and the Foreign Secretary himself, yet never used? What he did say was that Class Seven authorisation was confined to allowing agents to conduct activities such as breaking and entering and planting bugs which would otherwise be unlawful.

Just googled the Intelligence Services Act. I'm no expert at these things, but as young officers, we had to become familiar with the Army Act. I rather enjoyed the MML, the Manual of Military Law, and I felt comfortable working my way around it reading the notes in the margins and looking up the various schedules. So when I downloaded the Intelligence Services Act, I was heartened it followed a similar format with sections and sub-sections and sub-sub-sections. It didn't take me long to find Section 7 and read through it.

I also read Section 5. Not much difference, really. Section 5 talks about warrants; Section 7 calls them authorisations. Section 7 specifically relates to actions outside the British Islands, whereas Section 5 does not mention a geographical limitation. Both had to be signed by the Foreign Secretary, or by a subordinate nominated by him. Section 5 covers 'entry on or interference with property or with wireless telegraphy'. Section 7 covers 'any act'.

So why did the Chief of the Intelligence Service say Class Seven authorisation was used for 'illegal activities such as breaking and entering and planting bugs'? Surely such activities would be covered by Section 5. Perhaps I had missed something. In my view 'entry on or interference with property' includes breaking and entering. 'Any act' includes killing someone.

The clever thing about the wording of Chapter 13 is that

Section 5 talks about warrants whereas Section 7 dances around the possibility of legalising someone's death. Nowhere do the two terms come together. There is no mention of death warrants.

Tired now. Must sleep.

7

15 Sep 16

I woke early again this morning, my head buzzing with legal jargon. I also had some weird dreams. Of courtrooms and people in wigs and robes, and of Broadsword. There she was, in her pale dress – broderie anglaise, as I now know it – looking amazing, just as she did on that special evening when she came to my cabin. She was led into the courtroom and everyone clapped. She saw me and walked up to me with that big smile on her face.

Then I woke up. The courtroom dream started me thinking about 'C' being interviewed at Princess Diana's inquest. I imagined I was an eminent QC who was questioning a head of the Secret Intelligence Service in that courtroom under similar circumstances. Someone once told me the secret of examining a witness was never to ask a question to which you don't know the answer.

This is how I pretended it would go, with a pretend C I'll call Sir Courtney Capers, and a pretend princess called Jane. I must admit I've since done a bit of googling before recounting my thoughts here, but then any respectable QC would do their homework beforehand.

Me: "Sir Courtney, I too would like to thank you for being with us today at this important inquest. I trust it was your decision to be a witness and give evidence, and you were not cajoled into coming or persuaded in any way?"

Him: "No, not at all. I'm here today as a voluntary witness. Serious allegations have been made against the Service, and I take them personally, as I have already said."

Me: "I quite understand, but let me reassure you the purpose of this inquest isn't to make allegations. It's merely to establish how Princess Jane came by her death. I hope, and all of us here in this courtroom hope, that you might be able to shine some, umm, light on the matter [this stirs a murmur from the public gallery]. May I ask if you had to seek permission to come here today and give evidence?"

Him: "Permission? Of course not."

Me: "And you weren't ordered to come by anyone?"

Him: "Heavens no! As I have already told you, it was my decision alone."

Me: "Thank you, Sir Courtney. As you said earlier today, it's very unusual for a Chief of the Secret Intelligence Service – or indeed anyone from that organisation – to volunteer comment on an allegation of this nature. I believe you said it would be against policy."

Him: "Absolutely, but I believe in this case it's appropriate for me to do so."

Me: "So, you believe it's appropriate to put the policy of your erstwhile organisation to one side, and that the decision was yours and yours alone?"

Him, with a sigh: "Yes, as I have said. I believe it appropriate and it was my decision. Most certainly."

Me: "Thank you, Sir Courtney. I am most grateful for that. It is important that the court understands that answers you give will not be constrained in any way. With this in mind, could you just confirm that you are not constrained by any undertakings, promises or oaths which you might have given during your service which are still valid today?"

Him: "I beg your pardon?"

Me: "Well, for example, are you bound at all by the Official Secrets Act, or an Oath of Allegiance to the Crown, or perhaps an Oath of Secrecy, or Public Interest Indemnity, 'Crown Privilege' or any other gagging order which might prevent you from honouring the oath you took this morning: to tell the truth, the whole truth and nothing but the truth?"

At this point, the judge stops me and tells me that there may be matters which C cannot go into, but he was sure C would tell the court when this was so. I agreed, then continued.

Me: "Sir Courtney, I'll try to steer clear of such areas, but do please tell me if my questions stray into them. I think you would agree it would be better to tell us, rather than give us an answer which might either reveal a secret or perjure yourself. I would also add, for the benefit of the jury, that you are under no obligation to answer any questions which might incriminate you."

Him: "Incriminate me? Are you accusing me of a crime?"

Me: "Certainly not, Sir Courtney. Nobody for one moment is suggesting you might have done anything of a criminal nature. You are not on trial. We are simply trying to establish the cause of a tragic death. And if it is any reassurance to you, even if you and your Secret Intelligence Service had 'bumped her off' under the terms of the Intelligence Services Act, it would not have been criminal because that's the whole point of Section 7, isn't it? It makes an assassination lawful, doesn't it?"

I would make the pretence of going through my papers, but I know what I'm going to say next.

Me again: "Of course, I appreciate your wish to refute the allegation, and I would like to help you do this, once and for all. You see, by doing this, we would eliminate one of the causes of death which has been suggested. Previously in this courtroom, you kindly described in some detail the procedure under Section 7 which would be followed before any such authorisation would be given. Would you say this procedure has clearly been thought through?"

Him: "Absolutely. Much effort has gone into making sure any use of lethal force would only be used under the most stringent control."

Me: "Yet you said the use of lethal force plays, and I quote, 'no part in the policy of Her Majesty's government'. In which case, may I ask why so much effort has gone into developing this complicated procedure?"

Him: "The procedure was developed in case it ever had to be used in exceptional circumstances."

Me: "So, the use of lethal force does play a part in the policy of Her Majesty's Government – but only in exceptional circumstances. Thank you, Sir Courtney. Could you describe for the court an example of an exceptional circumstance where the use of force would be authorised?"

Him: "As I said, it has never happened during my time in the Service, so I cannot conceive a situation where it would be authorised."

Me: "Come, come, Sir Courtney. You, during your time as Operations Director, must have contributed to the 'much effort' that went into developing the procedure. Surely you must have given it some thought of how and when it might be used? Otherwise, there would have been no point in developing it. But let us move on. You said, I believe, that after the paperwork had been completed, it would come to you for further signature and then it would go down to the Foreign Secretary. Am I correct?"

Him: "Yes."

Me: "Who was above you in the chain of command when you were Chief of the Intelligence Service? Who did you answer to? In other words, who was your boss?"

Him: "The Foreign Secretary."

Me: "So after you would have signed the paperwork, you said it would go 'down' to your boss. That's an extraordinary turn of phrase, Sir Courtney. Surely paperwork of the nature you describe – part of a very carefully thought-out procedure – would go 'up' the chain of command to a higher level, and 'down' the chain of command to a lower level. May I ask you why you said it went 'down' to your boss?"

Him (irritated): "It is simply that the Foreign Office is in Whitehall which is down river from our headquarters."

Me: "So when you were at Century House, which is down river from Whitehall, the paperwork went up to the Foreign Secretary? Or did it depend on which way the tide was running? [A titter goes around the public gallery]. Or did it depend on the political tide of the moment? I put it to you that you did not really regard the Foreign Secretary as your boss, but more of a rubber stamp. One wonders who you did answer to, if anybody. Sir Courtney, may I ask you, very roughly, how many applications were made to the Foreign Secretary under Sections 5 and 7 of the Act between the time it came into force and your retirement?"

Him: "I cannot say, but they were required each time it was necessary to, to, to plant a bug, for example. Many times."

Me: "And were any of these many applications turned down by the Foreign Secretary?"

Him: "No, not to my knowledge."

Me: "To your knowledge, Sir Courtney? Forgive me if I misheard, but I thought you said all applications would be signed by you before going to the Foreign Secretary. May I ask you, though, did you ever have to 'lean on' a Foreign Secretary to sign an authorisation?"

Him: "Certainly not!"

Me: "So he just signed them? He was a rubber stamp, after all?"

Him: "No! In fact, I do recall on a few occasions there were discussions with the Foreign Secretary about such matters."

Me: "I assume these 'discussions' never included persuasion, coercion or blackmail of any kind. For example, if the Foreign

Secretary happened to have a secret which he was anxious to keep hidden, like having an illicit affair with, say, his secretary?"

Of course, at that point, the judge would stop me and say it was a preposterous idea to put before the court. I would turn to him and apologise if I had upset the court, but politely point out that I was saying exactly that, that such discussions would never be of that nature.

Me: "A truly terrible accusation has been made that, while you were Director of Operations, you made an application to the Foreign Secretary for a Class Seven for authorisation to kill Princess Jane. Would you therefore not agree that a corroborating affirmation by a person of integrity and high office that you did *not* make such an application might prove your innocence beyond doubt?"

Him: "Yes, I would agree."

Me: "May I suggest the best person who could do this would be the person who would've signed off the application, the Foreign Secretary himself? Your boss? If he stated under oath that you had never passed 'down' an application to him, this absurd accusation would be laid to rest forever."

Him: "Yes. But that wouldn't be possible."

Me: "Why's that, Sir Courtney?"

Him (red in the face): "You know perfectly well why."

Me: "But would you please tell the court why?"

Him: "Because he is dead, damn you!"

Me: "And how did he die, Sir Courtney? Tell us what happened."

Him: "He died of natural causes following an accident while hill walking in Scotland. He was airlifted out but died before they could get him to hospital."

Me: "Forgive me, Sir Courtney. But surely one dies either from an accident, or one dies from natural causes. It would be difficult to die from both, wouldn't it? Dying from one thing is bad enough, but dying from two would be most unfortunate. Perhaps it was a natural accident. But let's move on. Am I right in thinking that Class Seven authorisations can only be authorised for action outside the British Islands?"

Him: "Yes, that is true."

Me: "So, a lethal act could be authorised if it were to take place in a helicopter flying over the Atlantic Ocean a mile or so west of Cape Wrath, on its rather roundabout way to the hospital at Inverness?"

Him: "Are you implying that I personally or the Intelligence Service had anything to do with his death?"

Me: "Sir Courtney, you are hardly likely to want to dispose of a crucial witness who alone can prove conclusively you are innocent of the death of Princess Jane. Indeed, I can only think of one reason why you would want to get rid of that man. It would be because he alone could also prove conclusively that you *were* responsible for her tragic death. Now, if I may, I would like to resort to the more normal practice of me asking the questions – if you don't mind."

Me again: "You said previously, with some pride, that your organisation recruits people of proven integrity and character and does not tolerate any behaviour which falls below the high standards set by the Service. Would you say your Service, under your leadership, enjoyed a high sense of ethos, a culture of exemplary service, of loyalty?"

Him: "Most certainly. Any intelligence service must if they are to be effective."

Me: "I suppose the overriding culture of any intelligence service – its beliefs, its ideals, can be encapsulated in its motto. I note, for example, the Mossad has, or had, the motto 'By way of deception, thou shalt do war'. Sir Courtney, does your Intelligence Service have a motto?"

Him: "Yes. It's 'Sempre Occultus'."

Me: "And can you give us the English translation please?"

Him: "Always secret."

Me: "Always secret? So if you had applied for a Class Seven

authorisation to use 'lethal force' against Princess Jane, it is most unlikely that you would tell us, oath or no oath. Isn't that so, Sir Courtney?"

Him: "Look, I've made it quite clear it's NOT the policy of Her Majesty's Government to assassinate people–"

Me: "But you also made it quite clear that it's not the policy of the Secret Intelligence Service to answer allegations in court. Yet here you are today, doing just that. And it was your decision, and yours alone, to break away from that policy. One must ask the question, did you ever decide to break away from the policy of not assassinating people?"

All in my imagination, of course. But had it not been for the seriousness of the subject, it would have amused me, as I lay there next to Julie waiting for dawn to break.

8

16 Sep 16

Just read what I wrote yesterday. Then I thought if I were the cross-examining QC at Princess Diana's inquest, would I want to rake over these things? Would I really want to insinuate that my government had carried out some terrible deeds? What would it achieve? It wouldn't bring anyone back to life. It wouldn't gain any advantage for my country.

In fact the opposite. Any such revelation would do my country a great deal of harm. And for all I know, there might be good reason for a government to engage in acts which otherwise would be criminal. 'Quod est necessarium est licitum...' Acts which are necessary.

Perhaps in real life, if I'd been cross-examining him, I might have kept my questions well away from the heart of the matter.

If the Foreign Secretary is just a rubber stamp when it comes to Class Seven applications, it means 'C' decides on them. That's some power he holds, which reminded me of that quote: 'Power corrupts. Absolute power corrupts absolutely'. But on the other hand, he has a difficult job keeping the Nation safe, particularly in today's uncertain world.

Of course, you and I from would argue that killing the occupants of that car was wicked, whatever happened to be in the national interest. But we are not rulers. Princess Diana was one of the two people Tony Blair described in his book 'A Journey' as being a danger.

Danger is a strong word, much more so than the word troublesome. And look what happened to Thomas a' Becket, the troublesome priest. I'm not suggesting a casual remark by Blair signed her death warrant, or that a Class Seven application was ever submitted and signed, but a PM has a job to do, and he must do what's necessary in the best interests of the Nation. To do what is necessary is not a crime: the Doctrine of Necessity rears its very ugly head yet again.

Oh yes. I nearly forgot. The other person Tony Blair said was a danger? A certain Foreign Secretary.

You may not think the death of a princess has much to do with Mission Possible, but I think it might. If they can do that to the 'People's Princess', what could they – might they – have done to Eleanor? Even more worrying is this: what may they do to Eleanor if I manage to get her back home? Whoops. Am I doing the right thing?

---

19 Sep 16

Sunny day. Just remembered I must finish scanning the microfiche into my computer. Fiddly job. Then I must read through the scans and check if there's anything else of interest. Perhaps the newspaper pages hold some vital clue. I just hope I don't have to read all ninety-seven of them.

Afternoon. Done it. All ninety-eight are there. Dear old Mr B! He must have gone to a lot of trouble. Must get reading soon.

---

25 Sep 16

We have just returned from a few days in the Cotswolds. Wonderful! Did a bit of walking, and plenty of eating. Do we eat to walk – or walk to eat? I think the latter.

Now here's a thing! I've just found two more Class Sevens on that fiche. Remarkable! Unfortunately, both the name of the target and the signature block of the person authorising the action have been blacked out.

Neither has a photograph. Both use vague wording, stressing security and the 'interests of the Nation'. The first was dated before Eleanor's, the other much later. I couldn't think why Mr B had included them, but at least it proved that these things are used despite what was said at Princess Di's inquest.

So my search continues.

———————

26 Sep 16

Waded through the fiche documents this morning and found the nugget of gold! It's a letter from Mr B to me personally, on three consecutive photos. I've read it a couple of times, but I think it's important you read the whole thing as it is a vital part of your story. And I think you will find it interesting. My new computer has a character reading program, so I've been able to copy it in here directly.

4th March 2014

Dear Major Rayner,

When one reaches 90, there's not much to look forward to in life, or what is left of it. But instead one can take pleasure in looking back at the past, at one's happy moments, at one's achievements, the people one has loved and have loved you. But to do so, one has to open the box of memories, a box that also contains those secrets which one might prefer to leave safely under lock and key.

One of my pleasures was that our paths crossed in 1986. Your input to the study was of great value, and you have a right to be proud of what you achieved in those four short days. It also pleased me that you got on well with 'Mrs Grey', and that your brief liaison was fruitful. I loved her too, but I could have never had an intimate relationship with her. I am much older, but that was not the reason. I had a big secret which I could never have shared with her. The blood of her husband was on my hands.

He was a young man of 23 and a member of the Service, newly trained, recruited straight from university. He was bright, full of promise, of passion, but known to be an angry young man at times, as men of that age often are. But he threatened the Establishment, to the extent that he posed an imminent danger to the Nation.

I was co-opted onto the committee which heard his case, and having studied it in meticulous detail, along with all the factors involved, I decided, with my fellow committee members, that action was necessary. I could have taken the easy way out, and walked away. I could have argued strongly against the operation. But it would not have made any difference. Yet to this day, I cannot help but feel an enormous sense of guilt that I was a party to that young man's death.

Mrs Grey was a girl in her early twenties. They had been married for a few months. I decided I would do what I could for her during the months that followed. When she had recovered from the appalling loss I invited her to come and work for me. She was brilliant at her job, and we got to know each other well. She swore she would never marry again, but I think she yearned for motherhood. I hoped that one day I would be able to introduce her to an eligible young man within the Service, but I failed.

You came along, and I could tell that you two would get on. I hoped you would enjoy each other's company on that last evening, but neither she nor I expected it would lead anywhere. Afterwards, we discussed what kind of future you two might have had in front of you. And together we decided that she would remain as Mrs Grey, and you as Mr White, never to meet again.

I looked after her as much as I could until she disappeared fifteen years later. We missed her dreadfully. It was a tragedy. Like her husband before her, she had posed a threat to the Nation, and therefore was in danger. In a way, it was fortunate that the Intelligence Services Act had come into being in 1994, as it then became necessary to go through a much more lengthy procedure before action could be initiated. I was not involved, but I heard it was happening, and I was able to do something about it. I hope I had saved her life. I owed her that.

Also, I was able to copy the authorisation which you will find on the fiche. It might help you reunite her with her family: her son and her grandchildren. I am too far gone to undertake such a task, but I believe you can.

I have included two other authorisations on the fiche. They are powerful. They have protected me for many years. Please notice that three names have been blacked out. This is to spare you from the burden of a great secret. All three would be familiar to you, and neither person deserved to die.

But neither were allowed to live, because both had become a threat, in their different ways. Their demise was necessary but I would advise you against further investigation. It would serve no purpose. Some secrets were meant to remain secret. It is our duty to keep them that way. Sempre Occultus.

Return those authorisations to their rightful owner, in exchange for your broadsword.

Good luck and God bless.

After reading his letter, I had another look at the other Class Sevens. I couldn't understand why he said three names had been blacked out, because both targets and authorising signature blocks had been redacted: four in all. Perhaps he was just getting confused. It's bad enough at my age.

Or could one name have appeared twice? Then a rather bizarre possibility occurred to me. It's not something I would wish to share with anyone, but like the Lusitania, it may one day become common knowledge, and nobody will care much. In a few hundred years, perhaps those Class Sevens might appear on the equivalent of google images, as the death warrants do today of two former Royal personages, Mary Queen of Scots and Charles I.

――――――――――

1 Oct 16

I've thought a lot about Mr B's letter. It's comforting to know he thinks I can do it, but on the other hand, I feel even more under pressure to perform. But perhaps that's a good thing. The other day I started worrying whether bringing Eleanor back was the right thing to do. Then I wondered if I was just making an excuse for myself, an excuse to put my feet up, watch telly and forget about all this. These days I do struggle a bit, and this damp weather is not good for my old bones! I need a push to do anything. But Mr B's letter has given me a bit of one, so on we go.

Enough complaining. Let me tell you what I've done today. I phoned up Mr Bolding – although I had to hang on for what seemed like ages before I was put through. I thanked him for his help so far, and the most useful notes for the 'book'.

He asked me how it was going and when it would be published, and I said I'd let him know. I asked him if he could help me prepare 'an information' which my character could present to a court. I explained it would be nice to have a copy in the book. He said he would be delighted to do this if I could give him about a week.

---

16 Oct 16

I've been writing this 'final chapter' for a year now. How time flies by! I believe I've made good progress, but my time is running out. Julie says I should be slowing down at my age, but I feel I should be speeding up! So I will continue the fight, at best speed, but enjoying the odd tipple in the evenings, a walk in the countryside at weekends, some good eating and some kitchen bridge. And being a stepdad and a step-grandpa. And the secret knowledge that I am a real dad and real grandpa, too.

Good and bad has just happened. Good that Bolding has come up trumps with an excellent submission for the court. Bad he sent it to me by email. I'm not paranoid about security, but I did learn to be cautious about it from Mr B and 'affable Andy', whoever he might have been.

I should take comfort I'm not the sort of person likely to be hacked, or have my identity stolen, but to have Bolding's submission passed over the airwaves – or through the telephone lines – made me feel uncomfortable. You see, he referred to the evidence as being a government-issued top-secret documentation in my possession. I'm not supposed to have it. He put my real name on the submission. My fault. I should have said my character was Mr Purple or something.

But I suppose he thought it would be useful to have the submission in digital form so I could paste it into my manuscript.

---

20 Oct 16

Got a beastly cold! Mission put on one side.

---

26 Oct 16

Getting better. Must tackle that submission today. And pay Bolding's bill.

Looked through it again, and have made one or two changes – like Eleanor Lucille Titania Braithwaite instead of the mythical Martha. I'm slightly nervous about 'laying' it, of handing it in. Bolding suggested the County Court at Maidstone. Will sleep on it.

---

28 Oct 16

Not so hot – and it's my birthday! 74! Had a nice lunch with my girls – that's Julie and my step-daughters Frances and Fiona – at the Sussex Rifleman. This evening they are coming round for a high tea with the kiddies after they have picked them up from school. Hubbies are then joining them, which will be great. Bob's always interested in my views on things, and Michael's a great jokes man.

---

14 Nov 16

Still not right. And here we are, winter around the corner and the prospect of skiing! For me? NOT, as my grandchildren would say. They're right, of course. Those days are over.

Said I'd go to Sue's lunch party next week, her 70th birthday. Sue is Mike's wife. Mustn't give up on these things. I think I'll give her a pack of bridge cards.

9

20 Nov 16

I'm a bit better today. Why is it, I used to ask myself, that old people are always talking about their ailments? I now know. It's because their ailments are always affecting them. We're like old cars, bits dropping off, wearing out.

You're lucky if you have just one thing wrong with you. Most of us oldies have lots of things wrong with us. So when you are set upon by two muggers, one wielding a knife, it doesn't help much. But I'm jumping ahead of myself. I'll come back to that later.

I did make it to Sue's birthday lunch yesterday. Trains were good. Went first class, as a treat. Julie was teaching and couldn't make it, so there was just the one ticket. Also, I treated myself to a taxi at the other end and asked the guy to come back at three. I thought it would give me a good excuse to get away. These things can drag on a bit.

Over drinks before lunch, I met a friend of Mike's. An attractive young lady, in fact. I should tell you something. When I now see a pretty girl, I always smile at them. And it's amazing how many – most in fact – smile back. I'm not sure whether it's because they like the 'cut of my jib' as Mr B might have said, or, much more likely they know they are quite safe with me. Sad, in a way.

Anyway, Karen smiled back, and she was really nice. We chatted about Mike. Her dad had worked with him when he left the Army, and when he came down to their house, Mike used to tell her stories about the SAS. She doubted any of them were true, but as a young child, she found them fascinating.

After lunch, Mike asked me if I would help him with the coffee. I willingly agreed, knowing it would give us a chance for a chat. He launched in straight away.

"Ex SAS. Territorial. A bit of a reputation. . ."

"Sorry Mike, who are we talking about?" I thought it might have been Karen.

"Action Man. Possibly your Action Man. Come on, Gerry! Get up to speed! You mentioned him on the phone the other day."

"Just making sure," I said. "So, a reputation for what?"

"Look, what I'm going to tell you is all hearsay and mustn't be repeated, but there was a guy in the Regiment who had the nickname, Action Man. Late seventies, Northern Ireland, acting captain. Goes by the name of Timothy Turnbull. His bosses liked him, but the boys didn't. They thought he was unstable – something not quite right. Just as well he left when he did, if you ask me. If the boys don't respect you, you're finished. Joined SIS. Could you get the milk? There's a jug in the cupboard behind you."

"Sure," I said. "Anything else?"

"The cream. Someone might want it. Over on the table."

"I meant about Action Man. Any other info?"

"Actually, yes. From another source. Falklands '82. Special ops. Three Argy prisoners handed over to him for battlefield interrogation. Usual procedure, except he shot them dead. Apparently, they were US mercenaries. Story goes it would've been harmful to US/UK relations if they'd been sent up the line and knowledge of them leaked out. He should have just let them go, for fuck's sake. That's what I would've done. . ."

Mike poured the boiling water into the two cafeterias, then carried the tray through to the drawing room. I made a bee-line for Karen. I took a liking to her, possibly because she laughed at my jokes. Not many people do.

When it was time to leave, I said my goodbyes. Karen said she needed to get down to London and enquired if I was going by train. I said yes and asked if she wanted to share my taxi to the station. She said that would be very kind, so the two of us climbed in and before long we were there. We had a ten-minute wait, but then soon found ourselves sitting in a first class compartment all to ourselves. Most of the traffic was going out of London at that time.

She must have been quite well off for a young girl of her age; as a young man, I would not have dreamed of going first class. Perhaps she was on an expense account. For a party?

We chatted more, about this and that, and then she said something like: "Please, please don't be upset, but I need to talk to you about something. I was hoping I would meet you at the party; you see I have been told to, to pass on a message."

She paused, letting it all sink in, studying my face to see how I was taking it. Not well, was the answer to that. I hadn't a clue what she was talking about.

"Mr White?" she asked. It was clever because I smiled and thought of Mrs Grey, of Mr Black. It was a happy thought. She had me in the right mood, and by calling me Mr White she told me – almost – what it was about.

"Go on," I said.

"We understand you're trying to help a. . . umm. . . colleague of ours. We appreciate that very much. We want to help you." Another pause.

"How?"

"We might be able to find out where she is." She was watching me, seeing how I was taking it. "We think we can do this, but we will need your help also. In fact, we would need to work together."

"What can I do to help you, then?" I asked.

"We find that sometimes we work better by keeping a low

profile. Once the media get involved with what we are doing, things can get very tricky. The public have a fascination for our kind of work. They think it's glamorous and exciting, but really most of the time it's just a hard slog.

"Not that we mind if we succeed in the end. We like to. . .to make a difference. It would not help us if anything, ANYTHING were made public about our task."

"So you want me to drop the idea of a private prosecution?" That damned email from Bolding, I thought. She nodded.

"Anything else?" I asked, thinking of those Class Sevens on Mr B's fiche, and now on my computer.

"We would like our secrets back, please." I thought, here we go. Time for a tough negotiation. I decided to play dumb.

"What secrets are these?" I asked.

She could see right through me. "Any that you may have that you are not supposed to have?"

"I might possibly have some copies of some documents you may want, but if you think I am going to hand them over just like that, you can think again."

"OK. How can I persuade you to let us have them?" she asked.

"I will let you have them, only when I have proof that Eleanor is safely back in this country – or a country of her own choosing. And a guarantee that she and her family will never be subject to any action by SIS, directly or indirectly, which might do them any harm."

"Okay," she said. "Agreed."

This knocked me back a bit. She must have seen the expression on my face.

"We trust you. After all, we are on the same side, aren't we? Shake on it?" She leaned forward in her seat and grabbed my limp hand and shook it. Deal done.

"Now Gerald, is it true you're a keen skier?" She reminded me of Mr Blue. For the rest of the journey, we talked about skiing, how we started and where we had skied. I didn't tell her how my skiing had come to an abrupt end.

Finally, we pulled into King's Cross. Just as we stepped onto the platform she looked at her watch. "Oh my God. Look, I must fly. Great to meet you. I'll be in touch. Thanks for the chat!"

She didn't ruffle my hair. I don't have enough left to ruffle.

I caught the tube to Charing Cross and then the 6.37 to Sevenoaks. It was dark when I arrived, and I had a ten-minute walk to my car, across the main road and up St. Martin's Road. I don't know why, but I had a funny feeling I was being followed. It didn't worry me, as Sevenoaks is a reasonably safe town with a low crime rate. However, I had noticed a couple of hoodies hanging around the exit from the station. I turned to look back at them, and they were looking directly at me.

I walked up the hill to the sound of my heels clicking on the dry pavement. Apart from a young couple having a cuddle on the corner, the road was deserted. I finally reached the car, parked between two others, and as I went to open the driver's door, someone behind me shouted, "Hey Mister, have you got the time?"

I turned around, and there were the two hoodies about twenty feet away, striding towards me. I pulled up the cuff of my coat so I could see my watch, but before I had a chance to see what the time was, one of them lunged towards me and grabbed my keys from my hand.

"What the hell do you think you're doing?" I shouted at him, not realising at that moment what was going on. I was not so worried about the car, but on the bunch were my house keys and the keys to my office and workshop. No sooner had this happened than the other bloke came up to me and asked me for my wallet. He wasn't a man of many words. The Stanley knife in his hand said it all.

I decided not to be a hero. I made a point of not looking him in the eye, and I said, as calmly as I could, something like okay,

okay, I'll give it to you. As I fished my wallet out of the inside pocket of my blazer, he grabbed it out of my hand and chucked it to his mate. He then gave me an almighty push backwards. I tried to save myself, but my old legs would not move quickly enough, and I lost my balance and started to fall.

But then a third person, whom I hadn't noticed, somehow managed to catch me from behind and stop me whacking the hard pavement. Strong arms, I thought, as I was hoisted back to my feet. Then a voice said, "It's okay, just stay calm." It was a girl's voice.

As she said this, another person rushed onto the scene, heading at a sprint straight for the guy with the knife. Just before he reached him, he jumped up in the air and did one of those double kick things, striking the guy on the side of his chest with both feet at the same time. This sent him flying, and I heard the knife clatter to the ground. Then two people – both men I think – got out of the car in front of mine. One of them ran to the guy on the ground, turning him onto his stomach and yanking his arms behind his back.

The other person from the car ran toward the hoodie with my keys, but clearly, the hoodie didn't fancy his chances at out-running him and dropped the keys and wallet and put his hands on his head. Within about a minute a van arrived on the scene. It all happened so quickly. The hoodies were bundled into the back of it with one of my 'saviours' and drove away. The woman who caught me asked me if I was okay. I said I was fine.

And indeed I was fine. In fact, I found it quite exciting, although I was disappointed I hadn't contributed anything to seeing those blighters off. Another of the good Samaritans picked up my keys and wallet and gave them back to me. Some of my credit cards had fallen out, but using the torch on his mobile phone he found them all and handed them to me.

The girl then asked me if I was happy to drive home, and I said yes, perfectly happy, and then I thanked her and the other remaining good Samaritan for rescuing me. I think they were the couple I'd passed on the corner, but it was dark, and they weren't wearing any distinctive clothing, so I couldn't be sure.

Just as I was about to drive off, the young man tapped on my window. As I lowered it, he said, "I think this might be yours, sir."

He handed me the business card with Broadsword's name on the back, the one I had written on all those years ago. I thanked him and put it back in my wallet. Then I said a silent 'thank you' to Broadsword for watching my back, for being there for me.

As I drove the few miles home, I thought how lucky those passers-by just happened to be around when I reached my car. You hear a lot of complaints about young people these days, but I had just experienced the very best of human nature from a small group of youngsters who, with no regard for their own safety, had tackled my assailants to save me.

It wasn't as if I'd shouted out for help. They just waded in. I have some training in unarmed combat, but I could never have done a double kick as that chap did. It was impressive.

It's strange what you notice and what you miss in a situation like that. Until the girl caught me, I had no idea the courting couple were anywhere near me. I had not heard them approaching, and I don't think the muggers had either. I noticed afterwards that all my rescuers were wearing trainers. But all young people seem to wear them these days.

It wasn't until I got home that I started shaking. Julie opened the door she said, "What on earth's the matter? You look terrible!"

She helped me with my coat and guided me into the snug where I collapsed onto the sofa. She went into the kitchen and came back with a scotch and soda for me and a prosecco for her. She sat beside me and said, "Okay. Tell me about it."

Afterwards, I felt much better. We both agreed it had been a lucky escape, but to be honest, my main concern was not for me, but for 'Mission Possible'. Having just 'done the deal' on the train with Karen, I was anxious to stick around for a bit longer so I could see the thing through.

Julie suggested we should phone the police, but I said I wasn't hurt at all, I hadn't lost anything, and that the two hoodies had probably learnt their lesson. I added it would be nice if the efforts of my good Samaritans were publicly recognised. Julie said "Good Samaritans, eh? Very good Samaritans, if you ask me!"

We talked about other things, as we ate our supper on either side of the kitchen table. Julie told me about her day, and I told her about the lunch. Then we had a little cuddle on the sofa as we watched the ten o'clock news.

---

22 Nov 16

I have just read what I wrote a couple of days ago. And I have suddenly realised what Julie meant about my good Samaritans being very good. Someone was keeping a very special eye on me.

10

16 Dec 16

Nothing much has happened on the 'mission' front until today. Been putting up Christmas decorations, doing the Christmas cards, and generally getting ready for the festive season. It seems it was only a few months ago we were going through all this. But still, I like Christmas. It's hard work at my age, but the girls and their families are very helpful – and the little ones do enjoy it so much.

Back to the mission. Amongst the cards which arrived this morning, I've just found one addressed only to me from David and Karen. No surname, and at the time I just couldn't place the names. My memory is not that bad, but sometimes it's just slow. I usually get there in the end, but it can take an hour or so to google my addled brain.

Inside the card was an SD card which I thought would contain one of those round robin letters saying how fantastic the children had all been over the last year. Or a video clip of them starring in the school play. At least it might remind me who David and Karen were. But it wasn't a round robin. When I put it into the card slot on my computer, I was flabbergasted. What a Christmas present! Here it is.

To whom it may concern

In accordance with the Intelligence Services Act 1994, Chapter 13, Section 7 (8), the undersigned does hereby declare that any act which might have been authorised, planned or contemplated by Her Majesty's Government or any department thereof, involving Eleanor Lucille Titania Braithwaite, either directly or indirectly, is no longer necessary. Furthermore, it is declared that any current or future application under Section 7 of the above act which might involve Eleanor Lucille Titania Braithwaite or any member of her immediate family will not be authorised under the provisions of this section or any other section of this Act.

It was from 'The Office of the Secretary of State for Foreign and Commonwealth Affairs', and it was digitally signed by the man himself.

A result. At last. All we need to do now is wait and hope and trust that Karen's 'people' can locate Eleanor. And hope the 'To whom it may concern' includes Action Man.

---

28 Dec 16

Great Christmas. Probably best ever for me, as Karen's Christmas card gave me a big lift, just when I needed it. It's still up there, on the string across the bookshelves. As for the SD card with the round robin that never was, that's safely locked away. If I'm successful, it might be needed. A kind of insurance policy.

---

1 Jan 17

A Happy New Year to everybody – yet again.

---

4 Jan 17

Never thought I would hate the snow! But it does look lovely. Doctor coming here today. Sleeping in spare room. It's better for Julie. She kindly cleared a path for me to my office. Wonderful girl!

---

25 Jan 17

Not so hot these days, so when I got the text message from Karen, it gave me hope. It just said *In Buenos Aires raining hard but improvement is expected next week Karen xx.*

Dare I think the end is in sight?

27 Jan 17

Must just tell you this. I dozed off after supper, as usual, and I dreamed Mandy came round. Mandy of all people! My first wife! Said she had come to say goodbye. God knows where she was off to. Better get back to the house otherwise Julie will start worrying.

From: Bob and Frances Matthews
To: Daniel Braithwaite
Subject: Gerald Rayner
Date: 2 February 2017 09:45

Hi Dan – me again! Just to let you know we are having G-pa's 'bash', as he calls it in his notes he left, on Sunday 26th March at St. Jonathan's Country Club, just outside Sevenoaks. He said he wants you to be there and 'any member of Dan's family who can make it', to quote.

Basically, it's drinks then lunch with one or two speeches. He also wants a pianist and has given me a list of tunes he wants played – to be kept secret!!! He always had a bit of a weird taste in music, but the list was something of a surprise! Still, "Anything Goes" as they say!!!

Bob and I are trying to get out to Samoens this coming April with kiddies, and hoping we can all ski together. It'll be strange without G-pa leading us all. I know he missed last year, but now he has gone it feels different. Perhaps you could step into his shoes – or ski-boots???

Frances xxx

P.S. Found text below on G-pa's phone last night. Old fashion job, but I managed to share it, so I am attaching it. Don't know if he read it. I can't really understand it, but it seems to be from a friend of his. Just wondered if you know him, as I assume Gen is Geneva. If so, perhaps you could pass on the sad news:-

BS4DB – flying BA to Gen Wed week. Can hardly believe it, going to be a G at last!! With new 1 on way! Amazing coincidence U2DBs did finally meet.....Work it out, Dumbo! That's 2-1 to me I believe!!!! Thanks for everything. B would have been hugely proud of you, as I am. Some sunny day??? I owe you....

From: Bob and Frances Matthews
To: Daniel Braithwaite
Subject: Gerald Rayner
Date: 3 February 2017 09:08

Hi Dan –now hear this! I was lucky I got that draft diary off to you a couple of days ago, 'cos last night someone broke in to G-pa's office and took his new computer. Probably hoping to get a few quid for it down the Pub!

And they took an tuck box he picked up from somewhere. Who would want an old tuck box? Some people!

See you at G-pa's bash? Could you let me have numbers?

F xxx

From: Bob and Frances Matthews
To: Daniel Braithwaite
Subject: Gerald Rayner
Date: 12 February 2017 10:21

Cheers Dan. Five AND A HALF, eh? Congratulations all round, I guess! And a mystery guest??? Just the sort of thing G-pa would have loved.

See y'all on 26 Mar.

F xxx

PART 3

Coming Home

1

The school term had just started following the Christmas break. Anita Valdes walked slowly from the classroom, out into the shaded courtyard. The fountain was working again, not that this did much to cool the mid-day heat of an Argentine summer. Her visitor sat on the low circular wall surrounding it, waving his Panama hat in a lazy effort to waft the hot air around his overheated head.

The cream linen suit and white cotton shirt did little to help, other than making him look like something out of a Graham Greene or a Somerset Maugham. The slackened tie around the worn open collar of his shirt, the beads of sweat on a florid forehead, the spotted handkerchief held in the other hand, pressed into service as an improvised mop, reminded Anita of the Noel Coward song. Mad dogs and Englishmen.

Definitely English, probably from the Embassy. Of low rank, she thought, as she noticed the discoloured elbows of the crumpled jacket, the frayed brim of the Panama, and the worn out loafers on his feet. 'Down on his uppers'; she amused herself with the thought. He had driven to the school himself. She could just see his car outside the open gate, and she heard it clicking, like cars do when they cool down after a long, hot journey. The jacket and tie were a sure sign he was on official business. But why has he come here to see me, she wondered.

He had driven to the school himself. She could just see his car outside the open gate, and she heard it clicking, like cars do when they cool down after a long, hot journey. The jacket and tie were a sure sign he was on official business. But why has he come here to see me, she wondered.

As she approached him, he struggled to his feet, transferred the hat to join the damp hanky in his left hand, and introduced himself.

"Good morning. My name is Andrews. I'm from the British Embassy in Buenos Aires". He spoke in Spanish, fluent but with a strong English accent. Anita shook his outstretched hand as she continued to eye him up and down, trying to work out what he wanted from her. Old school, she thought. Upper class. Put a foot wrong somewhere along the line. He gave her a business card.

"Thank you. I am Anita Valdes. Good morning. You may speak in English if you prefer. Can I help you?"

She didn't want to get involved in small-talk, or offer him a drink, or suggest they went inside. She just wanted to get back to her class, her children. She'd been widowed some years ago – he was killed in a mining accident in Bolivia – and the short marriage had been childless. So for her, her pupils were her family. She loved them, and they adored her.

Her husband's company had provided her with a generous widow's pension, a regular income, paid monthly. This allowed her to work for nothing at the school in exchange for her humble abode in the grounds. At the end of each week, she would ask the headmaster how much she owed him this week, for the privilege of teaching such rewarding children. He would laugh and say not even the president could afford to pay her what she was worth.

The arrangement suited them both. For Anita, it also had another advantage: no work permit needed. That would have been tricky.

"Well, that's a relief!" said Andrews from the Embassy. "I must say your English is very good." To Anita, it sounded almost like an accusation.

"I've spent time in England. I teach English here." She said it with a trace of a Spanish accent.

"Ah well, that explains it!" he said. Anita stood there, waiting for him to get down to whatever business had brought him here, across those hot, dusty plains from the big city.

"Well, I wondered if you may be able to help us. You see we are looking for someone." Anita stiffened. "But please don't get me wrong, this person hasn't done anything wrong. No, no, everything is in order." And he fished inside the inside pocket of his jacket and drew out an envelope. "It's an English girl. We just thought you might know her, being an English speaker. Look. This is her."

He took the photograph out of the envelope and handed it to Anita. She looked at it, slowly stroked her chin, turned the corners of her mouth down, then put her head on one side. After a pause, she shook her head. "I am sorry, Mr Andrews. I do not know this lady."

It was almost 'Meester Andrews', and 'thees lady'.

She handed the photograph back to him. She remembered when it had been taken, at the end of their course at Fort Monckton. They had been told not to smile, to look serious, but they were all in high spirits, having passed, and the harder she tried to keep a straight face, the more she had giggled, her almost silent giggle. The photographer was a young man, and he had started smiling too and blushing. She never understood why some men became embarrassed when she smiled at them.

He was a handsome lad, and she thought it hilarious. In the end, he gave up, and her file photograph shows her with a broad grin. Mustn't smile now, she thought. But the seriousness of the situation at that moment was no laughing matter. At least she was wearing her glasses; black rimmed, plastic frames, and her long hair was drawn back into a tight bun. She was grateful Mr B banned photos in the brink tank.

Mr Andrews took the photograph and put it back in the envelope. "Well, thanks anyway for your time, Senora Valdes. Must dash. Got to interview five more suspects today!" he joked. Anita didn't think it was funny. "And if you do come across her, it would be awfully kind of you if you would give me a bell."

As he turned to walk back to his car, she relaxed. Then she said, "Why are you looking for her?"

Mr Andrews stopped and slowly turned around. Anita Valdes had been the twenty-ninth person he had visited that week. She was the only one who had bothered to ask that question. He used to be good at his job, very good. But the gods had not been kind to him, and his career had not progressed in the way that he once thought it might. Yet he still had that instinct, that intuition which can, on occasions, generate lucky breaks.

"We want to show her this." He took out the envelope again and pulled out a carefully folded sheet of paper which he handed to her.

People rarely smile and cry at the same time, but Eleanor did that morning, standing by the fountain. And so too did Mr Andrews, chiding himself for being a stupid old softy. Fair enough, he had done what he had been told to do, and his boss would be very pleased indeed and all that, as the rather embarrassing 'Whereabouts Unknown' could now be deleted from her file back at Section HQ. But what got him going was remembering the briefing he had been given, the full, sad, story – and the opportunity to give it a happy ending. Mission accomplished. Almost.

For her, it was like winning the match point of a Wimbledon final that had gone on for three and a half hours under a relentless sun. Driven to do her best, anxious not to let others down, the climax of two weeks of hard slog, preceded by months of intensive training. But for her, the journey had been nearly sixteen years.

She walked slowly back to her classroom, grateful for the fan on the ceiling which slowly circulated the warm, damp air. It was better than nothing. She decided siesta for the children would be early that day, to give her time to think. She would miss them. Mr Andrews had told her to ring him at the Embassy when she was ready to decide what to do.

———

The Embassy staff – the 'coordinating section' – were very kind. They sent a car to pick her up for the briefing. It took place in one of the air-conditioned conference rooms in the main embassy building. It consisted of a power-point presentation followed by the issue of credit cards and mobile phone with a world-wide tariff, the taking of photos, various forms to sign including the usual notification about official secrets.

After lunch, there was a less formal session of questions and answers. It reminded Eleanor of the 'inductions' one attended at the start of a new job. She was also reminded of what an old Baker-Streeter once told her: they never let you go.

Two young men gave the presentation, a sort of box and cox effort, explaining how the situation had changed recently which had made it possible for her to be safely repatriated to the UK if she so wished. They outlined to her the legal position, the documentation required, immediate travel requirements – to a country of her own choice – and on-going support. The monthly payments from the London-based holding company would continue if she could kindly provide them with change-of-bank details.

Arrangements would also be made during the first year for her return, if she wished, to visit the school where she currently worked. Over lunch one of the presenters, Alwyn, told her that a Gerald Rayner, a retired Army major, believed to be known to her, had played a significant role in achieving the change in her status. Gerald Rayner! she thought. From the brink tank. Danny's father.

Alwyn used expressions like 'he forced our hand' and 'he came up trumps'. *Was it all a card-game to them*, she thought. She smiled when she hoped she was no longer 'vulnerable'.

By the time lunch was over, she had decided her first priority would be to see her son Danny. The second, to find Gerald. The third to visit her parents in Sydney. Yes, her son and her parents would be located, and 'colleagues' would inform them of the situation at the appropriate time. No, she would be free to leave the country at a time of her own choosing, depending solely on flight availability to her chosen destination.

The flight would be first class, out of the embassy's allocation, no charge. Yes, the phone she had been issued with did have a list of likely contacts, and no, her number had not been given to anyone except the 'coordinating section'. No, Commander Bentley died two years ago.

She cried.

Then they handed her the bio, of who she was and what she had been up to since she went 'missing'. As if she needed reminding! Her role had come to an end. She was simply going to become herself. When she queried the need for it, Alwyn just said 'it's procedural'.

Also in the slim folder was a duplicate of her very own birth certificate, her marriage certificate and a slightly worn passport issued two years previously, complete with her photograph – the one taken just before lunch. And a valid UK driving licence.

She was told that the one thing missing, her death certificate, 'would be taken care of'. Alwyn said she 'would not be needing that for some time', and he laughed at his own joke. Not funny, if death has stalked you for sixteen years.

Before she left the Embassy that afternoon, she had been given the news that her son was living in Geneva with his wife, Helen – pregnant – and their two infants. The message from the Consulate said that if she wished to visit her son, they would provide accommodation in the city for as long as she needed it.

She accepted the offer there and then, and asked if a flight could be booked for her early the following month. She was told there were some embassy seats allocated on the 7th, and she was welcome to have one. A car would fetch her. Flight times would be confirmed by text.

On the way back to the school, in the embassy car, she took her new phone out of the box and read the brief instructions. The last one she had owned had been at least twice as big and half as clever. Eventually, she found out how to scroll through the contacts lists.

There he was, Gerald Rayner with his telephone number. She could have phoned him, there and then, but she decided to send him a text.

2

With the end of his middle finger, Dan wiped away the tear forming in the corner of his eye. It was the third time he'd read Gerald's story since receiving the package, and it still had that effect. Each time he was touched and saddened to learn how his parents met, loved each other but were unable to continue their brief relationship; and why Gerald was so upset about the news of Eleanor's death. It was the shock of this, of how she'd died that caused Gerald, an experienced skier, to fall off a chairlift in the French Alps on a bright sunny day.

The story was remarkable. It also contained a lot of Gerald's thoughts that helped to explain his behaviour; his attitudes to certain things. And it contained much about Dan's mother. Amazing things which came as a complete surprise to him. The nature of her work, for one thing, but also aspects of her character.

He'd never known his mum be angry, at least not how Gerald had described it. She had mentioned The Lusitania to him a couple of times, but she hadn't been emotional about it. As for Action Man or whoever he was, Dan could not recall ever hearing about him. Not the sort of thing you tell a young boy about, he thought.

However, reading about it did remind him of when he was about seven or eight, he had wanted the toy 'Action Man', popular at the time, but his mum had told him in no uncertain terms: no. Then she had added that it was just a doll – and boys don't have dolls.

Tantalisingly, the story also contained a promise that Gerald hoped to make amends before he died, to earn Dan's forgiveness for abandoning his mum, and for having what Gerald thought was a hand in her death. Dan had wondered how he would explain all this to Helen, things he himself was having a job to get his head around. It was only when the email from Frances arrived the following day that the pieces started to fall into place; the unsent email she had found on Gerald's computer, addressed to Dan: the diary.

Poor chap, Dan thought. He'd spent most of the last two years of his life trying to establish that Eleanor hadn't died at the World Trade Centre, and on his 'mission possible' to find her and bring her back to Dan.

Gerald believed he had made some progress, but Dan was inclined to dismiss the diary as evidence of an old man's wishful thinking. While he admired the trouble his dad had gone to, he did not go along with Gerald's theory his mum was alive and well somewhere, after all these years. She would've made contact somehow to let her son know she was okay. He just couldn't believe she wouldn't have bothered to do this if she had been alive.

It took him most of the day, on and off, to read the email properly. He had printed it out so he could read it wherever he was. Bearing in mind his dad was paranoid about using things like the internet, Dan was surprised the diary was in an email in the first place. But there again, it had only been in his drafts folder. Perhaps he was going to print it when he'd finished it. It was more than a diary. It was also a commentary – and it contained more secrets. Or ramblings.

The following morning he had another email from Frances about Gerald's memorial service. His father left some notes on what form it should take, and had asked if Dan and family could attend. He noted the date in his phone and asked Helen to do the same; 26th March, a Sunday.

Frances also asked if Dan might know of an old friend of Gerald's who had texted him saying he was flying into Geneva and hoped to meet up, not having heard the sad news. No name in the text; just what looked as if it could be an army callsign.

Then he had the phone call from the British Consulate in Geneva, not a million miles from their apartment. Could someone come round to see him, that evening, at about nine?

Helen answered the door. The 'liaison officer' was probably in her fifties, elegantly dressed and eminently presentable. She introduced herself as Mrs Marshall. Helen ushered her into their living room and suggested the seat by the window, opposite the sofa. Mrs Marshall turned down the offer of a drink but said she was very happy if both Mr and Mrs Braithwaite had something. She said it in a way that suggested it might be a good idea if they did.

Helen offered to leave them to it, not having the faintest idea what the purpose of the visit was, but Mrs Marshall suggested Helen stayed. Perhaps Mrs Marshall knew the children would be in bed, and that was why the visit was timed so late; maybe it was important to them both.

There was some small-talk, about the usual things, like the weather and the traffic in the city, and how nice she thought the flat looked. Then she got down to the reason for her visit.

"Mr Braithwaite, I have been asked to tell you that the Consulate here in Geneva is hosting the visit of a special guest." She paused and looked at Dan, then Helen, as if this had something to do with them. She then continued. "She is arriving next week." Again, she paused. One of her jobs was to break the news of a tragic death, usually of a relative, to UK citizens who happened to be in that part of Switzerland. This task was a bit different, but it needed the same care.

"She is flying into Geneva, via Heathrow, on the 8th. From Buenos Aires."

Dan sat there, looking around him as if he had lost something. Then at Helen, and then at Mrs Marshall. Suddenly he sprang to his feet and walked out of the room. Helen rose to go and see what was the matter, but Mrs Marshall stopped her by saying that it might be best to leave him for a while.

She asked Helen lots of distracting questions about the flat, the lovely furniture, the oriental rugs. They talked about the children and Helen told her about Number 3, due in May.

After about five minutes Dan returned. Helen said, "Darling, is everything OK?"

She saw Dan and Mrs Marshall exchange looks and saw her raise her eyebrows and give Dan a slight nod. "Hey, will someone tell me what's going on?"

"It's okay, Darling. It's okay. In fact, it's very okay. . ."

Mrs Marshall intervened. "Mr Braithwaite, would you like me to continue?" He nodded.

"Mrs Braithwaite-" she began.

"No, no. Please. It's Helen". She had always found 'Mrs Braithwaite' a bit of a mouthful.

"Thank you, Helen. That might be helpful, to avoid any confusion-"

"Confusion?" Helen interrupted her. "You're not saying there is another Mrs Braithwaite, are you?" Helen's mind was racing. Surely this woman hadn't come here to tell her that Dan had been secretly married before – or was still married but not to her – and that her husband was a bigamist.

"Helen, there is nothing to worry about." Mrs Marshall smiled for the first time since crossing the threshold of their home, as she could tell from Helen's frown that she had jumped to the wrong conclusion.

She continued. "There is another Mrs Braithwaite, but it's

Dan's mother." She left the words hanging in the air, allowing them to gently guide Helen's train of thought.

It worked. Helen thought about Eleanor, the stories, Dan's photographs. Her face softened, and she looked sideways at Dan, elbows on his knees, his hands supporting his head, covering his eyes. She remembered Dan telling her about how his mum had died, and that there had been no body to bury, no remains – except one charred and crushed handbag with a few bits of jewellery which had somehow survived. And the half-burnt photograph of a smiling twelve-year-old; the almost illegible writing on the back, which Dan reckoned was a message to him from his mum: 'until we meet again...'. He'd always assumed she meant in Heaven, whatever Heaven is. The necklace had formally identified her. The one he had given to Helen on the night they got engaged. The Dinny Hall.

"Have they found something?" Helen asked, realising how painful this must be for Dan. She knew DNA tests were continuing on some of the smaller bone fragments. She put her arm around his hunched shoulders.

"Yes, they have." A pause. Mrs Marshall was good at this. "They have found her. . .alive. . .alive and well." She smiled as she let the words sink in. "Eleanor Braithwaite is our special visitor."

She didn't have to produce the newly opened packet of Kleenex which she usually kept in her bag for these visits.

Dan went into the kitchen to make some tea, leaving Helen and Mrs Marshall talking quietly together. While the kettle was heating up, he slipped into his study and brought up Frances's emails on his computer screen. He printed off the one with the text message on the bottom, the one that had arrived that morning. He read it carefully. Suddenly it all made sense. Everything. Including why Uncle Dick had bought the chalet, that particular one. As 'a treat for the family', was what he'd said at the time.

He took the tray into the living room and with a slight tremble of the hands, he carefully placed it on the coffee table. Mrs Marshall accepted the offer of the bone china cup on a matching saucer and took her tea without milk or sugar. Helen and Dan had theirs milky, in mugs, and unusually for them, with sugar. Sometimes the old remedies work best.

Dan was the first to speak. "You know, I am going to find this very, very difficult. It's been 16 years."

He remembered the moment Uncle Dick had broken the news that September, the day before he was off to boarding school. He had seen the attacks on television, but it was a couple of days later that he was told his mother was missing. Then the handbag had been found. Other 14-year-old boys at the school were missing their mums, but not quite in the same way. They would see theirs at Christmas. He had to live with the fact he would never see his again, and he had to learn to handle the toxic mix of grief and anger, not helped by the absence of a body. No proper closure.

He soon made friends – boys do, finding themselves together, away from home in a relatively harsh regime of disciplined learning and servitude: of doing what you were told to do, not only by the masters but by the senior boys. It all helped the bonding process. Perhaps it had been designed to work that way.

His grandparents – he had only the one set – did fly back from Australia for the quiet memorial service held in the village church; suburb would be a better description. Understandably they were distraught, such proud parents, so broken. Dan found that he, as a lad of fourteen, was giving them more support than they were giving him.

Uncle Dick helped. He saw Dan most weekends during that first term and often took him out for tea to The Copper Kettle, a little cafe about twenty minutes' walk from the school. They would talk on the walk, and over their tea and scones. Uncle Dick explained to Dan that when a parent died, part of their physical body – their genes – lived on in every cell of their child's body. Their soul – their thoughts and ideas, their sense of humour and personal qualities like compassion and kindness, strength and determination – also lived on in the child, in their conscious memories and subconsciously in their minds.

He told Dan to remember this when he felt sad about his mother, or angry, and that he must behave like she would want him to, because she was there, inside him. In a way, he had not lost her. That small part of her physical being – and her soul – would be with him always.

Mrs Marshall then spoke. "Yes, you are going to find it very difficult indeed, both of you. But you must appreciate Eleanor will find it difficult too."

"But she was the one who decided to leave us," said Dan. "Me and Uncle Dick. She did the cutting and running and disappeared off the face of the earth. Why couldn't she have sent me a message, given me a sign? Why couldn't she have come back?"

"She *is* coming back, Dan. She is coming back to see you, and to meet Helen, and to be a grandmother to your children. It's going to be difficult for all of you. But let me just explain how we can perhaps help. We feel it's important you all take this one step at a time. For the duration of her visit, she'll have her own apartment within walking distance of our offices, and she'll be able to use the carpool when she wants.

"She'll be welcome to stay there as long as she likes, but we do expect that she may wish to make other visits, so she can come and go as she pleases. She'll have independence, but she'll be able to become part of your family if she so wishes – if you so wish it – gradually, at a pace that suits you all.

"Now, if you don't have any questions for me, I do have one question I would like to ask you, Dan. Would you like to pick her up from the Airport next week, or would you prefer us to meet her?"

He hesitated and looked at Helen. Her eyes said yes, he should do it. He was nervous about it because he didn't know how he would react, but then he remembered those words of his uncle's.

And he realised – for the first time – that inside him there was also a little piece of Gerald, and he wondered how Gerald, his dad, would want him to behave.

"I'll do it. Just email me all the details. I'll be there."

Mrs Marshall smiled at them both and rose to her feet. She fished out two cards from her handbag, and as she passed them across, she urged both Helen and Dan to give her a ring if they needed to.

Dan offered to go down with her in the lift, and she accepted. When they reached the lobby on the ground floor, she pressed something in her handbag to summon her driver, and while she waited for the car to appear, she turned to Dan.

"There is something you should know. Your mother didn't cut and run just to save her skin. It was done partly to save yours. It's true she had some, some, er, information which could not be disclosed at any cost. But others, other organisations were equally desperate to have that information and would have gone to any lengths to get it. Or bury it. Do you understand?" Dan nodded. He remembered the bit in Gerald's story, about his niece, and about shredding.

Mrs Marshall continued. "Thanks to the passage of time, along with a little help from Wikileaks and others, it's no longer secret. But look after her. The price paid was huge."

The black Bentley drew silently to a stop outside, and the liveried driver jumped out and opened the door for her. She waved to Dan and smiled, as she climbed into the back. He watched it glide off.

3

Dan thought about how it would go. He tried out a number of approaches and rehearsed them in front of Helen who was beginning to wonder if Dan had done the right thing in agreeing to meet Eleanor. His first concern was how to address her. Sixteen years is a long time when you're only thirty, and 'Mum' seemed inappropriate. And how would they greet each other? Should he shake her hand, or give the Gallic kiss on each cheek – or should it be three kisses?

Next, how would he feel when they met? Would he be able to control his emotions, whatever they might be? The simple things also concerned him, like whether he would recognise her. Or would she recognise him? He imagined the embarrassment of going up to her and saying 'Hello Mother', only to find the woman he'd picked was a total stranger.

But in a way, she *was* a total stranger. A wonderful friend and mother to him for fourteen years, but one who had led a double life. A mum who worked at the leisure centre teaching swimming and diving, water polo and life-saving, but also did secret work.

Secret from him, too. He knew she couldn't disclose this side of her, but it hurt him that the mother he loved was somehow more than the person she had appeared to be. And Uncle Dick was in on it! But he knew he had to be sensible, a grown man with his own family and his own business.

He also worried about what she would think of him. Would she smile at him from a distance, but would that smile fade as he approached her, as she looked him up and down and wondered about his dress sense, hairstyle or choice of shoes.

What if he was disappointed in her? A woman in her late fifties, fat with grey hair, embarrassingly dressed, wearing cheap perfume and experiencing a bad hair day. He made up his mind that whatever she looked like he would fake approval and smile broadly.

He hadn't confessed to Helen that Gerald was his father, so that was one item in his speech he didn't practice in front of her. But he would have to tell Eleanor about Gerald's story, and the earlier the better: that he knew all about her work, about her husband – and about how he was conceived.

He knew the airport well but was concerned about getting a parking space near to Arrivals. And then the drive through all that traffic. Where would he take her? Back to his flat, or hers? She might be tired, and the last thing he wanted to do was to inflict the kids on her after a long journey across several time-zones. Perhaps he would just ask her where she wanted to go. What a pathetic thought! No, as soon as he got the details of her flight, he would make a plan and present it to her as a fait accompli. Like his dad would have done, briefing his soldiers on their next mission.

He still wasn't sure how he would handle it when he received the flight details from the Consulate two days before her arrival. Then he had a flash of inspiration and extracted Mrs Marshall's card from his wallet.

"Mrs Marshall? It's me, Daniel Braithwaite. . . Yes, fine thanks. . . Yes, no problem. . . That's kind of you. In fact, there is something you could possibly do for me. Any chance of borrowing the Consulate car you came in the other night? You see, if I drive myself, I won't be able to talk to her, and if I hire a taxi, well, you know how smelly some taxis can be. . . Really? That's so kind. Fantastic."

The two of them arranged for the car to pick him up at 8:30 p.m which would get him to the airport in good time for the 9:45 p.m arrival. The driver would give him the bleeper; when he was ready to be picked up, the driver would meet him with the car at the VIP bay outside Arrivals. Eleanor would be travelling first class, so it should not take long for her luggage to arrive. But this would be picked up for her and taken to the bay.

They would then go straight to the flat, a Consulate asset normally used for visitors. The heating would be switched on, and a hospitality pack delivered – milk, fresh bread, tea, coffee, a bottle of wine. The VIP pack. Any dislikes? Dan remembered the story. He said to Mrs Marshall: no shredded wheat.

Dan's knowledge of sneaky-beaky stuff was confined to popular fiction and what Gerald had told him in the two missives. And what Mrs Marshall had told him in the lobby the other evening. Perhaps Gerald – Dad – had been wrong in assuming his mother fled from fear of being shredded by her own people. Maybe her people, or some of them, had arranged it all, to keep her safe – and him safe – until it was safe to bring her back.

The Class Seven might not have been a death warrant, but just an authorisation to 'take measures necessary'. To put her into hiding, into exile, whether she liked it or not.

The flight was uneventful. Eleanor managed to sleep for most of the first leg, from Buenos Aires to London Heathrow. It was a Dreamliner, with seats that converted into flat beds. The second leg to Geneva was a doddle, just over an hour. During the three-hour break between flights she did some serious airport shopping and used the facilities in the First Class lounge to have a shower and her hair done before putting on her new clothes.

She was pleased with how she looked. It had been a long time since she'd had the opportunity to wear something really smart – and in fashion. And this was a special occasion. She was also pleased she had kept her figure. There was something to be said for being on hormone replacement therapy.

During the hop to Geneva, she thought again of how she might handle the meeting with Danny. She received the message he would be meeting her when the Embassy car picked her up to run her to the airport in Buenos Aires. She knew he would be nervous. He would be the fourteen-year-old again, and she the mum. They would soon adjust to their new roles, of her the middle-aged retired widow, and he the young father and ambitious manager of his own business.

She recalled how Mrs T had put her at her ease when she visited her with Mr Black all those years ago. It was a good technique, to immediately start talking about something entirely off the subject of the meeting, distracting the person from thinking about what he or she should or would have to say. It breaks the ice and dispels the fear. But she must avoid the usual 'haven't you grown' expressions favoured by forgotten aunts and godfathers, which focus on the child and make them feel awkward. By the time the plane landed, she had worked it all out.

First Class has its privileges. She didn't have to wait with the hoi polloi around the carousel for her baggage. She quickly passed through passport control, but before she went through the doors to where everyone gathers to meet the passengers, she put on her new Raybans and hat. Then she waited and watched the automatic doors open and close in front of her as the first few arrivals proceeded through.

She spotted him, right in the front nervously holding up a millboard with her name on it. She couldn't believe it. It made her giggle. Did he really think she wouldn't recognise him? This handsome young man whom she brought into the world and fed and nurtured through infancy and up to puberty? He was the spitting image of his father, but so smart in that dark blue suit and highly polished shoes. Dan was looking anxiously every time the doors opened. Her boy!

She went ahead with the first part of her plan. Being careful not to look in Dan's direction, she strode purposefully through the doors and turned left. As she did so, she waved to an imaginary friend at the back of the melee of taxi-drivers, greeters and meeters, and headed off to the shop. She had placed the order online, using her new mobile. It was waiting for her, already gift-wrapped. All she had to do was sign the receipt.

The next part of her plan was to go back to arrivals, remove her glasses and hat and introduce herself to her son. But then her sense of fun got the better of her. She slowly made her way through the thinning crowd until she was right behind him. He was beginning to fidget like he used to as a boy when he got anxious about something. Then she said it, in a deep voice and with a slight Welsh accent, just like she used to ever since they had watched the film together when he was about ten. But it had the same effect.

Dan was beginning to feel embarrassed, holding the millboard up every time a woman appeared. He was too excited to just hold it up and look bored like the taxi-drivers. He felt conspicuous in his brand new suit. At least he'd decided at the last moment to take his tie off, which made him feel a bit more comfortable. But where was she? He wondered if she had a problem at passport control; perhaps she was travelling on an Argentinian one – or had missed the flight.

Then he heard it. Broadsword for Danny Boyee. He spun around. She laughed at the look on his face when she took off her sunglasses. The laughter lines, the blue eyes, the hair – more salt and pepper than ginger – but it was her. All he managed to say at that moment was one word, "Mum!", before flinging his arms around her, just like old times. She hugged him back, of course, giving that man's body a big squeeze, and, still giggling as the tears rolled down her cheeks, she ruffled his hair.

Neither of them noticed the people looking at them as they

slowly walked arm in arm through the arrivals area towards the exit, gassing away, smiling, and eyes only for each other. She would never have guessed that many of them assumed she was a famous fashion model or actress, a celebrity of some sort. And it would not have occurred to Dan that others thought he might be her toy boy, as she was far too young to be his mother.

Despite the minor deviations from both plans, the meeting went well. They were comfortable in the company of each other. Eleanor explained she wasn't allowed to tell Dan everything she'd been doing since she parted, and Dan said he understood. He told her about 'Dad' – he still hadn't got used to the name – how he owned the chalet next door to theirs – and that Dad had explained everything in his story and diary which arrived only a week or so ago.

"And we got to be good friends," he continued. "His wife Julie and her daughters and their families as well. We go skiing together – or at least have done so for the last few years. They're great. We get on really well."

Eleanor felt a slight pang when Dan mentioned Gerald had a wife, but she smiled. She realised it would be extraordinary if he hadn't. But she just wanted to meet him, to say hi, to say thank you. "So, your dad is happily married, is he?" She had to ask the question.

He looked at his mother. "Didn't you know? I'm so sorry. Last week. He died. . . I didn't realise. . . In fact, Frances – that's one of his step-daughters – is organising a memorial service for him in England, on 26th March, and we've all been invited. You too, if you're not too busy sight-seeing and babysitting."

Babysitting, eh? Eleanor was grateful for the chance to smile, at the kind and probably unintentional way her son had welcomed her into his family. Three days, she told herself. For God's sake, girl, pull yourself together. You only knew him for three days.

"Hey, Danny. I have something for you! But you mustn't open it until you get home. Promise?"

The drive from the airport went well. He was quite proud of his elegant mum, sitting next to him in the Bentley, looking like a million dollars. He asked the driver to take in a few of the more popular sights of the city which looked good at night. Neither of them was in a hurry to end the journey.

Finally, they reached her flat. They arranged to meet for lunch the following day, and she gave him a hug and kiss and packed him off as if she were sending him to school.

She felt happy and sad, as she kicked off her shoes in her new home and sank into the sofa in the living room. Happy it had all gone well, but sad about Gerald. But, as ever, she looked on the bright side. Although the present had been intended for Gerald, it was just as appropriate for Danny.

When Danny got home, Helen was asleep. He quietly got ready for bed and then remembered the present. He thought it might be chocolates or aftershave. But it wasn't. It was an Hublot. On the back was engraved 'For Danny Boy, from Broadsword, 2017'.

4

"Tell me what she's like, Danny," Helen pleaded the following morning.

"Well, where can I start? The truth of the matter is she hasn't changed a bit," he replied.

"That's not going to help me much, is it? I've never met her. And I've got to meet her this lunchtime. You might have asked before arranging it."

Dan had planned to take his wife and mother to a little lakeside restaurant just outside the city.

"Darling, you remember we would keep this week free, in case we had to help her with anything. Anyway, I checked on your phone just before I left."

"I, er, don't know what to wear. Or say to her. She might not even like me. Some mothers don't like the girls their sons marry, almost on principle. You do know that, don't you?"

"Darling, I can assure you; you'll be fine. And she will love you. You're her only daughter, for Heaven's sake! You'll get on like a house on fire. Think of all the things you'll be able to do together. And she might help with the children, and with the little one."

He wondered if Eleanor would be wearing that sensational outfit she arrived in. He thought it might be better if she didn't.

When they arrived at her flat Eleanor opened the door with a theatrical sweep of her hand and welcomed them in. Then she did her 'Mrs T' bit.

"Now, I know you are Helen, but Danny didn't tell me how pretty you are! Do come in and if you want to take your coat off, please do so. It's a lovely coat by the way, did you get it in Geneva? D'you know, I don't have a coat at all! I came from a very hot place, and it never occurred to me it would be this cold. Silly me! Perhaps you and I could go on a shopping trip together – I'll need some boots too, but I don't know what sort to get. You'll need to help me. . . Oh, and you're wearing a dress! Please excuse me for a moment; I think I'd better change out of these jeans. Do take a seat, or have a look round, or a drink? Danny, there's a bottle of something in the fridge, if you would be so kind? Back in a mo," she called out as she strode off to her bedroom.

Helen hardly got a word in edgeways. This wasn't the middle-aged lady she was expecting. More like a school-friend.

In the back of Dan's car on the way to the restaurant, it was Helen who was setting the pace as they chatted away, and she was the one pointing out the various sites to see, the good shops and restaurants she and Dan would recommend.

Over lunch, they talked about food and cooking, clothes and children, and Eleanor told Helen about the school in Argentina where she taught dance and drama, and English, to a wide range of age groups. She knows about kids, Helen thought.

As they lingered over coffee, Helen and Eleanor swapped stories about Dan's untidiness and his penchant for collecting junk. The teasing was a way of involving him in their conversation which did tend to drift back to girlie things if Dan didn't join in.

After the meal, they took a stroll along the bank of the lake. It was a beautiful afternoon, and the sun shone for them – and Dan lent his mum the old ski jacket he kept in the car. Not a great fashion item, but it kept the lakeside breeze out.

"Hey, guys," Dan said, looking at his new watch. "We really ought to be getting back. We have to pick up the kids –" He was about to say "the kids, Mum", but stopped just in time. He didn't want to call his mother that in front of Helen; he thought it sounded silly.

Helen sensed it and turned to Eleanor and asked what she would like to be called. "Well, nothing too rude, I hope! Mrs Braithwaite would be far too difficult, especially as there are two of us, and 'Eleanor' sounds so formal.

"What I would really like is to be called what I am: 'Grandma' or 'Granny' – whichever is available – by your children, and 'Mum' by you two. But I don't suppose you'd want to do that."

"That's OK with me, Mum," Dan said, without realising he'd already slipped back into the habit of his childhood.

Then Helen said, "And it's OK with me. Mum."

She laughed. They were both mums. It felt right, as long as Eleanor remembered who was the mother of Lucy and Josh.

The chattering continued as Dan drove home. They all agreed that Eleanor – Mum – would come back to the flat and Helen would then go off to pick up the children. The round trip wouldn't take more than half an hour or so depending on the chatter at the school gates.

Dan showed his mother around their flat, then plugged his photo stick into the television so he could show her his collection of family snaps. Him at his big school, playing rugby and featuring in the school play. Helen and him on their wedding day, then in Turkey on their honeymoon.

Eleanor tried not to let her sadness show, but Dan realised his faux pas and moved on to the ones of Josh as a baby, then a toddler, and then of him and Lucy together. The next ones were of them on their skiing holidays in the chalet. Some were of the little ones at ski-school, others of lovely meals in mountain restaurants.

"Hey, Danny. Can you go back one?"

"Yes, sure," he replied.

"Isn't that Gerald, your dad?" It was a group photo, on a ski slope with a big mountain in the background, everybody smiling and looking at the camera, except for Josh who was pulling one of his faces. In the middle was Gerald with his wife Julie on one side and Helen on the other – Dan was obviously taking the photo.

"Wow," Eleanor said. "Doesn't he look old!"

"But he *was* old. He must have been at least seventy-two when that was taken. When you two, you know, got together, he was only forty-three. You can't expect him to look the same."

"I know I know. But I never realised he was forty-three when we. . . 'you know'ed!" she teased, doing the inverted commas with her fingers. "I thought he was in his mid-thirties." She nearly added that he behaved as if he were, but thought better of it.

"So what did you make of him?" She wanted Dan to talk about him.

"He became a good friend. Such fun and the children loved him. We didn't see a great deal of him and Julie, only when they came out to the chalet. When I read his story, I felt I got to know him better. And his diary last week. That was a revelation. I did wonder if he was being slightly delusional about finding you. Then, well, here you are! Alive and well! "

"Your dad was an exceptional person. He had some great qualities. He was a what-iffer. Also, during our time together he never took anything at face value. He always wanted to know more, the whys and the hows. He was an explorer of. . . of possibilities. But he didn't delude himself.

"I'm not sure how to explain this, but think of people betting on horses. Some people bet on a horse because they're *sure* it's going to win. Others because they *think* it's going to win. But your dad was the type who would bet on a horse because he reckoned its chances of winning were greater than the bookies' odds.

"That's how his mind worked. He was an engineer. He was also a hypothesiser, a why-notter. A dreamer, but there was a certain rationality in his dreaming; it had a degree of logic about it."

She asked Dan if he had told Helen he was Gerald's son. Dan

replied no and Eleanor said it might be better if it remained that way, as it would be difficult to explain it. Dan agreed.

The front door opened, and there they were: her grandchildren. She went straight up to them. "Well hello! I'm your new granny, and if you don't like me you can take me back to the grannyshop!"

They looked at each other and giggled.

"Wow, that looks like a heavy satchel! Can I feel the weight? Goodness, you must be strong to manage that, young man."

"Excuse me," Lucy interrupted, "but mummy said we must intwoduce ourselves. This is my bwother Joshua, and I am Lucille. I am seven and my bwother is nine, but Mummy says sometimes he doesn't act his age."

"And she can't say her English r's pwoperly," Josh added.

Eleanor knelt down on the carpet next to Lucy. "It's easy peasy! Look. Watch me, watch my tongue. Rrrr! You just curl it up! Like you do when you say 'Lucy', but don't let it touch your front teeth or the roof of your mouth."

"Rucy. . .Rucy. . .Right!" Lucy beamed.

"Do you like football?" Josh intervened. Good, thought Helen, they're fighting over her already.

"Football! You're not a Chelsea supporter by any chance, are you Josh?" Eleanor asked. the question avoided the lie. And the truth would not have earned her any brownie points. Chelsea was the first team name that popped into her head.

"Chelsea? They're rubbish, man. Dad and me, we support Fulham. He took me there last year. Hey, come and see my things. . ."

Eleanor let Josh lead her to his football shrine in his bedroom, leaving Lucy practising 'Braithwaite'. She was beginning to sound quite grown-up, and a long way now from the 'Bwaifwaite' of a few years ago.

Helen turned to Dan. "Your mum's a right old Mary Poppins."

She wasn't sure if they needed one, with her not working, but then she thought of the new one on the way and decided to keep her mouth shut. A nanny could be useful, as long as she doesn't interfere.

Tea went well. There was a bit of showing off from both the little ones, and although Lucy called her Grrandma whenever the opportunity arose, Josh seemed reluctant to use her new name. If he tried to attract her attention in other ways, she pretended she hadn't heard.

Then he twigged it. "Excuse me, Grandma, can you. . ."

To which Eleanor replied, "Shush a moment, Lucy. Josh is asking me a question."

It made Josh feel important. With a late sibling on the way, it was important they both felt just as important as they always had been.

It was time for Dan to drop Grandma back at her flat, which brought protestations from Josh 'do you have to go?', and from Lucy 'when will you be rreturning?'. Eleanor explained she had a lot to do in her flat because she wanted it to look nice for when they all came round to see her. She suggested they all come for tea on Saturday.

As she said this she looked at Helen and Dan, raising an eyebrow as if to say would that be okay? At least she asked – sort of asked – thought Helen. She hoped it would not become an issue.

Well done that man, thought Dan, as he remembered the Story, and remembered Gerald's mission.

The visit to Grandma's turned into a sleepover for the children – because they were *so* good. Helen was relieved that Eleanor asked her if it would be OK. She was tempted to make some excuse like they didn't have their pyjamas or toothbrushes with them. But then she thought it would be nice to have Dan to herself for once – and to pretend for an evening they were back in Turkey, on their honeymoon, and he could treat her to breakfast in bed.

The sleepover gave Eleanor the chance to do some dance and

drama with the children. Josh thought break-dancing was cool, and Lucy said she wanted some tap-dancing shoes for her birthday. The ride home the following morning in the Consulate Bentley was a special treat because they had been so well-behaved. When they said goodbye to her and asked if they could come again, she said it was up to Mummy and Daddy but expected they would allow it if they were really, really good.

During the weeks that followed, Helen and Eleanor were able to fit in a few shopping trips together, each encouraging the other to buy things which they would never have dared buy on their own. They talked a lot and had fun together, but Helen sometimes wondered if Eleanor might take off and disappear like she had last time when Dan was fourteen. Her worry was the children; they would be heartbroken.

On one occasion during a shopping spree, they stopped for a coffee and cake, and Helen asked Eleanor if she had any plans. The reply surprised her.

"Plans? My goodness! That's something I haven't had for ages. I suppose I just want to contribute in some way. To be part of something, to help you – if you want me to – with the new baby, with Josh and Lucy. And Dan. But I want to stand on my own two feet, be independent, make a difference in the world. Achieve things. Certain things. Not for me but for. . . for friends."

Wow, thought Helen. A Mary Poppins with a mission. I hope she still has time for us.

Dan enjoyed the time he had alone with his mum to talk about old times, Uncle Dick and the leisure centre where she worked. And about Dad. It helped them both come to terms with it, to grieve in their different ways, for different reasons.

As for the children, they began by liking her, then appreciating her and her stories, then liking her very much, then loving her. Eleanor was not strict. To them, she was more of a big sister who could be quite naughty at times. But she had a way of making them want to behave well and to please her.

She never told them off. They quickly learned that if they squabbled Grandma would be unhappy, so they had a secret pact to be nice to each other when she was around. And before they did anything that might be naughty, they would ask her if it would be all right. Most of the time she would say, "Of course you may, my darlings." But on the rare occasions when she had to turn down such a request, she would say, "You can do that if you really want to, but I'd rather you didn't." It worked every time.

Eleanor's football skills improved – they could only go one way, but it made Josh feel he was an okay coach bearing in mind she was a woman. And Lucy surprised her parents by showing she'd inherited her grandmother's singing voice. Helen teased Dan by saying, "Odd how it skips a generation, isn't it?"

When Eleanor agreed to go with them to G-pa's memorial lunch, Dan emailed Frances with the numbers: five-and-a-half. He thought it an amusing way of saying Helen was expecting.

It reminded him of his mum's cryptic text message sent to Gerald the weekend he died, the one Frances had copied onto her email to him. His mum said she was going to be 'a G at last, and one on the way'. He then thought: how did she know Helen was pregnant, at that time, when she was still in Argentina? *Ah well, that's Mum for you.*

5

During one of their moments alone, Eleanor told Dan of her concerns about Gerald's memorial lunch.

"I'd love to come, and I'd be more than happy to help with the children, but I'm not sure about meeting his wife."

"Julie? She's great!" He noticed his mum's 'eek' expression. "Mu-um! It's not as if he were alive and you were still seeing him. You know, having an affair with him. All that was years ago, long before Julie met him. And you haven't seen him since. You're hardly 'the other woman'."

"You're right, Danny. But her husband has just died. This is the equivalent of his funeral for her. I'd hate to upset her. Do you think he ever told her about me?"

"I really don't know. The story he sent me did mention you, but there wasn't much to tell."

"There was you, silly boy!"

"No, what I mean is, he had no idea who you were, where you lived, and didn't even know your name. Hey! Hang on a sec."

Danny darted off into his study and came back a few minutes later with a box file. "Got it. It's here. He did tell Julie. When they got together."

"That's going to make it difficult. What did he say?"

Danny smiled. "Do you want me to read it out?"

"Oh, go on then," she replied. "Embarrass me."

"Here goes. 'Someone I met at a conference. . . Didn't know her name. Never saw her again. . . We made love all night long and the following day we blew up the Empire State building. Julie said' whatever' and changed the subject onto something more interesting.'"

"Yeah, yeah," Eleanor said, rolling her eyes. "That's a pretty accurate account of what happened, I suppose. But that's good. If that's all he said to her, I doubt she would remember. So will I just be the aged mother of a good friend of his, coming along to help look after the children?"

"Mum, you know it's not like that. I know the true position – and I know how you must feel. He was 'the one', wasn't he?"

"For all of three days. . .Excuse me."

She left the room returning after a few minutes. "Hey, Danny Boy. I've had a thought. There'll probably be quite a few people there, and they'll all be talking about Gerald, and comforting Julie. We're going to have to agree on what we say, and say the same to everyone."

"Good point. A sort of cover story, you mean?"

"Yep. I'm bound by the Official Secrets Act, so I can't say anything about my connection with Gerald, other than being the aged mother of a-"

Dan interrupted, "A good friend of Gerald's he met a couple of years ago. So I can't tell anyone he was my father?"

"'Fraid not."

"Not even Frances and Fiona?"

"Not even Helen."

Dan just sat there.

"I'm sorry, darling. But it's the only way. It's a mess, but you have to look on the positive side. To keep it under wraps is in everybody's best interest. Honestly, the alternative is even messier. If you tell the world you're Gerald's son, wouldn't you also be expected to change your surname to Rayner? Then would Helen and the children also have to change theirs?

"Look. You're Daniel Braithwaite, son of Eleanor Braithwaite. I was married to a Trevor Braithwaite who tragically died in a boating accident. Uncle Dick was your guardian when I was posted abroad, and you were told I was missing after the World Trade Centre attacks, presumed dead. All that is true. And it does not reveal State secrets. That's all the world needs to know."

"'Beauty is truth, truth beauty. . .' That's not very beautiful. Having to keep a secret like that hidden from Helen; my wife, for God's sake."

"It's a burden for you, yes. But think what a burden it would be for her if you did tell her you are Gerald's son, that she is really married to a Daniel Rayner, but she can't be told how it all came about. And eventually, she would have to tell the children – or keep the truth hidden from them. You would be doing Helen no favours.

"People think it is exciting to be 'in' on secrets, but it's not exciting at all. It's about as enjoyable as having a hole in your head. And sometimes that's what you end up with. Danny, I would advise you strongly not to tell Helen any more than she already knows." Dan knew she was right.

The conversation had taken Eleanor's mind off her other concern, the one she did not tell Dan about. Strangely, she had felt safe in Argentina. Nobody knew she was there, and until Mr Andrews came looking for her, she had got the impression that nobody was interested in her anymore. She also felt safe in Switzerland. True, Her Majesty's Government knew she was in Geneva – indeed they had kindly provided her with the air passage and apartment – but she felt she was a long way from danger. She had made few enemies in her career, but she knew how some people operated, even if it meant crossing boundaries.

Action Man – Timothy Turnbull – was one such maverick. He was a bully and a tough guy who always wanted to do things the tough way. She held him responsible for Trevor, and for her school friend. He was the sort of person who blamed others for his mistakes, and she did wonder if he would have preferred it if she had been killed on 9/11, or at least had remained lost forever.

At least she would not be staying in the UK for long; she had arranged to fly to Sydney to see her parents after the memorial lunch. But the prospect of a social gathering at a country club in Kent with many guests did not make her feel comfortable. And then there was the record of her flight booking from Geneva to Gatwick, so if someone had wanted to find out all about her movements, the information was out there.

So, on Saturday 25th March, the family Braithwaite, including Eleanor, set off for England to attend the memorial lunch for Gerald Rayner, a friend.

Invitations were 'Noon for 1 o'clock', dress: smart casual. Drinks would be served as people arrived, prosecco or orange juice – or anything else from the bar on the Rayner chit. Gerald had allocated a generous sum to cover everything. Frances's husband Bob arrived just after eleven to set up his computer and projector, and Peter the Pianist turned up shortly afterwards.

Frances gave Peter the list of tunes and explained about the mini 'sing-song' she had in mind; she had downloaded the lyrics to some of the numbers on Gerald's list and printed out copies which she put around the tables with the place cards, fifty-six of them.

It wasn't like a normal drinks party, with awkward introductions and the usual 'are you from these parts?', or 'did you come along the M25?'. Nor the small-talk, about the weather, the traffic, the strikes and what's-the-world-coming-to.

It wasn't like a funeral, either. No church service, no coffin with a dead body inside it, no vicar looking glum, no mournful organ music playing quietly in the background, no black ties or armbands, no wreaths. No undertakers pretending they were on the verge of tears, and no widow silently grieving behind a black veil, clutching a small laced handkerchief ready to dab away any tears. And children were invited.

Julie was taking it well. Her husband had died eight weeks previously so the tears had already been shed, lots of them. And it wasn't her first experience of widowhood; she had learned to be strong. This time she was the one being supported by her daughters. Previously she had been doing the comforting, helping two teenage girls come to terms with losing their dad. Not that they were free of grief for their G-pa, but they knew the roles had changed and responded remarkably well.

The first people to arrive were other members of Julie's family, all anxious to help. But there was little left to do. St. Jonathan's had done a great job setting up the seven tables with plated silver cutlery and sparkling glasses on pure white tablecloths, each with a vase of spring flowers. The screen had been set up in the corner opposite the grand piano, so when guests arrived, they saw a series of images of Gerald, from when he was a boy up to him enjoying his Christmas dinner three months previously.

Pre-lunch drinks were held in the adjoining conservatory, and this was where the guests gathered. Each one went up to Julie to greet her and pay their respects. She was attired in a colourful cotton dress and wore a bright smile. No widow's weeds for Julie. She had chosen the dress carefully; not the sort of thing she would choose to wear but it had to convey a message to her guests: have fun, enjoy yourselves. It's what Gerald wanted.

Her smile was no spray-on one but a genuine expression of her pleasure to see them. They said the usual words of condolences for which she expressed her grateful thanks, and if there was a spouse or partner she had not previously met, she was introduced.

As for her introducing the guests to each other, there was little need for that. Most of them had met before, either at school or university, or had served together, or had been fellow guests at weddings and birthday parties, christenings and funerals, or Christmas drinks, or Sevenoaks supper parties. What linked them all together – their one common purpose in being at St. Jonathan's on that day – was Gerald.

He too was there amongst them, not physically but in the memories of all those present. He was no less real than a computer program – or for that matter a digital image – able to exist quite independently of the computer on which it had originally been generated. Neither was an arrangement of molecules. And nor was Gerald anymore.

Typically, guests had left home that Sunday morning having had very little for breakfast in anticipation of Julie and Gerald's famed hospitality. So a glass of fizzy at midday on an empty stomach soon had its desired effects, and stories of Gerald were being freely swapped, sometimes to the accompaniment of roars of laughter, as some escapade or another involving him was being suitably exaggerated.

There was no need for sombre sobriety that day. Just a celebration of a life, a friendship. The children rushed around having fun. Nobody told them they must be quiet or stay close to mummy and daddy.

When the Braithwaites arrived, Josh and Lucy spotted Gerald's step-children and skiing companions, but they knew they couldn't dash off until they had said hello to Julie. The two families hadn't met since the previous April when they all went skiing together – the first time without Gerald. Hugs were exchanged, and Dan introduced his mother, Eleanor.

She was wearing her new outfit, the one she had on when Dan met her at the airport. But she was not feeling a million dollars this time. Apart from the kids and Dan and Helen, she knew nobody, and she could feel people were staring at her. It made her feel even worse. She wished she had her glasses on, the black framed ones. Julie noticed her discomfort and grabbed a glass from a passing waitress and took it over to Eleanor.

"Here you are my dear, have a glass of fizzy."

"Thanks so much. . . Mmmm, that's lovely. I'm so sorry to hear about your husband." She thought better about calling him Gerald. "I gather he was quite a man!"

"Well, that's very kind of you to say so. He's a wonderful husband. Sorry, I cannot get used to talking about him in the past tense. He thought very highly of your son. They became good friends. In fact, we all were, and the children all got on famously. Now, where has he been hiding you all this time, a glamorous mum like you?"

It made Eleanor feel slightly better, and she smiled. She was wondering how to answer Julie's question when Dan came across to see how she was getting on. "So what are you two girls plotting?"

"Just mum-talk, Danny boy," said Eleanor. "Now you must introduce me to Julie's daughters. I can't believe she's a grandmother."

Eleanor felt more relaxed, having winged it through the clashing rocks; and having met Frances and then Fiona and their husbands, she felt more confident about meeting other people, Gerald's friends. Which was just as well. First, a man of Gerald's vintage came up and introduced himself as Rodney, an old Cambridge friend, and another 'old chum' joined him. She thought they were very polite, as they both made a great effort to involve her in the conversation.

Eleanor then made her first mistake. "But he never said he went to Cambridge." She saw the puzzled look beginning to form on the faces of the two chums and immediately replied with a broad smile, "My son said he was at Sandhurst."

Rodney laughed. "He did go to Sandhurst, then on to Cambridge. But I'm not surprised he never told your son. Gerry was not the boastful sort, was he Nigel?"

"Not like you, Rodders! Eh? Oops, only kidding! Look who it isn't!" Another old man limped over to join the group, hesitating briefly to wave his walking stick at them.

Julie noticed Eleanor was trapped, and came over and grabbed her arm. "Now, come with me. I want to introduce you to a special person who is on his own." She said the words quietly and proceeded to steer Eleanor through the group to meet a man standing by himself, looking slightly out of place and uncomfortable among the gathering whose average age must have been at least ten years older than he was. He was elegantly dressed in a well-cut jacket and slacks, yet the open-neck shirt achieved the casualness requested of the invitation.

"Robert, I want you to meet Eleanor, the mother of Dan, a friend of Gerald's. He and his family live in Geneva and have come over just to be with us today. Isn't that kind of them!"

As Julie was saying this, Robert had already stretched out his hand towards Eleanor. "Hi, I'm Robert. I'm sorry, I didn't catch your name?"

The name was the last thing that caught his attention.

6

"So how did you know, er, Gerald?" It was the actress in Eleanor that enabled her to give Robert the impression she wasn't familiar with the name.

"He was my squadron commander – sorry, my boss – when I was a young officer in Germany. Too many years ago than I care to remember. Early eighties it must have been. He was a great boss, to us all, but he was particularly helpful to me when I landed in a spot of trouble. I heard later it cost him his career, but that's another story. What about you? Are you also living in Switzerland?"

"I am at the moment. I've recently retired – I was a teacher – and I'm spending some time in Geneva to be with my son Danny and his family. This evening I'm off to Australia to see my parents." Robert's half-smile faded.

"Are you still in the Army?" she asked.

"Me? No. I left shortly after my tour in Germany. I did a degree at Edinburgh – International Relations – then joined the Foreign Office. I'm on gardening leave at the moment before my next posting-"

"Ladies and gentlemen!" Bob's voice boomed out through the loudspeaker system, "will you kindly make your way through to the dining room and take your seats for lunch!"

It was like trying to get a circus on the move, but eventually, there was a drift towards the tables. Frances hadn't thought it necessary to have a master table plan, so guests had to go from table to table looking at the name cards until they found their place. It was fun, as it gave those people who had not yet met up a chance to say 'hello' and 'talk to you later!'. And there was a fair amount of shouting, things like 'darling, you're on the table by the window!' and 'Mike, you're next to me!'.

Frances had decided to scatter the children amongst the adults but made sure siblings were on the same table, so they didn't feel too lonely. Thus Josh and Lucy ended up sitting on either side of Bob.

The food was good and the wine flowed as Bob's slide show continued to loop and Peter the Pianist provided incidental music, just loud enough to be enjoyed but not too loud to make conversation difficult. The round tables were small enough to allow plenty of chat across them.

Bob was pleased to be between the Braithwaite children. He only saw them during the annual family skiing holiday, and he noticed a huge change in them since last April. Josh was beginning to learn the ancient art of being polite to people, and Lucy had grown in stature and confidence.

"Now Lucy, I hear you are going to have a baby brother or sister soon. What do you think of that, then?"

"I'm verry pleased," Lucy replied, "but my parrents left it a little late if you ask me. At least, I'll be able to help my mother with the baby, and we do now have another grrandma."

"So what are you hoping for, young lady? Another brother or a little sister?"

"I would prrefer a little sister. One brrother is enough, actually."

"And has mummy and daddy decided on any names yet?"

"Well, if it's a girl, it will have to have Titania as one of her names."

"And why's that?"

"It's our ladyname."

For a seven-year-old – going on twelve – Lucy had quite a loud voice, and her reply did not go unnoticed by the rest of the guests around the table.

"A ladyname?" Bob replied.

"Yes," Lucy said, as if she was agreeing that the weather was rather dull, "it's like a surname, but it's given only to girls. You see, if you are a girl, you lose your surname when you marry, which is very unfair, actually. So my great-great-grandmother gave her daughter a ladyname which she kept and passed down to her daughter and so on. It's Titania."

Josh sniggered. "Tit for short!" he mumbled, just loud enough to be heard by everyone around the table.

Lucy was unbowed. "Tit is another name for teat or nipple. Women have them and men have them, but at least ours work!"

Bob felt it time to intervene. "It's a lovely name – queen of the fairies, I believe."

"Actually, it comes from a boat."

All seven guests were waiting to hear more, and at least half asked the question in unison 'what boat?'

"It's a long story!" Lucy had inherited Eleanor's talent for telling a good story.

"Go on!" urged her audience.

"Well. It all happened over a hundred years ago. On a dark night in the middle of the ocean. Anyway, my great-great-grandmother – by the way, her name was the same as mine, Lucille. Although I prefer Lucy."

Everyone had the same thought: 'get on with the story!'

"Lucille was only four at the time, and when the iceberg hit, all the glasses on the table went flying. But she was a good girl and put on her life jacket and jumped into the freezing waters, clutching her doll which was called. . ."

"Don't worry about that, what happened next!!" everyone wanted to shout but didn't.

"I've forgotten her name. But she swam to the shore and was found, completely exhausted, by a nice man who took her to his home where he and his good wife looked after her and made her better!"

She looked at the faces around the table. Up to that point in time, she hadn't noticed them, all looking at her waiting for her to finish. Like any good storyteller, she had been immersed in her story. Then she remembered she hadn't quite reached the end. "Oh yes, the boat-"

"Ship," added Josh, rolling his eyes.

"All right then, ship. The ship was called the Titanic."

Lucy squirmed on her chair as her stunned audience remained silent. She thought she'd better explain. "You see, the nice man and his wife named her Titania after the ship!"

When the laughter and clapping died down, Josh had to say it. "I thought you said her name was Lucille."

It was Lucy's turn to roll her eyes, performed with hands on hips and a theatrical sigh. "Her second name was Titania."

"How did they know her first name was Lucille?" Josh taunted.

Frances came up to the table and whispered to Bob, "Darling, don't you think we'd better do the change thing. They're waiting to serve the dessert."

"Hang on, I must just hear this. It's priceless."

Another theatrical sigh from Lucy. "They didn't know any of her names. They had no idea who she was. So they gave her both names, Lucille and Titania, like me. Then she called her daughter Lucille Titania, and my grandmother the same and then me! So nobody forgets!"

"That's rubbish. Dad says your initials come from London Transport Bus, 'cos that's where he found you, in a cardboard box!"

More eye-rolling from Lucy. "I came from my mother's uterus, if you must know, and. . ."

Bob sensed it was time and switched on the mike. "Ladies and gentlemen! Or should I just say gentlemen, because I want all the men over the age of twenty – if there are any – to turn over their name cards. Now leave them there and go off and find your place where we would like you to sit for dessert and coffee. And take your wine glass with you!"

At which point Peter started playing the Benny Hill theme, as fast as he could, which brought shrieks of laughter from everyone present as dozens of old men struggled to the feet and went off in search of their new place. Some tried to walk fast like people appear to do so in old films, but others struggled a bit, some exaggerating their bad knee, hip or back to get more laughs. Finally, with a little bit of help from their friends, everyone was again seated, and Eleanor found that the man on her right was Robert.

"Eleanor! What a treat for me!" he said, deliberately exaggerating his pleasure to make it sound as if it was merely a pleasantry, uttered out of politeness to a middle-aged lady. "That grand-daughter of yours, Lucy, she is amazing! We have just heard the story of her 'ladyname' – and yours I believe!"

"Oh, that! She loves telling stories, and she can be very amusing, but she doesn't always get it right, bless her!"

"I did wonder that," replied Robert. "The four-year-old swimming to the shore clutching her doll? From the mid-Atlantic?"

"Exactly. At school, they did a bit on the Titanic: living history. But she's only seven, and sometimes she gets her stories muddled up."

"So tell me about Lucy's other story."

"Do you really want to hear about it?"

"I would like to hear about it from you," said Robert. "To hear the proper version."

"What I can do is to tell you what I was told – I must have been about twelve at the time. And the person who told me was my great-grandfather, Patrick O'Brien, who was really old. Now, before I go any further I should say he wasn't my real great-grandfather. He was the young man who found my grandmother and saved her life. At the time he was a farm labourer in south-west Ireland.

"One early day in May, many years ago, Patrick was working in the fields and heard a distant rumble from out to sea. He looked up and saw a ship far away in the distance, hardly more than a speck. He could just make out it had four funnels, so he knew it was an ocean liner. He often used to stop work to look at those ships, plying their way across the Atlantic, and he dreamt that one day he and his wife Meg would be on one sailing out of Liverpool to New York, to start a new life, a better one.

"But on this day, it was clear that tragedy had struck. The plume of smoke was clear for all to see, rising high into the sky above the stricken vessel."

Eleanor was in story-telling mode, unaware of using her hands to illustrate the rising of the smoke or the passage of a liner across the sea.

"Then there was a bright orange FLASH from on board the vessel." She said the word 'flash' loudly and suddenly, so much so that she jumped up a little in her seat which surprised her audience who by this time had gathered around her, having stopped on their way back to their tables to watch and hear her.

"About a minute later, Patrick heard another rumble, more of a whoomph, he said, and looked in horror as he noticed that the tops of the funnels were no longer parallel to the horizon. He realised the ship was sinking. He didn't hear the cries of the passengers but imagined them as he watched those funnels dip. And finally, he saw one end of that mighty vessel rise up high above the surface of the Atlantic before it slid slowly beneath it.

"He ran to the town to alert people to the unfolding tragedy off their coast. But others had witnessed the disaster too, and Patrick's mission had been useless. He ran back home to tell his wife Meg, and they hugged each other and cried as they imagined the horror taking place off their shoreline. They wanted to help, to do something, so they set off across the fields to the highest point on the coast overlooking the beach.

"From there, they watched in anguish the tiny black dots which they presumed were lifeboats, but were relieved to see a ship, a much smaller one, heading for the scene. They hoped all would be saved, that every passenger and crew member had managed to get into a lifeboat, and that the rescue ship would soon reach them and take them up on board and bring them safely back to port.

"They watched until the sun set below the horizon of the sea. When darkness finally came, they returned home wishing that there was something they could do.

"The following morning Patrick rose with the dawn, put on his overcoat and made his way down to the shore. He turned right and started to walk along the beach. As he rounded the headland, he saw the most terrible sight: body after body lying on the fresh sand as far as the eye could see, some with the gentle wavelets of the calm, cold sea lapping against them.

"He ran down the slope, hoping they'd swam ashore and were resting, exhausted after their ordeal. But as he reached the first one, he realised the person was dead. Then the next, and the next. He ran from one to another, hoping to find some sign of life. There were women, children and crew members amongst the dead on that beach. Some souls seemed merely to be sleeping, but their lifeless, discoloured, cold bodies confirmed to Patrick that they were gone. Others had suffered the most appalling injuries which no creature could have survived.

"As he ran along that beach, he noticed a wicker basket amongst the dead and the debris. It wasn't round like the one he and Meg used for firewood but oblong with a hood at one end, like a Moses basket. It was higher up the beach than the corpses, stranded by the receding tide. The extraordinary thing about it was that there were life jackets, five or six of them tied around the outside.

"But the basket was empty. Whatever had been its precious cargo had been lost at sea. Next to it was a bundle of clothes, which also had a life jacket strapped to it. Pat noticed it moved – or did he imagine it? Was it wishful thinking? He went up to it. It was a little girl, unconscious, blue hands and face, but breathing. Just. Patrick had found my grandmother. In her arms, hugged to her little chest inside her thick coat, sodden with sea-water, was a doll.

"He knew what he had to do, and as quickly as he could he unfastened the straps of the life jackets and removed the girl's wet coat. Then he undid his coat, and lifted her up still clutching her doll, and very carefully wrapped his coat around her, so that the warmth of his strong, youthful body, steaming from the run along the beach, would warm her cold, tiny, almost lifeless torso.

"He ran with her all the way back to the cottage, and as he got near, he shouted out to Megan to light the fire. As he came through the door, she helped him to the seat by their humble fireplace and carefully peeled away Patrick's coat, relieving him of his precious burden. She removed the life jacket and the wet clothes from the girl's body and swathed her in the dry, warm blankets which Patrick had brought from their bed.

"It was a good two hours before they noticed the colour of her skin had changed, and another two before her eyelids flickered. But they had saved her. She was on the road to recovery. Sadly, her baby brother – the doll – probably no more than three weeks old, could not be saved. The rigidity of that tiny body showed he must have died long before he reached the beach. Tragic, considering the efforts that little girl, an infant herself, had gone to save her charge.

"Perhaps in death, the baby had saved her by giving her a reason to struggle, to survive. Perhaps it wasn't merely the instinct for self-preservation that had enabled her to survive, but the love of another, of a tiny human form far too young to have been able to save himself. 'Greater love hath no man...' John 15:13.

"Patrick knew his Bible. But he wanted to add 'or woman', 'or girl'. But the life laid down was not hers. Her greater love had saved her. That little basket, with the life-jackets tied around it, had been her life-raft. The Lord works in mysterious ways, he thought.

"Within days rumours concerning the sinking were being talked about in hushed tones, in the shops and in the bars, and they reached the ears of Patrick and Megan O'Brien. It was then they decided to name their adopted child after that great liner, as a memorial to all those who perished, and as a reminder to others of man's brutality to man. And each mother bearing that name has passed it down through the generations, and I hope they will continue to do so.

"So, that's why I am Eleanor Lucille Titania Braithwaite!" She stopped. As if she had just delivered the happy ending her audience had been hoping for. But nobody smiled. Nobody spoke. Finally, Bob thought someone needed to break the silence and ask the question which was puzzling him and, no doubt, others.

"But surely the Titanic went down much nearer to the American coast."

"You're right, Bob. But you've got the wrong ship!"

Robert said it, quietly, but everyone around the table heard him. "Lucy. Tania. It was the Lusitania."

Dan was pleased his mother hadn't got emotional about it – or angry, as she had done with Gerald in the think-tank when they had argued about the rights and wrongs of it all. That was over thirty years ago; she must have been only twenty-six. She'd had plenty of time to get the anger out of her system. And he was relieved she was hardly likely to wander onto the other subject which had made Gerald wary, Action Man. But there was a big difference between the two. The sinking of the Lusitania was passed; over, a historical fact. Action Man may still be active.

Dan remembered how Gerald had got the impression Action Man was still around, in the organisation, probably climbing up the tree. Let's hope, thought Dan, he doesn't drop in here, or into her life – or into ours.

He also remembered his mother had shown another emotion when she was talking about Action Man: fear. Anger and fear. Two primitive emotions, often linked, which have similar physiological effects. What Dan had not considered was a third primitive instinct. Revenge.

7

The sombre mood around the table was quickly dispelled when Peter the Pianist reappeared and Frances took up the microphone to welcome him back.

"Hi Peter, very glad to see you have decided to stay, 'cos we'll be needing you to lead us in our singathon!!!" There were cheers from the crowd.

"But before we kick off with that, my mum Julie would like to say a few words."

"Thanks, Darling. Is this thing working? Oh, it is!. . . Well, I'm not going to keep you, I just want to thank you all very much for coming, and for your kind words of comfort, and about Gerald. I know he would have been thrilled to see you all here today, enjoying yourselves as I know he would have wanted you to do so. Thank you. "

Lots of applause, for Julie for her brief but brave speech, and for Gerald, their chum, mate, colleague, friend and boss – and, in one case, dad.

She handed the microphone back to Frances. "OK guys and girls, this is what we are going to do. G-pa – Gerald – has given us a list of songs, really oldies – like some of you in this room? Golden oldies, perhaps. Peter is going to play them, and we are going to sing along. Not knowing the words is no excuse, as you will find them on the table in front of you. So here we go. You'll all recognise this one."

Most of the assembled company groaned when Peter played the opening bars, but as soon as Frances started singing most of them joined in. It was 'Catch a Falling Star'. But it got everyone in the right mood, and the children did the actions.

The next was 'Some Enchanted Evening'. Someone had tipped Frances off, because she walked over to one of Gerald's old buddies, Phil, and handed him the microphone. As he climbed to his feet, pretending to look embarrassed, Frances signalled to the assembled company to keep quiet. With a brilliant lead-in from Peter, Phil began.

"Some enchanted evening, you will meet a stranger."

He had a good voice and did the expansive arm actions of an opera singer. However, when he reached the 'ger' of 'stranger', he was half a semitone flat. It was his party piece. As usual, it brought howls of laughter. It made people realise they didn't have to be a good singer to join in the fun, and for the remainder of the song, Phil was well supported by an enthusiastic chorus.

Next was the Beatles favourite, 'Do you Want to Know a Secret', which prompted Lucy to stand up and do her Pan's People impression which her new grandma had taught her. But when she realised everyone was looking at her she stopped.

The cries of 'More! More!' from a delighted audience persuaded Grandma to go to the rescue, and with the two of them dancing side by side, Lucy felt much more comfortable. At the end of the song, everybody clapped and cheered, including Eleanor, not realising that the whistles and cries of 'encore' from the men were for her.

As 'Pan's People' walked back to their seats, Peter played the opening bars of 'Anything Goes!', that bouncy Cole Porter song which Eleanor had used to teach her pupils tap-dancing, including her latest protege. So back onto the floor they went, and much to the delight of the crowd they danced and sang. And much to the delight of Robert, it was he whom Eleanor chose to advance on when it came to that special verse:

"If driving fast cars you like,
If low bars you like,
If old hymns you like,
If bare limbs you like,
If Mae West you like,
Or me undressed you like,
Why, nobody will oppose.
Anything goes!"

More cheers and applause. Frances was pleased with the way it was going. They got through the next two songs, even though there was a bit of to-ing and fro-ing as guests went to make themselves comfortable.

"Wow, guys and girls, that was fantastic! We are going to take a break now, then three more to go. So if everyone can be back in here, let's say, in 10 minutes?"

During the break, one of Julie's tennis friends came up to her. "What a wonderful party! I would think Gerald is up there in Heaven looking down on us all, having such fun, and he will be smiling!"

Julie smiled. In fact, she found it difficult to stop herself giggling, as she was tempted to say to her friend, known for her strong religious beliefs, 'He's not in Heaven, he's in formalin'.

'The Blue of the Night' quietened down the mood, but everybody sang and swayed in their seats to the enchanting melody. 'Danny Boy' followed, and when the end of the last verse on the song-sheet was reached, a lone voice, all on its own continued, without a piano accompaniment, without a microphone:

"Oh Danny boy, the pipes, the pipes are calling
From glen to glen, and down the mountain side
The summer's gone, and all the flowers are dying

'Tis you, 'tis you must go and I must bide.
But come ye back when summer's in the meadow
Or when the valley's hushed and white with snow
'Tis I'll be here in sunshine or in shadow
Oh Danny boy, oh Danny boy, I love you so."

Some onlookers admired Eleanor's acting skills, seeing the stage tear running down her cheek. Others thought it was a wonderful tribute to her fine son Dan. But Dan knew the tear was genuine, and that the song was not for him.

The last number was not 'Auld Lang Syne'. It was 'We'll Meet Again'. With everyone joining in, it sounded just like it did at the end of the Doctor Strangelove film, a bit sad, but not melancholy. A fitting farewell for Gerald; and from Gerald, as he had selected it and put it on his list.

Without realising, Eleanor had got to her feet and – as far as she was concerned – was Vera Lynn at that moment, singing in a forces nightclub. Robert was not the only one looking forward to that sunny day.

———————————

It had all gone well, but it had lasted much longer than anyone had thought. Dan was anxious about getting to Gatwick on time to catch the evening EasyJet back to Geneva, bearing in mind the plan was to go via Heathrow to drop off his mother. But at the last minute, Eleanor said she would get a taxi from St. Jonathan's, to save Dan time. It had been a bit of a squash on the journey over from Gatwick anyway, so they were all relieved, even though it brought forward the sad parting.

Accordingly, her luggage was unloaded from the back of the hired car and goodbyes were said, hugs and kisses all round.

Lucy was the worst. "Grandma, do you have to go?"

"Now listen, Darling. I'm going to see my parents, then in four weeks, I'm coming back to Geneva to see you, Josh and your mummy and daddy. And a few weeks after that, we'll have a new baby! And you and I are going to help Mummy look after it. Won't that be wonderful!" Lucy smiled at the thought.

Dan started the car and wound down the windows so they could all wave to Eleanor as they drove off. Josh said, "Mum, I need to go to the loo!"

"Oh, Josh! Why didn't you go earlier?" Dan stopped the car and sighed. "Go on, then. Off you go."

Julie came out and went to the car. "Dan, I forgot to give you this. It's a photo of Gerald when he was young. It was in his office with one of those sticky note things with your name on it. I think he wanted you to have it. It's the one where he's holding those long skis. Amazing, aren't they?"

Minutes later, Josh was back in the car, and off they went down the drive and out onto the main road. As they were heading down the drive, Josh asked, "Mum, what does 'abort' mean?"

Helen did not know how to reply. She felt conscious of the life growing inside her. "Well, darling, it depends on the context, on how it was said."

"Does it have anything to do with projectors?" Josh then asked.

"What?" said Helen.

"Projectors. You know, like the one at lunch projecting that man's photo, on the screen."

"Darling, those photos were of Gerald!"

"No, there were some of a much younger man. They were blurred, out of focus."

His mother laughed. "They were all of Gerald! Some when he was old – like the one with you in it pulling that face – but others were when he was much younger."

"Oh!" said Josh. "I get it!" He had never imagined that Gerald, the nice man they sometimes went skiing with, was ever a young man.

His mother smiled. That's nine-year-olds for you, she thought. "So, where did you hear the word 'abort'? Was it recently?"

"Yes," replied Josh. "It was when I went to the loo just now.

In that building. A man outside the window was saying 'subject not in focus, subject not in focus, abort, abort'. Or something like that. He was almost shouting."

Helen laughed. "Darling, I'm afraid I haven't a clue what he was talking about. Are you sure you didn't imagine it?"

Dan had been listening. He felt his stomach churn. Helen asked him if he was OK. He noticed his knuckles had gone white, as his hands instinctively tightened their grip on the steering wheel of the Ford Focus.

Eleanor did her double-hand wave as she watched the car disappear through the gates. She was sorry to see them go, but she had enjoyed the lunch and the entertainment much more than she thought she would. Somehow she felt she had got to know Gerald a bit better even though he hadn't been there.

On the way back into the building she met Robert. He wished her a pleasant flight, a good time in Australia and said he hoped that they might bump into each other again some time. He too loved Switzerland and was lucky enough to be posted there, to take up a new job at the British Embassy in Bern later that week. He apologised that he didn't have a card to give her, as they were being printed, but he wrote his name on a menu card – Robert Dunn – with a mobile number, saying that if ever he could be of service she should call him. She thanked him for his kindness, they said farewell to each other and parted.

Having done long haul less than three weeks previously, Eleanor was not relishing the much longer flight to Sydney. At Heathrow that evening, she would change out of her glad-rags and heels into jeans and a sweater over a light cotton blouse with her new pair of light slip-ons on her feet. Business was not as luxurious as First, but better than economy. Nevertheless, she was pleased she would have a 24-hour break in Singapore with the use of a hotel room.

As Dan drove away from St. Jonathan's down the steep sweeping bends of River Hill towards the M25 junction he was somewhat relieved to feel the brakes were working well, and he smiled to think how silly he had been to even think that they might have been in any danger. He made up his mind not to get like his father and start seeing monsters around every corner. Helen looked at him and saw the smile and said, "So what's on your mind, lover-boy?"

"Oh, just getting used to this car. It's funny when you hire a car, you never bother to read the handbook or get familiar with it. You just drive off. At least that's what I do. I don't even know if this is diesel or petrol. Not that it matters. . . Oh, no!"

"What's up? Do we have a problem?" Helen said.

"This is crazy. We're on empty! Almost. They couldn't have filled it up! Thank goodness we've got plenty of time. I'll stop at that service station, the one just after we join the motorway."

"Do you think we'll get that far?" Helen was worried about being stranded on the hard shoulder. She had heard it was a dangerous place to be, especially on the M25.

"I'm sure we can make it. I'll toddle along at forty," he reassured her. "You can go for miles on empty at that speed."

It was slow going, but eventually, Dan pulled off the motorway onto the slip-road and then into one of the refuelling bays. He noticed the police car at the end of the slip-road and was relieved he'd only had a couple of glasses of wine at lunchtime. But no sooner had he arrived than it drove off. Dan put in ten litres which was more than enough to cover his journey from Gatwick and back. He wasn't going to waste any more money, and he would have a word with Hertz about it when he handed the car back.

The flight was on time, and good news: they had not run out of bacon sandwiches and Twix bars. The weather was settled, and with the children both fast asleep the plane gently touched down on time on the runway at Geneva Airport. It hadn't been a full flight, and in no time at all they had retrieved their bags and were walking across to the multi-storey car park.

The drive back to the flat was easy as the traffic was light. Soon they were at home. "Here we are again, folks," said Dan, trying to sound cheerful.

"Yeah," was all Helen could muster up by way of jolliness.

Lucy said it all for the four of them. "I'm missing her already."

"Not to worry!" Dan tried hard to change the mood. "Just think of her arriving in Australia on Wednesday evening. Remember, it's autumn down there, beautifully warm, and Grandma will be seeing her parents. She'll have a great holiday with them, and in three weeks' time, she'll be back here! Isn't that great?"

"Three weeks? That's ages," said Josh, stifling a yawn.

"Can't you ask her to come back sooner?" asked Lucy.

"Come on you two," said Helen. "Bedtime. School in the morning!"

Dan started unpacking the suitcases. He put the photo-frame on his desk in his study, the one of his dad as a young man holding those old skis. He had enjoyed 'G-pa's bash' and meeting his father's old friends, even though he couldn't tell anyone he was more than 'a skiing friend of Gerald's'. He'd loved seeing those photos of him; and the songs – and Lucy, dancing with his mum! He too hoped the next three weeks would go by quickly.

8

"You've really screwed up this time, haven't you? First, you do a stupid deal which costs us an arm and a leg; then you let the fucking bitch go! Are you mad?"

Karen decided not to answer the question. She would wait until his rage had died down.

This was the first time she'd had a face-to-face with 'The Dope'. It was an unfortunate nickname for the new Director of Operations, but in the case of this particular incumbent, it was tacitly agreed by all lower ranks at Vauxhall Cross that the acronym for the post, D-Ops, was appropriate.

Fortunately, she had been warned about him when the summons had arrived. During her wait in the outer office she had breathed slowly and deeply and made up her mind she would remain calm and show no sign of fear, shock or anger. She'd been told he wouldn't offer her a seat and he would start standing, facing the window overlooking his beloved river. He would work himself up into a frenzy, then turn round and face her.

"Tell me, why the FUCK did you let her go BEFORE you got the fiche?" She let him continue. "Didn't it occur to you that the creep would double-cross you? You meet him once, you have no idea who he really is, you haven't a clue what he's like yet you trusted him!

"Believe me, girl, you've got a lot to learn about human nature.

Tell me, once he got his. . . his woman back, what incentive did he have to hand the damn thing over? What on EARTH were you thinking would happen? Did you really expect him to give it to you as soon as the Braithwaite woman landed in Geneva?"

Karen decided it was time to answer his question. "Yes, Sir. I did. And he would have done so, had he been given the chance-"

"Given the chance? So what chance did you give him? Eh? Look, girl. This is serious. I mean really serious! You failed. You'd better have a bloody good reason why this whole thing went pear-shaped, or you will be clearing your desk out, sharpish!"

Karen steadied herself. "Gerald Rayner didn't have a chance to hand over the fiche because he died."

The Dope moved quickly over to his desk and grabbed a file. He flipped it open and scanned the last two pages. Karen continued. "He died in his sleep, unexpectedly, on 26th January-"

"I know, I can read! I've got the email here in front of me. So what steps did you take to prevent this MFU?"

Monumental fuck-up. Karen knew the term, and she had to admit to herself that she hadn't allowed for Gerald dying suddenly.

"Sir, I did not foresee his demise." She wanted to say her crystal ball had crashed that week, but she thought better of it.

The Dope sat down at his desk and continued to read the file.

"And then you organise the removal of a wooden box from his office expecting the fiche to be there? Surprise, surprise! It's not! Then yesterday, on a Sunday, while Mum, Dad, Auntie Glad, Horace, Boris and Maurice were all at some party you send in two search teams – two! For a poxy little garage! And guess what? They can't find the fiche! So, your line manager orders you to take back the Braithwaite woman before she skips the country. And what happens? You screw that up too!

"Your hoity-toity, let's-be-nice to people approach hasn't worked, has it? So what are you going to do about it, eh? Come on! Tell me!"

Karen sensed the tirade was nearly over. "I'm sorry, Sir, that it hasn't worked out how we would've wanted it to. But I'll not give up. I'll find the fiche and hand it to you personally. Give me four weeks. I'll do whatever is necessary to get it back."

"You bet you bloody-well will, girl. If we don't get that fiche, Rayner doesn't get Braithwaite. Is that clear?"

It wasn't clear to Karen because Rayner was dead. "I understand, Sir."

"Go on then! Don't just stand there!"

Karen turned around and left the room. In the outer office, his secretary gave her a smile, as if to say that's how he treats everyone; don't take it too seriously.

The Director of Operations watched her close the door behind her, and he relaxed. He thought it had gone well, despite the fact that he hadn't been properly briefed that Rayner had died before Eleanor bloody Braithwaite was repatriated. But he'd shown strength throughout, and had made it clear to the girl he was very much the boss.

He'd only been in the post for a couple of weeks, and he felt it important to stamp his mark on his fiefdom. It irritated him that the Braithwaite woman was still on the scene after twenty years. She was weak, too soft, and he could never forgive her for bottling out in Paris. He'd put that episode to the back of his mind, but now the woman was back, he was worried. The last thing he needed right now was for her to frig up his career for the third time.

And neither could he ever forgive her sugar daddy, that old queen Richard Bentley, who'd poached her to work in his think-tank place after her stupid husband had shot his mouth off. If she'd remained with me, he thought, I would've knocked some sense into her; shown her the proper way to do things.

He had little time for Bentley. Old school, old-fashioned, never moved on from the Cold War. To be good at your job these days, he thought, you've got to be tough and play dirty. Him and his

Queensbury rules. And a traitor, too, taking photos of those Class Sevens and sending them to Rayner.

As for the Secret Intelligence Services Act of 1994, he despised it: see what happens when you have to fill in forms all the time! But what a lucky break the Service had got, with that long email sent from Rayner's computer to the son in Geneva. And the others received by the son, about the lunch. He hoped GCHQ would continue to come up trumps, and with any luck, the whole matter could be brought to a successful conclusion. Or termination? He smiled at the thought.

Until then he was under a lot of pressure. He understood the sensitivity of the documents on that fiche, and the need to retrieve it. If they ever found their way onto the internet. Not a nice thought. A scapegoat would be sought – and he might be it.

On the other hand, what if he were to walk into his boss's office upstairs and produce the fiche to him in person? With options to stay on after 65, he might just make it to that upper office himself. 'Sir Timothy Turnbull'; it had a satisfying ring to it. He would sort the place out. Get rid of the fluffy pink, and get the show on the road. Then retirement, and more time for the love of his life, The Mary Fifi, his precious boat.

At least he had made sure the girl, Karen or whatever her name was, was suitably fired up and motivated to do her job and deliver the fiche. And for his part, he would make pretty damn sure Eleanor Braithwaite didn't slip through his fingers. He read through the file again, then picked up the phone. He had some favours to call in. Bugger the 1994 Act, he thought, as he waited for the connection. Let's do it the old way.

After leaving Turnbull's office, Karen went to the ladies, locked herself in one of the booths and had a little cry. It was not an unhappy cry, just the release of emotional tension. She knew things hadn't gone well for her, yet she enjoyed that inner confidence of knowing she had behaved correctly and hadn't screwed anything up.

Shit happens sometimes and you have to deal with it. She would. But on her terms.

———————————

Having checked into her hotel room in Singapore, Eleanor made the most of the break. She hung up her clothes – the good ones she would wear for the last leg of the flight, for when she met her parents. She then put Robert's mobile number into her phone and threw away the menu card. She slept, read her book and went out and did some shopping.

With Dan's help, she had managed to face-time her parents a few times in the past five weeks, so it would not be a difficult reunion. It would be emotional, but all the explanations had been done, the inevitable questions answered or carefully deflected; the parents understood there were aspects of their daughter's life which they didn't need to know. And they knew what she looked like, and she knew what to expect of them. No shocks.

She was quite excited as the plane touched down; it was her first visit to Australia. But what she was truly looking forward to was staying with her parents and being their little girl again. It was, therefore, a shock and a disappointment when she was stopped at customs and asked to come this way, please. She was invited into a windowless office where a pleasant young man explained that random checks were carried out from time to time, and she just happened to be picked at random.

He asked to see her passport which he retained, 'in order to take a copy' – and her handbag which would need to be searched as well. She asked if she could keep her phone as her elderly parents were meeting her and she needed to tell them she was held up. The young man said, of course she could, and told her that after her luggage had been searched, everything would be carefully put back and that she should be on her way within twenty minutes.

After half an hour the man apologised for the delay and offered her a cup of tea or coffee. She chose coffee. When he returned with it, something had changed. The smiles were gone. Then, when the hour was nearly up, an older man in uniform came into the room and explained that prohibited substances had been found in her suitcase and under Section so-and-so of such-and-such an act she would be detained for further investigation.

When she asked how long this was likely to take, she was told it would be about three days, a week at most. She would be housed in the airport's detention unit, in her own room with en-suite facilities and able to retain some personal items. She would be taken there as soon as her room had been made ready.

9

The day following her ordeal with The Dope, Karen took a pool car down to Julie Rayner's house just outside Sevenoaks. She didn't want to phone ahead, as it might have had muddied the waters. So she was lucky to find Julie in. She hadn't worked out what to say, preferring to let things develop naturally.

"Good morning, Mrs Rayner, my name is Karen Shapley. I am so sorry to trouble you, but I wonder if you could help me. It concerns Gerald."

"You're not the Karen he met at Sue's birthday lunch, are you? He told me all about you! Come in, come in!"

"Mrs Rayner, I'm so sorry to hear about him, and your sad loss. . ."

"It's Julie. And it's been over two months. I can talk about him. Now, coffee? Tea? Why don't we go through to the kitchen? We can chat while I put the kettle on."

A good start, Karen thought, and she relaxed. "I heard he had a good send-off on Sunday."

"Oh that!" replied Julie. "Yes, it was good fun. Gerald would have loved it. Some of those songs he chose, though, very out-of-date stuff, but I think everyone enjoyed themselves. His skiing friend, Dan, came over from Geneva with his wife and family, and his mother as she was on her way to Australia, and a lot of Gerald's old army friends came along."

Karen made her move. "On the subject of his time in the Army, there is something that concerns my boss at the MoD. You see, we believe Gerald had a document in his possession, a confidential one which he should have handed in. To be honest, it happens quite often, but we have to account for such things.

"It didn't really matter when he was alive because he was very good at security, but now he's gone we need to make sure it doesn't fall into the wrong hands. If it did, it could be embarrassing. We don't want him remembered as someone who was careless about such things."

"I see what you mean! No, that would be awful! So how can I help? Would you like to look round his office? I have the key somewhere. . ."

"That's kind of you. But can I ask if anything has left his office after he died? Has anybody taken anything away?"

"The answer to that is yes. Someone broke in there and took his new computer and an old box somebody sent him. We don't have many break-ins here, but occasionally garden sheds do get broken into, and things like mowers are stolen. I gather they turn up at boot fairs."

"Do you know if anything else was taken? Books, files, folders?" Karen asked.

"No, nothing else has gone, to my knowledge. My daughter Frances checked everything – she was wonderful, as she had the ghastly job of going through his papers and things the day after he died. But apart from the theft, everything is how he left it in both his office and his workshop. Once we get the go-ahead from the solicitor, we'll let the family have a look round. I have two sons-in-law who would love to get their hands on some of his tools. You know he was an engineer?"

"I do, and I understand he was a keen skier, and you too, I believe?"

"Yes he was, and I still am. Nothing too extreme, mind! But he started long before I did. He must have been in his early twenties. Let me show you a picture of him. Hang on a sec. . .

"Oh no, I gave it to Dan. On Sunday. I knew it would make him smile. In those days the skis were so long, you wouldn't believe it. Anyway, I knew Gerald wanted Dan to have it as he'd put a post-it note on the glass with Dan's name on it."

"Well, I'm sure you did the right thing in giving it to him. You've been really helpful, but I mustn't keep you any longer. If I may just have a quick look in his office if that's OK?"

"Certainly. Come this way. . . Now, where's the key. . ."

Later that afternoon Karen was on a plane from Gatwick to Geneva. She emailed Dan from her phone before she boarded explaining she was a friend of Gerald and needed Dan's help – ETA at 7:05 p.m. She thought with a bit of luck she might have a reply by the time she landed.

She turned her phone back on as soon as the aircraft touched down, but no message. She would try his mobile once through passport control and customs. As she went through the automatic doors into Arrivals she saw the Gerald look-alike – but much younger – standing there with a millboard with her name on it as if he did this on a regular basis.

"I'm Karen. Are you Dan?"

"Yes. I got your message, but I thought I'd just come and meet you. I think I know what it's about, and I guess it might be better if we talked somewhere in private. My wife Helen knows nothing, and I think it's simpler that way. Why don't we go and have a coffee?"

They sat down opposite each other at a small table. The waitress came and took their order, and after giving them a bit of time for small talk, she returned with two Americanos.

Karen thought she'd better get to the meat of it. "Dan, we have a copy of Gerald's diary, the one Frances emailed to you shortly after his death. I assume you have been through it?"

"Yes. So I know about you and the deal you did with him, on the train. I assume you are that Karen?"

"Yes. And I know Gerald was your father. But we haven't seen the story he sent you, the one he refers to on the first page of the diary. But that doesn't matter. I think you know why I am here." She thought so far, so good.

"I guess it's because my father died before he honoured his side of the bargain. So you want the documents. That fiche from Mr B? The one he sent to my father?"

"Yes. We do."

"Fair enough. My mother has been found and returned. He would want you to have the fiche, and so would she. But I don't have it."

"We think you might have it without realising it. The framed photo Julie gave you last Sunday. We think it might contain the fiche. Where is it at the moment?"

"On the desk in my study, in the flat. Helen will be settling the kids. Twenty minutes from here. Do you want me to go and get it?"

"Why don't I come with you, wait downstairs in the lobby while you get it, then I can get a taxi back here. It'll save you a journey." Karen remembered her training: keep tight; minimise risk.

Deal done.

Soon they were parking in the basement of Dan and Helen's apartment block. Then Dan left Karen in the lobby while he shot upstairs. A few minutes later he was down again and produced the framed photo. He handed it to Karen, and she carefully peeled away the tape. There were two layers of backing cardboard, and in between was a microfiche sheet. She held it up to one of the wall lights and took a photo with her phone camera on macro-mode then zoomed in on the image and panned up and down. She could just make out the tiny silhouette of the lion and the unicorn crest on one of the photos.

"It's the one! Thanks, Dan!" She couldn't help smiling.

"A pleasure. And. . . er thanks. For everything." Dan was pleased he helped honour his father's obligation, and he still had the photograph of him.

"Bye. All the best. And to Helen and your children. And your mum, of course. Here's my card. If you need it."

Dan shot up the stairs to his flat, carrying the photo-frame carefully, so the glass did not drop out.

Karen put the fiche in her bag and apped for a taxi and within ten minutes she was on her way back to the airport.

She was pleased to have met him, having known his father. As for Eleanor, Karen had heard the stories about her – or rather legends – and was pleased she'd played a part in repatriating her.

While Dan was up in his apartment sticking the photo frame back together his phone sounded. It was a text from his mother: *'Arrived safely in Sydney, but detained on suspicion of smuggling!'* He fished out Karen's card and rang her. She was still in the taxi.

"Hi, Karen. It's me, Dan. Sorry to bother you, but you'll never guess what's happened. My mother has been detained at Sydney Airport. Suspected of smuggling, would you believe it?"

"What? You must be joking! Leave it with me. We'll get our people to look into it. And Dan, let me know if you hear anything else."

"Thanks, Karen. Will do."

"That would be great. I'll hang on to your whatsits till this is sorted, OK?"

"Cheers. Most grateful. Bye. Have a good flight."

As Eleanor sat there, contemplating her situation, she thought the worst aspect of it all was being in a foreign country without a passport. Without one, you are completely trapped – unless you can get to a British embassy or consulate which is willing to help you.

The thought reminded her of Robert Dunn, the man she'd met at Gerald's bash who worked for the Foreign Office. He probably knew all about that sort of thing. Then she remembered she'd put his number into her phone and decided to take him up on his offer of help. Maybe he might know someone in Sydney who she could contact.

About an hour later the older man in uniform returned and very sheepishly explained there had been a mix-up. Very regrettable, and on behalf of the Department of Immigration and Border Protection he would like to apologise to her and to her family meeting her. He said he would escort her personally through the airport to the VIP lounge in Arrivals where her parents were waiting for her. A porter would bring her luggage.

It was a wonderful reunion; lots of hugs and kisses, smiles and tears. Lots to talk about, despite the face-times, so much so that Eleanor had not noticed the smart young man standing by them, also smiling. It was her mother who introduced him.

"Darling, this is Alec who has been looking after us so well. He was waiting for us at the information desk after we were called over the loudspeaker. It was quite exciting, actually!"

"Hi. Alec Brown, from the Consulate General's Office. Welcome to Australia!"

"Thanks, I'm Eleanor. Eleanor Braithwaite. Oh, and thanks so much for looking after my parents. I think my luggage must have got mixed up with someone else's. I nearly got arrested!"

"Well, we couldn't allow that, could we? Not on your first day?" he joked. "When we got the call, we had to act fast. But tell me, how do you know Sir Robert? Is he a relation?" He could see the puzzled look on Eleanor's face. "Sir Robert Dunn? Our new ambassador in Bern?"

While waiting in Departures at Geneva airport, Karen phoned the duty officer in her section and asked for a sitrep from Sydney on an English woman, Eleanor Braithwaite, arriving from London and detained by Immigration and Border Protection. She also had asked if GCHQ could do a run on phone calls from Vauxhall Cross to Australia in the last seventy-two hours.

On the flight back, she carefully planned what she would do in the office the following day. It would be fun, she thought. She also wondered how that dope Turnbull would have done things. Probably an SAS team from The Increment, abseiling down from the roof, stun grenades, dazz-lites, traumatised children, hysterical mother, trashed flat. And he was worried about me using two search teams! He really ought to grow up. This is 2017, for Christ's sake.

10

Dan read the text from his mother that had arrived during the night: *'Freed! With Mum and Dad. All good! Lots of love Xxxx.'* He texted Karen with the good news. When it arrived, she was in her office having cycled in early to avoid the London traffic.

On her desk was the report from GCHQ stating that two days previously a call lasting six minutes had been made from the Director of Operations' office to a mobile number in Australia. This reinforced her hunch that The Dope was doing his own thing, yet again.

She went ahead with her plan and phoned up his secretary to arrange a meeting; she had a document he wanted. Less than fifteen minutes later the secretary called back to say he would see her straight away but only for five minutes because he'd made an appointment with C immediately afterwards.

Breathe deeply and slowly, she told herself as she got up from her desk, picked up the folder with the GCHQ report and went to The Dope's office.

"He's in a good mood for once," his secretary said, "just go straight in."

"Ah! Come in. Do take a seat." The Dope didn't get up from behind his large leather-topped desk.

"Thank you, Sir," Karen responded, realising he probably wouldn't remain seated for long.

"Now, I believe you have something for me, a very important document which you nearly lost forever? I just hope you've learnt your lesson not to make stupid deals with people you can't trust!"

Karen smiled and looked suitably chaste, but remained silent.

"So, shall we have a look at it and make sure it's what it's supposed to be?" He produced a magnifying glass from his desk drawer.

"I've checked it, Sir. It's genuine."

"Well! We'll see about that! Your record of getting things right leaves much to be desired. Come on, girl, hand it over."

"I can't, Sir."

"You what? Come on, don't be stupid. Give it to me this instant."

"I don't have it with me, Sir."

"You don't have it? Are you wasting my time? You told my secretary you had the damn thing."

"I did get hold of it, Sir, last night. Rayner's son gave it to me."

"Surely you haven't lost it already? What the hell have you done with it?"

"It's in a safe place, Sir. I cannot give it to you because I am holding it in trust until Eleanor Braithwaite is safe. Until she is safely back in Geneva."

It took a few seconds for The Dope to realise what Karen had said, and then the expected happened. He jumped up from his chair and slammed his right fist so hard on his desk that the photo-frame next to his phone fell flat. Karen noticed the photograph was of a boat. The white collar of his shirt emphasised the ever-growing redness of his neck. Then came the tirade.

"Don't you come your hoity-toity ways with me, you stupid little tart! If you think you can play games with me, you'd better think again, you FUCKING BITCH! Give me that folder NOW!"

And with that, he ran around his desk and snatched it from Karen's lap. With trembling hands, he ripped it open and scanned the single sheet of paper it had contained. He breathed out through flared nostrils.

"I'm going to get you for this," he growled, as he slid the GCHQ print-out back into its folder.

At that moment, the door opened and in walked C, his boss, the man himself.

"Ah, there you are, Tim. I thought you wanted to see me, to give me something important? Your secretary told me it was urgent but good news. And to be honest with you, I could do with some good news right now."

He noticed Karen, still sitting there, breathing slowly and deeply. "What's going on here?"

The Dope tried to hide his alarm and fright with a big smile. "Good morning, Sir. Oh, nothing much. This. . . this operative has, I'm afraid, let you down, and I was discussing with her how she might put things right."

"Really, Tim? It's not like Karen to make a mistake. What's she done?"

"Well, Sir. It's the Bentley fiche, the one with the. . . the things on it. She's lost it. I was hoping to bring it to you this morning as soon as she handed it over. But she can't seem to. . . to remember where she filed it. We were discussing where it could be."

"In that case, I'd better leave you two to get on with it. Let me know when you find it." C turned around and walked out of the office.

When the door was safely closed, The Dope towered above Karen, still seated. "You have failed me! You PROMISED me! You useless piece of. . . DIRT!"

The slight pause gave Karen the opportunity to speak. "No, Sir. I didn't fail you. I didn't break my promise. I said I'd get the fiche and hand it over to you within four weeks. I will do this; I will keep my word. Providing Eleanor Braithwaite returns safely to her home in Geneva within that time."

He could not believe what he was hearing. "Get out!" he screamed. "GET! OUT!"

Karen got up and walked, not towards the door but around to the side of the desk where her torn folder lay. As she picked it up, he snatched it away from her, his eyes blazing. She looked back at him and smiled, then walked out of the room. Her hunch was correct. But her smile was a mistake.

As she passed his secretary she smiled, "So what's he like in a bad mood?"

Karen went home early that day, back to her studio flat in Putney. She moved her bedside table out of the way and carefully lifted the corner of the carpet. She retrieved the stiff cardboard envelope on which she had written Dan's address in Geneva and walked to the post office.

The Director of Operations slumped in his chair. Why is it, he reflected, that I'm surrounded by idiots. This stupid girl has screwed up again, despite my advice. What is it about young people these days? They just don't get it. As D-Ops I'm not going to tolerate indiscipline, insubordination, and people like this girl going off and doing their own thing. He believed he and he alone had the strength and the experience to deal with this – and he would. He would do what was necessary.

His mood went even blacker when he received a text from a certain mobile phone in Australia. The Braithwaite woman had been released. It would seem you can't even rely on your chums anymore.

He knew it was unwise to bring the Braithwaite woman back from exile. He said so at the time but was persuaded that having the fiche back more than compensated for the risk of her being around. Now, she was free and the fiche was, well, anywhere: a double whammy.

It was time, he thought, for him to take over the reins and drive this project to its ultimate conclusion. To bury the evidence

– both 'items' – once and for all. It's no good being squeamish about this sort of thing. If you are going to protect the Nation, you have to protect the Service.

11

It's amazing how time flies by when you're enjoying yourself, thought Eleanor. The three weeks were nearly up, and all had gone well. Her parents had been wonderful and had taken great care of her, treating her as if she were somewhere between being an honoured guest and a patient convalescing after a long illness.

They showed her all the sights, and she told them about her new life, their grandson Dan, his wife Helen and about their great-grandchildren, Josh and Lucy. Most mornings Eleanor would get up early and face-time them in Geneva, and often her parents would join in the session.

Eleanor also kept in contact with Dan by text and mobile. They realised they had to be careful, and they chatted casually but in a code which seemed to evolve all on its own. Karen was Katie, Mr B was Brian, Julie became Andrew. Fiche became fish, then dish, then recipe.

Thus Eleanor knew Brian's recipe had been found and Andrew had given it to Dan. He gave it to Katie but asked if he could have it back. Katie said she would put the recipe in the post. So Eleanor knew Julie had given the fiche to Dan who had handed it over to Karen who had sent it back to Dan in Geneva.

Then one morning Dan phoned Eleanor. "Morning Mum, how are you doing?"

"And good evening to you, son! I'm fine – and you and Helen and the kids?"

"All good, thanks," Dan replied. "But I had a text last night from Katie. Poor thing. She fell off her bike on the way to work and is in Tommy's A & E with a broken ankle."

"Oh no! That's terrible! Hope she's out soon. It would be a shame if she missed the party. By the way, did you get the recipe back, the one she was putting in the post?"

"Nothing as yet. I'll let you know when it arrives."

A few days after this exchange, the subject of their chatter once again turned to 'the party'.

"Now Darling, I've made a few changes to my travel plan, because I want to stop over in London to see Katie, to make sure she's all right."

"Oh, Mum! You're not going to be late coming. . . back, are you?" He had wanted to say 'coming home' but then thought it slightly presumptuous.

"No, Darling, I'll be there as planned, arriving on the 15th, but I'm leaving here a day earlier. It's been wonderful with Mum and Dad, but they're working so hard to give me a good time, I think they'll be ready for a rest! I forget Dad's nearly 85 – and Mum's not far behind."

"Well, we'll all be looking forward to seeing you. Helen's doing fine. Obviously not skiing, but I took the little ones out last weekend. You should see the snow! It's wonderful!"

"'Fraid I'm not into skiing, yet – unless it's on water!"

"We're gonna get you up on planks in no time at all! After the party's been sorted."

"OK OK. But you're right about the party. We don't want anything to go wrong. But I've had an idea which might help. Talk to you about it when I get back. Bye for now, love to all!"

It was not totally secure by any means, but if their conversations were on the watch list, at least they avoided most of the hundred or so likely tag-words which would have triggered the trace-and-record software.

It was a grey, overcast April morning. The Director of Operations looked out across the river slowly flowing past his window some eighty feet below. He watched the craft – pleasure boats, barges and water taxis – making their way up and downstream and across from bank to bank. Seeing them reminded him of his Mary Fifi, but even the thought of his precious boat wasn't enough to blot out his concerns over the Karen Shapley.

When you want them to hospitalise someone, they waste three people; when you want one simple wet-job, they break an ankle. He clenched his fists at the frustration of it all. He had never liked The Increment, a 'rogue element' if ever there was one. They never listened. They always knew better. It made him think of the old adage: if you want something done properly, do it yourself. Well, he thought, maybe I should show them how it's done; I've done it before, I can do it again.

Eleanor arrived at Heathrow jet-lagged and exhausted. The grey skies and the damp air were a mighty change from what she had become used to. But she had things to do. The first was to rent a car, then find a hotel.

She decided on the Holiday Inn, being near the airport and with a parking space available. Having checked in, she hung up her clothes, had a bath and a snooze with the alarm on her phone set for 1:00 p.m. It would be enough to recharge her batteries.

To Eleanor, it seemed as if the couple of hours had been only a few minutes, but she sprang out of bed, got dressed, went down to reception and asked them to order a taxi to take her to St. Thomas's Hospital. It had been ages since she'd driven in central London, and she wanted to be able to look around rather than concentrating on the traffic.

As the taxi made its slow way along the Embankment, she looked across at the headquarters: Babylon-on-Thames, Legoland, Ceausescu Towers. A £200-million-over-budget in-your-face embarrassment. I wonder who's directing things now, she thought. On arrival at the main entrance to Tommy's, the woman at reception directed her to Chaucer Ward where she would find Miss Shapley in a private room.

Eleanor was not prepared for the shock. Karen was in a bad way. Her face was badly bruised, and it was evident from the contraptions around her left leg that it was more than a broken ankle.

"Hi, I'm Eleanor Braithwaite. My goodness, what have you been up to?"

"Eleanor Braithwaite? My God! What are you doing here?" Karen tried to sit up, and despite the obvious pain, she broke into a smile. "Eleanor Braithwaite? Well, that's amazing!"

"Lucky, actually – for me, I mean. I'm on my way back from Aussieland to Geneva with a quick stop-over here in London. Thought I'd just pop in. My son, Dan, told me you fell off your bike. Is that what happened? It looks like you've been in the wars!"

"Yeah, well I did fall off my bike, but with a little help from my enemies. I didn't know I had any, but here I am!"

"So what happened? Tell me." Eleanor turned around to make sure the door was shut.

"A few days ago I was cycling into work and came to a junction – which I know well – where I have to turn right. I moved over to the right-hand lane but kept to the left to allow cars to use the rest of it.

"In the central lane, on my left, was this thirty or forty tonner whatever it was – big artic – which was going straight on, but just before the lights changed, this motorcyclist drew along side me, on my right. I didn't really see him, as I was watching the lights. But as they changed, he gave me an almighty sideways push. Anyway, I went flying just as the artic was pulling away.

"It was like slow motion. Like being in a tumble drier. I screamed as I went under the side of the lorry. More in anger I think because at that stage I wasn't aware of being hurt. I think the lorry driver must have heard me because a moment or two later there was a great hiss of air brakes as the thing juddered to a stop. My left leg had gone numb, but I couldn't drag it away.

"I think it was the lorry driver who came round to see what had happened. Very poor English. Either a Latvian or. . . anyway, an eastern European. He was almost crying. But he had the sense to get back in his cab and reverse the thing to free my leg. That's when the pain started, and I think I must have passed out."

"Gosh, you were unlucky to have your leg trapped like that!"

"Unlucky? Actually, I reckon I was very lucky. You see, I ended up right under the lorry. If the shove hadn't been so violent, it would have been my body under that wheel, not just my leg."

"So, do you think the push from the motorcyclist might have been deliberate?" Eleanor asked.

"No doubt about it. He wanted me under those wheels."

"Hmmm. Any thoughts? Who would do this sort of thing? And why, for Heaven's sake?"

"God knows. You of all people must know it's hard enough in this job telling who your friends are, let alone your enemies. A few weeks ago I did have a run-in with the new Director of Operations. We call him The Dope. Between you and me, he's a bit of a prat, but I can't imagine him doing anything like this.

"He's a tough talker – and tries to bully people – but I think that's all it is. He did come and see me yesterday, believe it or not. Asked how I felt. Seemed more interested in looking around the room, out of the window. A strange guy. . ."

"What's his name?" Eleanor asked.

"Timothy Turnbull. Past it, if you ask me-"

"My God!" said Eleanor. Then to herself, quietly, 'Action Man'.

"D'you know him?"

"Know him? Yeah, I reckon I do. I don't think he likes either of us!"

They talked about other things, Dan, the job, and d'you remember so-and-so, what happened to her or him. Then Eleanor brought the subject back to Action Man.

"Tell me about Turnbull. What d'you know about him?"

"Well, I've only met him a couple of times, in his office. He was very much against the move to get you back. You know, in return for that fiche thing? The one Richard Bentley sent to Gerald Rayner?"

"Yes, I do know about that. My son Dan told me, about the deal you did with Gerald on the train."

Karen flinched in pain as she adjusted her position on the bed.

"Well, I think The Dope reckons the deal hasn't been honoured until he has the fiche. Perhaps I shouldn't say this, but I've got a feeling your detention in Sydney might have been his work. I asked for a phone run – from Babylon to Australia – and there had been a call from his office to a mobile there. It was the day before you landed."

"But why is he so keen to get the fiche back?" Eleanor asked.

"God knows. He seems obsessed by it. You know it's got some Class Seven forms on it?"

"Go on," Eleanor urged.

"I have a feeling they implicate him personally."

Eleanor sighed. She feared the worst. It all started falling into place. Paris. The forms would blow him clean out of the water, she thought. And indeed so could I, if ever I found myself in the witness box. Perhaps he wants to bury the fiche and me. And Karen, and Dan, for that matter.

Her thoughts went back to the days of the brink-tank. She never liked hearing Mr B relating to new scopers the story of the child kidnap, but in that hospital room she thought about it; and Lucy, and Josh. Her disappearance had kept her son safe from that type of threat, but she wondered if her return might put him and his young family in danger.

"Tell me, Karen, does he ever get away from his work? Does he go on holiday? Has he any hobbies?"

"Why do you ask?"

"Well, he has always seemed a bit of an oddball, if you ask me. Just wondered if he had changed much," replied Eleanor.

"You're right, he is a bit odd, but he does have that boat of his. I think that's his relaxation. I hear he goes and works on it most weekends when he is not 'in the field'. Not that he is much these days; he must be getting on."

"A boat, eh?" said Eleanor. "What sort? Sailing?"

"Not sure, although I did see a photo of it, on his desk. Looked like a launch to me, that kind of thing."

"Ah well, each to their own, I suppose. Look, I'd better get going. Take care and get well soon. I'll come and see you when I'm next in London." Eleanor reached across the bed and pressed the nurse call button. "Trust me, Karen," and she put her finger to her lips.

When the nurse arrived, Eleanor explained in hushed tones that her niece had planned to take her own life, and asked for her to be moved as soon as possible to a public ward where she could perhaps engage with other patients and a closer eye could be kept on her. And to make sure she has her mobile phone with her, so she can call me. In the meantime, someone should remain with her.

———

The Director of Operations made his plan of how he would deal with that wretched girl Karen. It was a good plan and would have worked had it not been for a most amazing bit of bad luck. As he entered the main concourse of the hospital, who should be coming towards him but the other bane of his life, Eleanor Bloody Braithwaite. As soon as he saw her, he pulled the brim of his fedora down, lowered his head and kept walking. Tough it out, he thought.

"Mr Turnbull!" Eleanor cried, just after he passed her. Everyone around must have heard it. He had to stop. "So what brings you to St. Thomas's?" she asked him.

Seeing her big smile made him feel better. "Oh, just visiting a member of staff, you know."

"It's not Karen Shapley, is it?" Eleanor asked. "Because I've just come from her bedside. Bad business, that. She told me she was deliberately pushed. The police are up there at the moment. Wasn't it lucky she got a good description of the motorcyclist! Attempted MURDER, if you ask me. Let's hope they catch him, eh?"

"Absolutely!" he replied. "And, er. . . what about you? Will you be in London for long?"

"No, just passing through. Why d'you ask?"

"I... er... just wondered if we might have a drink together – talk about old times. Perhaps I could pop in and see you. Where are you. . er. . . where are you staying?" he asked.

"Travelodge, Waterloo Road. Must dash!" she said, as she turned and strode towards the exit, leaving a very startled Director of Operations standing there.

He was proud of his quick thinking, his ability to respond to events, to be decisive and get things done. It's what got him early promotion. And on this occasion, it might just secure him his knighthood. In a flash he realised the Shapley woman, damn her, had probably passed the fiche to Braithwaite, and there she was striding out of the main doors of St. Thomas's: Braithwaite and fiche together. What he thought had been bad luck was, he hoped, exactly the opposite.

He ran towards the doors and through them, shouting her name as he noticed her striding northwards towards Westminster Bridge. "Mrs Braithwaite! Mrs Braithwaite! A word please?"

She stopped and turned around. He jogged up to her, puffing.

"Mrs Braithwaite! I am so glad to see you! I didn't recognise you at first! Er, may I call you Eleanor?" Eleanor said nothing. She just gave him her half-smile.

"Eleanor, look, I know we've had our differences in the past, but I wondered if the time has come to put those behind us, and, well, be friends. Here we are, after all those years, bumping into each other like this! Perhaps it's a sign, don't you think?"

"Well, Mr Turnbull, it's a bit of a coincidence, isn't it?"

"Oh, please call me Tim. It's not as if I were still your boss, is it?"

"Okay, Tim. Do you want to go and have a coffee?"

"Well, I thought it might be best. . . I thought I should at least invite you to dinner – on me of course."

"Why thank you," Eleanor replied. "Where had you in mind? The Ritz?"

He laughed. "I think you deserve better than that! No, I would like to invite you to dine with me on board The Mary Fifi."

He noticed Eleanor's frown. "It's a little ship! It's my little ship. You know, one of those that went to Dunkirk in 1940, to rescue our soldiers. To be honest, my little ship wasn't involved, but her sister ship, The Mary Jane. . . "

"Tim, that's very kind. I'd love to. But I could only do tonight, I'm afraid, as I am flying back to Geneva tomorrow evening."

"Capital! Tonight it will be! Now, she's at Cookham, but why don't I pick you up from your hotel at, say, 6:30 this evening and drive you down. I have to be in the office early tomorrow morning, so driving you back is no problem, none at all. I'll bring all the supplies with me, and I will rustle up something in the galley for us. I think you'll enjoy my cooking!"

"Sounds wonderful, Tim. But Cookham's near Maidenhead isn't it? I'm on my way there now. My grandmother used to live just outside the town, and we used to go to her house for Sunday lunch when I was about six or seven. I want to see if I can find it. I mean, why don't I meet you there, at the boat, at, say, 7:30?"

"Why not indeed?" He tried to smile at the thought, but he was anxious about the fiche. But on the other hand, if she had it with her now, she might well have it when she arrived at the boat.

The Dope explained where the country club was, where to park and how to get down to the boat. He said it was best not to call into the club, as they might get hold of the wrong end of the stick, seeing a woman on her own boarding his Mary Fifi. Rumours and all that, you know.

Brilliant, he thought. This could all go well.

12

Eleanor thought the walk into Victoria would give her time to think and get some fresh air into her lungs. She hoped Karen would be safe. Even Action Man – The Dope – wouldn't try anything at the moment, having been spotted entering the hospital. And with any luck, someone there would be keeping an eye on her, at least enough to deter anyone from trying anything.

She thought she'd better get cash, so she stopped by at a bank with an ATM outside and withdrew £1000. Her next stop was a branch of Maplin's. She told the young salesman she'd recently become a grandmother and needed a baby alarm.

He showed her the latest range of CQ-er-alirt modules which require no wiring and, with a special app – free with any module – she can operate the system from anywhere using her mobile phone! He was more excited about them than she was, explaining how the monitor would 'wake up' if there was any sound or movement, then telephone her iPhone and display a picture in real time of what was going on in the room, even in the dark. She could then use her phone to talk to the baby through the monitor.

He also said for a further £69.99 she could purchase another module which would operate a table lamp, or indeed any other appliance in the room, all through her mobile. He explained how they worked, and how easy it was to download the app and follow the simple instructions.

She decided to take the monitor and two switch units, as it might be useful to operate a fan. Yes, he said, we do a fan, a very good one, and it's over here.

Hang on, she thought. These things are all mains operated. She then explained to the sales assistant that in her daughter's house in the country they sometimes get power cuts, especially in high winds. Ah, he said. You'll need one of these.

He showed her a UPSU, an uninterruptible power supply unit. He said it's normally used for computers but would keep any appliance going for up to six hours. It's rated at five amps, so it could easily power a light and a fan. She thanked him and said she'd take the lot. And then she remembered the presents for the boys, some binoculars for Tom and one of those Leatherman tool kit things for Harry. And for Dick, a torch, one of those LED jobs you wear around your head. The assistant beamed. She paid in cash and left.

Her next call was at a Fones-R-4-U shop. She needed an iPhone for her nephew who was going to be ten next week. Just a pay-as-you-go thing, no contract or any paperwork to bother about. He's only a child. Yes, madam, we have just the thing for you.

Finally, she popped into a lighting shop, browsed around and found what she wanted. It was a small desktop reading lamp with one of those bright tungsten-halogen bulbs. She bought it – and a pack of three spare bulbs. Then she took a taxi back to her hotel.

She enjoyed the drive down to Cookham in her rented car, despite the heavy traffic. Quite different to driving the school bus, down to the village and back, along the dusty dirt road on which you would see more horses than cars.

It was the lushness of the English countryside which pleased her. So green after summer in Argentina and then autumn in Australia. She had left in good time recalling the old adage: time spent in reconnaissance is seldom wasted.

The Dope was pleased with himself. He reckoned he had a reasonable chance that evening of getting his hands on the fiche and eliminating the other source of evidence. The proverb about killing two birds with one stone amused him as he drove away from Vauxhall Cross down to his little treasure, his Mary Fifi.

He thought he'd play it by ear, confident his quick-thinking would enable him to exploit the situation in the best way possible with the minimum amount of fuss. He'd start with a subtle approach, put the wretched woman at ease, off guard. An aperitif, then steak 'a la Turnbull' with a glass of Shiraz. Then he would do the business. He had enough anchor chain.

Eleanor watched him arrive, through the binos from the opposite bank. Nice boat, she thought, if you like that sort of thing. He was carrying a plastic bag in one hand, and a bottle in the other. It was ten to seven and beginning to get dark as he climbed aboard. She watched carefully as he put down the bottle and the bag and lifted the lid of one of those rear locker things.

He took something out, then fiddled with a padlock on the rear hatch. Surely not, Eleanor thought. It can't be the key. A moment later he slid back the rear hatch and disappeared 'below decks', as Mr B might have said. She watched as one light then another went on in the main cabin, or whatever you call those rooms on boats. It was time for her to drive around and enter the lion's den. Here goes, she thought. Wish me luck, Trev.

The lights on The Mary Fifi made her easy to locate. It was the only boat on the mooring with any life on board. Eleanor guessed that at this time of year not many people are inclined to mess about on the river. He'd obviously been keeping a watch on the towpath for her. Because when she was about ten paces away, he appeared from below and nimbly climbed onto the wooden jetty to greet her.

"Eleanor! You made it! How wonderful to welcome you to my

modest little home here on the Thames. Now, let me give you a hand."

Eleanor had to make a conscious effort not to shudder as he took hold of her forearm to guide her down the short gangplank he had carefully placed in position ready for her arrival. And she was pleased she had popped into her bag the Leatherman lookalike. The blade was not long enough to be an effective defensive weapon, but it was better than nothing.

"Thanks, Tim. No, really, I can manage, thank you. . . Wow! What a beautiful boat! Oh, sorry, or is it a ship?"

"My dear girl," he was smiling. "You are quite correct either way. Technically she's a boat. But also a little ship, as I was explaining this afternoon. She's the exact twin of The Mary Jane. Mind you, I've done a lot of work on her to bring her up to this condition. . . but how rude of me. Let me take your coat and then I'll get some drinks."

"Tim, look, I wonder if I might use your loo, first of all. After that journey. . . "

"Of course of course. It's this way."

Eleanor locked the door noting that the lock seemed substantial enough, and it wasn't the sort you could open from the outside. Then she checked her mobile to make sure she had a signal. Fine, just a precaution. Pity the window's too small to crawl through.

"Ah, Eleanor! I've poured you a glass of sherry; you will join me in one, won't you?"

"Of course, Tim. But what I would love you to do more than anything is to show me around."

"How remiss of me! Come with me. And do bring your glass with you. We'll start up for'ard and work our way back."

She enjoyed seeing the boat, all its facilities and nooks and crannies. But hearing about it was another matter. The Dope went into far too much detail, explaining how everything worked, and what he had to do to bring this or that piece of equipment – dating back to 1939, mind you – into good working order.

But for Eleanor, it was worth it. For one thing, she managed to spill her drink on several occasions without him noticing, so by the end of the tour her glass was empty. No point in taking chances, she thought. And she also managed to find precisely what she was looking for. It was next to the galley.

When they returned to the saloon, The Dope poured himself another sherry and launched into his prepared speech, the subtle one.

"Now, Eleanor, I know we shouldn't talk shop on such an occasion as this, but I wondered if I could ask your advice."

"Sure, Tim. I would be glad to help the new Director of Operations. What's it about?"

"Well, some years ago your erstwhile boss Richard Bentley sent that fellow Rayner a microfiche. We are not sure exactly what's on it, but we believe it contains some secret documents. Apparently, Rayner promised to return it once. . . er. . . your good-self returned from, from abroad. Sadly, Rayner passed away at the end of January, and we don't have the fiche, even though you are. . . well. . . here, safely in the mother country!"

"So how can I help?"

"I'm wondering. . . thinking. . . of how we might proceed. C is adamant we get the fiche back. I was wondering about a reward. I mean, if you had the fiche, for example, would you be tempted to return it if you were, somehow. . . rewarded?"

Eleanor was dumb-struck. Is this the best he could manage? God help the Secret Intelligence Service, she thought.

"Hmmm, Tim. That's a tricky one. A bit naughty of him to die, wasn't it? Only joking. Actually, Karen mentioned something about some documents this afternoon. About being sent to a solicitor in Geneva. My son – Gerald Rayner's son – works out there and apparently a load of stuff was bequeathed to him by Gerald. So the fiche might be amongst that lot."

"So you. . . you don't have the fiche yourself, by any chance?"

"Me? Good Lord no! If I did, I'd give it to you. The last thing I'd want is for the Service to be embarrassed by some secret documents going missing! I'm proud of the Service, as I am sure you are."

"Yes, of course, of course. So what would you suggest?"

"Well, Tim. I think we need to find out exactly who has the fiche at the moment. Would you like me to ask my son? I could text him now if you like. I mean, while I do that, you could be getting on with the cooking. It may take a little while to raise him. Children being put to bed and all that."

"What a good idea. Please excuse me – and do help yourself to some more sherry. You can talk to me when I'm in the galley, you know. It's only a little ship." He chuckled to himself.

"Thanks, Tim. Will do."

Eleanor proceeded to text Dan in Geneva: '*Can you confirm that you have received the fiche?*'

After a few minutes, she called out to The Dope, "Good news! He's confirmed it's at the lawyers in Geneva!"

The Dope was not overjoyed with the way things were going. He had hoped Eleanor would have produced the thing there and then, but he accepted it was a bit of a long shot getting the two birds together.

It would have to be Plan B. But that was what it was all about, being quick on your feet, adapting to a moving situation, like that time in Ireland. He would hold the Braithwaite woman hostage and not release her until the lawyer sent the fiche. Then he would let her go; might let her go if she were nice to him. Otherwise. . . You have to do what is necessary.

At least they were getting on well. His charm offensive had worked, and maybe she would help him. After all, it wouldn't look too good for her either if the Paris fiasco became public. She was the one who jumped ship; who ratted out wrecking the mission.

"Tim! Can you hear me?" Eleanor asked.

"I certainly can. Any further news?"

"Yeah. Just got another text from Dan. Good and bad, I'm afraid. Good that the fiche is definitely at the lawyers in Geneva. D'you want their name and address?"

"No, not at the moment. What's the bad news?"

"Dan's being a problem. Over-protective son, I'm afraid. He's worried about me. It's all to do with when I arrived in Sydney. I was picked out at random to be searched, and they detained me on suspicion of smuggling. I thought it was just a mix-up, but Dan thought I'd been deliberately targeted.

"Just like his father, in that respect. A bit of a fantasist. Anyway, he's told the lawyers to send the fiche to the Guardian if I'm not back in Geneva by Sunday night! Honestly, how dramatic can you get! But I've just texted him back to assure him I'll be back by then, and that I'm in good hands at the moment."

"What?" The Dope, ashen, came into the saloon where Eleanor was sitting with her phone. They looked at each other for a moment. "Sorry, Eleanor, I didn't quite catch that. The steak was sizzling. What did you tell him?"

She passed her phone over to him. He read the message: "*Thanx darling am with Director of Ops SIS having a lovely evening on Mary Fifi, a gorgeous little ship at Cookham. See you at airport on Fri as arranged xx.*"

He didn't realise that – like the other message – it had not been sent. Nor that none had been received.

The Dope looked crestfallen. He realised he would have to let her go. But he looked on the bright side. At least he'd established a good relationship with Eleanor, and he reckoned she realised it made sense to co-operate with him for once and not be her usual contrary self.

Eleanor knew she'd won this round but wanted to make sure. "Look, Tim. I know how much this means to you, and the Service.

I'm going to make sure the fiche gets back to you personally, just as soon as I get to Geneva. Monday morning, Dan and I will go to the lawyers, get the fiche and post it back to you registered mail; air mail. You should have it by Thursday at the latest. Believe you me, we are together on this one. I know we have had our disagreements, but this time I'm right with you."

"Thanks, Eleanor. I appreciate your frankness. I have a good feeling about this. I think it's going to end well. Just make sure you do get back to Geneva on time. And take care of yourself. We don't want anything happening to you in the meantime, do we!"

The meal was surprisingly good. Perhaps it wasn't going to be the last supper for the condemned woman, thought Eleanor. Tim was gracious and polite – for Tim – and although his conversation was tedious, he kept his famed misogynistic disdain for women under some degree of control.

The dessert, in those little plastic tubs from M & S, slipped down well, and when he offered coffee, she accepted, saying it would keep her awake on the drive back to London. Not that she was sleepy. She was still on Australian time.

Time to wake up.

13

Eleanor waited on the jetty while The Dope turned off the gas, flicked off the main switch, checked all windows and then locked the hatch behind him. She pretended to be rummaging in her handbag while she watched him replace the key.

They walked to the car park together. The Dope urged Eleanor to drive carefully and said how much he appreciated her agreement over the fiche. Eleanor thanked him for a wonderful dinner and the guided tour.

She drove out of the car-park, up to the bridge and across to the town. Then back to the car-park. Having made sure there was no-one around and no other car, she parked the hire car, opened the boot to do a final check of her equipment.

———————

As Tim drove back to his flat in London, he smiled. The evening had gone well. He'd won over the Braithwaite woman and manipulated her into doing his job for him, of getting hold of the fiche. With any luck, the damn thing would be on his desk by the end of the week.

In the meantime, there wasn't a great deal he could do. He hoped he might return to The Mary Fifi on Sunday and take her out for a spin. Let her have some air. His planned trip on her, that night with the Braithwaite woman, upstream, under cover of darkness, would have to wait for another time. At least until he had the fiche.

––––––––––––––––––

In the deserted car-park, leaning into the boot of the hire car with her head-torch on, Eleanor plugged the lamp and the fan into the two remote switching devices which she had previously plugged into the power supply unit. She'd already downloaded the app onto the new phone, and now she tried it out again. One-ON. One-OFF. Two-ON. Two-OFF. Perfect.

It was time to test the monitor. In the low light-level in the boot of the hire car, it worked as well as it did in the shop. She was amazed at the clarity of the image. And the range. Her walk-past test confirmed it could detect movement out to fifteen paces which was more than adequate for her purpose.

The last check was with the remaining modified bulb. In her hotel room, she had prepared two, by very carefully crushing the glass. The first time she tried it, using the combination tool as a hammer, she had also crushed the element. The second time she placed the little bulb between the jaws of the pliers and gently squeezed. And then again with the last of her bulbs, thus ending up with two bulbs each with an intact element but without any glass around it. She'd tried one in the lamp and switched it on. The bulb lasted less than half a second before the unprotected element flashed itself into nothingness in a shower of sparks.

She had only the one left, so she could not repeat that test in the car park. All she could do was to inspect the element carefully in the light of her torch. It looked good, and using the pliers in the Leatherman combination tool, she carefully replaced the standard bulb in the lamp with the modified one. All she needed to do now was to gain entry.

Her plan had been to use the jack handle to force the hatch open. But now she knew where he kept the key, getting in would be easy. So with a spring in her stride, she set off from the car park with her bag of goodies, down to the towpath and back to the boat.

The difficult part was finding her way around without putting on any lights. But as her eyes got used to it, she could just make out the various items of ship's furniture and fittings which were of importance to her. And during her tour, guided by Tim a few hours previously, she had made an effort to remember the layout of the boat.

It didn't take her long to set up the various elements of her plan. It had been easy because she had scoped it. It reminded her of Mr B's puncture on the way to the airport. If you think it through beforehand, pretending you are there doing it, you are much less likely to make a mistake, or forget some vital element. But would it work? She was not sure.

By 2:30 a.m she was back at the Holiday Inn in West London. Nobody took any notice of her when she walked into reception to pick up her room key; the place was as busy as ever catering for stop-overs and short stays rather than holidaymakers. Fifteen minutes later she was asleep with both her mobiles on and on charge.

She surfaced at nine, read the papers over her Full English Breakfast, then ordered a taxi to take her to Tommy's. It was outside visiting hours, but Eleanor was able to have a quiet word with the girl on reception who phoned through to the ward sister.

Karen had been moved to a public ward, and looked none too happy about it. But Eleanor told it to her straight; you might be in danger. She quietly explained about The Dope, his history in The Falklands and Northern Ireland – and south of the border with special forces when he was a young man, barely out of school. How some of those operations, which were not out of the book and did not follow any convention, had hardened him – brutalised him – and possibly desensitised him to the sanctity of human life. It happens to some.

The success of those operations in strategic terms had earned him accolades and promotion which, in her opinion, had taken him beyond his level of competence: the Peter Principle in action. Some people were able to get through such experiences without it affecting their moral compass. Others, like Tim Turnbull, could not. He was a toughy, and when it came to matters of judgement, he would take the tough line, on the basis that it had worked for him in the past. This made him unpredictable and prone to doing silly and dangerous things. That's why Karen had been moved.

She thanked Eleanor for her candour and said it was a privilege to be talking to her like this, one to one. Eleanor, too, was grateful for the opportunity to share some of her experiences and concerns with a kindred spirit. She told Karen a little about Gerald, how they met, and what had happened at the leisure centre. It made Karen laugh. And Karen made Eleanor laugh when she recounted her meeting with him at a birthday lunch and the deal they did on the train afterwards.

They got on well. When it was time for Eleanor to go, she wished Karen a speedy recovery and said she would like to keep in touch. Karen said that would be great, and they swapped phone numbers.

14

Eleanor hoped Dan had not been waiting too long at Geneva Airport as it was approaching bedtime for the children and he would want to be back home helping Helen.

As she emerged through the automatic doors into Arrivals there was a surprise waiting for her. Dan was there – and Helen and Josh and Lucy. Dan wasn't holding up a millboard, but the two children were holding up a banner saying "Welcome Home Grandma!"

It was a good reunion. The children being there was a special treat for them as there was no school in the morning. Helen was enormous, but looking well and happy. And the children wanted to hear all about Grandma's adventures down under.

While Dan went off to pick up the car, Eleanor fished the presents out of one of her suitcases. Lucy loved her binoculars, and Josh thought his combination toolkit was 'epic'. They then made their way towards the exit and the pick-up bays, Josh carefully wheeling the heavily laden trolley.

Dan showed off his new car to his mum.. New to him, he explained. It was a people-carrier big enough to carry the family, all six of us, he said, plus pushchairs and all the accoutrements which a newborn would need. So there was plenty of room for Eleanor's luggage.

On the way back, Helen asked Eleanor if she would like to come for a 'sleepover' at their flat rather than go back to her place, but Eleanor replied she would be better off at her flat as she was still a bit jet-lagged and wanted to sort out her washing and get settled in again.

And she thought about the new mobile in her bag, the one linked to the monitor and remote switches. She worried it might be activated the following morning, and she thought about what she might do if it did suddenly come to life showing her an image of the main cabin of the Mary Fifi with a man walking down the companionway.

It seemed so simple while she was there, to eliminate the threat, to protect Karen from another nasty accident, and to achieve justice for her husband. But now she did wonder if she would go through with it.

Eleanor was grateful to Lucy for interrupting her thoughts and asking her if she might like to join them on Sunday for lunch on a paddle-steamer which would take them on a tour of the lake.

"Ooh, yes please, Lucy! I would love to do that. Tell me about the boat."

"Well, it's called the Simpleton-"

"The Simplon," Josh corrected her, pronouncing it correctly in the French way: Samplon, with the 'n' disappearing into the back of the throat to give the nasal sound. "Built in 1920," he added, "that's almost a hundred years ago! And she has a fourteen hundred horse-power engine!"

Lucy rolled her eyes. "We get on it here in Geneva, and it takes us to Lausanne and back, and they give us lunch on board!"

"Wow, it sounds like fun!" Eleanor turned to Helen. "Thanks, Helen, that would be nice. Thank you."

That Saturday for Eleanor was good and bad. Good to be back from behind enemy lines. Bad she had to face up to what she might have to do. She kept looking at her phone, the new one with the app which would operate the camera and switches on board the Mary Fifi. She expected it to leap into life at any moment. But it didn't.

She half hoped the battery had run out, or some other malfunction might unburden her of the awful decision she would otherwise have to make. And then she remembered she could switch the monitoring camera on herself from her phone. She did so. The image appeared, as clear as an HD TV screen. Nothing wrong there. And not a sign of life on board.

Emboldened by her ability to control the monitor, she thought she would try operating the remote switch she had plugged the fan into. She selected the option from the main menu, then hesitated when it asked her which appliance she wanted to operate. She was pretty confident the fan was One. Or was it Two?

She held her breath and selected One-ON. After a second or two she heard the distinct sound of a fan whirling. Then she chose One-OFF. The whirling sound died down and stopped. She was pleased she had made the thing work. Sort-of pleased.

It was mid-afternoon when the monitor phone pinged. She grabbed it from the coffee table beside her, and her heart started pounding when she looked at the image. Nothing had changed, but she heard the sound of a chugging engine. It was getting louder. Slowly it began to fade, until all she could hear through the phone was the quiet lapping of waves against the hull. These too died down. Then a message appeared on the screen: Switch off Monitor? Yes/No. She chose yes, sat back and relaxed.

Her mobile rang, the normal one, but it still made her jump. It was Helen asking if she would like to come over for supper, read the children a bedtime story, then stay overnight so they could all leave together in the morning to go down to the quay. Dan will come and pick you up, and would six be OK? I'd love to, she replied and went into her bedroom to pack her overnight bag, remembering to include both phones and chargers.

She woke early that Sunday morning. She wasn't sure if it was the remains of her jet lag or the worries about her plans. As she was anxious not to disturb the household she just lay there, faced up to her concerns and went through them in her mind, one at a time, as Mr B might have done.

Firstly, the technical side of things. She knew little about such matters, but the electronics – the monitoring camera, the two switch units and the mobile phone – all seemed to be working fine. The electrical devices – the power unit, the fan and the lamp – were all OK, although she couldn't be sure about the modified bulb. It looked OK, but she might have damaged the exposed filament while putting it into the lamp.

Then there was the whole concept of the thing. Before leaving the boat – for the second time that night – she had checked the gas was slowly escaping from the cylinder but it was a complete guess as to whether enough would leak out to do the job.

Being heavier than air, it would fill the boat from the bilges up to the vents on the deck – if there was enough of it. But she hadn't the faintest idea how long she should run the fan before detonation. She knew there had to be a mixture of air and gas to initiate an explosion because a spark in pure propane would be just that, a spark: without oxygen, there would be no explosion. As for the effects, she was reasonably confident they would be powerful enough to cause extensive damage. She knew about fuel-air bombs and how devastating they can be.

Secondly, she was still concerned about herself. She had no idea how she would feel about it when the time came to select Two-ON from the options on the screen, the one that would switch on the lamp. Would she be doing the right thing? Was it right to kill Timothy Turnbull, Director of Operations, Secret Intelligence Service? Was it justified?

At times during the last few days she had felt she had no option; it was her duty to prevent the greater evil of him murdering others, like Karen, who had done nothing to deserve it except get in his way. And where would he stop? Did her son, Dan, know too much for Turnbull's liking? Would he be under threat? And perhaps Helen and the children might get caught up in some hair-brained operation to silence her or Dan and end up as collateral damage.

At other times she tried to see it from Turnbull's point of view. He had a job to do. Not an easy one: and if he wasn't very good at his job, was that his fault? Were his experiences a mitigating factor in any way? Could he be forgiven for being a tough nut, for grasping the nettle, stamping out the fire, or any other metaphor for taking direct, swift action to prevent a greater harm to his nation which it was his duty to protect?

Her final worry was how she would be judged by others. It was not that she cared what people thought of her, but it was a litmus test. A test on her own judgement. The circumstances prevented her from discussing the matter with others, so she had no way of canvassing the opinion of the tribe, or perhaps the herd or the flock.

She remembered reading about the anti-war march in London in early 2003 that tried to persuade Tony Blair against invading Iraq. Over a million people took part, and for each one who did there were perhaps ten others who supported it. Few of them as individuals understood all the factors and all the issues involved, but together as a group they did. But Tony Blair turned a blind eye to the collective wisdom of the nation and started a war.

She had no such collective wisdom to guide her – and while she hoped the man in the street might support her intended action, she guessed her chances of being found innocent in a court of law were zero. There was the Doctrine of Necessity which justifies an illegal act if it prevents a greater evil, but not against a charge of murder.

Also, for the defence to be valid, the greater evil had to be imminent. She had no doubt that Turnbull – with his high rank in one of the greatest intelligence services in the world and with all his contacts in other services and in the military – had the experience and the capability to use lethal force whenever and wherever his warped judgement might demand it.

So, her intended action passed the imminence test – in her view. The final test was whether the greater evil which she foresaw could be prevented in any another way. Telling the Police? Demanding an interview with C? Leaking the whole thing to the Press? She concluded that her planned action was necessary.

"Grandma, I've brought you some tea." It was Lucy.

"Good morning, darling! How very kind of you!"

"I've already put sugar in it."

"I'm sure it'll be delicious." Eleanor waited until Lucy had left the room before tipping the contents of the saucer back into the cup. One mouthful of the sweet liquid was enough to make her wide awake and give her enough incentive to jump out of bed and into the en-suite bathroom.

15

The children raced ahead to join the queue boarding the Simplon. The weather was typical for the time of year, bright, warm sunshine, yet the mountain peaks around the lake still retained their white caps of snow in stark contrast to the vivid blue of clear sky behind them.

Around the shores of the lake the trees were beginning to show a slight tinge of green, a sure indication they were starting to spring back to life. A soft breeze gently ruffled the water, but there were no waves. The passage would be smooth.

Eleanor tried to join in the conversation and show an interest in Josh's explanation about the engine, and to help Lucy guess what they might be having for lunch. But Eleanor's mind was on another boat. She realised that if The Dope were to visit The Mary Fifi at all this weekend, there was a high chance it would be this morning.

If it had to happen, she would prefer to be alone in her flat rather than on a pleasure steamer with her family. But she had no choice. So she made up her mind to forget about The Dope and his boat and concentrate on enjoying the trip, the good weather, the fine views and the company. If 'it' happens, it happens. If it doesn't, or if I miss the activation for some reason, that'll be fate, she thought.

They were all standing on deck when the ship pulled away from the quay, finally on its way to Lausanne. Josh persuaded Eleanor to lean over the railings so she could see the 'actual paddles' thrashing round as they propelled the vessel forwards.

"Come on, Grandma. Let's go and see the engine!"

"Good idea, Josh! Which way do we go?" She looked back at Helen, just to check that Helen and Dan knew she had Josh, and with good humour, she let Josh drag her off.

"This way, Grandma. . . Just look at that! Cool!"

They were overlooking the exposed engine bay. Josh launched into a detailed explanation of how steam in the two great big cylinders pushed out the pistons and turned the huge crank which turned the paddles. Eleanor found it much more interesting than the lecture aboard The Mary Fifi. But eventually, the smell of the hot oil and the noise of the machinery persuaded both of them it was time to go back on deck.

Eleanor was leaning against the railings watching the foaming water slipping past the hull, with Lucy on one side and Josh on the other. Dan was with Helen behind her, making good use of the deck chairs.

Eleanor wasn't sure that the sound she heard was from her new phone, so she took it out of her bag to check. Her heart started racing. It was him on the screen: Action Man, The Dope, Timothy Turnbull, climbing down the steps into the main saloon of The Mary Fifi. She hoped the children hadn't heard him when the monitor picked up him saying, "What the fuck?"

But she didn't have time for speculating on such matters. From the menu on the bottom of her screen she selected One-ON, and when she heard the noise of the fan, she selected Two-ON. She noticed that The Dope had half turned, just before she heard the whumph and the screen went orange. Then almost immediately it went blank. A message appeared: 'connection failed'.

She looked across the lake at the far shore, her hands hanging limply over the rail. She let the mobile slip from her hand and drop over the side of the Simplon into the water of Lake Geneva, as the paddles propelled the steamer along at a steady twelve knots. She was confident no-one had noticed.

"Darlings, if you don't mind I'm going to sit down for a while with Mummy and Daddy."

Eleanor tried to work out how she felt. She knew The Dope had boarded The Mary Fifi and opened the hatch, as that is what had activated the monitor. She had even seen his image and his face when he'd started descending the steps into the main cabin. And she'd heard his voice and then what sounded like an explosion, and she'd seen the orange flash. So she felt reasonably confident the technology had worked. Whether she had achieved her objective, she could not say, but she guessed the probability was high that the mission had been accomplished.

It was a strange sensation. Despite her worries earlier, she felt she'd done the right thing: no regrets, no guilt, no remorse. Now, on board the Simplon, she felt a sense of calmness but no grief at all for Timothy Turnbull. Just a deep sorrow for all those who had suffered at his hand. For her precious Trevor. For Karen, for the teenaged girl he had cheese-wired in South Armagh because she had stumbled into his ambush and might have wrecked his operation. For the three Argentinian prisoners whom he gunned down to save him the bother of organising their transport back to base. And for others who might have suffered similar fates.

There was no proof, of course, that he had done these things, just rumours. Horrible things happen in war however you define 'war', and possibly, in times of conflict, circumstances could arise which justified such killings. Perhaps Timothy Turnbull did those things so he would achieve his mission, but Eleanor wondered if he was driven by loyalty to Queen and Country or by the personal ambitions of Timothy Turnbull.

Enough of that, she said to herself, and got up from her deck-chair and disappeared. A few minutes later she came back and went up to Josh. "I have something important to tell you!"

"What is it, Grandma?"

"The Captain has invited you to join him on the bridge."

"Wow!" he said, grabbing Grandma's hand and dragging her aft towards the centre on the ship.

It went down well. The Captain explained to Josh how the speed of the ship was controlled by this lever here, and how the engines were made to run in reverse by pulling another lever if you need to go backwards.

Josh was allowed to pull the cord above his head and was delighted to hear the high-pitched 'oooh' of the ship's steam whistle. And finally, under the careful supervision of the helmsman, Josh was allowed to take the wheel. The bright smile on his face took Eleanor's mind off the other matter. But when they returned to join the others, the thoughts resurfaced.

Was Timothy Turnbull just as much a victim as the others, in that his role and circumstances forced him into carrying out those extra-judicial killings? She could not say. Could her killing of Timothy Turnbull also be termed an extra-judicial killing? An eye for an eye, a tooth for a tooth, and an extra-judicial killing for a number of extra-judicial killings, she thought. Then another Biblical quote came to her mind. Those who live by the sword shall die by the sword.

———

Eleanor woke early on morning following the boat trip. She loved staying with Dan and Helen but on this particular morning, she was glad to be in her own bed, at home. She had slept well and had come to terms with what had happened, but her training told her the assignment was not over until the results had been validated. She needed closure.

So when she went to her little corner shop at lunchtime to get the English papers, she was disappointed not to see news of her achievement emblazoned across the front pages: 'PSYCHOPATH SPY KILLED BY OWN BOAT', or 'REAL-LIFE BOND BLOWN AWAY'.

But she bought the papers anyway – all of them, and returned to her flat to read them. Only the Mirror had a mention, hidden deeply in the middle pages, hardly a column-inch.

> 'Boat blast kills Mary Jane's twin. The Mary Jane, one of the 'Little Ships' which sailed to Dunkirk to help evacuate our boys from the beaches there, might have had a lucky escape, because a look-alike built at the same time was blown up on Sunday, not by a Luftwaffe bomb but by a leaking gas bottle. It happened near Maidenhead, Berkshire, on the River Thames.'

It was frustrating for her. Events on Sundays rarely received good coverage on Mondays, so she accepted she would have to wait until the following day to find out more. Surely, she thought, if someone had died they would have mentioned it. But then she realised there were other explanations. Perhaps he was trapped in the boat which had sunk, or the blast had blown him overboard and his body was gently floating down the Thames disguised as a log. Or that somehow he had survived.

Her worst fears were confirmed the following day. Again she had bought all the English papers – from another shop – and taken them home to read. Again, no big headlines, but tucked away in the middle of The Times was a small article describing what had happened.

> A man was critically injured on Sunday morning in a gas explosion on board a small pleasure craft moored on the Thames at Cookham, near Maidenhead. His name has not been released but he is believed to be the owner of the boat which was destroyed in the blast. He was found in the reeds next to the towpath two hundred metres downstream of the mooring, alive but unconscious. He was taken by ambulance to the local hospital with fractures and burns. Foul play is not suspected.

The article went on to describe the boat as being the twin of a famous 'little ship', The Mary Jane, which had rescued etc. etc.. It then recounted the danger of gas installations on small vessels, and how important it is to have gas appliances professionally installed and inspected in accordance with gas safety regulations. In this case, the boat had not been lived in, but a spokesman for Cookham Country Club which owns the moorings said cooking smells had been reported coming from the boat the previous Thursday evening suggesting the gas was in use at that time and had not been turned off.

Eleanor sighed. In some ways she was relieved she hadn't killed him. Another side of her hoped he would die of his injuries. But whatever the outcome, she had at least tried, and the loss of his treasured Mary Fucking Fifi was, in a very small way, some payback for Trevor.

As promised, she went and joined the family that evening for an early supper followed by a made-up bedtime story. While the children were getting ready for bed, Eleanor relaxed on the sofa and picked up Dan and Helen's daily paper. It was The Times. She could not resist turning to the article and reading it again.

Josh appeared. "Grandma, what's that you're reading?"

"It's The Times, Daddy's paper."

"But what are you reading about?"

"Oh, it's just some report on a boat that blew up because the owner had forgotten to turn off the gas."

"Blew up? Wow! Is there a picture?"

"No, darling."

He thought for a moment. "What's the boat's name?"

"I'm afraid it doesn't say."

"It should've been Napoleon!" he said with a bright smile.

"Why's that, darling?"

"Napoleon Blown-apart!" Eleanor looked at him. She could not raise a smile, even a pretend one. She wasn't in a laughing mood.

"It's a joke!. . . I made it up!. . . You see, his real name was Napoleon Bonaparte. We're doing him at school. . . Do you get it?. . . You see, blown apart sounds a bit like Bonaparte."

Eleanor put him out of his embarrassed misery. "Oh, I get it!

Yes, that's very clever. Ha! I like it! Blown apart!. . . Now, where's that sister of yours? It's time for our story."

"Grandma?"

"Yes, Josh?"

"Do you. . . do you have any secrets?"

"Secrets? Well! That's an interesting question! Because if you have a secret, it's best not to tell anyone you have a secret. So if you do happen to have one, the answer would be 'no'. And if you don't have a secret, the answer is also 'no'.

"So, young man, what do you think my answer would be to your question? What do you think I would say?" She was pleased she avoided the need to tell him an outright lie.

"It would be 'No', Grandma." He thought for a moment. "Grandma, why did you drop your mobile phone over the side of the ship this morning?"

"Drop my phone?" She felt her heart rate rise. "My mobile?" She reached into her handbag. "Look, here is my phone! And, hey. Hang on a mo. . . Look at this! It's one of you steering the ship."

"Grandma?"

"Yes, darling." She braced herself.

"When I grow up I want to be the captain of a paddle-steamer!"

16

A week later Eleanor got a text from Karen: '*Big boy dropped in this morning. Nice man. Kind of him. Have given him recipe which pleased him. Said I'd done well. BTW thanks for sending it. Told me Dopey was in intensive care cos his thingy went pop! Making good progress. How are you?*'

Eleanor replied: '*All good thanks. Send regards to big chap. Sorry Dopey poorly.*' She wanted to add 'rather than dead', but didn't. '*Keep me informed of progress.*'

She had to admit she was worried. Things hadn't worked out as planned. But she recalled the words of her instructor: shit happens – deal with it. Then her think-tank training kicked in and she what-iffed it.

As The Dope was in intensive care, it was extremely unlikely he would soon be out and about – at large, she thought, like an escaped lunatic. Indeed, if someone is critically injured, there's a chance they won't make it. But if he pulls through he's likely to remain in hospital for quite a few weeks. Burns take a long time.

So no rush. Not yet. But she made up her mind to use the time constructively to scope all possibilities. Perhaps he wouldn't have a clue how his precious boat had 'popped'. But the one she needed to concentrate on was the other one. That he saw the desk lamp, the fan, and possibly the baby monitor, and put two and two together. Even The Dope could sometimes come up with four.

Put yourself in his shoes, she thought. He might be a trifle upset she'd destroyed the love of his life, perhaps his one constructive achievement on this mortal coil. And he might not be too pleased she'd nearly killed him and caused him pain. Physical pain but also the pain of loss, of bereavement, not only for some silly old boat but for lost opportunities to fulfil life-long ambitions, to realise dreams, to become C, someone who is remembered. And he might react. Perhaps like a wounded animal.

He's going to try to kill me. Like I tried to kill him.

And for the first time she recognised that among her many motives for trying to kill him – to defend herself and others like Karen, to rid the Service and the world of an evil, to achieve justice for those he had killed – there was pure, unadulterated revenge for Trevor. Then she remembered a quote from one of her favourite books, The Girl With the Dragon Tattoo: 'To exact revenge for yourself or your friends is not only a right, it's an absolute duty'. She felt better.

She then thought: if I have the right of revenge, surely he does too – even though he's a shit of the first order. And she felt worse. And frightened. Not the selfish fear for what might happen to her, but of a mother fearing for her child and a grandmother fearing for Josh, Lucy and the little one due in two weeks' time. She'd destroyed something of Turnbull's which was precious to him. She had to face the question of whether he would he seek out and destroy something of hers which she loved and cherished.

She ached for the opportunity of talking through her dilemma with somebody, anybody; but this was impossible. It wasn't the sort of problem you could discuss with your doctor, your shrink if you have one, your local bobby or your parish priest if you were that way inclined. As for friends and loved ones, there was no way she'd frighten the life out of them by suggesting they might be in danger from a madman – or at least from someone who had killed before and would kill again.

You're on your own, gal, she said to herself. If only Mr B was around. He'd know what to do. But she told herself you know how he would have set about dealing with the matter; do what he would have done.

"Mr Turnbull! Mr Turnbull?" He could just make out a blurry image of someone bending over him. "You're in hospital, dear. You've had an accident."

Don't call me dear, he thought. Just stop this pain. It hurt to speak. His arm was agony. It hurt to open his eyes, to close them. He couldn't feel his legs.

"You're in the Royal Berkshire Hospital in Reading. Can you hear me?" He just managed to nod. "Are you in pain?"

Of course, I'm in pain, you stupid idiot, he wanted to say, but the dressings on his face made coherent speech impossible. He nodded again. He tried to raise his right arm, but it was restrained by something. Ah, he thought, that's slightly better, as the morphine pump was turned up a notch.

He had no idea how long he'd been there. He had vague memories of going to The Mary Fifi – must have been Sunday morning – and opening up and smelling the sickly smell of petroleum gas. Then a flash. . . Cold water, very cold. Swimming, and trying to stand, and to grasp the tufts of grass as he slowly drifted passed them.

He remembered his knees sliding along a muddy bank, his hands grabbing a tree root and hanging on, as the current swung him further into the bank. Crawling on all fours onto the bank, then the intense pain, then nothing – until this nurse woke him up just now.

At C's insistence, Karen was moved back to a private room at Tommy's. She much preferred it, especially when she had visitors. The consultant had explained to her, gently, the likely prognosis.

Karen found it hard to take: the strong possibility of being a spook with a limp for the rest of her career.

She understood that ankles and feet aren't meant to be crushed under the tyres of a 40-ton truck even though they're made of rubber. The good news was the scars on her face were superficial and would heal in their own in time. And the chipped elbow, well, she would just have to get used to that; the tenderness would go in time.

A colleague came to bring her flowers and the statutory bunch of grapes which they tucked into as they chatted. Karen learned that The Dope was in a bad way and was likely to be in hospital for at least eight weeks. He'd been severely burnt on the left side of his face, and his man-made fibre trousers had melted into his skin. Apparently, if he hadn't been blown into the water he would not have survived.

There wasn't a great deal of sympathy for him at Vauxhall Cross. His secretary was positively chirpy, and very soon after the news of his accident there were the usual grim jokes doing the rounds: his injuries were being blown out of all proportion, well blow me down, that's some blow-job Mary Fifi gave him – and of course his new name: petroleum blown-apart, which was as much a reflection of his leadership style as it was of the nature of the accident.

Karen was bucked up to hear the rumour he might not return as D-Ops when he was discharged. As for her getting back to work, she could hardly wait. C had been most encouraging, saying that everyone was missing her and that she was a highly valued member of the team and had much to offer the Service. And she thought with The Dope out of the way, driving a desk at Legoland might not be so bad. She enjoyed her text exchanges with Eleanor and hoped they would meet up again.

"Well, well, Tim, what have you been up to?" It was C, his boss.

It was difficult for The Dope to talk because of the injuries to his face, but he explained to C that the person who installed the stove had obviously not done it properly.

"Good Lord, Tim, that's terrible. But I thought you told me you'd done all the work yourself? Anyway, I have some good news. Karen got that microfiche back for us. It's safely under lock and key."

The Dope explained – as best as he could – that he knew Karen would succeed if she followed his instructions.

"But I thought she'd misfiled it?" C asked.

Again The Dope struggled, but he was adamant she had lied about losing it to cover up her stupid mistake of sending it back to that man in Geneva.

"Tim, be careful not to tire yourself. You've had a bad accident, and you need to build up your strength. Don't worry about us. We'll manage. You just concentrate on getting well again."

Finally, the Dope asked C how she was. When C replied that Karen was doing fine, the Dope didn't like to say he meant his Mary Fifi.

No-one else visited the Dope, except the duty officer every Thursday. And his driver, once, to drop off some stuff at Reception for him which he had specifically requested, from his office and from his flat. Among the bits and pieces he had asked for was a picture of a boat. It was all that remained of it.

The birth went according to plan. Dan was there, and it reminded him of the episode in Gerald's story about him hearing the faint cry of a new-born baby in the French hospital. It must have been a long way off, thought Dan, listening to Isaac, his second son, practising his newly acquired skill of breathing in air and bawling his head off.

Despite her previous revulsion at the thought of another brother, Lucy adored him from the start. Josh was delighted because the disaster of another sister had been averted. Helen and Dan were relieved all had gone well and that Zak was healthy and complete. And Eleanor was pleased with her new-found role as a hands-on part-living-in granny, nanny and general help. She needed the distraction.

Karen kept Eleanor informed of her progress. And that of The Dope, although few of her visitors seemed to care about him. But he was off the critical list. Neither Karen nor Eleanor thought this was good news, although neither mentioned it.

The Dope must have been improving because he was beginning to get bored. There wasn't much he could do, just lying there, and because his eyes were less painful when closed, he couldn't read or watch television for long. So he would just lay there with his thoughts, grieving for his Mary Fifi. All that work. All that money.

It was good the fiche was back. Bad the other bird – the other source of evidence – had flown away to Switzerland. A difficult country to operate in; few 'old chums' there, he thought. But somehow he had to eliminate the danger to him and the Service if the bird were to squawk.

Another thought troubling him was how he could possibly have installed that stove wrongly. He'd checked every joint. Or had he forgotten to turn the gas off at the bottle?

He went through his actions the night the Braithwaite woman came down. After coffee, he'd cleared away the cups and put them in the sink with the plates and frying pan and saucepan. He thought he'd turned off the gas, then the lights at the main switch as usual. Braithwaite left the craft ahead of him and waited for him on the bank while he locked up, put the key back in its hiding place, and. . .

Surely not, he thought. A woman, arranging a stunt like that? Anyway, she'd flown back to Switzerland on the next day. Then it dawned on him. She'd had an accomplice and told him where the key was, and he had planted some sort of bomb on board, wired up to a control point.

"The gitch! That ucking GASTARD GITCH!".". He didn't realise he was shouting, despite the pain. The duty nurse came running.

"Mr Turnbull! Are you okay?"

"Er, yes, I'n okay. Just had a nasty drean. Sorry."

Detailed planning didn't come to him easily. He was more of a seat-of-the-pants man. He knew the plan would have to be a good one, with a back-up in case things went wrong. It would be all his own work; no more relying on third-rate deadbeats, retired Walter Mittys, and certainly not The Increment. And none of that form filling, for fuck's sake!

The concept began forming in his mind. It needed to include an element of punishment to make her realise the terrible wrong she had done him – and the Service of course. Yes, he thought, punishment to fit the crime. And he began humming the Mikardo melody.

It would involve petroleum of some sort, and he would also take out what was precious to her. He hoped she would suffer a lingering death, long enough to realise her loved ones were going with her. As for collateral damage: get real, it happens.

As the weeks went by, his plans – A and B – developed, were modified and refined. His injuries were slowly healing, and he was told he might be discharged before the end of June. He told the good news to C when he came to visit him for the second time.

" You'll be glad to hear I'm being 'released' in June!" He could now talk properly. Almost.

"Ah! Well, that's good news." C's face looked as if he'd just been told his Labrador had died.

"But Tim, I'm anxious about you. You've been through a lot. I'm going to put you on sick leave, to allow you to convalesce, to get better. . ."

"How long had you in mind?" the Dope asked, fearing being out of the loop for too long, should C decide to hang up his hat.

"Let's just see how it goes, shall we? Now, here's a little present for you. I guess you don't have one, and these days we all need one!"

The Dope winced at the pain caused by his broad smile when he took the box out of the bag. It was a mobile phone. He was dreading it was a gold watch or its equivalent. "Thank you, thank you! Just what I need!"

"And the contract's on the house, by the way," C added. "It's all set up."

This will make planning a lot easier, The Dope thought. And the sick leave? An opportunity on a plate. He thanked C again as his boss turned and walked out of the ward.

"Hi Tom, Tim here. . . Well, getting there you know. . . No, Tom, a total loss. . . You don't happen to have Wayne's number do you?"

It was one of many phone calls he made in re-establishing his 'network', a collection of oddballs from whom he could 'call in favours', as he termed it. In reality, they were too frightened to refuse him. They knew he'd shop them or stuff them in some other way if they didn't do his bidding.

Among these were some 'old friends' from Paris, who were awfully kind in finding out for him some addresses in France. He liked France but didn't like Paris. It had been nearly twenty years, but the bad memories still haunted him. But what better way of convalescing than to visit another area of France, he thought, far away from that awful city. He'd heard that mountains in summer could be quite beautiful. And a little dangerous, if you're not careful.

He liked the name of the small town in the Haute Savoie. The Seven Mountains. Or in French 'Les Sept Montagnes', although it was usually referred to by its name in the local dialect: Samoens.

17

Eleanor knew what Mr B would have advised: 'the best form of attack is defence', quite the reverse of the well-known military maxim dating back to the American Civil War – and still evident in US military thinking.

He would, of course, have qualified his advice by explaining that if the forces are equal in strength, it's often better to let the opponent make the first move. Like in tennis, he had once said to Eleanor. He used to enjoy it when he was much younger but was never any good. He could run around the court and get the ball over the net but failed on accuracy and power. Yet he was quite successful, at the tennis party level, on a grass court in someone's garden in Sunningdale after a glass or two Pimms. His secret was not to attempt the winning line-shot, but just to get the ball back and let his opponent make the mistakes.

She also knew he would have been upset she was contemplating another attack on her adversary. He would have warned her about the cycle of revenge and urged her to see the situation from the other person's point of view. He would have advised her to bide her time. To wait. To let her adversary make the first move, to declare his hand, to raise his head above the parapet, show his colours. Then it would be the time for her to seize the initiative, surprise him, and drive her attack home.

In the meantime? Watch, and wait. Take precautions, be on guard. Don't underestimate your enemy.

While Eleanor was concerned about what The Dope might do, she was determined not to let it get to her. She'd scoped the worst scenario, but there were many others. And while he remained in hospital there was little he could do. Also, she felt safe in Switzerland, in Geneva; it was not as if it were a location with a high crime rate, where corrupt police were stretched to breaking point, where violence was just accepted as the norm. Although The Dope was a bit of a dope, he was not completely stupid. He was ambitious, aiming for the top job. He would make sure he didn't get caught.

Rather like she had.

Two things happened which raised her concern during the early part of the summer. The first was that Karen had texted her the 'brilliant' news that dopey was being released into the wild on 16th June. The second was that Dan had announced they would all be going down to the chalet in Samoens during the half-term break to have some fun.

Josh and Lucy were quite excited about the prospect. They had enjoyed winter holidays in France for three years, staying in the chalet next to the Rayner's, but the young ones had yet to experience the delights of Samoens in the Summer. Helen was happy with the plan, although she realised she would for much of the time be constrained by the demands of Zak, the latest addition to the Braithwaite family.

Eleanor was less thrilled. They all pleaded with her to come, but she had to weigh up whether they would be safer without her – or with her there. France was not Switzerland, and he has contacts in France, she thought. At least she knew there was a danger, whereas Dan and the Helen did not, and she wasn't about to wreck their summer with that knowledge.

She decided to go – and to enjoy it. Dan heard Julie would be there at the same time in the next-door chalet, with her younger daughter Fiona and her two little ones. Safety in numbers, thought Eleanor; seven pairs of eyes and ears.

Dan planned lots of activities for the older two children, rafting, crazy golf, the jungle gym and swimming in the lake, and of course, he would join in. For a grand finale, Dan had booked one night's accommodation for them all in a high mountain refuge only accessible up a steep mountain track, among the cows grazing on their summer pastures. Eleanor felt they would at least be safe up there, out of harm's way.

The Dope didn't mind the drive from London down to Dover, then the ferry across to Calais and the leg down to the French Alps. The holiday season hadn't really begun, and the autoroutes were almost empty compared to the motorways in South-East England. He was in his own car, which he loved driving, and he was able to pack away in the boot some items which he thought might be useful for the mission.

He had to stop a couple of times to fill up, and the smell of the petrol as it flowed through the nozzle of the pump into his tank made him feel quite sick. It had been over two months since the accident; yet whenever he smelt petrol it had that effect.

He had booked himself into a little guest house in a hamlet just outside Samoens, as he was anxious not to bump into Braithwaite before he carried out the other bumping he planned, the bumping off. However, he would find out where the two chalets were during his first evening. He thought the recce ought to be carried out under the cover of darkness, as the scars on his face did attract attention.

Nobody ever said to him things like 'whatever have you done to your face?' They just stared and said nothing, but afterwards, they probably said to their friends 'did you see that man with those dreadful scars?' It wasn't sympathy he was after, nor did their pity bother him. He just didn't want to be remembered.

The target arrived in the village on Day 3, by which time The

Dope had recced two observation posts from which he could study the house and watch movements from a safe distance. Having identified their car by watching their comings and goings during their first full day, Day 4, he was able to venture into the little cul-de-sac late that night and attach the tracking device.

The activities Dan planned had gone down well. Eleanor had been enchanted by the village, and Helen was getting to grips with handling the baby, ably assisted by Lucy. Julie and Fiona had kindly offered to have Zak for the one night they would be up the mountain, and Helen gratefully accepted. A night's uninterrupted sleep! she thought.

They left for the refuge after lunch on the Friday. The first leg of the journey was by car over the pass into the next valley where they drove up several hairpin bends before finally arriving at a cafe and a car-park beside a mountain lake.

"Here we are, guys. This is where we start walking!" He could tell from their ashen faces that both children felt a bit carsick, and he thought the sooner he could take their minds of it the better.

"Daddy, where are we walking to?" asked Lucy.

"I'll show you. Come round here. Now, can you see the top of that mountain I am pointing at?"

"Yes."

"Right. I want you to imagine the very top, the pointed bit, is the middle of a clock. Now imagine a line drawn from the middle of the clock down to the number four. Follow that line across and down, and you'll see the sloping roof of a building. Got it?"

"Yes, Daddy. But that's miles away!"

"Well, we have all afternoon. And when we get there we will have cakes and tea, then supper!"

Lucy thought that sounded pretty good. She looked through her super-duper binoculars at the refuge, and she was surprised it was so big. She had been expecting something more like a cowshed.

"Wow!" she said. Then she carefully followed the path winding down from the refuge, disappearing into the forest, then emerging further down, only to be obscured again by a fold in the ground.

Above the refuge, she noticed the trees became more sparse until at a certain level there were none at all, just a mix of green and brown slopes and jagged grey rocks and cliffs. But above those, high on the ridge behind the refuge, she spotted the patches of snow which, because of their orientation and altitude, had survived the summer sun.

While Dan retrieved the rucksacks from the back of the car, Helen took Lucy to the loos behind the cafe, and Josh went down the short path to the edge of the lake where a couple of fishermen sat patiently on the bank waiting for a bite. The weather was calm, and the passing clouds prevented the afternoon temperatures from climbing too high.

"OK, everybody. Just listen in," Dan began when the party had reconvened. Eleanor thought it was rather fun being under the command of her little boy. "We've got about three miles to go. But that's just the distance on the map. We also have to climb through a vertical distance of nearly 700 metres. That's like walking up the stairs to the flat a hundred times!"

He paused to let it sink in. "But we'll take our time and stop when people feel like it, and if anyone wants a drink, let me know and I'll pass you a water bottle. So, let's see. The time is nearly 2.30, so I reckon we'll be there at five, just in time for tea!

"Remember, this is the hard part. Tomorrow will be an easy descent back to the car, but if everybody's good – that includes you, Grandma – we'll have an ice-cream before we drive back to the chalet."

───────────────

The Dope had been disappointed that no suitable opportunity had arisen on Day 5. Just local trips. To the shops, the swimming pool and the riding stables. But Day 6 was proving to be of interest. The car had left with the target on board and headed off north, up the pass towards Morzine. He'd been able to follow it on the screen of his mobile, and having tracked it through the town, he'd watched it wind up a small mountain road with lots of hairpin bends.

Perfect, he thought. The road won't be busy, as it ends at a lake. And he saw from the map on the screen that the only way down from the lake was the very same road. Time to move, he thought. He sensed his opportunity had come. They were trapped.

He lost no time in getting back to his guest house, changing into his 'kit', specially purchased for the mission, and heading off in his car towards Morzine and beyond. He wasn't quite sure how he would play it. As a young man he had learned that one of the principles of war was to maintain flexibility, and over the years he had often hidden his lack of planning ability behind that principle.

When he reached the car park, he was pleased to see the people carrier there and relieved there was no-one around. It puzzled him as to where the target et al had disappeared to, as it was beginning to get late, bearing in mind the young children.

He waited.

Eventually, his impatience got the better of him and he boldly strode up the front door of the cafe and went in. It was getting dark. The man behind the bar said in bad English that they were just closing, to which The Dope replied, in equally bad French, that he was hoping to catch up with his friends who had come this way. The man explained that often people would walk up to the refuge and spend the night there, then return in the morning.

"Y-a-t'il une autre route down from la refuge?" The Dope asked.

"Non, monsieur. Zair ees only zer one way."

The Dope waited for the cafe owner to lock up and depart, then he set to work with the rock, the fishing line, the pull-switch and the C4 plastic explosive. He set the timer for ten minutes, on the basis that it would be impossible to drive down to the end of the hairpins in that time. The ten minutes would start when the vehicle pulled away, leaving plenty of time for it to exit the car-park and build up speed.

18

It was a beautiful morning. Overnight there had been a fresh dusting of snow on the high peaks, but the warmth of the midsummer sun was rapidly chasing it away. The Braithwaites awoke to the distant sound of cowbells, and Josh and Lucy jumped out of bed and opened the door leading from their bunk room onto the wide terrace of the refuge.

Lucy raced back for her binoculars and returned eager to study the stunning views surrounding them. The glasses were good ones, but for a child quite heavy. But by resting her elbows on one of the tables on the terrace, she was able to hold them steady and focus them properly.

"Come on, Luce. Let's have a go," said Josh.

"In a minute, I'm just looking at those cows over there. They're beautiful!"

"Hey, is that our car down there?" asked Josh. "It looks awfully small!"

"Well, we should be able to see it from here, because when we were next to it we could see this building. Here you are then." Lucy handed over the binos.

"Wow! These are good!. . . Yep! It's our car all right. But I can't see the number plate. Wrong angle. There's another car next to it. Right-hand drive. Must be a Brit. Here. Take a look." Grandma had taught them about sharing.

"Mmmm. And there's a person in it. . . He's getting out. . . He's stretching. . . D'you think he slept there? I mean, overnight?"

"Give us them back then. . . What a weirdo!" said Josh.

"D'you think it's that man we saw yesterday? The one with those scars?" asked Lucy.

"What? Scarface? The man looking at our chalet? Can't tell. Could be. Same stupid hat. . . He's just gone into the cafe."

"Come in, you two. Breakfast!" It was Helen. She'd slept well for the first time in nearly three months.

The Dope had slept terribly. He hadn't realised how cold it could be at night in the mountains, even in June, and although his seat did recline it was hardly like a bed. The people carrier was still there – so the people were still up the mountain with no way back except the ancient mule path leading right to his feet.

It's going to be a good day, he thought, and he hoped the cafe owner would soon return and open up so he could have his coffee and croissant. Or two, he thought. At that outside table, from where he could keep an eye on the refuge and the path down.

Once they started to make their way back, he would wait further down the valley for the sound of the explosion. Just to be sure.

It was during breakfast that Eleanor heard about the other car from Lucy.

"Well, darling, perhaps they are on the way up here. We didn't reserve the whole mountain, you know!"

"But Grandma, we saw the man stretching. He was on his own."

"Then he went into the cafe," added Josh.

"Oh well," said Dan. "I expect he's come up to the lake for a day's fishing."

Eleanor kept quiet. The guardian reappeared with another jug of coffee and swapped the empty bread basket for a full one.

"Come on children," said Helen. "Have some more of this

delicious bread. Try it with this home-made jam. It's scrummy! It's made from myrtles, little berries you sometimes see growing wild on the mountainside."

Josh tried it. "Epic!" he said. "Can we take some back with us?"

Eleanor finished and excused herself to find the custodian. She bought a pot of jam and paid the bill, and thanked him for a wonderful stay. He warned her the weather forecast wasn't good and suggested the sooner they were on their way down the better.

She returned to the breakfast table and had a quiet word to Dan about the forecast, suggesting they ought to make a start. While Helen chivvied the children on, Eleanor wandered out onto the terrace and looked down the valley. She could just make out Dan's people carrier in the car-park far below her, and the blue one parked next to it. Same colour as the one in the Cookham car-park.

Lucy was first out, complete with packed rucksack on her back and her large binos dangling around her neck.

"Darling, may I borrow those for a sec, please? Your binos?" Eleanor asked. "I just want to have a look at something."

Lucy could see her grandmother had them trained on the car park. "Grandma?"

"Yes, darling, I am listening."

"Josh and me think it might be Scarface!"

Eleanor put the glasses down and stared at Lucy. She couldn't help frowning.

"Sorry, Grandma." Lucy remembered being told not to make remarks about people with disfigurements, or to call such people names.

"Who do you mean, darling?"

"Well, the man down there. Josh thinks it might be the man we saw looking at our chalet yesterday. Josh said he had the same hat on. A thing with a feather sticking up."

Eleanor went to the bunk room to pack her things, and to have a think. Simple, really. Either a harmless tourist, on his own, driving a right-hand-drive car, having recently burned his face badly – or The Dope, out here, to get her, to get them. There weren't many more possibilities to scope, so she chose the worst. No time for speculation. Down? Stay? Up? She found the guardian.

"Excusez moi s'il vous plait, monsieur. Est-que c'est une route la-haut?" *Is there a way going up?*

"Mais non, madame. Il y a seulement la route en bas." *There is only a way going down.*

"Merci, monsieur." Eleanor turned to walk back to the room.

"A moins d'on se retrouve en Suisse!" he joked. *Unless you want to end up in Switzerland.*

She didn't have a clue how she would sell it to the others. She took Dan aside. "I want you to trust me. I want you to do exactly what I say. Don't ask questions. Do it. And support me."

He could tell from her expression she meant business. Over to you, Mum, he thought. You're in charge.

She got everybody together on the terrace. "I've just had a wonderful idea!" She put on her broadest smile and made eye contact with Helen, Josh, Lucy then Dan. She kept her eyes on Dan and let her smile fade. He knew what that look meant. He was back to being a little boy. It was her way of saying to him, if you don't do what I say, I will send you to bed for the rest of the day.

The children were both excited, trying to guess what her wonderful idea was. Normally, her ideas were pretty good ones, either funny, exciting or pleasing in some other way.

"What is it, Grandma?"

"Tell us, Grandma!"

"Well. . . " She had everybody's attention, not least of all Dan's. "Do you remember the film *The Sound of Music*?"

19

The Dope watched them through his binos gather on the terrace outside the refuge. He could make out five figures. Must be them. Rucksacks. Sticks. Two children, three adults.

Come on, he thought. Get ON with it! He wanted to be in Calais by the evening, then in London by midnight. He was on his third coffee. If I have to wait, he thought, I might as well sit here and enjoy the delights of a French petite-dejeuner.

He thought he saw some movement and lifted the binos to his eyes. About bloody time too, he thought. Any minute now they'll be out in the open, on the way down, into the killing zone.

He waited with the binos trained on the path below the refuge. And he waited. Then he noticed them, a group of five figures, two of them smaller than the others, climbing up a path, to the left of the refuge and above it.

"Where the FUCK are they going?" he said it to himself, but out loud. Through the glasses, he could just make out a path zig-zagging up the mountain, well above the tree-line, leading to a shallow saddle between two peaks.

He shot up from the table and dashed inside the cafe. He was livid but tried to remain calm. "Excuse me!" He had given up all attempts to speak the language. "I say! Anyone there?"

"Oui, monsieur?" Le Patron appeared from the kitchen, wiping his hands on his apron.

"Look, last night you told me there was only the one path down, and it looks as if I might miss my. . . my friends, because they've left the refuge and gone another way!" For him, he was being calm.

"Monsieur, you ask me last night eef zair ees anuzzer paz coming down zer mountain. I tell you no. Per'aps your friends 'ave gone up zer mountain, up zer ancient route for zer mules, to zer top."

"But, but once they get there, I assume that they will have to retrace their steps and come down here, to their car, the white one outside?"

"Oui, monsieur. Zat ees correct." The man shrugged, Gallic style. "Uzzerwise zay will find zemselves een Sweetzerland!"

The Dope slapped a twenty euro note on the counter and raced out to his car. He opened the boot and grabbed his rucksack and shot off up the path leading up the mountain to the refuge. Shit shit shit, he thought. What a bloody idiot! Surely it doesn't take the brains of an archbishop to realise I meant any path! Bloody frogs! On to plan B.

He was pleased he had packed his hunting rifle, his Remmy with the telescopic sight, with its barrel sticking up out of the top of his rucksack with a fishing-rod cover over it. And he took solace in the thought that two women and two children would make it very slow going for them, and they might well turn back before they reached the border. It wasn't as if they knew he was there, for God's sake!

As they set off up the steep path, Helen sidled up to Dan. "Danny? Tell me. What's going on? What's up with Mum? Does she think she's Julie Andrews or something?"

"I'm not sure, but I sense something's not quite right. I sense it's serious. She told me to trust her – and I do. She's taken over as leader of our little group. We mustn't make her job harder by questioning everything she does. A good soldier does what he's told, not because he's some sort of automaton, but because in a tight situation there isn't time to question every order-"

"Tight situation, Danny! What tight situation?"

"Look, I haven't the foggiest. Before we left, she told me to get four teaspoons. Just like that."

"Four teaspoons, for Pete's sake! What did you do?"

"I got four teaspoons," said Dan. It made Helen smile. Four teaspoons! Can't be that tight, she thought.

She was missing Zak. It came in waves. A sort of ache behind the eyes. She just wanted to get home. To cuddle him.

The Dope knew if they reached the border, Plan B would be difficult. He had a lot of ground to make up, but he was driven by thoughts of achieving the mission, of what it would mean for him and the Service. It would close the book on what had been a very uncomfortable chapter.

He was a good shot. Always had been, and he thought if he could get within two fifty metres and adopt a stable fire position, he would stand a good chance of succeeding. Just get those cross-hairs on the target and gently squeeze. But no capability to fire bursts, not like the LMG, the light machine gun, his weapon of choice in the old days, with two magazines strapped together with masking tape enabling a quick change when one became empty.

His 'Remmy' was a bolt-action Remington Model 700. No butt pad, muzzle brake or mercury tube, so it kicked like a mule. But The Dope didn't mind that. He liked to feel that thump into his shoulder, as the 180-grain bullet accelerated along the 22-inch barrel before being released on its supersonic flight to its target. It helped him to imagine what it would do to the target at the end of its flight, ripping into flesh and bone.

The sight was a Leopold VX3 with a six-and-a-half to twenty magnification, so he could zoom in on a target once he had acquired it. He would see her face. And wipe that silly smile off it, he thought, as he marched up the rugged path at a fast pace.

The children liked the idea of walking over into Switzerland, just like the von Trapp family in the film, escaping the Nazis. But Eleanor was careful not to push them too hard, and they frequently stopped to enjoy the views, listen to the cry of the buzzards circling high above their heads, and the marmots whistling their warnings to each other among the rocky outcrops.

"Grandma?"

"Yes, Lucy?"

"Will we get an ice-cream when we reach the top?"

"You certainly will, my dear girl, if you are good!" Lucy smiled at the reassurance and made up her mind to be extra good in the hope of getting an extra big one.

Josh looked up at the bleak and barren slopes leading up to the saddle. In places, he could just make out the path. A cafe at the top? A man selling ice creams? Dream on, he thought, but I'd better not say anything. Now he was nearly ten he must take these things on the chin.

Eleanor explained about the other animals they might see and said there might be a special prize if someone spots a chamois. Dan asked if that included him, and his mum said yes.

As they walked on, up the winding path, Eleanor took out her mobile phone and started tapping into it. Helen noticed.

"Danny. Look, she's texting someone. . . Who could it be? I mean, who walks up a steep mountain texting, along a path strewn with boulders where if you tripped you would probably end up in Morzine?"

"Haven't a clue. She's probably playing Candycrush." Dan replied.

"Don't be so flippant!" She was beginning to get irritated. It was Zak.

"Why don't you give Julie a ring?" Dan said it without really thinking. He didn't believe in telepathy and all that sort of rubbish, but he'd sensed Helen's change of mood without realising it.

"D'you think there's a signal up here?"

"Try it. Mum's obviously getting through."

"Okay." Without stopping. Helen swung her light rucksack round and fished out her phone from one of the side pockets. After a few minutes, Dan could tell from her smile that all was fine back at base.

———

The Dope was making good speed but finding it difficult to force enough of the thin mountain air in and out of his lungs. His mouth was dry and his throat sore. Had it not been for the adrenalin being pumped around his body at 150 beats per minute, he would have stopped, sat down on the nearest rock, removed his sweat sodden-hat and enjoyed the wonderful views which had escaped his notice.

He was gaining on them. He hardly needed the binoculars anymore. Every now and then he would catch a glimpse of them when the path became visible, and he thought about trying for a long shot. He assessed the pros and cons. An early hit would complete the mission; a miss would alert them to his presence. At long range, he would need to adopt a prone firing position – difficult on a steep slope, and it would take time to set down his rucksack, extract the Remmy, get down, test and adjust.

Worth it, he concluded, if only they would stop. Please stop, he thought, as he watched them slowly trudge across an open expanse of steep pasture. Stop, you bastards.

He noticed the clouds. As the light breeze gently took the air up the valley to the cooler heights, water vapour was being formed, but the sun was also at work warming the air again on its way up and evaporating the microscopic droplets of water. The result was that between the refuge and the saddle there was a layer of light, swirling cloud. Damn it, he thought.

———

Under Eleanor's instructions, the von Trapps had stopped to admire the view just before the path disappeared up a narrow re-entrant. They'd been walking for nearly three hours – and it was showing. When Eleanor asked Lucy if she might borrow the binos, Lucy gladly passed them over, relieved to be free of their weight for a while. Eleanor declared she was 'going to make herself comfortable' behind a rock. The others got the message and walked on.

She did go behind a rock, so she could rest the binos on the top of it as she carefully scanned the view down the valley. After a couple of minutes, she saw him, powering himself up the path below as it crossed an open grassy slope. She guessed he would reach her present location in ten to fifteen minutes. It was time for her to catch the others up and made sure they kept moving.

If only they could get into that cloud, she thought. She wondered how she might speed them up without causing too much unnecessary alarm. After all, he might still be just a tourist out for a hike.

As she stood and turned to start the ascent, she heard the crack and thump. Two seconds later she heard another. She was flat on the ground when it came. Not a German tourist, she thought; but he could have been a hunter.

She remembered being taught about cracks and thumps during the small arms module of her basic training, down on the ranges at Hythe on the South Coast in Kent. They were in the butts, the pit in front of the targets. The instructor said the crack was the sound of the bullet as it broke the sound barrier as it passed overhead at 2000 mph, the thump which followed was the sound of the gas exploding out of the rifle barrel at a more sedate 700 mph. The point was this: you could tell how far away the firing point was by the length of time between the crack and thump.

She couldn't remember the formula, but it was something like 500m for every second, 250 for half a second. Nobody was going to get their stop-watch out, but the lesson was simple. If the thump follows quickly after the crack, you can be sure the firer is pretty damn close. In this case, she reckoned the distance was around 250m.

She made good speed up the re-entrant and soon caught up with the group. "Grandma, we heard some bangs!" Josh seemed excited about the prospect of being shot at. The others were less pleased, and Eleanor saw the look in Helen's eyes.

She needed to reassure her. "Yes, Josh. I heard them too. I think it must be hunters down in the valley. I guess sound does funny things in a valley like this. It echoes around a bit and seems much closer than it is. Look, why don't you go on? I'll wait here, and if the hunters come this way, I'll warn them there are people ahead.

"Danny, give me a hand with this strap would you?" He came over. She gave him his orders, quietly, so the others did not hear. "Follow the track. Keep together. Keep going. Play a game – Nazis chasing you, Indians, whatever.

"Carry Lucy if you have to, sing songs, tell jokes. If the clouds lift, stop and lie down behind cover – to have a rest, to keep out of the wind, say whatever you want.

"When the cloud closes in, get up and keep going. Don't stop unless the cloud clears."

Dan wanted to say surely it's safer to move when there was no cloud and visibility was better, but he didn't. He just said his equivalent of 'Wilco, Boss!' It was 'yes Mum'.

The bloody clouds, thought The Dope. He needed something to blame for his two misses, rather than his heaving chest and trembling hands as he'd tried to keep the rifle steady. Whatever fitness he might have had before his accident had been lost through his stay in hospital, and one of the few types of terrain he wasn't familiar with were mountains – and he struggled with the difficult business of taking enough oxygen into his lungs.

He didn't have time to stop and recover. He struggled to his feet, swung his rucksack onto his back and using his precious rifle as a walking stick he continued. He had to keep going, keep climbing if he were to achieve his mission.

Then another gap in the clouds. He saw them for a moment before they disappeared. But hey! he thought. That's Braithwaite, standing up! Probably doing her lipstick. He fell into a prone firing position and wriggled, trying to get some degree of comfort on the stony track. He held his breath and tried again. Cross-hairs on the side of her head. A single shot, with that satisfying kick into the shoulder. But damn the woman, she had dropped to the ground just as he had started slowly squeezing the trigger.

The others heard the whine of the ricochet, not as loudly as Eleanor did, but it alarmed them. "What in Heaven's name was that?" asked Helen.

"Just a bullet hitting something hard and spinning off," explained Josh, as if it happened every day, like it did in his favourite computer game.

"Nonsense!" said Dan. "It's a... it's a screech eagle. They do it to frighten their prey, so it freezes. Nothing to worry about. Come on, guys. Grandma thinks she can catch us up before we get to the top! Let's show her what we're made of!"

Grandma hoped she'd last long enough to make it to the top. She'd seen the scree slope ahead and realised it would be quite a dangerous obstacle for them all. Through Lucy's binos, she had seen the steel wire rope strung across it, which at least would give them something to hold on to. But if they slipped. . . a long way down, at a steady 39 degrees, the angle of repose for loose shale.

Then after the scree, she could just make out the steep climb up across the odd patch of snow to the saddle. And over the top into Switzerland and safety and a happy ending to the film. I must be bonkers, she thought.

The clouds closed in again around her and she got up. She noticed the fresh chip in the top of the stone she had crouched behind. Back to the film, she thought, let's get on with it. Last reel.

Under the cover of smoke – in reality swirling clouds – she advanced up the hill at a good pace and eventually caught up with the others as they reached the scree slope.

"Hi everyone!" she tried to be cheerful. "Wow, this looks like fun! Nearly as good as the jungle gym the other day! Danny, you'd better show us how it's done. I just need to go to the loo again. All that coffee!"

She left them gingerly making their way across the loose stones, one by one, hand over hand along the steel wire rope. It was a slow process. She retraced her steps until she found a good position to assess the situation below her. Please, please don't go away, she pleaded to the clouds.

As she waited, she heard the sound of distant foot falls from further down the valley, the rhythmic thrump of rubber-soled boot on rough stone. She heard the occasional expletive, and if she listened very carefully, with her mouth slightly open as she had been taught, she could just make out the sound of someone puffing hard, panting. She made her plan.

She walked back up to the start of the scree and began crossing it. She looked up and saw patches of blue sky through the thinning cloud above her. The others were safely across, on the far side, slowly making their way upwards towards the ridge in the bright sunshine. Their silhouettes were magnificently illuminated against the dark blue of the sky, making them perfect targets.

When she reached the upper edge of the scree she stopped. It's going to have to be here, she thought. Custer's last stand. Keep your head, girl.

Keep. Your. Head.

Damn the clouds, thought The Dope. No chance of a shot in this stuff, but at least she wouldn't see him. He reached the scree slope and started to cross. It was hard work. He could just about hook his injured left hand over the steel rope, but with his rifle in his right hand, there was no way he could use the rope to haul himself up. He noticed the breaks in the clouds directly above him and realised they were thinning out as he climbed higher across the scree.

Then he saw her. The Braithwaite woman. With her back towards him, looking in a bad way, struggling up the rough path on the far side of the scree slope. He saw her stumble – and realised his chance had come. He dropped to his knees, unhooked his hand from the rope and took up a fire position.

She was no more than 75 metres away. Damn this thin air, damn these fucking stones, he thought; must steady myself. Aim, breathe out slowly and squeeze, he reminded himself. He was finding it hard to hold the stock of his Remmy with his injured hand, left elbow resting on his left knee, right knee on the scree. He struggled to slow down his breathing. Then a break in the clouds. Sunlight, a static target. Yes! he thought.

He fired. As he did so, he felt the satisfying kick as the butt-plate drove hard into his right shoulder. He instinctively resisted the impulse by digging the toes of his right foot into the scree. The stones beneath readjusted themselves just enough to make him lose his balance. He quickly moved his rifle down across his body, pushing the butt into the slope below him to steady himself. But the stones under the butt also moved, and continued to move. He toppled over and started sliding – then tumbling – down the 39-degree slope. He let out a scream, as he felt what seemed to be a band of steel tightening around his chest.

Time stood still for him. He was back in bandit country. He saw the girl, with the wire tight around her neck.

And he saw her eyes.

"Well done, you lot." It was Eleanor. "You okay, Helen?"

"I'm fine, thanks. What about you, though?"

"Oh, still in one piece. Hey, isn't it wonderful up here?"

The group had made it to the saddle, a sharp rocky ridge between two peaks. Along the top of the ridge was a fence; nothing to keep someone with any determination in or out, but at least it marked the border. Where the path crossed it there was a gate, but that too had seen better days, when every crossing point along the border had been permanently manned.

The ugly flat-roofed building just inside Switzerland was a reminder of those days long gone by, but it was kept in reasonable repair as rudimentary accommodation for the guards in case the border ever had to be shut. It was the Swiss way.

A few metres on the Swiss side was a square stone post about a foot high set in the ground marking the official border with CH inscribed on one side and an F on the other. Josh spotted it first and jumped over it, declaring his arrival in Switzerland before any of the others. Lucy then stood astride it, delighted at the concept of being in two countries at the same time.

Both children were whacked. They had been going for four and a half hours. They were hungry and thirsty, but the supplies of water had been consumed long ago. They were too polite to ask Grandma about the ice creams she'd promised them.

"Danny, could you let me have those spoons, please?" He thought she had really flipped this time, but he gave them to her.

"Now, you two first," she said, pointing to Lucy and Josh. "Come with me!" She took them behind the building where the fresh overnight snow had drifted, yet remained because it was in the shade.

"It's probably best to watch me, then you can try for yourself." Eleanor knelt down at the edge of the snowdrift and got out the jar of jam from her rucksack. With one of the teaspoons, she scooped out a good dollop of jam and rapidly stirred it round in the snow, ending up with a hole in the snow about the size of a large cup. In the bottom of the hole was a mixture of fine ice crystals and myrtle jam.

"Get your smackers around that!" she said, passing a spoonful to Lucy.

"Mmmm." Lucy smiled and closed her eyes. "Please, may I have some more, Grandma?"

"Of course you may, darling." It was Eleanor's usual reply if they wanted something. And, as usual, there was more to say. "Here's your spoon, here's the jam – and there's the snow."

Josh was next, and then he rushed off to get his parents so he could show them himself. They all thought it was the best ice-cream they'd ever tasted. Well, best sorbet, Dan thought, if you wanted to be pedantic.

The next surprise had not yet arrived, but according to the text message from her new best friend in Bern, it was on its way. Eleanor could relax. It was strange because as she sat down and leaned back on her rucksack, she started shaking.

It reminded her of Gerald all those years ago in the brink-tank, shaking when Mr B had briefed him about the bomb scenario and his niece being kidnapped. That was all pretend, of course, yet it had triggered the fight-flight response. With her, at this moment, high on a hill in Switzerland, the response had been delayed by twenty minutes or so. Dan noticed and came over to her.

"Do you want to tell me about it?"

"Not just now," she replied. "Later."

The wop-wop-wop of the Swiss Army helicopter brought everybody back to life as it made its way from its base in Martigny and then slowly descended onto the H on the flat roof of the building. The crew were delighted to take part in the surprise 'exercise' which had relieved them of the boredom of being on standby for mountain rescue, which didn't happen much out of the ski season.

And they loved having such enthusiastic passengers as the Braithwaite family. For Helen and Eleanor, it was a delightful way down to their car and then home. For Lucy, it was a wonderful way to look down on the Alps and enjoy the stunning views of Mont Blanc. Josh loved watching the pilot confidently handling the controls as he banked the machine around the peaks and ridges, finally coming to rest on the car-park by the lake and powering down.

Dan couldn't quite work it all out. The text messages. The hunters? But he was getting there. He looked forward to hearing all about it from his mother. But when they landed, she had work to do.

"Danny, why don't you settle Helen and the children in the cafe – get them some lunch. I need to check something out."

"Okay. Call me if you need me." By this time Dan had become used to taking orders from her.

Eleanor started by walking slowly around Dan's people carrier, looking carefully for any untoward sign. Had she not been looking hard, she wouldn't have noticed the fishing line. One end disappeared down the steep bank at the edge of the car-park, next to where the car was parked. She peered over the bank and saw a rock hanging from the nylon line.

The other end disappeared beneath the car, but before it did so, it went around the spot where the left-hand front wheel made contact with the ground. The tyre was like a jam cleat: it locked the line preventing it being pulled in either direction. Until the vehicle moved. World War Two stuff, she thought.

She lowered herself to the ground and carefully eased herself underneath the car. She found the line and followed it to the pull-switch. She could hardly believe it; the safety pin was still in it! What a twerp, she thought. Then, what a bastard. She gently eased the small cube of plastic explosive away from the petrol tank and placed it on the ground.

After the hamburgers and fries, they all piled into the car and Dan drove off. As he did so, the fishing line under the front was freed, and the rock around which the line was tied pulled it – and the pull-switch and the plastic explosive – down the steep bank into the forest. No sign of the attempted murder remained.

Always secret.

Within the hour they were back at the chalet in Samoens, sorting themselves out and getting prepared for the morning when they would return to Geneva. Eleanor enjoyed her time with her family, but given her various 'interests', she felt it might be prudent to retain her flat for the moment. There was talk of Dan selling up and moving the family back to London which might affect her own plans.

Helen was delighted and relieved to have Zak back. But realising her sleep was likely to be interrupted that night she decided to turn in early. While Dan saw Lucy off to bed, Josh and Eleanor found themselves alone in the sitting room.

"Grandma?"

"Yes, Josh."

"When I leave school. . . " He was already grown up, sort of. "I want to become a spy."

"Do you, indeed?"

"Yes, like you, Grandma." Eleanor looked at him. What next, she thought.

"Like you were, Grandma."

At least he used the past tense, she thought. After today, it might have been the pluperfect. She smiled at him and let him continue.

"Like in that story you told us. After we watched that film. The time when you were dropped behind enemy lines and got caught by the Germans, then escaped."

"But, Josh, that was only a story. I made it up!"

"I know, but that's what I want to be, like you were – in the made-up story."

When finally all the rest of the family were tucked up in bed and fast asleep, Dan offered Eleanor a whisky, as he usually did. But for the first time, she accepted.

"I had a feeling you might," said Dan as he poured and passed it over to her. "Right. I'm listening," and he sat down.

"Which version?"

"Your version. I'm a big boy, you know."

"Stop me if you have any questions."

"Sure."

"There was a hunter in that valley. He was hunting me. Us, if you like. Why? Dinntick. Er, sorry. You do not need to know why. Old scores, I suppose. But it was to do with that fiche. Or what it contained.

"Anyway, the children spotted him by the car, at breakfast time. They recognised his ridiculous hat because they had seen him snooping around here yesterday. He was armed with a high-powered rifle with a telescopic sight. I had nothing, so it was very much a one-sided affair.

"I had to use what there was around me, the cover of the clouds – and the scree slope. After you had all crossed it and gone on, I also crossed and waited for him on the far side. He couldn't see me because of the cloud.

"I had to get him onto the slope – it was my only chance. I couldn't allow him across it, or he would have seen you lot. D'you remember it was getting quite sunny?"

"Sure I do. Go on, Mum."

She sipped her whisky, then continued. "Anyway, I could hear him. He was puffing like a steam train. Which was encouraging. In that condition, he needed something to lean on, some stable support for an aimed shot. And there's nothing on that slope. Except for the rope of course.

"My fear was he would see me before he started to cross. So I stayed down, using my phone as a periscope. You know, on selfie mode. I didn't take any pictures. I just watched him. I don't think he'd seen me at that stage, because he started to cross, hanging onto the steel rope with his left arm. I think his hand was too injured to hold it properly. In the other hand, he had his rifle.

"I watched him on my phone. I heard him swearing to himself. He still hadn't seen me. I guessed – hoped, more like – he was about halfway across when I stood up, back towards him, watching him on the phone. The clouds must have cleared a bit and he saw me. He sounded like some animal. An angry one. A sort of snarl. His chest was heaving.

"He tried to lift the rifle up with just his right hand. It was waving around. I began to move off slowly as if I was very tired. I wanted him to think he had plenty of time. I pretended to stumble. I let out a cry of pain. I looked round. As I did so, he sort of smiled. He couldn't have been more than 80 yards away.

"I watched him. He knelt down, slowly. Unhooked his left arm from the rope. Took up a firing position, kneeling on the scree. Then held his breath and fired. The recoil must have unsteadied him. There was a clatter of stones. He tried to grab the rope but it was out of his reach. He tried to use his rifle to stop himself sliding, but the more he leaned on it the more it slid.

"Slowly at first. Then he lost his balance and he fell, sliding and tumbling. He let out a scream. More a cry of pain than of fear. He'd dropped his rifle by then. He was sort of hugging himself, sliding and tumbling down that slope."

She paused and sipped her whisky. Dan sensed she couldn't go on for a moment. "Mum, we heard the shot, and then we heard the scream. I thought it was you. I told the children it was the sound wild boars make when they are hit. You took some chance there. Did you think. . . did you, er. . .”

“Think I was going to die?” she asked. Dan nodded.

She took another sip. “They say it concentrates the mind, facing death. I thought ‘What would Gerald do?’ Your dad. He would have worked it all out. I tried to do the same. I pretended I was him – old Smartypants.

“I guessed the gunman would go for the head-shot – sure way of achieving a kill with a single shot. With a bolt action, there’s not much choice: you can’t double-tap. I was watching him, and I knew he hadn’t adjusted the sight, at least not since his arrival at the scree.

“His last shot had been at a longer range, probably over 300 metres, so I reckoned if he hadn’t changed the setting, at that short range it would go over my head. All I had to do was to let him shoot. Anyway, he was breathing so hard, I doubt if it would have hit me.

“So. . . that’s it, really. Thanks, Gerald. . . ” She paused. “And Danny?”

“Hmm?”

“Thanks. You were brilliant. Well done.”

“It’s okay. . . What happened to him? The gunman, I mean.”

“Oh, I walked down the slope, found him still breathing, called rescue services. . .” She saw Dan’s face. “Of course I didn’t! I came straight up to where you lot were, to make the ice-creams. You’ve got to get your priorities right, you know.” She paused.

“It’s peculiar. You get a feeling about these things. I don’t think he will be bothering us again. Or anybody else, for that matter.”

It was time for bed. It had been a busy day.

“Mum?”

“Yes, Danny?”

“What d’you call that concoction of yours?”

"What?" She yawned. "Do you mean with the jam and the snow?"

"Yeah," he said, yawning; it was catching. "Yep, the ice cream thingy. It must have a name."

"That? A name? It's jam snow."

They sat there, sipping their whisky.

"Mum?"

"Hmmm?

"Was it. . . was it him?"

"What d'you mean 'him'?" She looked puzzled.

"Dad told me about him in the story. When you were young. Action Man. Was it Action Man?"

Her look answered his question. "Good one, Mum!"

There was a long pause."Can I ask another question?"

Eleanor's eyes were closing. "Go on then."

"Why did you go?"

"Go where?"

"Why did you leave us?"

"I thought I'd explained. I had to stop him reaching-."

Dan interrupted. "No! Not that. Twenty-six years ago. You left us. You disappeared. Why?"

✻

THE END

✻

Thank you for reading this novel. I hope you enjoyed it and found it interesting. If so, I would be most grateful if you would be kind enough to review it on Amazon. It need not be a long one; any review helps to raise the book's profile among the many millions of books on their website.

A Balance of Evil is the first book of a trilogy about Eleanor Braithwaite. The second one is A Burden of Secrets in which Eleanor struggles to explain to Dan why she disappeared all those years ago. It's not easy as she has to confront her past and reveal some uncomfortable truths about herself, and some disturbing secrets about her work. Like this book, it is set against a background of real events.

The third book, A Bodyguard of Lies, will be published in 2018. It is set in 2020. Eleanor is on a skiing holiday in the French Alps with her partner, Robert Dunn, when disaster strikes in the mountains high above them. Terrorism is suspected, and her boss in London asks her to retrieve some vital evidence before anyone else can. She and Robert succeed, but for some reason, London is more interested in destroying it. She is determined to find out why.

AUTHOR'S NOTES

This novel is a work of fiction. However, what may seem to be the most fanciful elements of the story – the high-level source, the Cold War strategies and the 'suitcase bombs' – are mostly factual.

The source could well have been Colonel Stanislav Lunev, a former Soviet military officer. He worked as a GRU Intelligence Officer in the United States until he defected there in 1992. According to him, some RA-115s were secretly hidden in caches in the States in the eighties, and some did go missing. The FBI have denied this, but, as Mandy Rice-Davies might have said, they would say that, wouldn't they.

Mr Green's 'generic' is similar in structure to the Twin Towers but smaller in size. A full description of the real towers can be found in the NIST report which can be downloaded from the internet. The NIST investigation cost $16million and lasted something like three years. Over 200 staff contributed to it. Their main objective was this:

'To describe *how the aircraft impacts and subsequent fires* led to the collapse of the towers after terrorists flew jet fuel laden commercial airliners into the buildings'. (My italics)

NIST acquired and organized nearly 7,000 segments of video footage totalling in excess of 150 hours and nearly 7,000 photographs from over 185 photographers. They and their contractors compiled and reviewed tens of thousands of pages of documents; conducted interviews with over a thousand people who had been on the scene or who had been involved with the design, construction, and maintenance of the WTC; analysed 236 pieces of steel obtained from the wreckage; performed laboratory tests, measured material properties; and performed computer simulations of the sequence of events that happened from the instant of aircraft impact to the initiation of collapse for each tower.

It is a tragedy that their studies stopped short of investigating the mechanism of collapse after initiation, as their brief explanation of a block of storeys free-falling under gravity and crushing the storeys below does not comply with the laws of physics. The sums are surprisingly simple and can be done by anyone with some basic knowledge of applied mathematics.

Among the writings on the subject, two scientific papers were produced which attempted to take over the study where NIST had stopped, one by Bazant and Greening (and others), the other paper just by Greening on his own. They set out to prove that the towers collapsed directly as a result of the planes impacting into them, and that they had not been brought down by controlled demolitions.

The first was entitled 'Collapse of the World Trade Center Towers: What Did and Did Not Cause It'. This is an impressive paper, full of complex mathematical formulae, esoteric graphs and diagrams and long words like comminution (crushing). Here is an example of the wording used.

'The key idea is not to use classical homogenization, leading to a softening   stress-strain   relation   necessitating   nonlocal finite element   analysis,   but   to   formulate   a   continuum energetically equivalent to the snapthrough of columns.'

The paper's first error occurs in the first few lines. It states that allegations that the towers were brought down by controlled demolitions rest on the towers falling at free-fall speed. This is not so; free-fall speed is rarely achieved in a controlled demolition, except in its early stages. Certainly, a rate of collapse of less than free-fall speed is not proof that no explosives were used, as the paper claimed.

The second error in the paper is that it assumes a controlled demolition using explosives and a gravity-driven progressive collapse are mutually exclusive; they are not. In a controlled demolition, explosive is used to initiate the collapse, and then gravity provides most of the energy to break up the structure as it crashes into the ground.

The third error – or misleading statement – is that the authors have worked out the energy to crush all the concrete in the towers, then say that a controlled demolition would require 316 tons of TNT placed in holes drilled into the concrete on every storey to achieve this. This is not so. In a controlled demolition, most of the energy comes from gravity.

The most serious error is the statement that only 7% of the total gravitational potential energy available is necessary to crush the concrete, and that the remaining energy is dissipated by frictional and plastic deformations, and ejection of air and other debris. The authors have overlooked the kinetic energy of the tower just before the end of crush-down, after most of the tower has already been crushed and the air and the other debris have already been ejected.

The paper's final sentence was clear:

'These conclusions show the allegations [of controlled demolition] to be absurd and leave no doubt that the towers failed due to gravity driven progressive collapse triggered by the effects of fire.'

Just below this, in small print, was an acknowledgement:

'Partial financial support for the energetic theory of progressive collapse was obtained from the U.S. Department of Transportation through grant 0740-357-A210 of the Infrastructure Technology Institute of Northwestern University'.

He who pays the piper...

When Dr Frank Greening – one of the co-authors – came to write his own paper, he was much more able to communicate his thoughts to mere mortals. His aim was to show that 'the observed collapse events could have occurred without the help of explosives'. Indeed, in his conclusion he stated:

'An analysis of the energetics of the WTC collapse events has shown that the kinetic energy of the aircraft collisions and the subsequent gravitational energy released by the descending blocks of floors were quite sufficient to destroy the twin towers in the manner observed.'

Unfortunately, he failed to take into account the kinetic energy of the storeys, *after they had been crushed*, when they finally hit the ground at over 100 mph.

His paper is interesting, because in 2014, eight years after he wrote it, he changed his mind. He now believes molten aluminium from the planes reacted explosively with water from the sprinkler systems and other materials, and these explosions caused the collapses.

He could be right. Some of the molten aluminium could well have found its way down lift-shafts in the centre cores, all the way to the bottom of the basements, where water would have collected; a lot of it. He has presented his latest findings to NIST, but they are not interested in investigating it further.

All quotes in the novel by Bush, Blair and Netanyahu are correct, as are statements made by Blair in his book 'A Journey'.

The sinking of the Lusitania is well documented, and the quotes attributed to Churchill are correct. There are accounts of how attempts were made to save the babies on board by tying life-jackets to their carrycots.

Gerald's information on the London Bombings (7/7) is correct.

Information and video footage covering the Charlie Hebdo attack in Paris are available on the Internet. Gerald is right to be suspicious, as no alternative explanation has ever been given for the picking up of the shoe by one of the terrorists after they shot the policeman.

The Intelligence Services Act 1994 can be read in full on the Internet, as can a full transcript of Princess Diana's inquest from which Sir Richard Dearlove's quotes were taken. Gerald's imaginary cross-examination of 'C' was included to demonstrate the utter futility of putting the head of a secret service into the witness box in such circumstances: whatever MI6 may or may not have done, the answers are always going to be the same.

Jam snow is delicious. Try it.

The views of the characters in this book are not necessarily those of the author.

Any resemblance between the fictitious characters in this book and real people is entirely coincidental. Sort of.

25098800R00193

Printed in Great Britain
by Amazon